The March of Time

Pat McDonald

Strategic Book Publishing and Rights Co.

Strategic Book Publishing and Rights Co., LLC
USA | Singapore
www.sbpra.net

For information about special discounts for bulk purchases, please contact Strategic Book Publishing and Rights Co., LLC. Special Sales, at bookorder@sbpra.net.

ISBN: 978-1-68235-591-6

Dedicated to:

Caroline
You are greatly missed.
R.I.P

Acknowledgements:

Caroline you told me, "Do me proud." I can't ask you how I'm doing or tell you how much I miss you. This one is for you.

I thank Jane for introducing me to the Highlands of Scotland where we roamed freely on all those wonderful holidays we took. Although this is a work of fiction, somewhere in this book are a few of those treasured moments (some are strange, others are sweet) recorded for perpetuity which only we would remember.

Without these times I would not have been able to put my Private Investigator Bart Bridges in this setting. Some of the places may be real, others a product of my imagination; I have taken poetic licence with most of them whilst creating my imaginary castle right in their midst. However, my characters are a product of the same imagination entirely; none are meant to represent anyone living or dead.

PROLOGUE:

It is a sleepy village, somewhere in the Highlands of Scotland, nestling in the shadow of the white capped Cairngorms. Not yet winter when, it is told, the whole place becomes buried in snow, often cut off from civilisation surrounded by mountains in the glow of a weak sun.

Some say this is the highest village in Scotland, whilst others name that one Tomintoul letting the dispute rumble on through the years. The hill climbs up to the duck pond at the top where an abundance of water fowl grow in number, fed largely by tourists or walkers who come into the area. It is popular by virtue of its many documented walks.

The Brae is sparsely populated, with quaint cottages dotted along its route, thinning out as you climb to the pond at the top. At the bottom of the hill, just as you leave the village, therefore, considered to be one of the village shops, is a house built onto at the front, to provide premises for a 'shop'; once an art gallery of sorts, selling paintings, sculptures and the many locally produced greetings cards.

*Recently closed down, the shop has a new sign: **The March of Time**. At the side of the name someone has created a caricature of a white rabbit in a top hat, his ears poking out at the crown. The large stomach is covered by a waistcoat in paisley design showing the strain at the button fastening, it matches the bow tie he wears at his neck.*

The rabbit (or hare) is holding an opened fob watch as if checking the time; the chain attached to the watch is hooked into the pocket of his waistcoat.

The door to The March of Time suddenly opens revealing a short stout strange looking man wearing a waistcoat with a matching bow tie; he turns closing and locking the door behind him.

The sound of a cacophony of chiming clocks begin their ritual synchronised chorus to herald in midday, as the man hurries up the Brae to disappear down the track leading to the village's only pub where he eats lunch every day.

CHAPTER 1

The day light is overshadowed by heavy dark clouds, there being no sun to speak of, making threats by one or two flakes of snow fluttering in the poor visibility. She turns off the A9 at the Stirling services when tiredness begins to affect her eyesight. She parks her car as far away from prying eyes at the services, the need for coffee taking precedence over her urgent need for flight.

She pulls the hood of her coat around her head more for disguise than to keep out the bitter chill of the wind buffeting against her thin body and she begins to walk towards the main building. Avoiding people is difficult at such a popular tourist stop. The crowd of people dismounting from the National coach near the entrance are hard to avoid. When she gets nearer there appears to be a crowd clustered around one poor woman lying awkwardly on the icy ground having fallen whilst negotiating the slippery kerb of the walkway to the services entrance.

She moves past as quickly as she dares in the conditions, her head bent, concentrating on her own precarious steps. She hears shocked whispers of 'ambulance coming', 'broken hip' and 'pain' filtering from those gathered around the prone woman. She hurries on past to avoid any likelihood of chance conversation, the accident is after all none of her business. She is far too cold to stand around outside like they seem to want to do. She feels she may never get warm again.

Once inside, the comforting heat of the café with an aroma of filter coffee emanating with a hissing whoosh from the state of the art equipment, draws her to the small queue, grateful she arrived before the hordes of people from the coach. They will almost certainly visit the toilet facilities first whilst she can wait until later.

The queue moves quickly until, with her coffee and a snatched packet of shortbread biscuits in her hand, she makes her way to the farthest vacant table in the corner of the café, where she can observe the passengers from the coach as they cluster together in their concern, all wondering what is going to happen to them now they have a casualty. They sit attentive as their driver announces they will be continuing their journey in half an hour without their injured passenger. She blots out the low muttering as she eats her short bread letting the sweetness linger in her mouth for much needed comfort whilst the hot coffee warms her body with each sip.

Her mind does not move away from her need to flee. She has no vision of an alternative life, just an assertive belief she can disappear as long as she keeps moving onward away from her past. She needs the long sought after solitude, undisturbed by human contact with the much required time to heal, to discover who she really is. Solitude will give her the chance to reflect on her life.

Her choice of direction was determined by a need to surround herself with natural beauty as a stark contrast to the 'ugliness' of her life so far. In her desperation to escape there was only the choice to go to survive, or else stay and die a long slow death. The misery began with the one 'unhealthy' relationship she will not miss at all. The trigger that made her 'run' was the very last beating she took, only waiting long enough for the tell-tale signs to fade; she knew next time would be her last. She ran.

The only thought poking through her hazy mind is perhaps her impulsiveness at taking this huge step in winter, better to have been made when the weather was warmer, less threatening. She knew she panicked. She tried to push away the image of the poor woman lying on the icy ground who appeared to be broken under the huge Gortex coat someone threw over her. The idea this woman could have been her mingles with her mounting fear of discovery. The difference being she would be lying there alone having no one who really cared about her in attendance.

Reluctant to leave the warmth of the café she forces herself to rise, visit the facilities where even the heat of the hand dryer makes her want to linger. The women in the queue behind for the dryer glare at her when she peers round at them making her rush out once more into the cold of the ever increasingly dull day. The weather worsens as she travels north. The bitterness of the wind increases buffeting her car with its force. She daren't stop again knowing she would eventually be climbing up to the signposted ski resort at Glenshee which she needs to get past before nightfall. Her legs ache with the constant driving position and her head throbs from the unwelcome thoughts passing through her mind; even so she presses on.

The only plan she made, just a mere possibility, now seems the feeblest of ideas, was to find a Bed and Breakfast place amongst the many she knows must exist. She wants somewhere temporary, to start out from; later to find a more permanent place to live. She imagines B&B's would be in abundance outside of the seasonal tourist months, only a matter of making enquiries from someone local.

She has no real idea of the seasons for paying guests or whether guest house owners went away to find warmer climates in the winter months, closing down until the Spring. She hopes there would be winter ones open for the skiing season. These she imagines will be clustered around the few ski resorts with lots of people milling around. In that, she was certain she didn't want to find herself.

Eventually, passing through Blairgowrie she begins the climb up to Glenshee, where the signpost marked as the A93 road will take her to Braemar. The sheer relief of getting this far is offset by the strain on her legs which now begins to feel unbearable from having to use a low gear and putting pressure on her far from new car. Her hope is she can get further, at least to be close to some kind of civilisation if she happened to break down.

Many times she regrets her impulsiveness, her darkest fears of being found frozen inside her broken down car eventually doesn't seem quite so bad, at least a blessed release from the living hell she is running from.

She reaches the summit where the Glenshee Ski Centre stands forlornly empty, with no sign of real life or any of the snow needed to bring the place to life. Only the hillside sculptures, two seated figures, overlook the road as if in anticipation of her arrival. She notices the figures look away from each other, each viewing a different scene. Their backs separate them from making any kind of connection. She is certain they represent a married couple; the body language tells all.

She considers stopping, abandoning her journey on, to sleep in her car. The thought beckons as her fatigue grows with the cramps in her legs begging for rest. She is greatly relieved she brought a sleeping bag and the blankets she nearly left behind. At least she still possessed the instinct for some things at any rate; all else that was rational has long since been hammered out of her.

Once over the top the descent allows her to ease the pressure on her legs as the road winds down into the village with a view of a church steeple and the abundance of fir trees beginning to catch the flakes of snow on their branches. On impulse she turns left towards the centre of the village which also seems as deserted as the Ski Centre up top. *Who would turn out on a day like this?*

She cruises slowly past a large hotel with no lights showing, either abandoned or closed, she cannot tell. Next there is a Co-op store with dim lights. At the end of the village a café is also closed making her stop to turn her car around to leave. She stops outside a quaint shop which according to the overhead sign is **The March of Time,** displaying all kinds of time pieces in its window. The shop fascinates her especially the painted picture at the side of the name, a rabbit in a top hat checking the time by a pocket watch, makes her smile for the first time since she began her mammoth journey.

She flicks her windscreen wipers to displace the loose flakes of snow as she stares at the shop wondering whether you could make enough to survive from the selling of clocks. Then she spots the hand-crafted notice on the door offering the service for mending all clocks, watches and time pieces. *Even so*, she thinks, *do people actually get their clocks mended?* They are more likely to throw them out or buy something new.

She sees movement to one side of the notice somewhere deep inside the shop. In panic she puts the car into gear to pull away, she is far from ready to have any kind of conversation should the proprietor of the shop come outside to try to entice her in to purchase a clock she has no use for. Time is not something she wants to measure, at least not until she is sure she is safe.

She decides to press on with her journey even though she has no idea where she is going. Visibility begins to diminish with the light of the day making her feel even colder. Overcome with weariness she has a need to stop. She sees a sign for an inn showing dim lights of occupancy. She pulls up outside the front even though an arrow points to a rear car park. She doesn't know how weak her legs are until she tests them on the short distance to the Inn door from where she is parked outside.

When she pushes through the door she is greeted by a roaring log fire, the crackles and sparks a welcome sight. She sits down as close as she can possibly get to the fire there being no other people in the bar. She takes in its features as she begins to thaw out. There is a limited menu of food available chalked up on a blackboard behind the tiny bar. All she really wants is the 'Soup of the Day' with a coffee except there is no one there to take her order.

Through a hatch at the back of the bar she can see a large room with a pool table next to stacks of tables and chairs. A giant of a man, as broad as he is tall, dressed as a chef sluggishly makes his way across the room towards her, seemingly with difficulty. Wheezing, out of breath he has sufficient left to inform her the kitchen is now closed, lunch time is finished and he has switched everything off.

When she tells him she has come many miles, only needs some hot soup because she is chilled to the bone, he relents saying he could manage a bowl of soup with a sandwich. However, the bar is closed. He can oblige her with coffee if she doesn't mind instant.

Even though she barely converses with the man when he brings her order, she asks him if he knows of any local places, preferably B&B's in the area. This Inn is residential he tells her and is currently closed until the spring like a lot of places. He offers her directions scrawled on a piece of paper to a reasonable place he knows of, if she doesn't mind going a bit further on. Now revived by soup and a sandwich, going further seems more appropriate than turning back to retrace her journey. Always moving on, appeals to her sense of flight taking her away from the past, closer to a new beginning.

CHAPTER 2

Bart hovered behind the door of his shop drawn there by the sound of a car or more precisely the grating of the gears by someone nervous perhaps. He could make out the thin pale face of the driver, a young woman, her auburn hair covered by the hood of her coat was poking out masking the shape of her face. He was right she did look nervous or maybe even scared.

Just like you?

The sound loud enough to be heard above the noise of all the clocks in his shop spooked him making his heart race. He watched the girl, her age he placed in her early twenties, was sitting staring at his shop out of the driver's window. She looked upwards to the name he chose to display above the door, thought he saw her smile fleetingly, everyone did. The picture of the rabbit he knew most people found amusing especially those who knew him because the rabbit was dressed like him with waistcoats and matching bow ties.

The caricature was suited to the shop's name, **The March of Time,** a play on the March Hare from Alice in Wonderland, whilst the white rabbit was distinctly different. Since his move he changed the name from his former shop where he established himself as a clockmaker on joining the Witness Protection programme in the very quiet seaside town of Wainthorpe-on-sea. A quiet place where hardly anything ever happened until the man next door to his clock shop was found brutally murdered. That was when everything changed.

The shock made him reassess his own position having changed his name from Bart Bridges, the once Private Investigator, who found himself entangled with some seriously bad people placing him in great personal danger, to become Cyrus Bartholomew, clockmaker. This was his cover (his 'Legend' according to the police) that made him feel reasonably safe, except he was neither Cyrus Bartholomew nor was he a real clockmaker. He did, however, mend clocks, something he taught himself to do and felt comfortable with. Nonetheless, he still thought of himself as Bart, he could never quite get used to being Cyrus.

The girl in the car trembled with the cold; her pinched face was blue, whilst those forlorn eyes he imagined radiated panic as he watched her. He leaned forward to get a better view of her, saw the pale face frown as her body first stiffened then began to shake. She suddenly reached forward to engage the gears to back jerkily away.

She must have seen him move. He tutted at himself, *not much of a private investigator if you allow yourself to be seen and to scare away your subjects!* He walked towards the door, caught a glimpse of the car disappearing along Main Street. He switched the 'open' door sign to 'closed', turned the key in the lock knowing no one was going to come now. There hadn't been a customer all day. He laughed wryly having clearly frightened away the only potential one.

He slid the bolts on the door locking him in. No local nonsense for him. The locals may rarely lock their doors up here in the Highlands, was something he would never be able to bring himself to do. He would not mention this to anyone coming into his shop or even those he met in the pub. Safety was ingrained in him ever since his 'exile' in dropping out of his old life. He didn't think he would ever feel completely safe again.

Since his moonlight flit from Wainthorpe, leaving his Witness Protection life behind completely, he'd informed no one. He felt much happier out on his own. He even destroyed the telephone number of his Witness Protection minder, 'Steve'. He felt sure he would never make contact with him again. The only regret was leaving behind the only real friend he ever made, Jayson Vingoe, who he did miss especially their regular chats about forensic evidence. Bart Bridges, also the once Scenes of Crime officer, like Jay (only they called them CSI's these days) became a Private Investigator, yet he was unable to forget his training or his forensic skills which gave him a keen eye for people and places which came in handy later.

Out of the glass in the door he stood looking at the sky, overcast with heavy snow clouds. When he came here last year, he missed the worst of the winter weather. People at the pub suggested conditions could get so bad they were often snowed in. Something even the snow ploughs coming through clearing the main roads couldn't stop. When the snow fell it came quickly, often many feet high overnight. How they laughed, telling him he wouldn't stand much of a chance outside given his height.

Bart Bridges (Cyrus Bartholomew) was short and plump like the picture of the hare on his shop sign. He knew how he appeared to people, he never quite got used to some laughing at him. As far as he could remember, Jayson Vingoe was the only person who never did. Yes, he missed his friend Jay more than anyone in his previous lives. Bart sighed deeply as he saw the first few flakes of snow fluttering past his door. He wondered if he would be able to get out to the pub at 12 o'clock tomorrow for his midday meal, as he did most days, if the snow came with a vengeance.

He turned back moving behind the shop counter to his work area, a table laid out with the pieces of a large Grandmother clock he was repairing. The individual parts were placed in an order only he knew the significance of. The flash of the face in the car and the pieces suddenly reminded him of Emily, back at Wainthorpe. A fifteen year old school girl who was the only person he'd ever met who shared his fascination for time pieces, whom he taught how to mend them, after school or on the weekends when she helped him in his shop.

His mind recalled another young lass back at Wainthorpe; an illegal Eastern European girl, frail and unkempt who worked for a time as a waitress at the golf club where he sometimes ate lunch in the clubhouse. She shared the same frightened look the girl in the car outside did. He knew the feeling of being pursued. Briefly he wondered if he ever shared the same haunted look sufficiently for anyone to notice. Not that anyone ever really saw him. He was mostly invisible to people which was a rare quality to have as a Private Investigator.

He glanced towards the door, spotted two more large flakes of snow drifting past. He reached down under the shop counter to touch the baseball bat he kept there concealed from view. The motion, a reflex, was an urge he often had, its smooth surface always made him feel a little bit safer. You could never be really sure when you might need it. At least when the snow came he would feel happier being cut off from the outside world with no one able to get through the mountain pass into the village.

CHAPTER 3

Long after she finished eating she sat basking in the warmth of the fire. With no other customers her patron, the chef, retired back to his kitchen. With no paying guests she wondered what he could possibly have to do. Eventually she left the warmth of the dying fire, returned to her car where she sat contemplating the hastily scribbled directions in a nearly indecipherable scrawl. Spurred on by the need to get as far away as she could, she started the car and drove away as the snow began in earnest.

The instructions, together with what she remembered of his quickly spoken words, directed her away from the main road to Aboyne. At Crathie she turned along what the chef called the 'Old Road' running parallel, where she began to count the right turns off, eventually taking the fourth, *or was it the fifth*. She wasn't sure now which, there was meant to be a post box on the corner she couldn't spot. Why a post box out here when there was no sign of houses or any kind of life, seemed odd as she climbed the inclined lane at the fourth turn.

Visibility diminished as the snow increased. The gloom would soon become full dark with night approaching fast and there being no actual street lights she could see. She was in two minds whether to turn around to retrace her journey, then where would she go? Without a postcode her satnav moved on showing her a meaningless map whilst the stilted male voice urged her to take the next right or left turn where there was none. She switched the satnav off leaving her to drive in complete silence except for the sound of the car's engine. When the car laboured she changed down a gear.

The car crawled its way up the incline where she could see the outline of a cottage, one with a flickering candle in the window. She felt like she was driving around in circles now, noticing another similar cottage; she wondered if everyone placed a naked flame in their windows out here. After another two turns, the poor visibility, with intermittent use of her wipers to move the snowflakes, made her stop outside of yet another cottage with a candle in the window. This one looked the same as the last one. The windscreen wipers stopped across the glass as if frozen to it. She could no longer see the road in front of her so she decided to ask at the cottage about the address the landlord at the Inn wrote down on the piece of paper sitting on the passenger seat beside her.

The pathway led to the open door stretching out before her, each step felt harder for someone so fatigued, her movements like walking in slow motion towards the silhouetted figure standing waiting in the doorway. At first quite hazy, the blurry shape was accompanied by two dogs, standing still one each side of her like sentinels watching her progress up the pathway.

They showed little curiosity, neither of them barked at her, a stranger. They stared at her motionless; she assumed assessing if she posed any danger to their aging mistress whom she could now see clearly. There was no greeting wag of the tail or hint of a sniff. They turned to run back inside having made their decision she was no threat, leaving the old lady, alone at the door.

"Come away," the elderly grey haired woman greeted her in a very Scottish way, "You'll be perished wi' the cauld and wanting a glaise."

When she got near enough to register her sweet face, the woman smiled, stood back into the hallway to let her visitor come inside out of the snow, as if she was expected. It seemed natural to enter, by now she was far too tired to think of doing anything else. She barely registered anything other than the hallway was a room with a piano directly ahead whilst a Grandfather clock to one side struck a quarter past the hour as she stepped inside. She let the old lady lead her through to a large kitchen at the back where the two dogs lay stretched out in front of a kitchen range with a blazing log fire in the middle.

Much of the evening's conversation was lost on her, hearing hardly anything the old lady spoke about because of the constant rushing bitter wind outside drowned out all sound, much like whispers in a dream. The hot chocolate drink warmed her inside giving her a rosy glow as well as bringing hot-aches to her hands. Afterwards the old woman led her upstairs to a spare bed already made up in one of the rooms. She neither questioned the fact nor did she object to it, she knew nothing after her head lowered onto the pillow because she fell fast asleep.

It turned out to be the best night's sleep she ever had before or since. Her advanced state of fatigue, from the distance she travelled away from her past life, must have produced a stark sense of wellbeing to allow for it.

*   *   *   *   *

When she woke up next day the bedroom was bright, even though she could detect no sun shining through the curtains at the window. Far from seeming strange the room felt familiar and cosy. She knew exactly where she was and oddly felt like she'd come home. She thought instantly of the kindly face of Elizabeth Elspeth Grant, the frail woman she met the night before. She had no memory of her saying her name; most of the conversation was one way, so she thought she must have heard it.

By the time she dressed and went down stairs into the hallway she found, to her surprise, the whole contents of her car sitting on the floor to one side of the piano. She was forced to reassess the strength of the person who retrieved her luggage. Elizabeth didn't look like she was able to have undertaken such a task.

On entering the kitchen again the logs in the fire place burned as brightly as the evening before, except now a large black bottomed kettle sat at the front on a shelf with steam rising from the spout. She noticed the fire supplied the means to heat the range in between twin ovens, one on either side. She inhaled the deeply delicious smell of baking bread filling the room, mingling with the aromatic freshly ground coffee she could detect. Also something much sweeter she couldn't quite place, cinnamon or vanilla she guessed. She had never seen such an antiquated means of cooking outside of a history book. Somewhere to the left of this configuration a conventional cooker sat in a corner with three hot plates underneath an eye level grill none of which showed any sign of use or responsibility for the enticing smells.

The old lady, for she must have been in her eighth decade, took down a tea cloth from the rail beneath a mantelpiece over the range with which she unlatched the door to the right oven. She caught a glimpse of a crusty cottage loaf of bread. Elizabeth took out the tray, the loaf's crust browner on the side nearest to the fire – no oven fans here for even baking. She placed the loaf on a wooden bread board in the centre of the large kitchen table, where a dish with golden butter sat next to a three segmented jam dish with orange marmalade, homemade blackcurrant preserve and at a guess either raspberry or strawberry jam.

She smiled at the girl, "You will be hungry no doubt?" She moved to take the kettle off the boil, "Will ye take tea or coffee?" she asked pouring hot water into a teapot before she replaced its lid covering the pot with a brightly knitted tea cosy to keep the brew warm.

The whole scene, a step back in time, made her feel safe, something she hadn't felt since early childhood; one that didn't last as long as it should have. Nevertheless the echo of the feeling still lingered.

"Coffee would be nice," she replied. "Thank you for letting me stay the night," she was feeling the need to convey her gratitude for rescuing her, the snow having come on heavily at the time she invited her in. "You needn't have brought my luggage inside," The comment sounded a little ungrateful so she quickly added, "It's much too heavy...."

"Not at all," she cut in. "I think you might see why I did if you were to look outside."

With this the old woman moved over to the back door whilst the girl watched the two dogs follow her, once again standing either side of her when she pulled the door open.

She was shocked seeing the snow standing some three feet in height in an abundant blanket across the back garden as far as the eye could see, rendering the whole garden featureless. One or two trees grew out of the white carpet obliterating everything apart from snow laden branches hanging heavily from the weight. There was a recently cleared pathway cutting across the garden to the snow camouflaged outbuildings which were barely distinguishable shapes, their roofs heavy with snow.

The snow had been scraped away to give access to one of the doors. The old wooden entrance was split in two unequal halves so the top could be opened leaving the bottom half closed in place, like a stable. She was shocked by the piled up snow either side, testament to the amount of work that had gone into clearing the paths. This was something a frail old lady ordinarily might be incapable of doing.

"It's for the dogs," she said simply. At the reference to them they both looked up at her making no move to go outside. The snow was still falling heavily. "Go on!" she ordered tetchily as they both moved reluctantly out into the garden. "Now you can see why I needed to empty your car?" She grinned watching them tread tentatively away. "I think you might have some difficulty finding your car this morning – when the snow comes I'm afraid there really is no way of getting out. The snow ploughs don't come this far out, they only do the main roads to keep everything moving – it's much like this the whole winter I'm afraid."

She turned back towards her visitor as the dogs came scurrying back inside, wet from the falling flakes, they flopped back down in front of the fire. She quickly turned to close the door to keep in the warmth. She crossed to the fire picked up another log from the log basket at the side, to stoke the fire where the flames began to devour it.

The kitchen light flashed briefly struggling to stay on. "Ah," she went on, "Another reason to keep yon blaise." She sounded like she was talking to herself as she used the long handled poker to shift the log into the flames. "The electric is prone t'fail – mebbe off for hours so we have to resort to oil lamps or candles."

"Yes, I noticed the candle in the window last night," the girl said, knowing the candle drew her. The old lady smiled as if she knew and the candle had been a deliberate ploy.

"Old habits die hard," she mumbled. "It was something ma mother did when the weather turned bad – it's the only way to show anyone where we are. There are no street lights out here to give direction." She seemed to fade off into thoughts of another time as she gazed into the fire watching the flames jump into life to greet the newly placed log. She stood for a few seconds as her guest watched her mesmerized by the dancing flames. "It's always nice to have someone to talk to."

She felt a little guilty as her own intentions were quite the opposite. How do you convey to someone who spends most of their time alone you envied them?

The old lady picked up the steaming kettle again; she watched her carry the awkward load to the worktop where she poured the hot water into a waiting cafetière with freshly ground coffee already at the bottom. Immediately the rich coffee aroma burst into life challenging all the other smells. She put the kettle back on the fire, the top of the cafetière lid in place, leaving the plunger standing upright. She placed the coffee on the table in front of her, making the table seem fuller or maybe it was the cups. The girl saw hers was a large round bowl shaped cup sitting on its own white saucer. Elizabeth's was a delicate bone china flowery patterned 'old lady's' cup, neither of which seemed out of place for the present company.

"Thank you," The girl murmured as Elizabeth poured milk into her own cup, then offered her the jug. She shook her head, watched her place the jug down next to a sugar bowl filled with sugar lumps on top of which perched a tiny pair of silver sugar tongs.

She marvelled at the effort she must have gone to in providing these things. What she didn't consider, given the isolation she found the old lady living in, was how she would have fresh milk, never mind how she would keep anything cold when the electricity failed. Not until she saw her fetch a bottle of milk from a wooden cupboard outside the back door did she realise the snow provided a natural means of refrigeration.

After she took her bags upstairs to the guest room where she slept the night before, she gazed out of the window across to where she abandoned her car the night before. She could see a snow drift she assumed was her car, now covered entirely by snow. Comforted by the scene outside, she realised if she couldn't get out, then no one would be able to get in. Not that anyone knew where she was.

CHAPTER 4

"My goodness!" Bart's unheard cry of shock reverberated around his empty bedroom, there being no one else present to hear him. He had just pulled open the heavy duty curtains he was now accustomed to having ever since his seaside years when his next door neighbour (he discovered much later after his murder) grew marijuana in his green house. The powerful lights he used during the night shone directly into his old bedroom at the back of his shop keeping him awake.

Bart smiled at the distant memory *you would be hard placed to try it here* crossed his mind as he took in the view across the basin where the village sat surrounded by low mountains. The terrain lay under several feet of snow masking any features apart from the tops of houses. The forest of fir trees was covered all over except at their very tips where the snow had been shaken free by the force of the sweeping wind. He could see the drifts of snow were thicker in some places producing waves of snow like the swell of a white ocean.

He moved across to the second window on the adjacent wall, drew back the drapes giving him a view of the bottom of Main Street and the 'turning circle' used by coaches full of tourists as well as the local bus service. Everywhere the snow rendered everything featureless. He could see the roof of someone's car outside a house on the road to the Linn of Dee, buried under several feet of snow, with only a side mirror giving a clue to what lay beneath. He lifted his gaze to the sky which was still full of snow, now coming fast, adding to the depth and he understood the humour expressed by those in the pub about his lack of height being risky in bad weather.

The day before, as he watched the young lass in her car outside, he saw the first of the snowflakes begin to fall and had promised himself a walk up the road today to the one Co-op shop in the village selling groceries, with a separate trip across to the butchers to stock up on provisions. He didn't expect this much snow quite so soon, he realised he'd left food buying far too late.

"What now Bart?" he asked himself as if he were talking to someone close by.

He wasn't sure he possessed an implement sturdy enough to dig his way out of this amount of snow, certainly not as far as the grocery store on Main Street.

First, he needed to check exactly what food there was downstairs. He was a creature of habit, always eating at least one meal out each day. He hardly ever kept food in quantity at home. His next door neighbour around the corner facing the turning circle, was one of the local cafés, being one of the primary reasons he chose to live here when he came to view the 'old gallery' he eventually turned into his clock shop. A café close enough to pop out for lunch, or tea, even breakfast if he had a mind to do so. He doubted whether 'The Griddle Iron' would be open in this weather even though Max and Steph, the owners lived on the premises. Who would come out to eat in this kind of snow storm?

After he made himself a bacon sandwich with the last in the packet, he took his breakfast with a coffee into the shop just as all his chiming clocks hanging on the walls, dangling from the ceiling or free standing, began their nine o'clock synchronised routine. To most people hearing the noise for the first time was either a fascinating experience or else they ran back through the shop door to escape the assault on their tympanic membranes. Bart no longer found this amusing especially if he was in the middle of serving someone. Even though most people found their way back once the noise ceased, there was the occasional customer who didn't bother to return, whilst at least one he knew of made off without paying for the wrist watch they held in their hands.

Bart left his breakfast on his work table amidst the clock pieces to go over to the door which he unlocked and unbolted. Opening up he was immediately faced with a wall of firm snow nearly up to his waist. He stood looking out at the falling flakes wondering how much snow would constitute a record depth in the Highlands.

He heard a chugging noise, sounding like someone mowing a lawn somewhere in the distance. He shook his head smiling at such a ridiculous notion. As the sound grew nearer he began to frown unable to identify the source or lean outside to search for its owner. As the noise grew louder he waited until he saw a spray of snow shooting towards both sides of the road.

A small machine with angled blades at the front, a flashing light above a small cab was towing a trailer making slow progress down the hill past his shop leaving a channel free of snow behind it. The driver of this mini snowplough sat in the cab, glanced across at Bart who recognised his face from his many visits to the local 'pub'. He would have been hard pressed if asked his name. The pub was the only one in the village, half way up The Brae, hidden behind the sparsely placed cottages. The Moor Hen was the only place, other than the bars at the two hotels in the village (one of these was currently closed for renovation), where you could purchase a pint and a bar meal.

After he arrived in the village, he used the hotel bar on the main A93 Glenshee road where he'd stayed whilst scouting for a place to buy. At the time he got to know the manager who provided him with a good deal of local knowledge. When he moved to Scotland permanently he chanced upon the Moor Hen pub one day whilst out exploring the immediate countryside. In the summer he joined the local golf club after taking a much longer walk beside the River Dee. The clubhouse bar was a little basic, quite impersonal, being housed in a pre-fabricated structure. Even so, being a solitary person, he could ring the changes, whilst trying hard not to court too many people's attention or engage in any overly familiar associations. As a non-golpher he found the clubhouse useful to indulge one of his interests, 'people watching' which was much of the basic work of his previous occupation as a Private Investigator. He expected never again to meet anyone he felt he could call 'friend' like Jayson Vingoe back in Wainthorpe-on-Sea and he preferred it that way.

Bart closed the shop door blocking out the sight of his temporary imprisonment to return to his rapidly cooling bacon sandwich which he ate ravenously whilst sitting idly fingering the pieces of the Grandmother clock laid out in front of him. He tried to picture the contents of his integral garage feeling relieved he put his car away after he last used it. Often lazily he left the vehicle out front where the young woman stopped the previous day outside his shop.

In his mind's eye he searched the neatly packed garage space for anything he might use to scoop away the snow from his doorstep and the narrow pavement down The Brae to join the expanse of pavement The Griddle Iron used in summer as a pavement café extension to their premises. Nothing came to mind.

He didn't own any gardening equipment, like a spade, because his back garden was a courtyard he had so far failed to complete having decided one day he might fill the small space with garden furniture surrounded by planters to add a bit of colour. This was a project in waiting taking second place to sorting out the shop's hundreds of precious time pieces which took precedence over anything else. When time marched on he forgot about the garden entirely. Winter in Scotland he discovered came early with a vengeance if last night's snow was anything to go by.

He picked up his empty breakfast things, took them into the back scullery where he washed them whilst he stared out of the window at the white over space he thought of as his back garden. A small featureless yard with only a plastic coated washing line strung across to hang his smalls out to dry. He stared in fascination to see even the washing line managed to retain a couple of inches of snow balanced across the swaying length. As he watched a sudden gust of arctic wind blew the snow off sending an icy spray across the air.

Bart began to make a new mental list of things he needed to pay more attention to whilst silently chastising himself for his lack of foresight, until now he hadn't been so lax. He always prided himself on his readiness for any new situation. After all he was once quite a good Private Investigator, even with his give-away unfortunate looks he didn't easily blend into the crowd. He liked to think his appearance was distinctive (some thought strange), in any event unique.

There was, Bart believed, something appealing about living up here at a much slower less stressful pace lulled into a near comatose state. The contrast to being in the Witness Protection programme was stark, never knowing whether any of the villains from his past life would come looking for him. Mostly, he'd survived in a hyper-vigilant state. He was like a car with the choke always out putting pressure on the engine. *Now there was a metaphor to come out of nowhere.* He often wondered whether one day he would have a heart attack brought on by all the stress. Only now, having slipped into a much more sleepy way of living, did he realised he'd lost all the hitherto anxiety he used to have.

His attention was drawn by the sounds from the shop. He was always attentive to the noises his clocks made especially any 'odd' unexpected sounds he couldn't quite place. He was reminded once more of Emily with her acute hearing, tuned into the rhythm of the ticking, the chorus of chimes, especially the noises the cuckoos made. Emily was the one who detected the irregularity of the clock with the 'bird' missing its beak, as well as always being a half beat behind the rest of them at the noon chimes.

He knew the sound he'd just heard couldn't be put down to that particular clock because he no longer owned it. He gave Emily the clock as a gift when he left, partly because he was never able to correct the irregularity himself, no matter how hard he tried (and he certainly did try). He knew if anyone could, Emily would be able to.

More importantly he left the clock with her because he was never really sure whether his 'bouts' of unconsciousness (or black outs) that only happened if he found himself in the shop as the midday chimes commenced, were anything to do with the cuckoo clock. He preferred to vacate the premises going each day for an early lunch to the pub just to be on the safe side. As a creature of habit the precaution was hard to stop, so he still did.

He listened again, heard only ticking clocks, he wandered off into the garage through the internal connecting door in search of anything with which to dig his way out.

CHAPTER 5

After a good night's sleep it seemed the most natural thing in the world to be sitting there with the old woman having breakfast. Whether because of Elizabeth Grant, the cottage or the snow cutting them off from the outside world, a sense of absolute wellbeing settled over her making her feel totally safe.

Later, once they finished eating, after she took her bags upstairs to the room she slept in the night before, the old lady took her outside to the stable block. She didn't expect them to be occupied in the way the building was intended, by any kind of animals; after all a woman of her years would have no use for horses. Part of her did consider she might have a goat tucked away in one of the stalls from which she got her supply of milk. She found herself holding her breath waiting for Elizabeth to open the door, thinking one might make a bid to escape its confinement.

Elizabeth pulled open the top half of the door to allow them to peer inside, grinning as if she knew what the other woman's thoughts would be. She saw a veritable food store of things. Stacked up to one side was an abundance of firewood with a coal scuttle standing ready at the side. The rest was given over to shelves of bottled, canned or bags of food of all descriptions.

"It isn't always quite this full," Elizabeth explained seeing the girl's total shock at the amount of produce stored there. "Autumn is the time we begin to collect for winter, so you have come at its fullest – by the thaw you will see why this is necessary. By then no doubt you'll be craving a wee take out meal." She gave a chuckle whilst the shock registered on the girl's face that a somewhat 'modern' practice would be known to the old woman. She was fascinated by this antiquated way of living, whilst take-out food was the furthest thing from her mind.

Elizabeth Grant opened the bottom half of the door allowing her to move inside where she beckoned her visitor in with, "Come," and a wave of her hand.

She moved slowly around inspecting everything stored there during which the old lady explained to her the fruit was from the garden. She pulled open a draw in an old chest showing an abundance of apples carefully laid down in the draws all individually half wrapped in newspaper. She explained apples were okay to store like this, it was the pears, she pointed at a row of jars of pear halves bottled in syrup, that needed to be prepared, "They ripen too quickly to keep any other way," she explained.

She ran her finger along the rows of jars marvelling at the variety of fruits there were on the shelves noting blackberries, gooseberries, blackcurrants, redcurrants being the ones she thought she recognised.

"It must take such a lot of work," she remarked.

"Not really," the old lady smiled. "Most of the fruit I give away." She didn't say to whom, but remembered the lack of neighbouring houses visible as she drove around in the snow storm, so she couldn't imagine who she meant. Perhaps she missed them with the lack of visibility due to the storm or the practice of displaying a guiding candle wasn't universally used during a power cut to draw her attention to any other homes. At the time Elizabeth Grant appeared to be pretty isolated, lacking people surrounding her to give anything away to. The isolation appealed to her even more.

Before they went back inside the old lady pointed to a large bag on the floor, "Would you carry one of those inside for me?" The paper sack contained dry dog food weighing many kilos she assessed when she picked one up, wondering once again how someone as old as Elizabeth could manage one on her own. She hefted the cumbersome bag up with difficulty into her arms leaving the old woman to close the stable door.

The two guard dogs sat inside the cottage's back door watching as she crossed the yard, only moving to allow her (with their food) passage into the cottage. The only sign of anything close to 'normal' canine behaviour was a slight raise of the nose to sniff the air.

"You are strange," the girl mumbled under her breath which neither of them seemed offended by.

The old lady joined her carrying a large square wicker basket filled with an assortment of things including apples. "I'll make us a pie for after dinner dessert, do you like apple pie?" She nodded her assurance offering to help. "It's nae bother," was the reply.

Once inside Elizabeth took her on a tour of the cottage, not that there was very much left for her to see. The one bathroom was downstairs off the hallway which she was already familiar with. The room contained a bath with a separate shower stall she used earlier in the morning; the heavy wooden plinth she stood on was still wet in places.

There was a small front 'parlour', a very pleasant sitting room which looked rarely used as she imagined the old lady spent much of her time in the large kitchen where the firewood crackled. The grate in the parlour was empty with another full log basket in a small hearth beside a glass fronted iron framed fireguard showing an embroidery picture of a hunting scene.

The frilled chintz sofa matched the chairs. They showed no particular signs of wear; the whole place was obviously seldom used. She noted the absence of a television realising the old lady had no use for such a device. She was probably totally oblivious to happenings in the world outside.

"Nice," was her only comment as they stood in the parlour doorway.

"Mostly where I receive visitors," which explained the not 'lived in' look to the room. She didn't ask her who her visitors might be, nor did the old lady offer the information, she merely closed any further discussion on the matter with the closing of the parlour door.

The young girl waited patiently behind Elizabeth as she slowly climbed up the stairs leading firstly into her own bedroom containing one large bed with brass bestead rails. Everything was neat with an assortment of crocheted doilies on the dressing table where matching candlesticks and trinket boxes in silver plate were displayed.

A sturdy old oak wardrobe to one end, a side cabinet next to the bed where an old style 'teas-made' took pride of place, were the only additional furniture in the room. Elizabeth watched her walk over to the one window with a view of the surrounding landscape, currently an expanse of all white with a hillside in the distance showing hundreds of snow-covered fir trees a common feature in Scotland. She imagined the view to be spectacular during other seasons of the year, but hard to tell with a generous blanket of snow covering all things and the snow still falling heavily.

Despite the arctic scene outside, the room was pleasantly warm which surprised her as she could detect no central heating in the cottage. The old lady smiled again as if reading her thoughts pointing to the wall at the side of the bed, "It's directly over the kitchen. The chimney runs behind the wall." She walked over to touch it. The girl followed her finding the stone pleasantly warm to the touch. "These stone walls retain the heat otherwise they relay the cold in from the outside."

She walked away expecting her to follow, "Unfortunately not so in your room." This reference to the room being 'hers' surprised her; she would have expected her to say the back room or at least the guest room. Next she led the way to the smallest room which looked out onto the back garden where you could catch a glimpse of the roof of the stable block through the window if you stood in the doorway.

Elizabeth nodded for her to enter, whilst she remained standing outside on the landing. The room appeared singularly cell-like with only a small iron-framed bed and a table up against the wall inside the door. The only other feature was the deep sill of the window where two more candlesticks stood alone without candles. To look down into the garden you would have to lean across to get a view below.

As if expected she walked into the room, moving over toward the window. In doing so she passed through a band of ice-cold air across the room before she got near to the window, making her cross her arms around herself, grabbing hold of her upper arms on each side she rubbed them to try to warm herself up. She turned to face the old woman who stood expectantly staring at her.

"Did someone die in this room?" The question came automatically without any real thought on her part.

Before Elizabeth could form a reply the line of books standing in a row on top of the dressing table inside the door fell over like a pack of dominoes might do if set up to flick the first one over. She neither jumped, nor uttered a sound as she watched the girl's reaction, before she turned away leaving her there. She followed, again walking through the icy cold causing her to shiver. As she passed the dressing table she set the books upright again mumbling, "Sorry," to the room – she had no idea why she did so.

CHAPTER 6

The unproductive search of his garage left Bart wondering how to extricate himself from his enforced imprisonment. He could hear the chiming of his clocks from inside the garage. When the sounds subsided, other odd scraping noises came echoing through the eventual silence. He crept back gingerly along the connecting passageway once more entering his shop, caught a glimpse of the flash from the snowplough's warning light and heard the 'lawnmower' engine labouring somewhere close by.

He opened the shop door discovering he failed to relock it after he opened up earlier. *My word Bart, now there's a first,* he thought, far from his usual anxiety at slipping up on his security precautions, he felt quite liberated. When the door was fully open again he found all the snow previously blocking his doorway, had been removed. In its place he found two Co-op carrier bags containing groceries.

He stepped out onto the door step to watch as the small snowplough moved away back up the hill with its tow truck full of similar carrier bags. Sitting amongst them he recognised Alastair the landlord of the Moor Hen who smiled and waved a greeting.

"We're serving lunch today from twelve o'clock," he shouted at Bart. "See you there?" not so much a question more like a very tempting invitation.

Bart waved back quite overwhelmed by the bonhomie as the procession of 'aide' made its way slowly up The Brae to deliver similar rescue packages to other stranded people.

"Oh my!" Bart exclaimed out loud, a veritable lump in his throat, he had never before experienced such kindness.

As he stooped to pick up the bags his protruding backside knocked against a long handled snow shovel he failed to notice propped against his shop window which he caught before it fell onto the bank of snow on the pavement. He held the shovel in front of him, its length nearly as tall as him, with a large black scoop head attached. He'd noticed these at the Esso garage on the A93 just outside the village when he last went for petrol, he now realised they were an essential requirement for life up here in the Highlands when the snow came.

He glanced once more at the disappearing snowplough now stopped at a cottage farther up The Brae and saw Alistair was delivering more emergency provisions. He could also see the handles of many more snow shovels slanting across the back of the tow truck, "Oh my!" he repeated.

He left his shovel in his doorway leaving the shop door wide open, whilst he took the bags inside. He began to dress himself in boots, a woolly hat, gloves and his old duffle coat. He went outside to christen the snow shovel by doing his bit to shift the snow from the pavement all the way down the road to join his neighbour Max clearing snow from the front of his café. There were others who came to assist him, progressing further out into the road to clear the 'turning circle' for the local bus service to get through.

He met people working alongside him he neither knew nor recognised and they toiled on without speaking to conserve their breathing, as if there was a predetermined plan. He realised this was the most exercise he'd taken in a long time and he could see his breath expelled in the cold air vapours in front of him. By the time they finished clearing the whole turning circle he felt completely exhausted, standing to one side he leaned on the shovel to get his breath back watching some of the people as they walked away. The others followed Max into the café where he could see Steph standing behind the counter inside. Max returned to the door to beckon Bart inside, "Hot drink?" he shouted smiling amiably.

Bart placed his shovel against the corner of the café feeling obliged to follow, reluctant as he was to join in with any group chat. The last thing he needed was a heap of personal questions. Accordingly, he took a seat as far away from the main group of disparate people, most of whom seemed to know each other. He settled sideways on with a view out the front of the café marvelling at the snow piled up to one side, most of the people having propped their shovels against this high wall of accumulated snow.

On the table in front of him a copy of The Scotsman periodical caught Bart's eye. He picked up the small publication randomly flicked through the pages showing mountains, cascading waterfalls and snowy scenes beneath which the articles appeared out of focus. As a reflex action his hand went in search of his spectacles in his waistcoat pocket, which he removed when he put on his heavy duty pullover. Then he remembered leaving his glasses sitting amidst the clock pieces when his attention was first drawn to the noises outside to go in search of a spade.

It seemed like hours ago. He glanced at the café clock on the wall. A huge station clock he admired the first time he came into The Griddle Iron, not only because of its enormous size which took a good deal of space amongst the pictures displayed on the walls, but because the clock fascinated him. Never before had he seen a clock moving backwards, anti-clockwise, yet seeming to show the correct time. It was like looking at a clock in a mirror. The time was nearly half past eleven with the whole morning nearly gone.

"*Heavens!*" Bart thought as Max approached him with a mug of hot chocolate piled with a head of thick cream sprinkled with cocoa powder.

Bart's hand automatically moved towards his pocket to search for some money to pay him. Max reached out to touch his arm in a gesture of 'stay' indicating no need for any reimbursement. "Thanks for a job well done," he said, which made perfect sense when you considered the help he'd received to give access to his café. Bart's eyes were drawn to movement outside as the local bus appeared down Main Street turning without effort to draw around in front of the café coming to a halt on the newly cleared turning circle.

The doors whooshed smoothly open allowing several people out including a man heavily clothed in what appeared to be mountaineering attire. He rushed towards the café moving hastily through the door up to the counter where he was joined by several of the group of snow shifters who all huddled together with Max for a discussion.

Bart heard the man's initial words of "Call out" as he passed by then watched him as they spoke urgently together. After this group discussion, with the exception of one man who went to sit back with the group and Max the rest of them left the café together to jump on board the waiting bus. The doors closed again, the bus moving away around the circle and back along Main Street.

Max walked over to the window where Bart was sitting, to stare in the wake of the bus.

"I do wonder at the stupidity of people," Max announced as if speaking to himself.

"What is it?" Bart could sense something significant was taking place.

"It's a call out," he replied. "They are mountain rescue volunteers, some walkers haven't returned." He paused as if in awe of the situation needing to find the right words to continue, "Feared lost," Max walked away back to his wife behind the counter. Bart watched as they spoke quietly together. He glanced back through the window up to the nearest piece of high ground covered in fir trees, shaking his head.

Bart had lived there long enough to know the difference between the hill he could see in front of him and the mountains that made up the Cairngorms. He knew this part of the world drew many ramblers, walkers and climbers of all descriptions ranging from enthusiastic exercise seekers to serious mountaineers with all the others in between.

He heard local talk, often delivered with the greatest of distain, about a category of 'stupid' people who neither heeded the danger warnings getting caught out when the weather changed quickly, as it was prone to do, nor did they have any understanding of their own abilities (or lack of them) and ventured out to places way beyond their capabilities.

Bart listened to the talk around the café instigated by the man left behind, he picked up that the three people in question were hikers staying in a local B&B, who hadn't returned yesterday from a walk seemingly caught out by the sudden onset of snow. They had been out there all night.

Bart shivered, regarded the slope of snow covered fir trees before him as the flakes of snow drifting past the café window were once again floating about in the wildly buffeting wind. He finished his hot chocolate, stood up to leave, hoping the snow wouldn't come back with a vengeance to remove all hope of finding them alive. He felt the brief guilt as he also selfishly hoped the snow wouldn't stop him getting a hot meal at The Moor Hen. He left the café with a wave of thanks to Max and Steph for his drink.

He absently picked up his newly christened snow shovel from the corner as he walked around onto The Brae, the short distance up his recently cleared pavement back into The March of Time. His mind was lost somewhere half-way up one of the snow covered mountains where he imagined three frozen bodies were buried. *How on earth could you find anyone in all this snow?*

As if in greeting the clocks suddenly clicked into a synchronised chorus beginning their quarter to the hour chimes. He stopped briefly to listen for any 'wayward' time piece out of sync with the rest. He could hear nothing out of the ordinary, knew he must get changed swiftly to be out of his shop and away to the Moor Hen before the twelve o'clock chimes began – he was still sufficiently fearful of his previous experiences to want to be out before then.

He knew he no longer possessed 'the' one cuckoo clock he feared the most. It now belonged to Emily back in Wainthorpe. This thought gave way to the notion he must check on her to see if she was.......well, simply to check on her. He was comforted by knowing Emily suffered no inexplicable effects when she stayed inside his old shop at midday. The very day she discovered *the* cuckoo clock with the bird with a missing beak and its faltering chime. This was one reason he left the clock with her.

*   *   *   *   *

The cuckoo clock hung on the wall above the bed, its two long trailing mechanisms just reaching equal lengths as the countdown chimes to twelve noon began.

Emily lay on her bed below the clock where she had been watching a You Tube video about Steampunk clocks and cogs; she looked up at the clock. This was her pride and joy, given to her by Cyrus Bartholomew as a parting gift before he left. It now began the striking of the midday hour. She waited.

It was another test run after her many attempts to correct the fault. Cyrus told her if anyone could rectify the irregularity, she could, which is one of the reasons he gave it to her, although not his only one. She waited, not daring to breathe, for the tiny door at the apex of the roof to open at the first strike of twelve.

The faint sound of the clock reversing signalled the anticipated opening of the door in the clock, then sprang forward, releasing the cuckoo clock's tiny wooden bird with no beak; springing out through the door "cuckoo", the first of twelve repeated motions, back and forth, back and forth.

She let out the breath she held with a sigh once again.

Of course, there wasn't many other clocks in this her bedroom to synchronise the sound against like there had been in the shop.

Nothing to mark time with, to show it was slightly out of time, a half beat behind because of the briefest reversal before it struck, as if someone put a finger against the clock's minute hand to pause the movement for a half beat before letting it go forward once again.

She knew, no matter how many times she dismantled the clock, putting it back together again, she would never be able to get back the missed beat of time. She felt compelled to keep on trying in the same way she knew was necessary to adjust time, she read somewhere once, to compensate for differences between clocks on satellites to those on earth.

It was all a matter of making sure that time moved forward together like it was supposed to do.

*   *   *   *   *

The small squat figure dressed in a duffle coat and Wellington boots, shot out of number one, The Brae, otherwise known as The March of Time, as if he was being pursued by a grizzly bear or a fire-eating dragon. He rushed straight up the snow cleared channel running down the centre of the road. Bart Bridges (a.k.a. Cyrus Bartholomew) slowed his pace only after the echo of his many clocks became a distant whisper. He had only just vacated his shop in time before the cacophony of sound began to herald in the beginning of the afternoon.

The boots made him slip a few times on the journey up The Brae. About half way up he met the road off to the left, turned down this lane towards The Moor Hen public house situated at the bottom overlooking the memorial games park. This was the place where once a year this quiet sleepy village turned over night into the mass gathering of more people than Bart had ever seen in such a tiny place at any one time. This he witnessed himself, also getting his first glimpse of royalty when the Queen's cavalcade went past him as he stood outside the café below his shop. Today, however, the park was marked by deep white drifts of snow he knew would remain for several weeks.

The side road leading to the Moor Hen had been cleared, probably the first to be done, because this was the site of the owner of the small snow plough Bart saw earlier. He now observed the vehicle standing silently inside a garage-like structure near the public house, the doors wide open with the engine off and no flashing light showing, hearing the subtle tick of a cooling motor.

A sensible vehicle to own if you live up here hidden away in a dip on a hillside Bart thought pausing briefly to take in the strange machine he felt could easily be an amateur built construction, likely made from a lawnmower engine. Somewhat amateur in its design, the plough was certainly nothing like anything he ever saw before, however, no one could fault its effectiveness. *Hats off to ingenuity.*

He moved over the short distance to where the outer door to The Moor Hen stood open denoting the pub to be ready for business. Before he got to it, his nostrils picked up the enticing aromas of an assortment of hot food mingled together making his stomach rumble and his earlier bacon sandwich fade into memory.

He pushed open the inner door revealing the subdued lighting of the open plan bar room which he could see already contained many people dotted around at various tables. For the first time, since he became a patron, he noticed how most of them were solitary people rather than couples or even families. This pub seemed to him to be a meeting place for the solitary, single, alone and perhaps even lonely, except for the one young couple he passed as he made his way to the bar who sat hunched together whispering, might belie his theory.

He was met at the bar by the smiling face of Alistair the landlord who didn't ask him what he wanted, he stood waiting with a whisky shot glass in his hand.

"The usual," Bart announced. Before he could add, "Bell's whisky", Alistair turned with his hand under the optic, pushed the glass upwards and waited until Bart gave the instruction, "Double" before he repeated the action. "Wonderful smells," Bart added nodding towards the food counter where a large tureen sat (usually containing soup of the day) showed a glowing red light, next to a large baked potato oven. Sunk into the counter a line of many serving trays were covered with lids to keep their contents hot.

The whole arrangement Bart always thought, on his daily sojourn up here at lunch times, seemed to him like an institutional canteen found in any school dinner hall or Her Majesty's prisons across the land. Bart knew, however, the food would taste infinitely better than either of those places, not that he had ever been on the wrong side of the law to attest to it.

His career found him working for the police as a civilian Scene's of Crime Officer for many years because his stature had been against him, he was on the short side. If there hadn't been a height requirement, he would have definitely joined the regular police from the start. The closest he came to investigating crime was, after he left the police to set up his own business as a Private Investigator enduring mostly routine marital breakdown work (collecting evidence required for divorce proceedings) or more often than not, 'finding people' for unknown reasons. This was the area of his work which resulted in him having to enter the Witness Protection programme when he became, he often thought, a 'none' person. To prove it, here he was, out on his own, a rogue who escaped from the Scheme hiding up in the harsh climate of the Highlands tucked somewhere in the shadow of the Cairngorms.

Bart paid for the Bells, moved over to what was now his regular corner, for he could, indeed, be classified as 'a regular' by Alistair and any one of these disparate (or desperate?) people who like him spent each day together, yet apart, in the same pub. Except, however, for the young giggly couple he hadn't seen there before whom he now observed had given up their quest of laughing taking to canoodling together which brought a frown to his face.

After settling for steak and kidney pie, mash potato, cabbage and with a generous ladle of gravy which he ate with an unusually ravenous appetite after his snow shovelling exercise, he settled down to read the complimentary newspaper he'd picked up from the pile at the end of the bar, happy in the knowledge *he* needed no company or unwanted conversation.

CHAPTER 7

After her ghostly experience in the smallest bedroom she found Elizabeth in the kitchen making another pot of tea, the table already set out with the cups, milk jug and sugar bowl once again. Although she couldn't say for sure if the table was always set, she was sure there hadn't been enough time for Elizabeth to organise it. In addition, a plate of home-made biscuits now joined them which she later found to be still warm from the oven.

"Coffee?" Elizabeth asked.

The girl was sure they must only have finished breakfast, even though she could see no sign of the breakfast crockery. She heard a clock chime from another room stopping to count as she heard eleven strikes. The old lady noticed her listening, "The grandfather clock in the hall keeps excellent time for eight days, if you keep it wound up," she said pouring hot water onto the ground coffee in the cafetière.

When they sat down at the table Elizabeth asked, "Well?" as if the word was sufficient a question for the other to know what she meant.

From nowhere the girl found herself saying, "The cottage doesn't seem to like me." The feeling came upon her whilst she straightened the books in the back bedroom.

"Oh, it's early days," the woman answered. "I'm sure the cottage will get used to you."

She was surprised, expecting a rebuke at such a strange admission, or something along the lines of "don't be silly". Nevertheless, her comment made absolute sense to her, not once did she question why the cottage would be able to get used to her given her intention to leave to find the B&B written on the piece of paper.

Yet she felt quite relieved, she automatically asked, "Do you think so?" She couldn't understand why it mattered so much to her.

This may have been the first weird conversation they had, although this wouldn't be the last. There were many more during the days to follow whilst they spent time there together. The only one they didn't have concerned her original intended destination or any plans she might have for the future. That one wasn't broached by either of them, any thoughts of moving on melted away when the big thaw came. Somehow, the girl's thoughts of her future seemed to get lost as did the piece of paper the landlord of the Inn gave her.

The days moved on in their endless snow bound captivity as they lived together in natural harmony whilst she slowly learnt the old woman's ways and the ways of cottage life. The life suited her giving her a feeling of safety which she never felt before. One incident in the beginning made her realise perhaps her being there was for the sake of the 'cottage', only a brief thought because as the days passed by she began to forget what brought her there. How she found the cottage was an even bigger blur.

The incident occurred one night when she was woken by the sound of crashing coming from downstairs which she immediately put down to the dogs fighting. She could hear no barking or growling, then she hadn't heard any sound from them at all. During one of the many power cuts she was forced to carry a lighted candle from her room to investigate the disturbance in case either of them was hurt. She found both fast asleep alongside the glowing fire in the kitchen. She could see nothing amiss, so she took the opportunity to place a couple more logs on the fire to maintain the warmth before she went back to bed.

It was next morning when she went for a shower she found the bathroom door difficult to open. She pushed the door with some force in order to open a small gap. Slipping her arm through the narrow gap she could feel the shower plinth standing propped against the inside of the door as if someone tried to barricade themselves in against anyone entering. Explanation would be difficult, as technically a dog (or even two working together) couldn't have opened the sliding shower door, lifted such a heavy wooden plinth, place the same on end up against the door and got out of the room. In fact, no human could have done either.

After this incident the feeling of being unwelcome in the cottage began to fade. She couldn't say this was because the dogs suddenly began to act friendly towards her, she didn't believe their nature allowed them to be anything other than what they were. They didn't even exhibit any real affection for each other as you might expect two dogs living together to do.

Not long after this Elizabeth died and the day after, the German Shephard (she realised she never knew his name) went outside into the garden not to be seen again. The disappearance of the dog was as unremarkable an incident as Elizabeth's passing, which seemed an inevitable end to her gradual taking over of the running of the place. Elizabeth eased her passage with an unobtrusive skill to take full responsibility of the cottage workings. Elizabeth Elspeth Grant in turn appeared to run down like an old clock slowly at first, until she petered out. She wasn't really ever sick, she always seemed tired needing more naps and sleeping a lot, until the time the girl was unable to wake her up.

The day after Elizabeth died the Grandfather clock in the hall stopped. When she noticed, she remembered Elizabeth's assurance the clock was a very good timekeeper if kept wound up. She tried hard to revive it the way the old lady showed her, however, nothing would work, at least not for many seconds after which the pendulum ceased to swing.

It has stopped in sympathy was all she could think of. She missed the rhythmic ticking more than the chimes every quarter of an hour.

Without the sound of the clock the cottage was as quiet as the grave, apart from the occasional creaks of the structure itself which were as eerie as the silence.

CHAPTER 8

The days following the first snows of winter gave Bart the undoubted conviction he would never feel warm again. When the snow began to thaw his world was filled with the slow dripping of water. Whether from the icicles hanging from his gutters or the snow on the roof, he always seemed to be in the wrong place to catch either a drip down the back of his neck or a gust of snow spray off the roof, catching him a direct hit in the face.

The antiquated heating system in the house barely put out sufficient warmth to enable his aching hands to manipulate the most delicate of tweezers or the other instruments he used to mend clocks. There was none at all in the shop, so tinkering with them required him to purchase some fingerless gloves which took some getting used to. They either made his hands way too hot or very itchy, both equally distracting.

He would need a new heating system if he was to survive in this climate, but in the meantime he managed with an old electric fan heater he found in a second hand emporium years ago when he first moved to the East coast. Why he always chose places with the most savage of weather he didn't know – *perhaps a tropical island would suit me more* – then such a place he knew was native to a range of creeping creatures he could never get along with.

He found himself undertaking less of his hitherto beloved clock mending, leaving a range of time pieces he purchased with the intention to restore them. Instead, he concentrated only on those brought to him for repair, which were very few during the snowy season. Consequently, he was left with much 'time' on his hands to fill. He read a lot more, took a great many snoozes in between until, as a Christmas present to himself, he upgraded the heating system in the house.

After he reassembled the Grandmother clock he hung it on the wall in the corner of his shop, there to stay until its owner dug their way out of one of the regions many castles to collect their antique timepiece. He was now without a commission and not really inclined to begin one of the many clock restorations awaiting his attention. He took, instead, one of the fob watches he picked up as a job lot of assorted silver watches at an auction many years ago. He kept them together in a small sea chest in his shop. Many people admired the chest when they came into the shop to inspect his clock collection. He doubted it was worth much in monetary terms nonetheless he admired the box with its leather straps, metal catches and faded labels; the scratches depicting a lengthy exotic travel history.

He spent the first couple of hours of the day carefully stripping the fob watch down, laying out each piece from left to right across the table covering in the order he removed them. Once done he went into the back room to make himself a cup of coffee, as the clocks began their half past eleven chimes. Together with a packet of hob nob biscuits he returned with both through to the shop.

He was halted by the vision of a young woman standing perfectly still in the shop staring at the range of larger clocks, Grandfathers, Grandmothers and the many hanging cuckoo clocks. She was so still and not having heard her entrance or the tinkle of his shop bell over the door, he began to wonder if she was a spectral vision. From what he could see of her face her skin appeared pale, almost translucent, made paler by being framed with long dark auburn hair. The white coat she was wearing made her appear like an apparition. A wave of fear ran up his spine in an involuntary shiver making his skin crawl.

It was only when, to his relief, she moved slightly he could tell she was real. She turned as if she sensed him watching her.

52

Instantly he remembered her, the young woman who parked outside his shop when the first snows of the season began. He especially recollected her because she seemed to be so afraid, like she did now, reminding him once again of Emily.

"Hello," his voice lowered to a whisper in case his usual loudness scared her. He knew he could be too resonant most of the time. She didn't smile as most people would on being addressed. She stared at him, with a vacant expressionless face he could not quite fathom. "Can I help you?" he asked as he walked over to his work table to deposit his drink and biscuits, then turned to her once again. "Sorry it's quite cold in here," he apologised in the hope she would recognise he was no threat to her. He was well aware his pudgy doughy face with his bushy eyebrows often had an adverse effect on people. Certainly babies or young children found him frightening; more often than not they fled his presence crying hysterically. "The old heating system has, like me, seen better days. My upgrade was the rest of the house only!"

The latter comment brought forth a twitch to her lips that didn't quite make a full smile. "Do you mend all clocks?" she asked without moving over to the counter.

"I certainly try," he assured her, "I have only ever failed with one rather wayward cuckoo clock of my own."

"Why was that?" She asked. This was something Bart hadn't stopped to consider before. The question quite stumped him.

"Do you know, I really have no idea," he admitted honestly shrugging his shoulders. "I think perhaps the bird was very wilful, much like me he possessed many defects," now he grinned as if mocking himself. He pointed to his face, "No beak!" In fact, this was partly true since Bart's nose resembled a piece of clay someone stuck in the centre of his face, pressing down hard with their thumb. He began to laugh his usual raucous laughter which this time drew a smile to her face.

"You say 'had', do you not have him any longer?"

Bart viewed her with renewed interest her having picked up the fact.

"No," he confessed reluctantly. "I gave the clock to my assistant at the time who……" here he wanted to explain about Emily's uncanny talents, however he checked himself because he thought he shouldn't speak about her in such a personal way to a total stranger. "As a parting gift," he chose to say.

"You gave someone a broken clock as a gift?" she sounded slightly reproving.

"Yes….well no, not actually broken," how could he explain to someone the half beat out of sync without sounding completely eccentric? "The clock was fully operational, merely suffered a bit of a hiccup which only myself and my assistant could detect…..you might say she took him to 'foster'." He grinned broadly at the image of Emily living with a wayward bird with no beak.

"I see," her reply didn't hint at understanding what he was talking about. After a pause her next words came with an urgent rush, "I have a Grandfather clock that has stopped completely…….no amount of winding will get it to go again."

"Ah, well sometimes you can overwind clocks," he offered with great assurance.

She appeared puzzled, "Can they be unwound?" she asked which took Bart by surprise and all his will power not to burst out laughing again because she was so very serious.

"Their mechanisms can be dismantled and then reassembled to release them from this state, yes," he assured her. "If you want to bring it in, I can take a look at it." His words seemed to send her once more into a reflective state.

She shook her head, "I can't," she frowned shaking her head. "Could you possibly come to the cottage to look at it?" The idea of taking the clock away from the cottage left her feeling quite panicky, she couldn't explain why.

Bart saw the same look of fear pass over her face he saw the first time he spied her sitting in her car outside his shop. He suddenly felt an overwhelming need to help her. "Yes, I think I could if there's somewhere I can lay out the pieces safely so they would remain without interference......" She looked even more puzzled now. ".....out of the reach of children," he explained.

Her face brightened, "Ah, I don't have children, there's only me."

"In that case, I can certainly take a look for you."

"Good," she seemed relieved and moved swiftly towards the door as if to leave.

"Hang on!" Bart shouted interrupting her progress; he picked up his order ledger, "Can I take some details, perhaps make a definite arrangement?"

She moved back to the counter looking down at the book where Bart was flicking through the pages. He kept meticulous details of each of the clocks he mended, which he added to with what he did to restore them to working order.

"Can I have your name and address?"

It stopped her momentarily in her tracks, he watched as she pondered the question. After too long a pause she managed, "Elizabeth Grant," which Bart Bridges, the Private Investigator, instantly noted was a name she didn't seem quite comfortable with. His canny instinct, a sixth sense he possessed when he intuitively knew someone was lying to him, became roused. He wrote the name down and waited for her to give him the address.

She surprised him with, "I have a problem with the address." Bart glanced up at her enquiringly, saw her stark embarrassment. "Well actually I don't know it," she added.

"You don't know your own address?" He tried hard not to sound like he was criticising her or in any way doubted what she was saying.

"I can draw you a map," she added brightly as if she'd just thought of the idea. She turned, seemed to run out of the shop leaving the door wide open and Bart somewhat stunned. He walked slowly after her over to the door, recognising the small dark red car he'd seen once before parked in exactly the same spot.

Elizabeth Grant opened the hatch back, leaned inside the boot of her car and after a moment found what she wanted, closing the boot. Bart turned quickly returning to the shop counter, picked up his pen and was poised over the ledger page when she rushed back inside holding a book of maps. She proceeded to flick through the book until she found the page she was looking for. She ripped the page roughly from the book, laid it down on the counter to show him the route to the cottage where she now lived alone.

Bart made notes with the extra information she gave, like a post box on the corner of the fifth turning on the right observing the slight hesitation in her voice.

"I'm sure I shall find you," he replied. "If not I can always ask someone the way."

The idea seemed to halt her once again until after some contemplation she agreed, "I'm sure someone will know where we are."

They fixed the day for the following Tuesday which Bart thought gave sufficient time for the thaw to take away most of the accumulated snow. He heard talk at The Moor Hen it took a long time for the snow to completely clear on that side of the Balmoral estate. He stood in his shop doorway as he watched her drive away, realised conditions must be passable to allow her to get out to visit his shop.

The encounter left him intrigued which had nothing whatever to do with his anticipation of seeing her 'broken' Grandfather clock. She interested him partly because of the idea anyone would live in such a remote spot without owning a telephone, because when he asked for her number in order to confirm his intentions on the following Tuesday in case the snow came again, she told him she didn't have one. Even more surprising, was when he asked for her mobile number, knowing these days one was considered an absolute essential for anyone of her age, she shook her head.

Most thought-provoking of all was her reference to 'someone will know where *we* are' when she already claimed she lived alone.

CHAPTER 9

The girl drove back to the cottage with a fixed stern face clutching tightly onto the steering wheel. She was annoyed with herself for making one or two 'slips' in her answers to the strange looking man's questions. Why did she give him her name as Elizabeth Grant instead of either her own name or a new made up one? So far she hadn't even considered she would need to decide on a name since she arrived in Scotland. She had to admit there was something quite natural about using 'Elizabeth Grant' when she heard herself say it out loud. Somewhere in the recesses of her mind lurked the idea she was now the 'new' guardian of the cottage, therefore the 'new' Elizabeth Grant. In order to denote the change in succession she would call herself 'Beth' if the clock man ever used the name Elizabeth.

The thing troubling her more was using the word 'we'. She wouldn't be able to explain to anyone she used the term correctly, either because she meant herself and the cottage, or even because she didn't feel like Elizabeth was actually gone. She often talked to her out loud if she ever needed an answer to a question about the place, after which the answer came naturally into her mind. She thought explaining this to anyone else would be impossible.

When she arrived back at the cottage driving straight into the back yard she found a small white van parked there; a young man was unloading a large sack, she recognised as dog food, from the van's back doors. She smiled as she was reminded she didn't actually live alone. She lived with her companion the Foxhound terrier she now called Sandy.

When he saw her car pull up alongside his van he returned the smile.

She got out calling, "I only need one sack," as if he'd asked her how much dog food she wanted.

"Oh?" he queried watching her open the kitchen door to let her furry companion out. Uncharacteristically, Sandy bounded over to the man wagging his tail, making a fuss like they were old friends. Her mouth opened in shock watching this alien spiritedness she hadn't seen before.

"You know each other?" more of a statement than a question.

He fussed the dog, roughing its ears which 'Sandy' seemed to take great pleasure in.

"Yes, we're old friends aren't we buddy?" he asked the dog adding, "Where's your friend?" as if he might answer him.

The dog raised his head first on one side then the other, with large sad eyes, as Beth answered him, "The other dog ran away, we haven't seen him since."

The man didn't respond, merely returned the sack to the back of his van, "I've left one inside the stable already."

She took out her purse walking over towards him taking out a £20 bank note to pay for the food. He put out his hand to stop her, "No need it's already taken care of."

Surprised, she put the money back in her purse toying with the idea she ought to ask him in for a cup of tea to be sociable like she knew Elizabeth would have done.

"I'll pass on a drink today," he said cheerily as if the invitation was already made. "I'm running late. I've got lots to do to catch up."

She merely smiled, greatly relieved to avoid another encounter. The last thing she needed was to face the strain of making conversation with a whole lot of personal questions about herself or the old lady.

59

She went back inside calling Sandy who stood in the same spot watching the van back out of the yard and drive off. Nonetheless, he followed her inside, ran straight into the parlour onto the couch in front of the window where he stood on his back legs with his front paws on the sofa back, staring out at the road as the van drove away.

She took this encounter as the first show of emotion by the dog wondering at the back story between the two of them. If she ever invited him in for a drink she hoped she could find the confidence to ask him about it, as well as what he meant by payment for dog food was 'taken care of.'

*   *   *   *   *

With the thaw continuing, when Tuesday came round, Bart set out for his pre-arranged visit to 'Elizabeth Grant'. He briefly stopped off at the Esso garage to settle up his debt for the snow shovel in case he forgot completely. He also took the opportunity to purchase a book of street maps of the local area which he thought might come in handy if he ever needed to do another 'house call'.

He found what he wanted, paid for both adding a Mars bar in case he got peckish later. The book of street maps by the date was an old one. In this part of the world there weren't many large scale developments requiring the maps updating.

Armed with the single map page ripped from Elizabeth Grant's book, he turned off the A93 at the turning for Balmoral Castle at Crathie village following the route for the 'old road'; on the B976 he found himself counting the number of turns off to the right.

Along this stretch of deserted road the thaw was less pronounced with a covering of snow still lying thick at the side of the road. He thought he wouldn't much like to be driving out here after dark. When he spotted the post box it was only a flash of red which caught his eye making him stop to reverse slightly in order to take the turning. He began to make his way up the incline stopping often to check his bearings against the notes he made.

He spotted the tree out of the driver's side window which made him stop again to admire the long strings tied to its branches, attached were coconut shells in tiers. When he examined it closer he was surprised to find, instead of the snow you would have expected to collect inside each shell, they contained either fresh bird seed or water. The shells were arranged in pairs, the one above like an umbrella shielded each dish below from the elements.

"Oh my!" he exclaimed looking around him for any sign of the creator of the feeders. He spotted the cottage opposite out of the passenger side window, knowing instinctively this was the one he wanted.

"Well, I'll be….." he exclaimed whilst thinking, *why didn't she tell me about this landmark feature?*

He moved forward turning into the open gates when he recognised her car he parked alongside of it. The back door opened, Elizabeth Grant emerged accompanied by a tan and white dog walking sedately at her side, stopped when she did, sitting down to wait patiently for him to get out of his car.

So this is the 'we', Bart thought, one mystery solved.

"Hello," she greeted. "You found us then?"

"Excellent instructions," he told her. "I spotted your elaborate bird feeders!" he pointed across to the tree admiring it once again. "It's ingenious!" She followed his eyes to the tree as if seeing it for the first time. She made no comment. "Although, the post box is still almost entirely covered in snow," he added as he took out an old Gladstone bag from the boot of his car. "I'll get my tools…..then perhaps you can show me my patient," he laughed heartily at the image of himself as a doctor. Well it wasn't too far from the way he viewed himself as a clock doctor. There were many occasions when all a time piece needed was a bit of encouragement with a friendly 'bedside manner' and others a full 'surgical' overhaul.

Bart, the clock doctor, followed her inside absently stroking the Foxhound terrier as he passed him.

"You must like solitude," he remarked as he entered the kitchen. He was met by the warmth of a blazing fire in the middle of the range and the mixture of aromas of fresh ground coffee beans, vanilla, cinnamon and other things he couldn't quite place.

The table was laden with an array of tea things. On a two tier cake stand was a mouth-watering mix of biscuits and cakes. An additional plate held a substantial Victoria sponge sandwich with strawberry jam oozing out of its centre, sprinkled on the top with icing sugar.

Bart trapped another "Oh my!" inside as she said, "I thought you might need something before you start, having travelled all the way out here."

"Goodness, this does look good," he declared, his mouth already beginning to water in anticipation.

"Tea or coffee?" she asked.

"Coffee would be excellent!" he boomed.

Bart watched her from his seat at the table as she busied herself lifting the heavy kettle off the fire grate, pouring boiling water into the cafetière already waiting with newly ground coffee. She brought the cafetière to the table with the plunger standing tall.

"Help yourself to cake," she ordered whilst Bart examined her closely. At a guess she would only be in her twenties yet she reminded him of his own maternal Grandmother who made excellent teas when he was a small boy. He stared in fascination at the bone china cup and saucer she poured milk into which he thought was Royal Albert Old Country Rose. The memory was now dim, yet certainly the familiar pattern reminded him of the one his grandmother used to have a complete set of. It brought him a long forgotten feeling of happiness which he savoured as long as he could whilst thinking about his Gran.

"The cake does look good," he declared as he cut himself a large slice. She smiled, took the knife he placed back down to cut a smaller piece for herself.

They both covered the ensuing silence with the taking of refreshments, neither of them wanted to make small talk or to have to think about what to say.

As the silence grew longer, Bart eventually asked, "Where do you keep the clock?"

She seemed relieved to be asked, immediately jumping to her feet, "It's in the hallway," she left the kitchen expecting him to follow. He picked up his coffee mug and carrying the tool bag he followed her out into the hall. When he saw his commission he stopped immediately staring at the mahogany Grandfather clock before him.

"Oh, my!" Bart exclaimed. "Now this is beautiful!"

She glanced from the clock to Bart and back again sensing how quiet the cottage was without the ticking of this clock, like the cottage's heart was no longer beating. She watched Bart walk over to the mahogany cased clock, where he ran his hand down the shiny wood whilst gazing lovingly up at the clock's face with its ornate top between which the arch displayed pictures as well as around the face itself. He glanced over at Elizabeth Grant absolute delight spreading across his face.

"It's a beautiful piece," he said reverently. "Nineteenth century no doubt, either a James Wiseman or a James Peat, I would have to examine it further to tell you exactly which."

"Can you mend it?" she asked eagerly.

"I'll certainly try, young lady," he stroked the wood tenderly once again. "These clocks are worth quite a lot of money, you know, they can fetch a good price at auction. This one is in wonderful condition, how long have you had it?"

She looked on a little perturbed by his question, now unsure of what Elizabeth told her about the clock.

"Err....I'm not sure exactly, it's been in the family for a long time," she found herself saying.

"Indeed, very well cared for, I can see why you would want to maintain it." He continued, a little nervousness having crept over him. "I'll see what I can do. I may have to seek some specialist advice." He could see his words cheered her somewhat.

"Good," she said. "I'll leave you to get on.....I really do want to hear the tick again." She nearly used the word 'beat' instead because she realised this clock gave the cottage its life, without the sounds it now seemed dead. She had also been feeling lonely without those sounds or at least since Elizabeth passed on which was truly strange given her previous craving for solitude.

She walked away to the kitchen leaving him alone in the hallway. When she turned back, he was standing as still as before sipping the remains of his coffee, staring lovingly at the clock.

CHAPTER 10

Bart kept reminding himself, every time he felt the bitter chill of this awful weather, the reason he chose such an out of the way place was to avoid the likelihood of being recognised by anyone from his past. He dropped out of the Witness Protection Programme to 'lose' himself after he spotted the copper from his past, Barney Johnson, out running alongside Detective Braithwaite back in Wainthorpe-on-sea where he felt reasonably safely hidden for a couple of years until the murders began. His mind flitted back to the seaside retreat of Wainthorpe-on-Sea.

*   *   *   *   *

On yet another Sunday morning ritual at The Silver Teapot café with his pile of Sunday tabloids, he sat in the same window seat with the two views. One was up Main Street where he could see his clock shop **Time and Tide**, *the other view along the seafront promenade where the beach huts stood looking out to sea.*

This particular Sunday he was distracted by the dog walker throwing the ball across the sand for the scurrying terrier to fetch. Then the two joggers as they appeared out of the coastal trail from the direction of the golf course. Two men in running shorts with hooded tops pacing each other as they approached the beach huts, moving towards where he sat inside the café, he watched them until he recognised who they were.

Braithwaite, the fidgety copper who touched his cuckoo clock, the one with the bird with a missing beak, ran alongside the other cop 'Cyrus' was meant to leave behind in his old life. He was the one shot by the hired killer to take him out; only it was the brutal killer who succumbed to the ferocity of the cop's faithful four legged protector.

Seeing someone from his past he took to be a sign. 'If this is not an omen nothing is', he immediately thought about moving on and setting up somewhere else.

Cyrus wondered how many times he would have to move on, how many changes of name he would have to make. He'd allowed himself to become too complacent by making the very first friend ever. How could he have let it happen?

*   *   *   *   *

It wasn't going to be easy if someone really wanted to find him. Someone like him could never really hide because when you looked like he did, five foot four inches tall, squat with the physique of the Michelin man, you immediately stood out in a crowd however hard you tried to hide. Yet as a young boy he appeared like an angelic choir boy. Ironically, Nature intervened laughing at his expense. By the time normal hormonal urges should have kicked in, they missed giving him the growth spurt his contemporaries experienced. Whilst everyone around him went through the pains of growth, Bart remained forever short – grown into Bartholomew Bridges, the Michelin Man.

As age applied its cruel magic, his doughy face took on a grey moulded complexion he knew no woman found remotely attractive, forever condemning him to a bachelor life. Together with his early penchant for fine whisky, the occasional cigar or two, his features moulded into a comical real life caricature of an aging choir boy. Only the pale blue somehow innocent eyes were left as witness to his former youthful beauty, which gave him a trusting quality that came in handy as a Private Detective.

Bart was sitting in his shop at his work bench industriously working on the silver fob watch he'd stripped down to its individual parts, when the tinkle of the bell made him raise his head to observe a man entering the shop. As was usual the new customer failed to see him sitting there bent over his task, because the shop counter obstructed their view.

The man, like most people, was instantly assaulted by the huge quantity of time pieces, especially the noise the mechanical ones made. Ticking, chiming clocks were an acquired taste, you either loved them or else you hated them. On this occasion he couldn't tell which type of person this man was, so he sat quietly watching him. There was no point in getting to his feet if this stranger was about to bolt for the door, having entered as the half hour chorus was about to begin.

When the cacophony commenced the man became perfectly still as the various chimes made perfect timing with each other which eventually brought a smile, one which Bart felt was a little crooked, to the man's face. Bart stood up slowly to his maximum five foot four inch height. The stranger watched him rise above the counter as if in slow motion seemingly summoned by the clocks. He was rather surprised.

Bart took in the slim build with a shaved head, accompanying the sharp skeletal facial features. Bart's immediate thought being he must be so cold without a hat on. When the stranger smiled exposing long rabbit-like front teeth, giving him a predatory quality, Bart didn't much take to him.

"How do you do it?" The man asked, his too high pitched voice added to his feral quality.

"How do I do what?" Bart's deeply resonant voice in stark contrast bounced back at him.

"Get them timed together," his pale grey eyes settled on Bart making him want to shiver by their watery coldness. He was not encouraged by the man's sensitivity to his clocks.

"Ah," Bart admitted, "It's not an easy task and one which requires much patience and dedication."

The man sucked his lips as if he had begun to salivate and needed to avoid the dribble. Surprised, Bart noticed he had no eyebrows. Rather than check to see if his eyelashes were also missing he glanced away around his shop saying, "I am doomed in my love of horology which requires total commitment."

The man followed his gaze examining the selection with the same smile (or smirk) fixed on his face giving the impression he was mocking him, "It must be a nightmare when the clocks go back."

"Indeed," Bart agreed not wishing to enter into further discussion with someone who looked to be laughing at him. "Can I tempt you with one?"

He stared back as though not understanding someone might enter a shop with the intention of purchasing something. After a moment he caught on, "Oh, no thank you," he laughed at such an absurd idea. He reached inside his coat producing a photograph of a dark red Vauxhall Astra car which Bart didn't need to know the registration to recognise when the man thrust the image under his nose. "Have you seen a car like this around here?" he asked, the smile now disappearing from his face becoming a serious predatory mask.

Bart took the picture to scrutinised closely, "Is the car stolen, officer?" he asked watching the expression on the man's face for any signs of changing again.

"I'm not a police officer," the man revealed testily.

Bart saw a shiftiness about him that reinforced his instinctive dislike.

"Let me guess," Bart ventured. "You're a debt collector trying to reclaim it?" His instinct to boot him out of his shop was growing proportionally with how much the man was making his skin crawl. By the expression on his face the feeling was mutual.

He took the photograph back, reaching once again inside his pocket for a second picture which he also thrust with a flourish at Bart.

"What about her?" he asked abruptly.

Bart took hold of the photograph of 'Elizabeth Grant' obviously captured at a much younger age pretending to look closely. He could see even at this age she already possessed a haunted expression reminding him of Emily, so he determined she had been unhappy for a very long time.

"Pretty girl," Bart commented. "What's she done?" Bart could see the man was holding back his irritation at all the questions. "Is she a runaway?" Bart asked, after all it would make sense. He turned the photograph over in his hand saw the name with the addition 'aged at eighteen' on the back. He remembered the kind of photographs he was given when he was a private investigator in the business of finding people.

"Not exactly," the man said. "Her husband is looking for her."

"Ah, run off with his car has she? Is he local?"

He shook his head, "No, the car was caught on camera heading up this way," he disclosed vaguely.

"So she's wanted for a fixed penalty," Bart suggested.

"Well, let's say he's not too pleased to have to pay the fine back there," he laughed now. Bart thought no doubt he got the full force of his temper over it.

"I don't get to see many people driving their cars being in here most of the time," Bart began trying to sound more reasonable. "We get snowed in a great deal at this time of the year," he thought he sounded like a longstanding local. "There's really no going outside for months, let alone driving a car," he nodded towards the door. "If I do see it where do I contact you?"

The man responded reluctantly to the funny little man, fished into his pocket producing a business card which he handed over to Bart.

"I'm staying at the hotel for a couple more days before I go back down, so if you see her or the car, let me know?" He took the photograph out of Bart's hand before he moved towards the door.

69

Bart glanced at the card, "What name shall I ask for?" The card merely showed the name of the ABC Detective Agency, something he had done under the same circumstances.

"Selwyn Jones," he imparted as he opened the door to leave.

Bart watched him walk away towards main street thinking about the girl in the picture, a younger version of the Elizabeth Grant who asked him only a few days before to call her Beth which he could tell immediately wasn't her real name. Now he just had it confirmed.

He spent the last few days since his call out to her exquisite Grandfather clock, thinking about her. There was a sadness that seemed to emanate off her in waves, as did the stark loneliness he felt she showed. What prompted his curiosity more was the innocence of her character. She showed absolute relief that brought her running out of the kitchen, when he very quickly released the clock's mechanism to get the chimes going again.

Despite what he told her, he knew it was almost impossible to over wind a Grandfather clock, so first he tried to move the pendulum to ease the spring, then the clock's hands gently. When he heard the ticking begin, he stood back waiting until the hands reached the first quarter of the hour to begin to chime. This was when she came hurrying from the kitchen at the sound. He felt very much the fraud not having done anything tangible to get the mechanism going again. He would have to say it recovered all on its own.

He watched her straining for the sound of the clock's loud ticking which made her close her eyes, listen intently uttering a sigh with profound relief as the smile came to her lips and spread across her face. She put her hands together as if in prayer giving thanks.

"Thank you," she breathed. "I owe you so much!"

In fact, he refused any payment telling her he was only too pleased to be able to see such a wonderful Grandfather clock ticking again. No amount of entreaties on her part would induce him to accept any. He advised her to leave the clock a good seven days before attempting to re-wind it again.

Although he was really pleased to get the chance to 'mend' such a specimen, his real pleasure came from being able to bring such a rapturous reaction from its owner. Anyone with this kind of love for clocks he considered deserved to be helped, there was no doubt.

CHAPTER 11

In the ensuing hours the PI's visit greatly worried Bart. It horrified him the man pursuing 'Beth' could stumble upon someone like himself who actually met her or even knew where she was living. The long range weather forecast warning of further heavy snows for the north of Scotland unnerved him especially if Selwyn Jones was to get snowed in the village; the idea filled him full of dread. He would rather have him outside with no way in. He would feel more comfortable as far as his own position was concerned, to have the private investigator as far away as possible. Instinctively, he neither liked him nor did he trust him.

He of all people knew of the variety of methods open to someone to find a person which would surprise anyone else, but gave Bart clues on the things to avoid at all costs if you were in a mind to disappear. He took great pains himself when he purchased his own runabout car in order for it not to be traced back to him or any of the names he had used. Identity through ownership made him think twice about owning another car. However, the sheer isolation of the Highlands made driving essential especially at his advanced age. His physical state gave him little choice in the matter even though he tried hard to maintain a certain level of fitness through keeping up his ritual walks.

Travelling anywhere by public transport was dependent on available service routes of course. The isolation of where Beth lived gave her two opposing chances of staying hidden; remoteness was a bonus, however, driving the car her husband owned, he thought was a bad move.

It raised a red flag to Bart's previous methods when Selwyn Jones mentioned the fixed penalty ticket for a camera violation, which her husband would have been notified of, being the registered owner of the vehicle. A person would know if they were spotted whilst driving a car, by the camera flash. These cameras not only registered the speed of the vehicle but also the place, both of which are recorded on the penalty notice.

As far as Bart could recollect there were no fixed penalty traffic cameras this high up for the direction of travel to be determined, so how could the man from the ABC Detective Agency know where she was travelling to? Bart himself knew there were 'other' kinds of cameras usually within cities using number plate recognition. These were searchable by the police who used them to monitor the movement of some very serious criminals who were known by their cars and their routine criminal activity.

This Automatic Number Plate Recognition (ANPR) system was often referred to as the 'ring of steel' around cities. This system belonged to the developing 'intelligence' arm of modern policing. Bart knew it wasn't beyond the bounds of possibility, although very rare, for someone working as a private detective to have contacts inside the police. Much more likely, of course, if you once worked as a police officer yourself, as many ex-police officers went into private investigation upon retirement from the police, their links with someone still serving would already be established.

He assumed Beth's story involved the likelihood of any one of these possibilities, the most serious being she was still using her husband's car. The idea alarmed him so much he felt an urgent need to warn her about Selwyn Jones.

Two days later, therefore, as Bart turned into the gates of the cottage once again he was shocked to find the yard completely empty; her car was nowhere to be seen. Of course, being without a telephone or a mobile, he was unable to contact her to arrange the visit. After having driven half-way to Ballater for certain purchases, he continued on to Aboyne where there was a large emporium selling the widest variety of items. He found what he was looking for there and then started to drive back along the 'old road' home in order to drop by Beth Grant's cottage.

Now sitting in his car at the cottage, he wound down the driver's side window to listen to the absolute silence which seemed strange given the elaborate construction of bird-feeders on the tree outside in the lane. He couldn't hear one chirp of a bird which gave him the strange thought they must all have flown south for the winter, not that he knew anything about migrating birds.

Bart shivered as an icy blast of wind hit the side of the car making the whole vehicle rock like a carnival ride. He closed the car's window. It occurred to him perhaps she might already have disposed of the car, might even be at home. He got out of the car to knock on the kitchen door expecting at the very least to hear the dog bark. There was no sound at all from inside.

He felt an overwhelming urgency to speak with her even though she might react badly. However, self-preservation dug at his thoughts, warning him he shouldn't get involved, until a flash of the predatory private investigator's image made him throw caution to the wind. He got back into his car for shelter cutting off the biting wind and where he could feel a little of the remaining warmth from the heater. He was in two minds whether to switch his engine back on.

As if on cue the dark red Astra pulled up beside him, the girl's eyes settled on his face, a gentle smile on her lips, yet her eyes were requiring an explanation for why he was there.

He got out of the car again, taking the full icy blast of the wind. As she rolled down her window he enquired, "How is the clock doing?" She sat for a moment with the window open. He saw doubt flick across her face which concerned him, she might feel alarm at his being there. "Look," he added hastily, "I need to talk to you, there's someone looking for you." He tried his best not to sound too alarmed but he could see he was failing badly. She suddenly appeared frightened. "Can we talk inside?" Then he added, "I have to sort your car out first?" he moved towards his boot without waiting for an answer.

Once out of the car she stood watching him carry a heavy tarpaulin folded into a large thick square.

"Take out anything you need," he instructed her as he began to unfold it. She picked up quickly what his intentions were. As if on cue a few flakes of snow drifted past whilst she ran around to the boot, lifted the hatch back to retrieve several shopping bags which she left outside the kitchen door. She then opened the passenger door to get a large box of green groceries. After depositing them with the other bags she went back to help Bart to cover her car with the tarpaulin which he secured to the ground by placing loose rockery stones at each corner. Once done, he helped her carry everything into the kitchen.

He noted the Foxhound terrier lying in front of the smouldering logs opened his eyes long enough to register their arrival before going back to sleep again. Beth threw more logs on the fire before she stood waiting for an explanation.

"What a very strange dog you have there," Bart commented whilst thinking how he could tell her his news. "I'm sorry if I've frightened you, missy," he apologised.

"Beth," she reminded him.

"Only it isn't Beth or indeed Elizabeth Grant that much I do know...." She gasped. "I believe your name is Lily Johns." The statement made her visibly wobble on her feet. She staggered over to sit down at the table.

"Oh!" was all she could manage.

"It is, isn't it?" he asked gently.

She shook her head, "No...I used to be Lily Johns," there was a quiver in her voice as if she was finding speaking difficult, "once, before....."

There was no doubt in Bart's mind she was terrified of something she was shaking so badly.

"Johns was my maiden name," she managed. He could see her mind retreat into the past.

"Not your married name?" he suggested. She shook her head again not giving her actual name. "I saw a picture of you shown to me by someone I believe is employed by your husband to find you."

He heard her moan, saw the tears begin to fall silently down her cheeks.

"How....?" the one word was squeezed through closed lips before her fist came up to cover her mouth.

She now appeared so wretched he again thought of young Emily who once cried like this when she told him about being bullied at school.

"I didn't tell him I knew you or I'd seen your car," he tried to reassure her. "Are you aware you were caught out by speed cameras driving up here?"

She showed genuine bafflement, "No, I'm sure I wasn't," she said. "I made certain."

Bart didn't expect this response, "Really sure?" he asked. She nodded.

"According to the Private Investigator your husband received a fixed penalty notice his car was caught speeding....."

"His car?" she asked utterly bewildered. "No. It's my car, I have the registration documents. I can prove it's mine."

"Ah, now that puts a different perspective on things, the picture he showed me was definitely the car out there."

"I don't doubt you," she said with a bitter inflection to her voice. "He'll try anything......" her voice broke once again.

Bart explained everything he knew about Selwyn Jones from the ABC Detective Agency as she sat listening in silence her large sorrowful eyes now looking resigned.

"I thought I could escape....." she shook her head. "....how can he know where I am?"

"Well, actually he doesn't.....I believe it's the car that has been spotted," when she scowled he went on. "Most places have vehicle number plate recognition, which I suspect he or the dreadfully creepy man he's hired, have some illicit connections to," when she stared at him for some explanation he went on, "It's a police software system primarily used to spot criminal activity."

She nodded, "It's hard to get away from someone who has daily access to those things.....it was foolish of me to try."

"Is he a policeman?" Bart asked taking the hint. She nodded. "Then, definitely not easy," Bart agreed. "Although, not impossible." He smiled knowingly. "I have something else for you," Bart jumped up leaving the kitchen to go back to his car. When he returned he held out a box with a pay-as-you-go mobile.

"Out here you need one of these, it's untraceable," he assured her. "And it gives us a chance of staying in touch or for you to call me if you need any help."

She sat staring at the phone. "I left mine back there," she sighed resignedly. "I knew the police could trace people through mobiles and also cars." She said rather sadly, "I thought I would be safe if I was careful and got far enough away, then he wouldn't be able to."

"If you had a garage where you could leave it until we could get you another one," Bart saw her face brighten at the idea.

"I do," she said simply. She rushed out the back door into the yard with Bart following after her.

At the farthest end of the row of out buildings there was one with double wooden doors looking more like a barn which Bart hadn't noticed as he drove through the gates. She opened up the doors. Inside Bart could see gardening tools, an old fashioned 'push' mower together with some old wooden garden furniture.

"It's a bit of a mess really," she admitted. "I could put the car in here for now. That doesn't solve my being out here without transport to be able to get provisions."

"Well let's solve one problem at a time," Bart dived inside. "Will these bigger things go in the other out buildings?"

She nodded as they both set about the task of moving everything out which would obstruct a car being driven inside. Once inside they covered the car again with the tarpaulin sheet. When all the other items were put away, they went back inside to discuss future plans.

"Are there many people up here who've met you or who might be able to identify you?" Bart asked.

She shook her head, "Actually today was the first time I've been out shopping since I got here," she paused thinking, "except for Elizabeth's funeral."

"Elizabeth?"

"Yes, this is her cottage, an old lady who she took me in when I got lost in a snow storm."

"So who does the cottage belong to now she's dead?" he asked, a simple question Beth couldn't answer.

"I don't actually know for sure, I rather think she wanted me to take it on."

"Is that why you call yourself Beth Grant?"

"It seemed the most natural thing do when you asked me for my name. I believe she wants it." The new Elizabeth Grant sat smiling for the first time since she heard the news she was being actively pursued.

"I think it's a good idea to keep the name," Bart said whilst thinking, *I should know identification by ownership is far too easy.*

CHAPTER 12

Beth stood at the kitchen door with Sandy at her side watching the clock man leave, giving him a sad wave. She gazed upwards at the slow fluttering snowflakes as they descended lazily knowing by morning there would be another blanket covering everything. It prompted her to run out to close the gate *against intruders, not that the gates would keep anyone out if they really wanted to get in.* She fetched the snow shovel from the stable in readiness to dig a pathway for Sandy next day like Elizabeth taught her. If an eighty year old woman could do it, so could she.

Sandy was always reluctant to go outside even in clement weather. He spent most of his time asleep in front of the fire or else alert up at the window in the parlour as if expecting someone to arrive or something to happen. She could never imagine him as a hunting dog, she didn't want to think about what they did to the poor fox. She preferred him as he was.

Beth absently picked up the mobile from the kitchen table checking the settings after exchanging numbers with Sirus. The one name, 'Sirus' with his mobile number came up. She knew instinctively this wasn't his real name either, just like 'Beth' wasn't hers. At least they had something in common. In everything else they were worlds apart. He'd asked her if she could manage another snow fall out here alone, cutting her off from the outside world? Also if she could cope without having to use her car before he got the chance to get her another one. She laughed then saying, "There's no driving a car out of here until the snow thaws," which was why she had stocked up with fresh vegetables. This was something he must do also before he got home.

She stood in the hallway listening to the ticking of the Grandfather clock, the familiar heartbeat of the cottage. She moved upstairs to her own room, the one which used to belong to Elizabeth being the warmest with the chimney behind the wall at the side of the bed. She lay down on the bed closing her eyes. She recalled, a few short weeks ago, when Elizabeth asked her to do the same whilst sitting beside her on the bed. "Close your eyes, dear," Elizabeth had said on that occasion. She then revealed what she often felt when she sat reading in bed at night. Beth felt the bed ripple as if the old lady had stood up making the mattress move, like she was still beside her.

The cottage she told her used to belong to one of Queen Victoria's ghillies, a particular favourite of hers. As the story went he became so ill he took to his bed. She visited him until he died, sitting beside him on the bed. When Beth first felt this happen to her she liked to believe Elizabeth was close by to give her comfort.

Thinking about the concerns Sirus told her about, she felt the bed move as if someone just sat down next to her. Knowing her husband was searching for her using a private investigator filled her full of dread. The feeling someone sat beside her made her anxiety begin to subside, her confidence in Sirus to grow. His taking charge, helping her to hide the car, gave her an overwhelming sense of relief; partly because the funny little man gave the cottage back its heart beat. She was grateful to have him as a friend. She lay there smiling feeling the bed ripple again before she opened her eyes. Of course, there was no one there.

The one thing she was now sure about was the cottage accepted her, happy to have her take care of it. She felt sure she would never be found there, and is why she never put a lighted candle in the window.

*   *   *   *   *

Bart stood at the Esso garage with the petrol pump nozzle inside the tank of his car gently squeezing the last drop he could to give him a full tank. He watched the flakes of snow scatter with the wind's icy blast creating a blizzard around him. He knew later the snow would some with a vengeance cutting him off again from Beth, leaving her completely isolated. In one sense not a bad thought if she could manage the time alone. At least now he could check on her by phone.

He paid for the petrol, walked back to his car at the pumps glancing up towards the lights of the hotel a short distance up the hill where the village began. His major concern was whether Selwyn Jones was still in the area. The thought of the creepy man made him shiver as the icy cold wind cutting across the open farmland, where the Esso garage stood exposed to the elements, buffeted against him.

He drove carefully up the slippery incline towards the hotel where an empty car parking space near the front door prompted the thought, *hopefully this was where his car was parked*. On impulse he veered over towards the empty space, to park up. It was half past one. He was hungry, knew he'd missed his pub lunch at The Moor Hen and wondered if he might get something to eat at the hotel.

From his last chat the manager told him they were now offering a small lunch menu for any passing trade or any of the few guests they might have during the winter months. Most passing drivers naturally stopped on this main route to enquire about food. In season, the hotel was a breakfast with evening meal hotel; their main guests being from arranged tours were usually out somewhere visiting a landmark at midday. The new free standing swing sign board outside merely said: 'FOOD – small lunch menu available.'

Bart stood in the silence of the hotel at the reception desk listening to the eerie quiet. He could smell no aroma of food, just a lingering odour of wallpaper paste. He was in shock at the awful black and white thistle wallpaper that greeted his eyes when he approached the desk, which was new since the time he stayed there.

"Oh my!" was his forceful disapproval on seeing the entire entrance hall redecorated with the singularly shocking addition.

The exclamation was loud enough for anyone to hear had there been a human being around to pick up the comment.

He turned to wander along towards the bar, could see no lights at the end of the corridor where the dining room was, found the bar open with no one serving behind the bar, even though the optics were lit. The room was completely empty. If anyone had been in earlier they certainly were somewhere else probably having an afternoon siesta in their room which is what Bart would be doing now at the side of his fire in the back room in the shop if he wasn't quite so hungry and in need of something to eat.

He sat at the first table near the one window staring outside at the fluttering snow lazily beginning to cover the ground.

"Well, hello!" The voice of the manager paused him in his musings.

"Ah, Philip, how the devil are you?" Bart boomed back. "More to the point what the hell is that mess out there?" he asked pointing towards the refurbishments in the foyer.

"Ah, you don't like our new décor?" The manager came in and stood next to bar grinning broadly.

"Tell me the choice wasn't your idea?" Bart suspected as manager he would have no say in the matter, the hotel being one of a chain of many others across Scotland owned mostly by a coach tour company.

Philip Miller was an Englishman, like himself, whom Bart struck up an immediate bond with when he arrived to take over temporarily from the previous manager. She was a young woman of little experience, thrown in at the deep end when the company introduced an all-inclusive tariff (as much alcohol as you wanted with your evening meal with a late bar) as an experiment to draw customers away from their rivals, ending with disastrous consequences. "Alcohol and people do not mix well, my friend," Phil told Bart after which he confessed himself to be a recovering alcoholic. His candidness struck a chord with Bart resulting in a rare attachment for him, after which he would never offer to buy him a drink as he did the first time they met.

In fact, he watched on many other occasions when the tourists tried to do the same. He noted how affably Philip Miller always refused drinks even when they persisted. Some people Bart realised took the refusal of their offer as a personal rejection.

Phil on the other hand would often say, "Have this one on me," giving them a free drink Bart knew he paid for himself later or once or twice he heard him say, "Perhaps another time when I'm not on duty." Bart realised he was strictly never around whilst off duty.

Phil laughed at Bart's reaction to the new décor, "Not to your taste?" he enquired. "Now there's a thing!"

Bart remembered the old décor, as being much darker and went well with the tartan themed carpets throughout and certainly been more tasteful.

"It's a bit 'sudden' for me," Bart declared.

"And doubtless a 'job lot' they got quite cheaply!" Phil was still laughing. "I can honestly say even in my worst times whilst drinking I would never have chosen something quite so hideous!" Phil turned to the bar, "Your usual is it?"

Bart always marvelled at how, as part of his job, Phil managed to cover for an absentee barman knowing how tempting pouring out drinks must be.

"Actually, I was wondering if I could get a bite to eat.....missed my usual lunch and coffee would be nice."

"There's soup left and chef can do a sandwich," Phil said. "I was about to have mine......I'll join you if I may, since there's no one around?"

"Brilliant! Even better, I do need to run something past you."

CHAPTER 13

When Bart left the hotel after lunching with Philip Miller he drove his car with extreme care in the emerging snow blizzard with a brief stop off at the Co-op to grab a few essential groceries. As he edged his car into his integral garage he knew he might be putting it away for a number of days or even weeks. The uneasiness he felt was not entirely due to the treacherous conditions he drove through, more from the conversation with his 'friend' at the hotel.

They settled down in the dining room with their cock-a-leekie soup, some fine ham and mustard sandwiches the chef generously added to with 'extras', healthy salad garnish and a portion of golden chips on the side. Initially eating in silence with deep sighs of enjoyment, before Bart sat back sated in his chair to sip his coffee, he raised the subject of Selwyn Jones with Phil. He produced the man's business card for the ABC Detective Agency to identify who he meant.

He waved the card under Phil's nose asking, "What can you tell me about this character?" Testing him, knowing full well his name didn't appear anywhere.

"Oh, him!" The manager remarked distastefully after a mere cursory glance. The ensuing silence did not augur well for Bart's curiosity. He waited until he offered, "You know I'm not really allowed to discuss our guests don't you?"

"He told me he was staying here," Bart answered in his defence. "He came into the shop asking me questions whilst flashing a couple of photographs at me." He wasn't about to discuss Beth if he didn't have to.

"Which he also did here," Phil scowled his disapproval sounding angry, "To both the staff as well as the guests! I was forced to have words with him to stop pestering people."

"So you know what he was asking about?" Bart ventured. "I assume he showed you them?"

Phil nodded, his face like thunder, "The thing is I'd already seen them before he arrived here," he confessed.

This immediately alarmed Bart. "How so?" Bart's stomach did an involuntary flip and he found it difficult to look at him.

"He didn't recognise me, thank goodness," he sounded relieved, as he went on to explain, "I've just got back from three days over at one of our sister hotels in Oban. It was my annual AA meeting. I was there as a guest with the rest of our group, sitting in the bar together after dinner when in comes our friend the 'walking cadaver'." At this Bart couldn't hold back a huge guffaw of laughter at such an apt description. Phil also smiled, "he's what my mother would say needs a 'good pan of stew and dumplings'.....she believed this to be a remedy for most ills especially anyone looking on the undernourished side of thin."

"So was he showing the same photos over there?" Bart's curiosity was now raised.

Phil nodded again, "A young girl in one, a dark red car in the other?"

It was Bart's turn to nod, "Did he give any explanation why he was looking for them?"

"He approached us as a group, there were probably about ten of us there. He handed us the pictures to pass around asking if we'd seen either of them saying something about the young under aged girl was a runaway and the car stolen."

Bart tried hard not to let out a tell-tale sound of surprise to show he'd given him different information.

"When I saw him again harassing my guests I got a little angry," he frowned with distaste. "Apart from which my staff were trying to serve at table. I have to keep an eye on them. It's a new Spanish lot, they've just started and I need to train them up. I mean they can barely speak English anyway so this creep was putting the fear of God into them!" He became a little embarrassed as he went on, "We've had a bit of bother with immigration lately - a couple of Polish ones with false papers got arrested here recently - they were deported! Having flash Harry poking around, as well as immigration, makes everyone a little nervous. Certainly it did me personally, anyway."

"Is he still around?" Bart slipped in the question as Phil paused with his story.

"No luckily he left early this morning," he nodded towards the window where they could see the snow looking heavier. "I didn't need the likes of him getting snowed in here spooking my staff. He'll have driven over the top at Glenshee before this lot started."

Bart did think twice about asking him in case the personal question offended him, yet his face when he mentioned Selwyn Jones was quite grim, so he pressed on.

"You say he bothered you personally?" His need to know was greater than possibly causing offence.

"It was having seen him over at Oban, you know, showing up here like he'd followed me, I thought was a bit of a coincidence." Bart nodded in agreement. "Felt like he deliberately followed me back here until he brazenly started flashing his pictures about again," he could see Phil thinking about him. "I thought the Company were checking up on me," he went quiet for a moment. "This really is my last chance of staying in the job, a double whammy if you like. I got put here to sort the place out after the last manager," he then realised Bart wouldn't understand what he meant. "The place isn't *the* liveliest of our hotels, there are no sea views. It's a quiet village with not much night life to speak of outside our own entertainment."

Bart understood, this was after all why he chose the place, once again going for quiet being the least likely to draw attention.

"You say 'double'?" Bart prompted after reflecting on himself.

"The other unwritten 'clause' in my last chance contract was, or rather is, to attend Alcoholics Anonymous meetings as well as to stay off the booze!"

"So they put you in a place where there is all-inclusive raucous drinking?!" Bart heard about the 'new' experiment from Alistair, the landlord at The Moor Hen who was mightily disgusted with the competition as a lot of his regulars took to using the hotel bar instead of his pub as their 'local'.

"The experiment was short lived, drawing more of a local crowd than enticing more tourists up here. They decided it was proving less profitable than they imagined," he laughed. Bart could hear the faint relief in his voice. He had also learnt from Alistair the foreign barmen they employed couldn't tell the difference between the paying guests and the casual locals, as they saw the same faces each night, so were giving free drinks away without knowing. He remembered Alistair asking him, *how can you compete with that?*

"So you thought they were checking up on you?"

"The thought did cross my mind when I first saw him arrive here," he said. "Clearly he showed no recollection of seeing me over at Oban when I plucked up the courage to confront him about bothering my customers." He scoffed, "Not much of a detective if you ask me. I don't think any of my staff could understand a word he was saying at first until they got a full translation making them really scared. One of them came to me to warn me the staff might mutiny!" he frowned fiercely. "You see his story had changed since Oban, the girl become an illegal who disappeared from her job on the west coast!"

Bart was really surprised at the man's brazen stupidity.

"Really?!" he exclaimed in disgust.

"I was about to ask him to leave when he checked out this morning at seven o'clock, didn't even wait for breakfast at eight," Phil confirmed. "I didn't have to think up an excuse not to have a room available if he was planning on staying more than the three days he was booked in for," he stared over at Bart for his understanding, saw none, so he went on. "The usual 'we're full' or 'I'm expecting full tours' in wouldn't do, it's the wrong time of year," he explained. "And.....I could hardly say we were closing for refurbishment," he laughed again. "You can still smell the wallpaper paste!"

Bart laughed heartily again, "Then you might want to replace the décor disaster with something a little more tasteful!"

Phil saw the funny side, "True, I'll keep that in mind should he show up again!"

Bart's stomach lurched at the thought Mr Cadaver might come back, "What is the likelihood?" he dared to ask.

Phil shrugged, "I'd like to say I could refuse him a room......the truth is most of the bookings are done through the 'tour' arrangements on their website – we do have 'casual' drop by ones, these are very few," he explained. "I do have him on my 'black list' though."

"You have a 'black list'?" Bart asked intrigued.

"The company does, it's computerised!" he confided. "This is in confidence!" he added quickly. Bart nodded there was time enough to explore the concept with him on other occasions.

They both glanced out of the nearest window at this point noting the swirling snow was beginning to settle now which made Bart jump up announcing he must get his car put away before the threat turned into a reality forcing him to leave his car to walk the distance back home.

Once his car was snugly garaged, Bart sat locked in The March of Time in his favourite chair by an open fire, a glass of his beloved Bell's Whisky in hand, contemplating the many stories Selwyn Jones was prepared to tell about Lily Frances (nee Johns) his thoughts wandering to her unknown husband and why he was so persistent in finding her. This kind of obsession was familiar to Bart. He came across similar during his years as a Private Investigator, skilled in finding people, sometimes on behalf of some quite unsavoury characters.

If anyone ever came close to such an obsession there was usually a reason, like the wife (or husband) who took off with the family jewels or at the very least all available liquid assets cleared out of a safe or a joint bank account.

Beth didn't fit any of Bart's stereotypes of these 'runners', she was far too scared to mess about planning that kind of departure. As to her pursuer, he didn't even know his full name, only the last name Frances after a slip by Beth when she showed him her car registration document.

However, he did know two other things about him. He was able to pay for the professional services of the Detective Agency on his police salary which wouldn't come cheap. Also Mr. Frances, whoever he was, really wanted to find his wife or.....yes, a third thing, he must be desperate sending someone to search the whole of Scotland for her. This might be the basis for a conversation he was yet to have with 'Beth'.

CHAPTER 14

The world turned white overnight; with the cold came the draughtiness. Bart stood in the doorway at the back of the shop listening to the clocks ticking. He clutched a mug of hot coffee in both hands for warmth. Even the old khaki cable knit sweater he wore over various other layers of clothing, including thermal long johns, barely helped. He appeared like an aging bull frog, even rounder than he normally was. On viewing his image in the mirror earlier only reinforced the analogy and for him to think *you are no Toad of Toad Hall!*

The bags under his eyes were extra saggy today due to his disturbed night worrying about 'Beth' stuck out in the middle of nowhere with only one strange dog for company. He couldn't rid himself of the image of her being pursued by a 'walking cadaver'. The description didn't seem quite as amusing during the night as yesterday when he first heard Phil Miller use it.

Déjà vu brought back his own fears, as a fugitive from the very dangerous Toni Maola - a name he would rather forget. He was adrift somewhere in the world, also a fugitive from the law, who wanted him on several counts of murder. Bart Bridges was one of the key witnesses with information related to his crimes, which put him into the Police Witness Protection Programme to await Maola's capture when once again he would have to expose himself to danger in order to give evidence against him.

Now Bart or whatever his latest name was, he sometimes needed to think hard to recall it, was a fugitive from the police Witness Protection and doubtless would be sought by them if Maola was ever brought to trial.

Why does danger pursue you wherever you go?

Satisfied the clocks were in perfect harmony, he left the shop returning to the crackling fire in the back room to sit in his comfy armchair. He put the coffee down reluctantly on a small table at the side of him, leaned in towards the pile of wood, to toss a couple more logs into the flames. He poked them with the iron poker to evenly distribute them amongst the half-burnt wood to get the heat going. He was reminded immediately of Beth's antiquated kitchen range, thoughts of her pushed all others away except the one, *was every solitary person in the world running away from something?*

That he, Bart Bridges, once seeker of runaway people, should end up one himself was hugely ironic. He took a little comfort from the knowledge his own experience in finding people provided him with the means to evade anyone looking for him. The same knowledge that told him he shouldn't get involved with Lily Frances as this could leave him wide-open to being discovered himself. *Anonymity was the best kind of disguise......making friends with anyone was to be avoided at all costs.* Advice he always kept until now.

Even though Bart knew in this modern technological world the prospect of anonymity was almost impossible. The development of the internet's social media was a huge people finding platform which he initially shunned in all its aspects. That is until the internet engine rolled ever onwards to other areas of people's lives, like when internet banking took off in a big way making using money of the cash only sort virtually impossible. Hell, he'd heard people even did their grocery shopping on line these days, delivered straight to their homes!

Wouldn't work up here, Bart thought, even Tesco would be hard placed to get through during the snowy season. However, he hadn't seen the shelves at the Co-op store on Main Street empty, a limited choice maybe, never completely out. The hotel must manage, as they kept going even towards Christmas when their menus flipped over to a month or more of festive fare offering the full Turkey dinner with Christmas pudding for weeks!

Thank goodness I don't live there, must feel like Groundhog Day every day! He chuckled to himself as he knew Phil Miller lived in a cottage at the back of the hotel but ate mostly all his meals in the staff dining room, like the rest of the staff. He remembered a barman once telling him you could spot the staff because after eating the meals for weeks they took on a grey pallor.

Bart dozed off in his chair waking up after half an hour, a cold cup of coffee at his side with a fire needing to be fed again. After another two more logs he moved over to the kettle, put a few rashers of bacon in the frying pan on the hob and two slices of bread in the toaster. As they began to fry he stood watching the white world flutter past his window in huge flakes thinking once again about 'Beth Grant' (*a Lily by any other name*) ideally wondering what she did when her bread ran out.

He did notice when sorting out her car, the stable-like buildings contained a massive amount of food. At the time the sheer amount took his breath away. This kind of resourcefulness meant she wouldn't go hungry then he recalled when he was over there 'mending' the Grandfather clock, the smell of baking bread pervading the cottage. Maybe he should take her example by becoming more resourceful for times like this severe winter which he believed might prove to be the norm up here.

He idly turned the bacon over in the pan to brown the other side, pushed the button down on the toaster sending the soft white bread to its doom. He flicked the kettle back on to boil again, put some new instant coffee in his mug; all this without taking his eyes off the mesmerising snow.

After breakfast he would search out his old lap top, the one he got as a concession to the modern technological world which he hardly ever used. He was much happier in the ticking world of clocks whose mechanisms he did understand.

He needed to do some searching, find out about Lily Frances (nee Johns) along with anything he could about her husband. He would begin by looking up the 'walking cadaver', Selwyn Jones. He also needed to find a car for 'Beth' or at least find out how he could dispose of hers. He was confident it was safely hidden away for now; he felt perhaps it was better to get rid of it altogether. Personally, he would like to see the whole thing crushed into a cube!

Once back beside the fire with a bacon sandwich he removed the cable knit sweater and proceeded to log on to the laptop he salvaged from his old life. He wasn't very experienced with computers, what he did know he learnt many years ago when the police force he worked for as a SOCO began to be computerised, they installed a fingerprint database.

He only used their systems until much later, as a P.I., he taught himself to use this very same laptop to interrogate the internet until he learnt the basics. When he became Cyrus Bartholomew, clockmaker, he didn't use the laptop much at all. There was no need to and he certainly didn't want to join the social media frenzy. Maybe he was too old or just plain anti-social – he told himself he possessed no desire whatsoever for friends, imaginary or otherwise.

He sat for a while until he finished his coffee whilst contemplating where he should begin. At the google search box he typed in *ABC Detective Agency*, pressed 'search' to pull up pages of agencies in many different towns. He had forgotten how frustrating the whole search facility could be. He had no idea which town Lily Frances' came from or knew anything about her background to be able to choose correctly.

Why did so many private investigation agencies call themselves ABC? He supposed for no other reason than using 'A' put them at the top of the search list giving them the chance to be chosen first. He was sure most people wouldn't ever get down to even the second level never mind the others. Out of frustration he abandoned the task completely.

He picked up the pay-as-you-go mobile he purchased at the same time as Beth's. Up until now he didn't keep in touch with anyone from his past for security reasons. The one he used as a Private Investigator was taken by the police as 'evidence' in his 'dealings' with Toni Maola when he was a client. Until now there was no reason to replace it. When he pressed the only number in his contact list he heard the ringing for what seemed an age.

CHAPTER 15

When Beth came back inside after clearing the pathways she was bright red in the face, perspiring greatly from the exercise. She tried her best to ignore the dog, who tentatively scooted out a couple of times to lift a leg against the high bank of snow leaving tell-tale yellow rings. She could see him standing watching her until she turned her back so he wouldn't be observed. *What a strange creature you are.*

She was greatly surprised when she heard the Grandfather clock strike eleven showing her how long she had been outside; once again marvelling at the old lady's seemingly effortless accomplishments when the same things seemed to exhaust her. She sat down at the table having filled the kettle, placing it back on the shelf at the front of the fire to boil. For the first time she thought she ought to buy an electric kettle to use when the electricity was working to save time. Maybe there were other things she could do to make life easier.

She idly picked up the mobile from the table in front of her, heard a text message pop up telling her she missed a call. Initially she was spooked until she saw the call was from Sirus, no doubt checking up on her after the heavy fall of snow overnight. She waited for the kettle to boil making a cup of instant coffee which she bought with the other provisions she got herself the day before.

She returned his call barely hearing the ring before an out of breath Sirus answered with a relieved, "Thank goodness!"

He sounded so alarmed she asked, "What's wrong?"

"You didn't answer, I got worried," he said calming down, obviously pleased to hear her voice.

"No, I was outside clearing some of the snow away for Sandy and to get to the supplies in the stable," she forced a little laugh not wanting to offend by telling him to stop fussing.

"The idea is you keep the phone on you at all times," he scolded making her feel like a little girl.

"Point taken," she agreed to appease him. "I didn't think clearing a path would take me so long. I'm not used to having a mobile," then she remembered how her own was often denied her. Martin only gave it to her when 'he' wanted to check up on her; he always checked afterwards in case she made any calls. She didn't want to openly admit a mobile brought back bad memories for her.

"How are you managing otherwise?" he asked.

"Fine, there's always something to do." Perhaps this was an odd thing to say, she knew. Then living there was strange altogether as time somehow didn't seem to be as tangible as it once was, always seeming to get away from her somehow, even if she would be hard pressed to tell anyone just how.

"And the clock?" she heard him ask making small talk, "Is still keeping good time I hope?"

She hadn't considered checking on the clock's time keeping, what mattered was the hearing the chimes; at other times she now barely noticed the gentle ticking. "Yes, I think so," she sounded unsure having nothing else against which to compare the accuracy, until she thought about the time shown on the mobile phone which was 11.04. "Yes, it's in keeping with the time on the mobile having just struck eleven – I counted." She beamed with satisfaction knowing Sirus sorted the problem. "What's the snow like in the village?" She asked needing the distraction from her ritualistic cottage life.

"We are well snowed in. I think Alistair will have his work cut out, or rather his mini snow plough will."

"Who is Alistair?"

"He's the landlord at the village pub I go to for lunch *most* days," Bart doubted he would be able to today unless Alistair's snowplough once again came to the rescue.

"Oh? I didn't see a pub when I drove through.....'" Sure there was a couple of cafés, two hotels, she couldn't remember seeing a public house.

"Ah, you wouldn't drive past the pub," he assured her. "It's hidden behind the cottages half way up The Brae, the road where my shop is at the bottom," not for the first time he thought it an odd place for a pub. There was no such thing as 'passing' trade; you needed to know where The Moor Hen was to go there.

"Oh, I see," she said. "The only one I've been to is the Taigh-òsta on the road to Ballater the day I came here. I stopped for something to eat." *How long ago was that?* She suddenly remembered the piece of paper where the owner wrote the address of a B&B which she didn't find. The piece of paper seemed a distant memory now also.

In the following pause Bart tried to think about how he might broach the subject of Selwyn Jones.

"Hello? Are you still there?" she prompted thinking he might have cut the call.

"Yes.....can I ask you a few questions, Beth?" he sounded tentative.

"Okay," she agreed doubtfully, not wanting to talk about her former life.

"I wondered if you maybe came to the Highlands from Oban?"

"Oban? Where is that?" she asked which threw him a little.

"It's on the west coast of Scotland."

"This is the first time I've been to Scotland," was her simple reply.

"So, no relatives over there?"

She went quiet for a moment before answering, "I don't have any relatives." Bart wanted to say 'Oh', didn't because it would sound like he doubted her. "Why do you ask?"

"I found out from Phil the manager at the hotel our 'friend' the private investigator was over there a few days before he arrived here, also asking about you."

He couldn't see Beth's face yet was sure she would be registering genuine surprise.

"I don't understand why he would go there?" Bart could hear by her voice she didn't understand.

"Exactly what I was wondering myself if what he told me is true about your car being spotted coming here, then why go to Oban?"

"I don't remember much about the drive up to be honest, I got really tired. I do remember the M74 then stopping at Stirling services. To be honest I wasn't exactly following a route," she felt like crying as she remembered the woman who broke her hip. The panic she felt was clearer than the actual journey. "I kept on going until, like I told you, I got lost in a blizzard which made me stop…..that was when I found Elizabeth…." She didn't add because of the candle in the window.

Bart could hear the catch in her voice; he really didn't want to frighten her any more than was necessary. "Does your husband have any connection to Oban, any relatives over there perhaps?"

Another pause ensued whereby he could imagine Beth trying to control her emotions at the mention of him.

"Not as far as I know……he's Welsh. I never heard him mention Scotland." *Another reason why I came here.*

"Can I ask you why you chose to come here, say instead of maybe going south or even over to Ireland?"

"I thought here might be more peaceful, not so many people." Bart understood perfectly well he'd done the very same thing. "I didn't consider Ireland; there would by necessity be a border to cross. I thought there was too much chance of being spotted." She didn't tell him she didn't have a passport with which to leave the country, it would open up potential admissions she was kept like a prisoner and not allowed to go anywhere.

"Yes, true, it's much easier for someone who has access to databases.....which reminds me, I expect our friend Jones is likely to be local to your husband.....where would that be?" The question wasn't very subtle, Bart knew, but he really needed to get some I.D on her husband.

Once again Beth was drawn back into the past, "It would probably be Newport," she said.

Now Bart could understand why she drove north to Scotland, he imagined she wanted to put sufficient distance between herself and her husband.

"Okay," Bart said. "The good news is our friend has moved on, at any rate, probably gone back there having drawn a blank."

"You know this for certain?" she asked eagerly.

"He checked out early before we got this round of snow. I believe so, he would have got over Glenshee before we got snowed in again," he couldn't help thinking *unless he went the other way*, which he knew would bring him closer to where Beth now lived.

As if she sensed what he was thinking she said, "I know a lot of places are closed to visitors, like the guest Inn I called at on my way here."

"Yes, it's the right time of year. He really did draw a blank," Bart wasn't sufficiently knowledgeable about the area to know how many hotels there were north beyond the village. "When the weather picks up we'll have to look to getting rid of your car."

"Yes…..it's fairly safe where we've put it, isn't it?"

Bart heard the plea in her voice which signalled the need for some reassurance. He made a mental note to look at ways to dispose of cars as his thoughts now turned away from the image of a crushed metal cube in favour of using the vehicle as a decoy away from where she was living. If her husband really did have the means to identify registrations this might come in useful. "We'll see," he said cryptically.

CHAPTER 16

The opportunity presented itself sooner than Bart anticipated. His first choice to find a way to scrap Beth's car, to crush it into a cube would be the most satisfying, he realised this wouldn't solve the problem of the over-zealous Selwyn Jones. He felt sure the man would return after the snow melted. He knew *he* would never have given up on a hunch when he was a P.I. From what he saw of Jones he recognised a certain determined predatory streak.

No, he wanted to divert attention away from Scotland, try to make it look like Lily Frances left the UK altogether. That meant he needed sufficient clues to entice the search away; to make sure Selwyn Jones would follow.

What Bart feared the most was drawing attention to himself. He couldn't risk taking her car somewhere himself knowing her husband had access to police tracing data. He was, of course, too physically distinctive to allow himself to show up on a chance speed camera photo or to be caught on CCTV footage to be identified, after all the police would already be looking for him having dropped out of Witness Protection. Getting personally involved would undermine all the subterfuge he'd gone to in getting this far away from the police *and* his pursuers.

This was the second time he changed his name, always being unable to get used to a new one. He feared the most having someone call out his new name, Sirus Jeffries, then him failing to respond to it. The last time his name changed from Bartholomew (Bart) Bridges to Cyrus Bartholomew, keeping the latter gave him a certain familiarity, an excuse to still think of himself as 'Bart', even though after two years the few people he got to know called him Cyrus.

This time a different spelling of the name Sirus kept a similar familiarity with his previous identity. The 'Jeffries' came as a bit of inspiration on his part, directly from his paternal grandmother's side of his ancestry. Her name was 'Gefyres' which he knew was Greek for 'bridges' because his father changed the Greek spelling to the English 'Bridges' when he came to the UK in his late teens searching for work. He met his mother and the rest is history as they say.

He could only speculate why he was given Bartholomew as his first name. The name did have origins in a strong Greek orthodox background. The ancient church of Christ and the Apostles, as St Bartholomew is not mentioned in the Gospel of John, yet he was believed to be one of the twelve disciples. Bart, however, having been a lifelong atheist, something else he has spent many years concealing even when someone referred to his biblical first name. Nonetheless, he missed it now taking comfort in knowing his new last name recognised his roots.

The idea about disposing of Beth's car came to him during one of his lunch time excursions to The Moor Hen where he found a diminished crowd of loners and where Alistair received him with his welcoming shot glass in his hand only to be disappointed when Bart shook his head. "I'll have a coffee with my lunch today, thanks," because he wasn't feeling one hundred per cent. He felt he needed to keep his wits about him in order to solve Beth's car situation.

Bart rubbed his temples with his hands, "A slight chill I think," he added as a reasonable excuse.

Alistair returned the shot glass to its row of fellows looking somewhat disappointed. He nodded over to the sparse array of regulars, "Maybe it's something going round," he said. "Can't tempt you with a medicinal brandy?"

Bart shook his head again looking around the room he noticed even the 'star-crossed lovers' were subdued. They leaned in towards each other where a weak looking beer with two straws allowed them to share it.

"Doesn't look too good," Bart commented nodding over towards them. He disapproved strongly of their public show of affection, whilst not being too prudish to feel sorry romance seemed sadly absent.

"Ah," Alistair observed. "Like most newlyweds when reality hits the honeymoon, as they say, is definitely over."

"Newlyweds?" Bart sounded surprised. They seemed to Bart way too young for anything so formal. At least the young girl he assessed was barely of age even if the boy was a little older.

"I believe so," Alistair confirmed. "Something he let slip when they first appeared."

"Not local then?" Bart assumed them to be a local couple of kids meeting here to hide from parental disapproval.

Alistair shook his head leaning closer towards Bart, "I think they might be one of those Gretna Green elopements."

It shocked Bart to think the landlord might have such a keen sense of assessing his clientele to know such a thing. "They told you?" he sounded doubtful.

Alistair's head shook slowly, "Nope," he admitted. "Saw a picture of them taken on their wedding day with the identifying Gretna icon showing – I believe it's an anvil? I saw the picture on their table when I was clearing away their plates. They had just arrived, still marvelling at their new status and shiny wedding rings, like the couple of kids they are – proud to have pulled the whole thing off, I reckon!"

"Ah," Bart was impressed with Alistair's deductive skills. "So what's ailing them now?" he asked observing their downcast countenances.

The landlord preened, he was clearly proud of his own powers of observation, "In a word – money." Bart's face took on an enquiring look. "He's been asking around about possible work. I don't think they expected to be staying up here quite this long – didn't anticipate all the snow."

"And they've decided to stay now?" Bart began to wonder how much of Alistair's thoughts were speculation.

"I hear they are looking for something with accommodation," he nodded knowingly. "Maybe they are coming to the end of affording their B&B."

Bart realised Alistair in his position must hear an awful lot of personal information about people, even with an enquiring ear for deductions. He made a mental note to be extra careful not to give anything away about himself.

"You know for certain?"

Alistair leaned in even further intruding on Bart's personal space, "One shandy, two straws and....." he nodded over to them. "They put in an order for one plate of chips, two forks," he touched the side of his nose knowingly looking pleased with himself.

Bart suddenly felt sorry for the young couple even if he previously secretly envied their young love. Clearly they were devoted to each other, not something he knew about himself.

Bart suddenly felt decisive, "I'll have today's special, landlord and give them whatever they want, I'll pay!"

He picked up a newspaper from the counter to take to his usual table in the corner to wait for his lunch. He couldn't miss out on the opportunity to strike up a conversation with the young couple.

CHAPTER 17

Fortunately it was only a few more weeks before there was to be a rare break in the normal winter weather pattern, due Bart was convinced to global warming. There was reports all over the news across the world according to meteorological specialists everywhere, earth quakes, tsunamis, hurricanes, tornadoes and even a surge in bush fires, were having devastating consequences. As a result they were expecting a prolonged period of unseasonal highs which would give an early 'spring' like spell to melt away the snow which would allow Bart to consider enacting a plan he was devising.

What gave him the confidence to approach the young couple directly came when he heard another of Alistair's speculations. Alistair touched the side of his nose as he told him about a man (he called him 'the walking skeleton') who was a private dick – here he showed Bart the card for the ABC Detective Agency which he took from a shelf behind the bar. Of course, the business card was identical to the one Selwyn Jones gave him, as was his description. Bart pretended to examine the details endeavouring to look suitably surprised.

Alistair told him he wasn't too pleased when the man moved around his customers showing them the picture of Lily Johns and her car but was sufficiently close to 'love's young dream' to register the sheer relief on their faces when the man found out the girl in the picture wasn't his wife.

"It was as if they expected a private investigator to be pursuing them, don't you see?" Bart remained suitably blank to show he didn't see at all. "I think yon lassie is a runaway," he sounded triumphant in his deduction looking to Bart for recognition of the fact. "She looks barely of age, don't you think? I could see they were both spooked by my detective friend."

"I see," Bart's thoughts moved on to gestate the germ of an idea which he hoped would be beneficial to everyone.

*   *   *   *   *

At first the young man Warren Doyle and his wife Anna were a little cautious even though they were getting close to desperation as the days progressed. Their search for non-existent work drew them closer each day to homelessness, which neither of them wanted to find themselves in, certainly not in such inhospitable weather. Even with a tent and sleeping bags they wouldn't last long out in the open. This was made clear by the story doing the rounds about the missing walkers from the B&B they were staying at who, they were informed, were eventually found dead.

They would need to move on soon anyway. What this strange little man was proposing gave them a chance with the means to get as far away from Anna's father as they possibly could. Maybe even start a new life somewhere warmer than this snowbound empty place. After a belly full of hot food inside them the idea grew infinitely more attractive.

The couple sat together eating their meal Bart bought for them whilst they discussed what they would do about his proposal. When they finished their meal Anna went to the ladies leaving Warren to go over to speak once again with Bart.

He stood contemplating him for a moment, "Okay, we'll do it, only we need to know precisely what you expect of us."

"Good," Bart felt a little relieved. "We have time to work out the details." He handed Warren some money already wrapped in the newspaper he'd been reading. "Meanwhile, you'll need to survive here until the next thaw comes," Bart pointed at the newspaper telling him the proviso was they were to speak to no one about their plans before they left.

All subsequent arrangements they made secretly at The March of Time. Only Alistair ever knew of Bart's generosity in buying them one bar meal.

"That was kind," was Alistair's comment made to him when Bart came to settle the bill after the couple left. This was the last time the landlord saw them either before the big thaw came or after. If he was ever to be asked about the young couple, his memory of them moving on would have differed with other people's by one or two weeks. Of course, the B&B owner recorded the exact date in the register when they moved out, then memory has a way of distorting after the passing of time.

The only actual piece of evidence Bart received later came in a pictorial form sent by the Doyle's from the deck of a P&O ferry. Just like most other young people the picture was a selfie showing them ceremoniously slipping a pair of number plates into the sea. It could have been any sea (of which Bart could only guess at). He wasn't really interested in knowing exactly where Selwyn Jones, Private Investigator from the ABC Detective Agency, would spend a number of months searching for a dark red Vauxhall Astra driven by a Lily Frances, as long he stayed as far away from the Highlands of Scotland as possible.

However, from time to time he did receive the odd picture of one curious sign post or another. The photographs contained no identifying features to show who sent them. There was enough to give a hint somewhere in the world a young couple were making good from the once kindness of a stranger. The very last one he received was a picture which read, 'DO NOT FEED' with a silhouette of a Koala bear which made Bart smile before he deleted it.

CHAPTER 18

Bart's first winter, before the installation of a new heating system at The March of Time, felt like the longest ever. Time stood still with everything frozen in the coldest winter on record. Conditions were made worse by his being without a car, having given his own (an early used Peugeot 208) to Beth when he took the Astra in readiness to give to the young couple he met only briefly. He felt isolated, frozen in endless days of inertia.

It surprised him the day he heard the shop bell tinkle as he was passing through from the back with a new mug of coffee in hand, to find Beth silhouetted in the doorway against a backdrop of rare winter sunshine, her face glowing from the chill of the early spring-like weather. Her welcoming smile cheered him instantly as she curiously beckoned him to join her outside, then promptly disappeared like the apparition he thought she was the first day she came into his shop.

He found her outside standing next to a small white van parked in the space immediately in front of the door. Both of her hands were held out to the side like a magician's assistant would after making the vehicle appear as if by magic from nowhere. Bart's double take was enquiring.

"I've got a part time job," she was every bit as excited as she sounded, "With wheels!"

After persuading Bart to close the shop to go with her to fetch his car from her garage, she explained how she plucked up the courage to invite the groom from the nearby castle stables (who was delivering a new sack of dog food) inside for a cup of tea like Elizabeth would have done.

"He offered me a job helping out at the stables, cleaning out, making deliveries, that kind of thing!" Bart could hear the sheer joy she showed in being able to have her first ever job, a decision she made for herself. "It's not much being part time, but I love it!"

Not wanting to burst her bubble, Bart didn't ask why a groom would be delivering dog food and she offered no explanation. Likewise she didn't explain how Elizabeth took Sandy after foxhunting with hounds came to be banned in Scotland resulting in most of the dogs being fostered out to various people until, the gentry believed, Parliament would come to their senses and lift the ban.

Bart's car remained inside the garage covered in the tarpaulin where her red Astra was previously, not that she needed to use it, she merely turned over the engine once in a while to keep the battery charged. That much she knew about cars having learnt its significance the hard way, she could still feel the rebuke of a lesson hard learnt.

"Are you sure you won't need this until I can get you another....?" Bart began even though he felt relieved to have his Peugeot back especially since his advancing arthritis troubled him the most during the harsh weather.

"No, really I have use of this van whilst ever I work up at the castle stables.....not only for making deliveries....it's so I can be flexible in my working days." She grew thoughtful, "Getting another car would be difficult I think unless...." She faltered.

"......unless you give them your real name on your driving licence?" Bart finished for her.

"Yes," she said simply, "which I don't have....I left my licence back.....there," *in my previous life.*

"Didn't the stables need a look when they gave you the van?"

Beth shook her head, "To be honest I was surprised when Fraser offered me the job. No, not even when he told me I could use the van….. He didn't even ask me if I could drive….he must have assumed I could!" It was so easy she began to have a real sense of freedom for the first time.

Bart passed one or two comments. He didn't want to spoil her obvious pleasure by casting any doubts over the arrangement, apart from which he felt a great relief to be able to have his own car back. He really had no explanation (other than the weather conditions) as to why he wasn't seen around in it. He realised how much he relied on his car when he first carried some shopping bags back from the Co-op on Main Street. Someone he recognised from the pub yelled over to him, "Car broken down?" He felt obliged to mumble something about trying to get fitter having become too lazy during the harshest parts of the winter.

By the time he'd walked the short distance home he was out of breath, so he was right. "You need the exercise!" he told himself out loud whilst he got his breath back. Afterwards he made more trips purchasing less each time to ease the burden of carrying them home.

As he drove back from Beth's cottage he promised himself he would keep up the exercise by maintaining his walking regime.

CHAPTER 19

Bart stared transfixed at the hands of the clock on the wall in The Griddle Iron watching them move backwards. Ordinarily the phenomenon would have brought a smile to his face. Today, however, his face appeared perplexed as he thought about the telephone call he just received before he vacated the shop for an early lunch.

"One of our house special burgers with homemade tomato relish," Max announced interrupting his thoughts by placing the plate in front of his only customer of the moment. When he caught Bart's pensive expression he asked, "Are you okay, Sirus?"

Bart emerged from his contemplations, peered down at the plate, a juicy burger, sweet potato chips with salad garnish and he inhaled the meaty aroma. "Excellent!" he bellowed in his usual way. "Who wouldn't be fine with such a platter?"

Max grinned, "Let me know if I can get you anything else." He moved away leaving Bart to his lunch.

The conversation which perplexed him was with the Laird's secretary, Thomas Galbraith which left Bart in an unsettled mood. Initially, he wasn't surprised to receive the call having expected someone from the castle to make contact, either by telephone or more likely to turn up at the shop, to fetch the repaired Grandmother clock. With the bouts of heavy snow coming fast, coupled with very little in the way of thaws in between them, he'd almost forgotten about the clock, having hung it up on the wall in the corner of the shop amongst the rest of the clocks. Once in a while he was reminded as he routinely wound them and because the task took so long he'd promptly forgotten about the castle's clock again by the time he finished the round.

He promised himself once or twice he would telephone the Castle to remind them or else drive there himself but there wasn't the urgency to issue a bill for payment for the repairs because he neither relied on the money from repairing clocks nor did their infrequency give much of a boost to his finances. In fact, there was sufficient money to live his simple life from the interest on his savings to sustain it. Apart from which the weather kept him from venturing out altogether.

When the telephone call came he was somewhat baffled. He realised the call wasn't from the man who brought the clock to him, who at the time he assumed was the Laird himself, both by the way he dressed as well as spoke. The request posed by Thomas Galbraith didn't even mention the clock. The formal request was on behalf of Laird Duncan Munro who wished to speak with Mr Jeffries in person if he would "kindly call at twelve o'clock on Tuesday to meet with him."

There was no hint about why the Laird wished to meet with him. Upon receiving Bart's agreement the man merely concluded, "Good," brusquely terminating the call. Bart was left at first irritated by the man's abruptness which eventually eased off into bafflement because he didn't ask about the repair to the clock, or even if he achieved or completed them, nothing.

*   *   *   *   *

By the time Tuesday arrived Bart's misgivings lessened a little, they were replaced with the anticipation of visiting his very first castle. He climbed into his Peugeot 208 setting off for the castle with the Grandmother clock safely encased in a soft blanket in the boot to cushion the delicate mechanisms during the journey. The prepared invoice for the repairs which he itemised in some detail was wrapped inside the blanket with the clock.

He drove over to the Castle with no real idea of what to expect never having been inside a castle in his life, he did feel a certain level of excitement at the prospect. He was completely taken by surprise when he saw it. He drove for what seemed like miles after turning in at the elaborately ornate gates with its austere gate house standing guard like a brooding gargoyle did on the guttering of many a cathedral walls

The extensive drive meandered up a winding tree-lined road which eventually twisted to the right where Bart was suddenly presented with the magnificent majestic castle structure with its symmetrical twin towers. Castle Daingneach's external appearance made Bart stop the car to take in the spectacular sight. Grand it was, whilst there was something primordially cold about the sheer grey stone walls which sent a chill through him as he stared at its battlements. He imagined in days gone by they would have given the occupants an obvious advantage in detecting advancing armies presenting a threat to them. He found himself searching the battlements for anyone who could be watching his approach in the same way. The prospect of being observed made him engage the gears of the car once again to finish his journey towards it.

He didn't have sufficient time to debate with himself whether he ought to be searching for a tradesman's entrance, his concentration was monopolised by the loose chippings he drove onto immediately in front of the castle. He felt the car slip instantly he heard the tyres of the Peugeot begin to make the unmistakeably loud crunching sound. *If no one spotted him from any of the vantage points of the battlements surely they must have heard his arrival?*

He skidded to a halt in line with the castle's front door which stood open. Relieved there were no other cars parked on the vastness of this forecourt when he opened his eyes (which he must have closed as a reflex against the slipping sensation), he saw the figure of a man striding towards him from the open front door. His first thought on seeing him was 'Indiana Jones' one of his favourite adventure movie series. However, this man reminded him of the alter ego of his hero, a fusty old Professor of Archaeology. He was all corduroy trousers, a beige knitted cardigan with leather patches at the elbows with his hair standing on end looking in need of a good comb. This was no adventurer, there the likeness ended.

He got out of the car smiling a greeting. However, the stern faced man was not smiling which made Bart look down towards his tyres for any evidence of skid marks on the shale surface which might have incurred an angry response from the owner of the face. Bart was no Sterling Moss. He couldn't see how you could arrive in any other smoother way.

"Mr Jeffries?" The enquiry was formally made although the face remained harsh while the bearer's voice was surprisingly tremulous. Bart wondered how long he would take to get used to his new name; hearing it spoken also made him feel slightly guilty at the duplicity of the pseudonym. He wondered if he ought not to have come at all making the Laird send someone over to pick up the clock as he originally thought would happen.

"Yes!" Bart managed in his normal forceful way. The sound seemed to echo in what he now recognised was an eerie silence surrounding this formidable place.

Perhaps, he thought, the sheer height of its intimidating walls created the echo repelling all other sounds. He could detect no bird song or other wildlife noises which drew his attention to the absence of any nearby trees, other than the forest of fir trees some distance away. Those standing sentinel beside the driveway ceased as the castle came into view.

It all smacks of some ancient means of fortification.

"Thomas Galbraith," the 'adventurer', come historian, announced without a glimmer of a friendly gesture. *Ah, the Laird's secretary.* "The Laird is attending to some business, he won't be long……if you could follow me I'll show you where you can wait." He walked away expecting Bart to follow him stopping halfway to the front door. When he turned to glance back he realised Bart wasn't following him. He was in fact bent inside the hatch back of his car, lifting out an old blanket from the boot after which he managed to close the hatch by the use of an elbow.

Thomas Galbraith appeared more irritated than curious whilst he waited for Bart to join him. Without saying a word he turned once again continuing towards the main door through which he disappeared leaving Bart to progress under the weight of his prized clock which he tried to cushion against any sudden jerky movements.

The castle's presence made him feel overlooked, somehow insignificant. Such a strange feeling made Bart feel nervous. When he entered, following Galbraith, he was immediately struck by the contrast between the brightness of the noon day sun outside, having to squint to focus and the gloominess of the interior. As his eyes adjusted, he could barely make out what the poor electric light revealed.

Apart from the open door which was rather unimpressively small for a castle, Bart realised there were no windows to let in any light from outside. The high interior walls were imposing, completely covered in fighting weapons, swords, spears, shields, axes and other quite gruesome armoury Bart felt intimidated by. He was given no time to take in this massive collection as Thomas Galbraith stood half-way up a flight of stone steps once again waiting for Bart to catch up with him.

He seemed none too pleased at his lack of progress watching Bart stop at the bottom of the staircase to take in their steepness. Bart clutched the blanket containing the clock tighter, knew he needed at least one free hand with which to aid his climb by holding onto the bannister at the side. As if in sympathy his arthritic knees twinged when he began to climb and not for the first time he considered how he might get himself registered at the GP surgery in the village. This in itself was difficult with no previous medical history he could possibly declare to a new doctor. His progress was slow, his knees taking the brunt of the climb as he followed the Laird's grumpy secretary.

Sometime later, his thighs still complaining, he caught up with the man at the end of a long corridor where he was shown into a rather impressive library with floor to ceiling stacked shelves of old books. Bart noted they were sets of leather bound volumes.

The farthest wall was hung with many large oil paintings of what Bart assumed were family portraits, the largest being the Laird himself dressed, he thought, in the family tartan, his distinctive ginger hair and beard he remembered gave him an almost savage appearance which contrasted greatly with the cultured voice he remembered when he delivered the clock.

Bart deposited the blanket on a nearby table to relieve the strain on his arms; he massaged each one to bring back some circulation. He pointed towards the picture of the Laird saying, "Impressive," which only attracted a cursory glance from Galbraith otherwise he ignored him completely moving instead towards the door at the farthest end of the library.

"Take a seat, I'll tell the Laird you're here," he disappeared leaving Bart quite alone.

CHAPTER 20

Left alone in the castle library Bart sat down on a heavy leather chair relieved to be able to get his breath back from carrying the Grandmother clock, he desperately needed to give his aching legs some reprieve. When Thomas Galbraith returned he was carrying a tray with two silver pots and several cups and saucers. The inevitable plate of traditional Scottish shortbread accompanied the rest. After placing the tray on a small table at the side of his guest he asked, "Tea or coffee?"

"Thank you, coffee please." Whilst he poured Bart took the opportunity to scrutinise the man close up. His first impression being Thomas Galbraith seemed quite nervous, he barely made eye contact. The second thing he noticed was his hand shook visibly whilst he poured the coffee. Bart began to wonder about the Laird's effect on his secretary, for he could hardly take responsibility for producing such a reaction.

"The Laird will be along shortly, he has nearly finished," he disappeared once again leaving Bart alone to take in his surroundings in more detail.

He spent the intervening time walking around the library breathing in the heady mix of mildew and old leather smells of the books. He could make out the faint dustiness of the volumes on the higher shelves which were inaccessible to normal human reach. To dust higher he knew would require 'specialised' cleaning attention. He deduced this particular castle was not open to the public, at least not inside.

After his inspection Bart stood in front of one of the two small windows in the room gazing out across the castle grounds towards the forest of fir trees in the distance. The land in between held a range of outbuildings together with a terraced arrangement of carefully laid out grounds including a walled in garden set with rows of assorted plants and bushes he imagined were vegetables or fruits.

Another area was partitioned by carefully cut hedges creating a boxed pattern of low neatly trimmed hedge shrubs planted for their resulting design which one day, if they grew sufficiently tall, might create a maze. Close to the castle there was a long row of stables he already knew about from Beth and was where she now worked. He could see someone leading a horse by its bridal.

One thing Bart was sure about, this castle was built to defend against any invasion. He didn't have a 360 degree view from where he stood, he thought, perhaps the battlements afforded the opportunity to detect or repel anyone's approach.

"It's impressive isn't it?" the voice behind him took him by surprise as he hadn't heard anyone come in.

When he turned Bart was surprised to find a man perhaps in his late fifties, his brown hair receding slightly was at the temples peppered with grey. He was wearing a dark green woven tweed jacket, one might expect a country squire to wear, a white shirt with grey slacks.

He was smiling, "My apologies for keeping you waiting, I wasn't expecting to be detained quite so long." His faint Scottish accent was barely discernible. "Duncan Munro," he offered Bart his hand as he walked closer to shake hands.

Bart glanced over towards the painting of the man with the fiery red hair and wild beard inwardly laughing at his previous assumption he was the Laird. Duncan Munro followed his gaze towards the picture, "I'm nothing like my ancestors am I? I'm not vain enough or have sufficient patience to sit for hours whilst some overpaid portrait painter commits my image to canvas for historical validity. These days we rely on photographic evidence," Bart found his laugh compelling.

"Is that why they all look so glum?" Bart asked gazing at the centre portrait of the kilted giant whom he recognised from his appearance in his shop, the conveyor of the Grandmother clock, who was more soberly dressed on that occasion.

Duncan Munro took in the direction of his gaze laughing heartily.

"You might be right. In those days the gentlemen were all portrayed as fierce fighting stock whilst the ladies were stoical companions." He nodded toward 'red beard', "In the case of my great, great uncle Seumus by all accounts he was as fierce as he looks there." He caught the frown on Bart's face.

"Great, great….?" Bart asked surprised.

"Yes, on my mother's side," he added which didn't provide Bart with much of an explanation.

Instead of raising the issue puzzling him, Bart asked, "Is that the Munro tartan?" His only knowledge of tartans being they are identifiably clan based.

"Actually, no, the Black Watch was regarded at the time as a universal fighting tartan which a few clans chose to wear," he explained. "Seumus Grant I dare say wore the Black Watch tartan for that purpose. He was known or should I say infamous for his fighting skills. The Campbell's, the Munro's and others also wore it for their scraps!"

"Your great, great uncle was a Grant?" Bart's question held a faint disbelief about it. The Laird was familiar with curiosity about the name difference.

"Aye," his accent suddenly became more marked. "He was also renowned for the sowing of his wild oats. Doubtless he has many a bastard offspring scattered around Speyside," he looked over at Bart for comprehension of the reference, saw none and continued,

"Grantown-on-Spey is where the Grants settled," he finished leaving Bart to note he must look up the history for himself when he got back home.

They were interrupted by the entrance of Thomas Galbraith carrying another identical tray of refreshments. He took the first one, leaving the room without uttering a sound, except for a furtive glance the Laird's way which Bart couldn't fail to notice.

"Forgive my secretary," Duncan Munro apologised. "He's of a nervous disposition, we aren't all fighting stock!" Again he laughed loudly at some hidden joke.

Once drinks were dispensed they settled on a sofa and a chair, the Laird went on, "I expect you are wondering why I asked to see you?"

Again Bart felt himself drawn further into this curious situation, so he chose to say nothing merely nodded expectantly.

"There have been some strange things happening here lately," he began which immediately peaked Bart's interest.

"Oh?"

"Yes," he continued, "I was detained by a call I needed to take from the local police."

At the mention of the Police Bart suddenly felt uncomfortable. He tried not to shift in his seat remaining focussed on the Laird's narrative. He nodded to indicate his attention.

"One of my ghillies has gone missing, we think maybe about a month ago. At the time we thought perhaps he'd gone away for a break – they seldom do you understand. Mungo MacLeod has been here for a very long time." Galbraith returned to the library where he stood discretely on the periphery listening to the Laird talking. "I have, however, reported his disappearance to the police now believing perhaps he may have deliberately left taking with him an item or even items of the castle's artefacts." He waited for Bart to comment.

"I see, you believe he has stolen from you?"

"Yes," he confirmed. "One of my domestic staff has noticed we have a clock missing from one of the corridors."

Bart seemed to jerk as if surprised. Once again he scrutinised the picture of Seumus Grant then turned back to Duncan Munro.

"Does he by any chance resemble the picture of your great, great uncle?"

The other two men stared at each other looking startled.

"How could you possibly know?" Duncan Munro asked surprised. "I suppose there is some resemblance, at least in colouring. Mungo isn't quite as wild or fierce; neither is his hair or beard."

He could see Bart seemed a little relieved. "That's true," Bart agreed, "which is why at first I thought he was you when I met him some weeks ago. When I was shown into this room I saw the portrait, which did seem to rather confirm my assertion."

It was the Laird's turn to look curious, "You've met him?"

Bart stood up, walked over to the table as they watched him retrieve the blanket he'd brought in with him to reveal the prized Grandmother clock he had been repairing.

"Well, I'll be damned!" exclaimed the Laird. They both came over to examine it.

Bart moved on swiftly to explain how the clock was brought to him at The March of Time and he'd spent the intervening time restoring it to working order.

"Not stolen then?" Thomas Galbraith asked.

"Not unless he intended me to mend it first," Bart suggested. "When exactly did you notice he was missing?"

The Laird grew pensive, "Ah, that is what the police just asked me." He glanced over at his secretary searchingly. "We did think initially he may have taken a short break even though it was uncharacteristic of him. When someone mentioned they hadn't seen him for a while we became concerned especially after someone noticed the clock was missing from outside in the passage."

Bart tried hard not to show any reaction to this. He thought their concerns were more for the clock than for the ghillie. Duncan moved across to pour himself another coffee. Bart could see he was troubled. "I'm ashamed to say our attention was drawn towards the absence of an artefact inventory......well at least as far as the many clocks are concerned. We do have a comprehensive one for the weapons dating back as far as Seumus Grant because this was his prized collection." The Laird sat back down.

"Did Mungo MacLeod take many of his clothes or personal items with him?" Bart asked.

Duncan Munro looked sharply over at Galbraith as if he expected an immediate answer.

Bart saw him squirm, but he remained silent.

"Has anyone inspected his room....?" Bart began.

"He doesn't live in the castle, he has a ghillie's cottage on the estate," Galbraith filled in.

"Okay," Bart acknowledged patiently. "So presumably someone checked in case he was taken ill?"

"Of course, but he wasn't there. Everything seemed to be in order," Bart noticed Galbraith remained quite nervous wondering if they checked only for the missing clock.

Bart wanted to ask many more questions which he resisted, his enquiry would have been more commensurate with his former role as a Private Investigator rather than the clockmaker he was now supposed to be. He took a hold of his curiosity which was likely to give him away, merely commented, "Well I dare say the police will ask a lot of questions when they look for themselves at his circumstances," he decided to leave well alone in case they were drawn to suspecting him, however, he did have one more question he needed to ask. "If you didn't ask me here today to bring back your Grandmother clock, then why am I here?"

Duncan Munro laughed, "Didn't Thomas tell you why I asked you here?" He glanced once again at his fidgety secretary seeming to gloat at his discomfort.

Bart shook his head not wishing to report his Secretary was very abrupt with him and if he didn't have the castle clock in his possession which needed to be returned, he wouldn't have come at all.

"My secretary has the task of stock-taking the contents of the castle....all the collections, some of which will already be extensively recorded, therefore will only need verification." He explained making Bart wince at the enormity of the undertaking for one person to perform. He began to feel quite sorry for him and could understand why he was so miserable. "Of course, perhaps such a task would appear almost impossible for one person, even where they have experience," the Laird conceded, "Which is why we have split the task into recognisable specialties. In the case of the many time pieces we have about the place, I invited you here to ask if you would undertake the task of categorising them for us, if necessary to identify any needing repair. I would like to offer you a retainer for this maintenance role in the future."

"Ah," Bart declared. "You are aware I trust, I have my own clock business with my shop?"

"Yes, indeed," Duncan replied. "I wouldn't expect you to take on a full time role. There is no timescale attached to it. Of course you wouldn't be expected to undertake any mending on site, unless you thought that appropriate, if you require to be at your own premises. You were recommended to us by one of our new staff who mentioned your work as being both knowledgeable and impeccable." Bart knew immediately Beth recommended him.

He smiled. "Would this be something you might consider?"

"I would," Bart replied immediately because he couldn't resist the idea of being able to enjoy the many clocks the castle held, some he surmised might be rare. "I can't imagine you would have so many clocks to make the proposition untenable," he peered around at the library's massive collection of books. "It wouldn't be like having to account for all these books!" he bellowed catching the perturbed expression on Thomas Gailbraith's forlorn face. He knew immediately this task belonged to him.

"Splendid!" The Laird beamed. "At least you have made a start with this Grandmother clock."

CHAPTER 21

Just as abruptly as he entered, Duncan Munro was called away. Bart found himself driving away from the castle after a promise to undertake his new role, his mind consumed by speculating on the whereabouts of the mysterious Mungo MacLeod. He tried to remember anything significant about his meeting with him when he came into his shop bringing the rather fine broken Grandmother clock for him to repair.

On his way back home he stopped at Aboyne to visit the large general emporium he often visited whenever he was passing and from where he bought the tarpaulin to cover Beth's car. He would always find some useful item for his repair work or other more domestic household equipment he needed to replace. He usually entered the premises with no intention of buying anything at all, yet always left with one or two bags of assorted items.

Today he was half-way round the store, already having filled a large shop hand basket with a variety of things – firelighters, packets of biscuits, a jar of coffee, batteries, an omelette pan together with a rather fine biscuit tin with a picture of the Queen's Royal guards resplendent in their red uniforms. He was standing examining the electrical fuses, trying to decide which would be the most likely needed, when he heard a gentle voice behind him, "Hello."

When he turned Beth was smiling broadly, "It's fascinating isn't it?" She looked about her at the vast array of things on offer. "I love this shop."

"Ah, yes indeed. I can't pass here without coming in to browse," he lifted his basket to show her the items he already picked out to buy, "I always come away with lots of things I never intended to buy!" They both laughed. "You aren't working today?"

"No, I usually work, Monday, Wednesday, Friday," she offered.

"I've just been up to the castle, I wondered if you were there. I understand you recommended me for the clock inventory?"

Her blank face told him everything, "Err, I don't know what that is. Someone did ask me if I knew anyone who was knowledgeable about clocks. I naturally told them about you at The March of Time, as well as how you mended the Grandfather clock…..did I do wrong?" Everything about her showed the worry she felt.

"No! Of course not," he put in swiftly. "Actually not at all," he tried to reassure her. He took out his fob watch from his waistcoat pocket to look at the time, "Look would you like a coffee and a bite to eat, there's a lovely little café around the corner, The Black-faced Sheep. Do you know it? There's one or two things I'd like to discuss with you," he said.

"Yes, I love the place, not that I've been there too often…." Her voice faded. Bart could see she still felt she needed to be cautious about being seen anywhere that might draw attention to herself.

The emporium they were currently in was large, spread out over a wide area which rarely, Bart knew, attracted large groups of people. In fact, the lay-out was set in such a way as to provide some nooks where a person could hide or at least be able to dodge most of the other customers. This was the first time he spoke to anyone other than the checkout clerk at the till.

"I usually find myself attracted to the back room of the café where it is quieter. If the corner table is available, being on my own, I usually sit facing away from anyone should they come through to visit the rest rooms."

He could see Beth's face flush a little, "Me too!" she admitted.

When they finished their shopping they paid for their purchases and left the shop together.

"I'll leave these in my car," Bart pointed to where his Peugeot was parked nearby. He searched the small parking area for Beth's white van.

She realised what he was doing, "I walked here," she smiled shyly.

Her admission shocked Bart knowing how far away the cottage was from the centre of Aboyne, "My word, that's quite some distance."

"Maybe, but it's a lovely walk," she added not telling him how she felt a wonderful sense of freedom to be out walking on her own. "It's such a nice day."

"Well put your purchases in my car, I'll drop you back home on my way."

She hesitantly followed him over to the hatchback where she left her shopping with his in the boot. Slowly they walked around the corner to the café where they could see one or two tables occupied in the front of the shop.

As they got to the door Bart suggested, "If the back room is full or we can't get the corner table we don't have to stay." He felt she needed the comfort of an 'out' should she want one.

"Okay," she agreed as she followed him across the room to the back with her eyes averted to the floor looking intently where she was treading. They found the back room completely empty.

"Excellent!" Bart moved over to the corner table where he pulled out the nearest chair for her to sit with her back to the room. He moved to sit facing her from the corner spot.

"Thank you," she whispered almost inaudibly.

They sat in silence studying the menus for a while before either of them spoke again.

"I guess at some point we both have to begin to live our lives normally," Bart commented being the first time he made reference to himself in such a way as to identify with her situation.

Beth studied his face to see if he really meant there was the similarity between them, both fugitives from something abhorrent. He merely nodded acknowledging the fact. She now understood they shared a common bond.

"Which is why you have helped me?"

He nodded again, "Perhaps one day we may be able to share some of our past," he said quietly. "For now," his voice took up a normal resonance, "I will have the seafood platter!"

After the waitress went away having taken their orders they were left quite alone in the back room of the café.

"What can you tell me about the ghillie who is missing from the castle?" Bart asked unexpectedly.

After a pause to assess the question she replied, "I've only heard mention about him this week. I haven't met everyone who lives or works there because I'm working in the stables. Of course I'm out in the van often, making my deliveries."

She could see Bart frown, "What exactly do you deliver?"

"A lot of dog food to the people who foster one or more of the hunting hounds," she said. "My Sandy is one of them, not the other dog."

Then she went on to explain about the hunting fraternity's hopes for a reversal of the fox hunting ban. The Hunt, she told him, was one of the castles more lucrative industries until then, leaving them with the horses and hounds to maintain with a reduced income.

"Did your other dog die?" he asked not ever having seen it.

"No, err well as far as I know. He disappeared around the time Elizabeth died." She became contemplative so he tried to change the subject.

"Has anyone suggested where Mungo MacLeod might have gone?" Bart slipped in.

Beth sat for a moment thinking before she answered. "Like I said I haven't met all the estate's staff yet. He was someone I just heard about. I did overhear some of the others talking about him when I sat having a coffee in the gift shop café where we take our breaks," she revealed. "I wasn't really paying close attention because their chat sounded like idle gossip. I didn't want to be drawn into those kinds of conversations."

Bart listened patiently, "What do you mean by those 'conversations'?"

She seemed flustered, blushing slightly wondering if she sounded silly.

"I think if they can talk about someone's personal life who is a longstanding employee they seem to like….then it wouldn't be too long before they could focus on me. I have to admit I want to keep well away from any gossip. I even thought I might have to give up my job working there," she seemed genuinely nervous. "When Fraser hinted in an emergency staffing situation I might be called upon to do a stint in the gift shop." She gave a gentle smile, it would be tempting though. I love the idea, you know?"

Bart thought the gift shop would certainly be a more suitable job for a pretty lass like her, rather than mucking out stables. He didn't say so, not wanting her to misinterpret his words.

Since he didn't comment, she added, "It's only at certain times of the year the grounds and the gift shop are open to the public," she frowned and once again he noted she was scared by the thought. "Apparently they get a lot of coach tour visitors stop off for a break to take refreshments, so the chances of being spotted…." Her voice trailed off. He saw her give a shudder.

"Did you pick up any of what they were saying about Mungo MacLeod?" Bart slipped in.

"Only he seems to be well liked by the castle people I work with. There was some talk about him having a lady friend somewhere in the locality."

130

"Really? Did they say who?" Bart was now intrigued, his private investigator curiosity was on full alert.

She shook her head, "No," she seemed to be pensive again. "The only thing….." she began before shaking her head again then closed up.

"What?"

"I'm not sure I heard right or even if I only got an impression….the trouble with gossip is it can be deadly!" she suddenly sounded really angry.

"Can you tell me what impression you got, I promise I won't tell anyone," Bart assured her.

"If I tell you, that makes me as bad a gossip as they are." she sounded self-critical.

"I don't think that is true, after all the man is missing. Now the police are involved they will certainly be asking for any impressions, however small or seemingly insignificant they might be." He notice how she jumped at the mention of police involvement, the idea really spooked her. "I have a similar issue in not wanting to get involved with the police," he confided. "I can't avoid doing so because I did meet Mungo MacLeod when he brought me the 'missing' clock to be repaired." She stared at Bart with renewed interest. "At least you can say you never met him can't you, so you wouldn't have anything to offer their investigation." She was instantly relieved by the idea. "I will tell you, Beth, it did use to be my business to find people, so part of my natural instinct to seek out information has been revived," he grinned at her producing a tentative smile.

"As long as you don't think badly of me…."

Bart frowned again, "I am asking you for your impression of what people are saying because I respect your opinion."

She seemed quite relieved. After a pause she went on, "It was when they were talking about his 'lady friend' there was a lot of giggling, you know, nudging each other. I thought I heard someone say maybe they've run away together. Then some other voice though I couldn't tell you exactly whose, seemed to whisper 'Thomas won't like that'."

Bart's expression changed to one of contemplation, "Thomas being Galbraith, the Laird's secretary do you mean?"

"I assume so. I did notice someone kick Fraser's foot under the table."

"And you think they definitely meant him disapproving of MacLeod having a 'lady friend'?"

"Seems so......you can see how it's gossip. I wouldn't want Thomas Galbraith to think I might be gossiping about him." Bart noticed how alarmed she became at the idea.

"Why?" Beth's head went down and he sensed her discomfort. "Beth?" he prompted.

When she raised her eyes to his he saw the haunted look she often showed when talking about her husband. "He is very creepy," she admitted.

"Can you explain in what way? I have to admit I took an instant dislike to the man, yet I would have difficulty telling you why."

She seemed a little encouraged by his remark. "Instinct, I would say. I don't like the way he watches me....it's like.....well I've been there before."

"Do you think he's a threat to you in some way?"

She thought hard then went on, "It's more the way he looks at me. He stares in a way I don't like, intense and unnatural, yet he comes over as being quite nervous. I'm not even sure nervous is the right word. Mostly he doesn't smile...."

"You can say that again!" Bart interjected.

"....but when he does his smile is quite strange!" she shivered again. "I've only seen him a few times. Mostly when I first started working at the castle when he came to the stables….it was like….he came to inspect me, after which I would see him hovering in places you wouldn't expect him to be, just standing staring."

"You mean he was watching you?" Bart tried to sound casual not wanting to make her any more nervous than she already was. Beth nodded slowly.

They sat in silence drinking their coffee for a while then someone came through to the back room to use the restroom. They waited until they left in case they were overheard.

When they were gone Bart plucked up the courage to ask, "I wonder if I could ask you to keep your ears open for any chance remarks from anyone, I'm sure there will be a lot of 'gossip' emerge when the police begin their questioning. I know it's asking a lot of you," he suggested.

Beth smiled broadly. Bart couldn't help thinking how much her face changed from one of solemn prettiness like the portraits in the castle of the female stoic ancestors, into a full blown beauty.

"You mean like an undercover sleuth?" she grinned impishly.

Bart laughed out loud at her sudden playfulness. "No!" he said with mock severity, "I don't want you poking about into anything, only to listen if their discussions mention anything about Mungo MacLeod. Soon I will be working there on odd days when I start my clock inventory, so will be doing the same." *Only I will definitely be poking about!*

"It will be nice to have you there some of the time," she sounded genuinely please. "Maybe we can meet up in the gift shop café to debrief," once again she deliberately made reference to being 'undercover'.

Bart held up a chastising finger to curb the sudden enthusiasm she was displaying as a family of five people entered the back room to take up the table next to them.

The parents of the two children were noisily sorting out where everyone would sit as the elderly lady stood being shouted at, "next to me Momma!", by a sweet little girl who was trying to cover the seat of the chair next to her with her hands so her brother wouldn't sit on it. Meanwhile, grandma glanced directly at Bart with an embarrassed smile.

He leaned over towards Beth, whispered, "Our cue to leave?" She stood up without even looking at the family, turning to leave.

The journey back to drop Beth off at the cottage was conducted mostly in silence before Bart headed home to sit quietly by his log fire with a glass of his favourite Bell's whisky. He needed the peace to think about his day at the castle as well as the missing ghillie Mungo MacLeod.

CHAPTER 22

Early Sunday lunch at The Moor Hen saw Bart at his usual table in the quietest corner buried behind one of the Sunday broadsheets whilst he waited for his roast beef dinner. As it was still early there were very few of the other regulars in evidence. The smell of roasting meat was making his stomach rumble.

Alistair, the landlord, brought over another Bell's whisky with some cutlery and a jar of English mustard.

"Thank you kindly," Bart took in Alistair's subdued face.

He nodded at the bar's lack of clientele, "Where is everyone, Sirus?"

At the sound of his false name Bart's conscience jabbed him. "They'll be here, it's early yet. Who could resist the smells?" He sniffed the aromas emanating from the kitchen which he knew would be floating in the cold air outside enticing everyone in range to enter.

Alistair wandered back behind the bar as Bart turned another page of his newspaper revealing the classified ads section he would normally have skipped over, going straight for the paper's sporting section. This time he stopped, his attention drawn to a sketch of a clock, one he could see was a caricature of a Swiss cuckoo clock. Thinking this was an advertisement for clocks he read the small one line of writing underneath.

Bird with no beak seeks Time Lord in the same continuum (and number)

Bart's heart skipped a beat. He immediately thought of Emily who had certainly been on his mind of late. He was reminded about her talking to him about the space-time continuum when she speculated on the subject of time travel one day. On that occasion their conversation was about the difference between the time on Earth and time in space which needed to be adjusted to compensate for the difference between clocks on Satellites to those on Earth. She was particularly intrigued by the accuracy of Atomic clocks used as the standard for international time distribution and a way to control the wave frequency of television broadcasts, as well as global navigation satellite systems such as GPS. Yes, *she* was so bright for a fifteen year old school girl she made him look at his previous opinion of children in general. At the time he suspected Emily was never really a typical child; certainly nothing like his impression of them. She was wise beyond her years even though she made the comment, "I wonder how Dr Who dealt with time on the various planets he visited?" He was taken by surprise reminding him she was, after all, only a child.

She went on to say, "I shouldn't think it's a problem for a Time Lord though." He was unfamiliar with the subject so he didn't know what she was talking about.

Could this possibly be a message from Emily?

Alistair appeared walking over to his table with a large plate of roast beef and Yorkshire pudding. He reluctantly put the paper down at the side of him.

Alistair placed the substantial meal in front of him announcing, "I've got Rolly Polly pudding with custard if you've any room left after this!"

Bart acknowledged Alistair's portions were so generous even he might find the pudding a bit of a challenge.

"Hmm, I'll let you know!"

The truth was he found the classified ad considerably distracting. He was having constant thoughts of Emily ever since he confided to Beth at their first meeting he gave a 'broken' clock to his young assistant before moving up to Scotland. This confession was the catalyst keeping Emily at the forefront of his mind.

Was she telling him she still had the same telephone number and asking him to telephone?

If so why the cryptic message?

His first thought whilst he worked his way through his meal was perhaps there was some news about the wayward clock because she mentioned 'the bird with no beak'. *Maybe she solved the problem?* The reference to 'continuum' which they also discussed as something that keeps on changing slowly over time might be significant. Perhaps the clock somehow progressed until it came into line with other time pieces. *Steady Bart how likely is that?*

Bart reprimanded himself for inferring so much from one single sentence. Of course, this could have nothing to do with the cuckoo clock which he was sure was responsible for his bouts of unconsciousness if caught inside his shop when the noon day chimes began. He certainly hadn't experienced them since he arrived in Scotland leaving the clock with Emily.

Yes, even so, you've taken no chances, always vacating the shop before the noon chimes begin.

The voice in his head reminded him, which of course was true bringing him here today before twelve as he did on most days.

He glanced around the pub noticing there were many more people now which seemed to have cheered Alistair considerably. There was even a whole family, a party of seven people. One of the teenage children was feeding the jukebox, pressing buttons resulting in a blast of some heavy music making Bart wince, raising the noise level so all the patrons were talking in louder voices in order to be heard.

It was too much for Bart. Consequently he took himself off home after paying for his dinner, passing on the repeated invitation to sample the pudding. He patted his substantial belly under his waistcoat, as he assured the landlord the Aberdeen Angus beef was of the finest quality which prevented him from trying the pudding. He was in effect, full up.

No one noticed him surreptitiously tear out the classified ad's page from the newspaper thinking the whole page was less likely to be missed than if he tore the strip containing the ad. Bart couldn't take even the slightest chance of drawing attention to himself. Any hint of his whereabouts he was sure someone like Toni Maola would use to track him down. He knew he would never do so personally he always used someone 'professional' like he used him, Bart Bridges the Private Investigator skilled in finding people. If Maola ever searched for him the reason would be because he was facing trial for his crimes. *That* would mean the police would also be looking for him to testify as a key witness. At first, he felt safe in the Witness Protection Programme, at least before he got spooked, his instinct making him run.

When he left, he told no one he was going before he disappeared, except for last goodbyes to Jayson Vingoe at the golf club. Their friendship meant a great deal at the end. He knew Jay would be okay. He too was a solitary person, now having just found his 'soul mate' in Agatha he was no longer alone. He wondered if they were married yet.

Emily was different. The closest he came so far to finding anyone who shared his love of clocks. She was a natural with an ear for them, before you added her deep fascination for them. He regretted losing the contact, even toyed with the crazy notion of taking her with him when he left.

As what? A sorcerer's apprentice?

He laughed cynically knowing the backlash an elderly man absconding with a young girl would attract. The idea would have been preposterous. Consequently, he left her the clock with the bird with no beak by way of compensation because he knew how much helping in his shop, Time and Tide, meant to her. He felt guilty because his running away took this away from her. The cuckoo clock he thought would help to ease the loss, he told her. After she guessed he was going, he left the clock because he knew if it could be corrected of its fault she was the one who could do it.

Even so, he would never be rid of the image of her face after she asked him, "Take me with you?" her voice pleading like she knew he would disappear even though he hadn't actually told her he was going.

He shook his head, "Surely you can see that is impossible….after Peter…?" At first she was shattered by the rejection which gave way to a sad understanding. Peter, her cousin, was abused by a paedophile living a legitimate life in their community. Emily was witness to every word of his retelling his ordeal to the police. She couldn't fail to understand what it would seem like if he…….if they……. were to disappear together? She merely nodded in the sad way she often did, taken the cuckoo clock and walked away.

Now this message in classified ads, what did it mean?

CHAPTER 23

After the large Sunday lunch inside him Bart fell asleep in his arm chair in front of a blazing fire. He slept soundly for a good couple of hours. When he woke, the fire was low and the room much gloomier than before he fell asleep. He woke with the immediate feeling something was wrong. He was nearly panicky, couldn't quite remember either a dream or whether something happened to make him feel this way. He rubbed his eyes trying hard to think whilst his head resisted, the low throb making him feel fuzzy.

He automatically placed another log on the fire to revive the embers, gave the new wood a good poke with the iron three pronged toasting fork he unhooked from the fireside tool set which he once used to toast bread on his open fire. He remembered how this fascinated Emily who hadn't seen such a thing before.

Emily!

She jumped back into his mind prompting him to search for the newspaper page. He found the ad on the small table beside his chair. This time he had no doubt whatsoever Emily placed the classified ad with the caricature of a cuckoo clock because she knew the drawing would catch his eye. He would intuitively understand she wanted him to make contact.

Here was the conundrum. She wanted him to know her telephone number was still the same, he was sure. The problem was he no longer had his original phones, either the shop's land line or his old mobile. He got rid of the first when he moved, destroyed the latter along with the sim card later. The mobile once contained a small collection of contact numbers he accrued after entering Witness Protection. Two of those numbers were Emily's.

He felt sure she would have tried his numbers first, finding they no longer existed. The ad was a clever way of trying to contact him because he knew Emily was a smart girl. He also recalled the Hobb's house phone was ex-directory so he couldn't look the number up in the old way. *Did they still produce telephone directories these days?* On line was now the source of just about all information.

He moved over to put the kettle on feeling the need for a strong cup of coffee to perk up his senses. Whilst he waited he got out his lap top, a half formed idea circling around in the fuzziness of his head. He took his lap top back to the armchair in front of the now crackling fire. He logged on to his computer.

In the Google prompt he typed – The Silver Teapot, Wainthorpe-on-sea, waited for the inevitable list of non-related references to pop up. He was already anticipating disappointment, after all the tiny seaside café run by Thelma Hobbs, Emily's mother, would hardly have a website. The corner café was barely one up from a greasy spoon not warranting such an elaborate way of advertising. He doubted even Max at The Griddle Iron around the corner would have one. His place was up market compared to the cheese-on-toast, egg and chips place he remembered by the sea.

He was surprised when he found the café listed under 'where to eat in Wainthorpe-on-sea' an initiative instigated by Wainthorpe Council with a view to attracting more visitors there. Bart assumed there would be a need after the murders reached even as far as the national newspapers.

The information was very basic across all the eateries covered. There was a picture of The Silver Teapot, its opening hours recorded below, reference to 'home' cooked fare which Bart thought stretched their simple menu. There was a telephone number. *Yes, Bart you haven't lost your touch!* He found a piece of paper, to record the number. According to the opening hours the café was 'closed' on Sundays (out of season) which surprised him as he always went there on Sunday mornings to read the pile of newspapers he bought from the news agents on the way there. Perhaps Wainthorpe was even more deserted now because Thelma Hobbs obviously thought Sundays no longer worth opening up for at this time of the year.

He sat contemplating for a moment until his need to satisfy himself the number was indeed the café's prompted him to call it. He wanted to hear if there was any message left on the answer service or even if he could recognise Emily's mother's voice, so he rang it.

Of course, he would have no idea what he might say if Thelma Hobbs did answer; a strange man asking to speak to Emily wouldn't do. The phone began to ring which was encouraging. On the fourth ring he was about to abandon the call when he heard the click which he supposed was the answer service cutting in.

"Hello?" was almost a whisper, too quiet for his diminishing hearing to make a judgement on the identity of the speaker.

He remained quiet listening in case they spoke again.

Louder this time, "Hello!" this definitely sounded familiar.

"Hello," ventured Bart.

There was a small gasp followed by, "Time Lord?!" It was definitely Emily's voice.

"Yes," he admitted.

"Five minutes……give me your number." He gave her the number quickly after which the phone went dead eventually giving way to the dialling tone.

Five minutes for what?

He placed his mobile next to his coffee mug on the side table, took up his drink which he sipped slowly as he waited.

What was all this cloak and dagger stuff about? Why was Emily in the café on a Sunday if the place was closed?

Time moved on past five minutes, he could see when he glanced down at his mobile phone screen. He was checking once again when the screen lit up as the phone began to ring showing an incoming call number he didn't recognise. These days his contact list only contained Beth's number.

Even so he answered cautiously, "Hello?"

"Thank goodness…. it's me……Emily!" she sounded out of breath. Also there was the noise of rushing wind and the pounding of waves against the shore.

Speaking loudly so she could hear him he shouted, "Emily, it's good to hear your voice, is everything okay?" He thought he detected signs of distress in her voice.

"Yes," she seemed to be gulping air. "I mean, no…..just a minute….." he heard the movement of the phone, a loud knock of something hard against the phone, followed by a sudden utter silence as the sound of the wind and waves receded. He feared she cut the line. "That's better," she suddenly said.

"Where are you Emily?" He asked beginning to worry about her.

"It's okay I've slipped inside the beach hut," he could hear her banging around. "Such awful weather, it's freezing out there."

"You've broken into a beach hut?" He sounded alarmed.

He heard her giggle, "No…..the hut is ours, only I don't have a key. They use it more for storage these days being near the shop." She seemed less out of breath now. He imagined her sitting down on a deck chair. "I've always come here when I want to get away from them…everything….. to be quiet."

He could sense the same loneliness he once saw in her when he lived there. The same sadness which he recognised the very first time he met her after she asked him if she could come into his shop to look around. That was also a Sunday in The Silver Teapot when she was waiting on tables. On that occasion she assured him she wouldn't touch any of the clocks like the other children did because she knew he disliked children. Even in the days after he gave her a job at Time and Tide because she loved clocks, she never seemed like a child, always appearing mature beyond her years.

"So the shop is open today?" he asked which contradicted the opening times shown on line.

"No, we no longer open on Sundays," she sounded melancholy. As if realising why he asked she added, "I go there in case you might call in answer to my ads."

"Oh!" Bart exclaimed. "This one wasn't the only one then?"

She laughed, "Err, no, there's been a few!"

He was shocked, "Sounds expensive....how can...... you afford....." he was going to say, *"How can a schoolgirl..... afford,"* however, he didn't want to offend her.

She laughed again, "Thanks to you, for teaching me about mending clocks I can earn some money. Since you left there's been a gap in the clock mending market! I've kind of filled in....placed a couple of adverts one in the paper shop, the other at the café," she spoke with obvious pride. "It was doing clock mending gave me the idea of the message." She giggled reminding Bart she was perhaps only a child after all. Even so Bart couldn't help being impressed by her entrepreneurial acumen, in one way he was quite pleased.

"As long as the clock mending doesn't interfere with your school work," he hoped what he created didn't distract her from her studies, then checked himself for thinking like a surrogate parent chastising her. She didn't answer him, only gave a nervous cough. He decided to change the subject, "I'm thinking there's a reason you have contacted me?"

What he heard next filled him with apprehension.

Emily presented him with a stilted picture of events beginning with the time he left Wainthorpe. Initially she thought the policeman who came to ask her for his contact details must be part of the enquiry team connected to the murder of his neighbour Mr Claymore, at the Art Gallery next door to his clock shop. Later she heard he was only asking questions about him wherever he went. He came into the café often speaking to local people, soon realising no one knew how to contact him. She previously met a number of the policemen because of her cousin Peter's involvement but he didn't seem to be working with them or was even known to them.

Bart asked her, "Did you get a name? I assume he left a card or a means of contacting him again should you hear from me?"

"If he did I can't remember whether he mentioned his name. He didn't leave his number with anyone I know."

"Okay, did you see him again?" Bart asked.

"Not for a long time. Not until fairly recently when he showed up again at the café."

"What was he asking this time?"

Emily went quiet at the end of the line, before continuing, "It's difficult because he was different." He could tell she was struggling to articulate her thoughts.

"What impression did he give you to make you think he was different?" Bart didn't want to influence her by making suggestions as to different types of mood. "Can you picture how he was?"

"Well, he seemed really worried, like my Dad looks when he doesn't make his quota of insurance sales each month," she said. "He wasn't, like, as friendly as he was when he came before, you know." She didn't want to tell him she found him a bit scary, like he was threatening her.

"And did he say why he wanted to contact me?"

"No.....well apart from you having some special information to help him in a case. He insisted if I ever heard from you to make sure you contact the number he knew you had."

Bart knew immediately this definitely was his Witness Protection handler. His thoughts flittered back to his last day when he met up with Jayson at the golf club to say goodbye. He stood warming himself in front of the open fire, took out the piece of paper with Steve's number which was meant for emergencies only and threw it into the flames after deciding to sever all contact with Witness Protection. He watched the paper curl up, consumed by the fire, the numbers written there disappeared. Could Maola have been arrested after all this time?

If true then Maola would know Bart could testify against him, which meant he was in serious danger if Maola set his mind to find him to stop him. He realised he had gone quiet thinking about the ramifications.

"So you've been trying to find me because of him?" Bart asked wondering how long she had been placing ads in the classified section.

It baffled him when she replied, "No not really."

"Why then?"

"I saw your friend, the big man who does forensics?"

"Jay?"

"Yes! He came in the café recently…."

"How recently?" Bart interrupted.

"Err….two, maybe three weeks ago."

"Yes, that is recent," he agreed talking out loud. "And what did he say?"

"He was strange, he asked me to step outside where we stood in the street. He kind of pointed along the promenade where the shops are all closed up for the winter, like he was trying to show me something or ask me something. Then, when I looked at where he was pointing he whispered, "If you know where Cyrus is, tell him Jay needs to speak to him urgently." She sounded really mysterious, "He told me never to speak to you in the café or at my house, they weren't safe."

Bart's stomach churned and he knew he needed to seriously consider his own safety.

He started with, "What about the phone you're using?" He didn't want to scare her by telling her he knew how easily mobile phones could be tapped into.

"Don't worry, I did some digging on the internet to see what would be the safest way to talk to you if I found you – this is a pay-as-you-go I keep switched off except for now."

He wanted to say 'good girl' which he knew was patronising, instead he asked, "Ever thought of being a Private Detective when you leave school?"

"Hmm," she said in a way Bart found curious.

"What's wrong, Emily?" he asked picking up vibes all was not well.

"I've left school," he couldn't make out if she was pleased or not. "Didn't have much choice...." Obviously she wasn't too pleased about it.

What she revealed next probably upset him more than the idea he might be being sought by dangerous criminals. She told him a tale of woe in the aftermath of the Wainthorpe scandals resulting in a serious decline in the café's income due to people boycotting the town as well as locals avoiding the café in particular. How her father lost his job because his boss considered him a liability to his business, being so closely connected to the murders. How school became almost impossible for her to be there. She thought her parents were about to split up, they have put the café up for sale and her mother is insisting she goes with her back to live in Grimsby where she grew up.

Bart felt bad for her, "What about your exams?" he asked astonished. He knew she was going through a rough time at school yet showed real promise academically.

"I'm not taking any because the only thing I want to do is work with clocks." Her voice got angry now, "There is no way I'm going to live in Grimsby!" she shouted defiantly. "I'm going down to London, there must be somewhere down there I can work with clocks!"

Bart was horrified, "You can't, you're only a child...."

She laughed cynically, "No, I' not. I'm seventeen soon......'*they*' can't stop me!"

"Look, London isn't the place to go," Bart pleaded. "It's dangerous. Accommodation is too expensive, without an income you'll end up on the streets, in all kinds of danger." He knew only too well from his P.I days having seen some awful things happening to young boys and girls who ran away from home. He knew about all the pitfalls having worked on so many tragic cases in the 'finding people' business.

"Isn't London where *you* are? You can get lost down there easily if you need to......" She obviously gave the matter a lot of thought. "Even if you don't have a clock shop any more, we could find one, work together again." She sounded eager but he heard the glitch in her voice, his heart went out to her.

"Oh, Emily," Bart sighed.

CHAPTER 24

After her conversation with Bart at The Black-faced Sheep, Beth found herself paying a lot more attention to the other castle workers she came into contact with whilst trying not to be too obvious she was listening. No doubt coming over as aloof, she always tried to avoid them by taking her breaks sitting alone in the corner reading a book. They tried to get her to join them, leastways initially, they did. Now she needed to try to avoid looking too eager to join them in case they got suspicious.

The next time she worked at the stables an opportunity arose at break time. The café was particularly busy for the time of year with the corner table already taken there was only a few vacant seats. Usually she would leave taking a take-out snack back to the stables to sit alone on a bale of straw to eat it. Instead she decided to go over to Fraser's table where a group of Castle employees sat alongside an empty chair.

"It's busy today," she asked the group, "Can I join you?"

She was warmly invited to sit down by a couple of grinning younger men she only knew by sight. One she recognised worked with the grounds maintenance team, the other at the stables, a young groom who spent most of his time exercising the horses, neither of them had she spoken to before. She deliberately avoided most men she came into contact with, whilst instinctively avoiding eye contact having no desire to see what might be reflected in their eyes.

On the other hand she knew who the woman was. The stylish, smartly dress woman in her forties introduced herself as Joy when she met her during her first few days at the Castle after she popped into the gift shop where she worked, to have a look round. Beth saw Joy frown when Fraser pulled out the chair next to him for her to sit down. Clearly he was delighted to have her there, not so Joy.

Joy gloated a little, "Aw has someone beat you to the corner?" Unlike her name, Beth knew, there was nothing whatsoever joyous about her. Beth didn't know how to answer her. She sat down opening her triangular packet of sandwiches.

The young groundsman laughed, "Nobody puts baby in a corner, eh?" which prompted the woman to glare his way at the reference to the classic film, Dirty Dancing.

Beth chose to ignore them both asking, "Do we have a coach trip in?" referring to the number of people sitting or queuing for refreshments at the counter. In winter the place kept limited opening times, was virtually deserted relying mostly on takings from the people working there.

"Aye, a down side to working here," Fraser grumbled. "They'll all be tramping through the stable block having a nosey around. When we tell them it's out of bounds they'll say they didn't know!"

"Can't read more like!" The groundsman muttered. Even though he was only in his early twenties he had already developed an outdoor rosy-cheeked complexion that all-weather working imprinted on his face. Beth stared at him enquiringly, so he obliged. "Three foot high signs everywhere to tell them, yet still they come!"

"Don't mind 'Worsel', he doesn't like his photograph taken!" They all laughed at the young groom's comment except Worsel.

"Bloody tourists!" he complained. Worsel carried on moaning, "Anyone would think they'd never seen someone working a'fore........they ask such stupid questions!"

For Beth's benefit Joy explained, "He gets asked what the Latin names of the flowers are a lot which he doesn't know....."

"Yes, I do!" he snapped back not liking to find himself the centre of attention or being mocked. "It's not my job to give guided tours of the grounds is it?" Beth watched everyone snigger at his expense, "Anyway, we aren't open yet. They shouldn't let them in!" He stormed out of the café.

Beth felt a little embarrassed for him. She could see how Joy was enjoying his discomfort which now endorsed her initial impression of her when they first met. She was left needing to be wary of her. Fraser spotted her flushed face smiling at her encouragingly.

"Whose job is it to show the public round?" Beth asked to cover up her own discomfort.

"Well, no one's really, they are left pretty much on their own to look around the gardens," Fraser admitted. "So I'm sure you can argue we ask for it. He's right about them ignoring the signs though, they are there to direct them. They do wander about where they shouldn't, in some cases even do damage."

Beth was about to ask what kind of damage when the young groom jumped in with, "Apart from which there are Health and Safety issue," he now looked as angry as Worsel did before he left. "They seem oblivious to the fact you can get a mighty kick from a horse which can be lethal. They always want to touch them.......some of the horses can be very spirited."

"Is the Castle itself open to the public?" Beth asked, hoping she wouldn't sound too naïve. She could do without incurring any disdain from joyless Joy.

Fraser shook his head, "No, but there has been some talk lately they might." He glanced over at Joy inviting any confirmation of the fact. She too was scowling now.

"There are too many valuable artefacts around inside the castle which they would need to make safe," she could see Beth didn't understand so she added, "Some people will steal just about anything if not screwed down! They often do from the gift shop, the grounds, even the toilets!"

Whilst they were talking the Laird's secretary Thomas Galbraith came in joining the queue at the counter. He spotted Beth sitting talking to the others, coming over after he was served. He sat down without being invited in the place Worsel just vacated. He was blatantly listening to their conversation whilst staring straight at Beth.

She noticed the subtle shift in their behaviour as the conversation moved on. They appeared more subdued now. Beth supposed because he was the Laird's Secretary they felt a need to be more cautious in their obvious grumblings about the castle's customers.

Fraser turned the conversation on to Galbraith, "Beth was asking whether the castle itself is open to the public."

Galbraith appeared uncomfortable with the question. He made no attempt to open up the packet of sandwiches he was holding or take a sip from the bottle of water he held. He placed both down on the table in front of him.

After an unnatural pause he replied, "The Laird does have it in mind," he revealed reluctantly. He found them now all staring in anticipation of him continuing but he seemed to hesitate.

Beth began to wonder whether he was shy or perhaps his reluctance to develop a conversation was a communication problem. She observed even those he instigated himself he found difficult. She didn't mind having no qualms in not pursuing them. On this occasion, however, she was keen to discover whether the castle would open its doors in order to attract more people, which alarmed her greatly because of the chance of being recognised by someone who knew her husband.

"When?" she heard herself ask him as no one else seemed to share her curiosity.

Thomas Galbraith looked sharply across at her. He seemed extremely uncomfortable with the question which she now regretted asking.

"Oh, not until he's got all the castle inventories done," he disclosed eventually.

"Inventories?" the young groom queried.

Galbraith glared at him, "Everything inside has to be accounted for, recorded in some detail, then valued…..for insurance purposes," he added the latter quickly.

"Wow! That's one hell of a job," Fraser acknowledged. "We were just talking about the things stolen from around the place….."

His voice faded as he saw the shock on Galbraith's face.

"The point is," Galbraith began irritably, "How do you know if something is missing if you don't know what you have in the first place?"

His anger was picked up by Joy, "Only if you do a stock take….which is one hell of a job comparing stock to till receipts I can tell you….CCTV is fine but you can't spot them stealing stuff if you're doing your job serving when there's busloads of them in!" She delivered this with great anger. As if she sensed their critical stares she went on now looking straight at Beth, "If my stock is down, the comeback is on me, makes me look like I'm not doing my job!" Beth lowered her eyes not wanting to incur her wrath further.

"Then there's the cost of all the security measures needed," Thomas Galbraith added.

"Security?" Fraser questioned. "You mean putting stuff in display cases?"

"Yes partly," he went on. "You have to have the really valuable artefacts made secure or removed entirely to a safe place for insurance purposes, like they do in museums, otherwise your insurance becomes so expensive it's untenable or they refuse entirely. Apart from which they wouldn't pay out on something valuable being stolen if we were shown to be careless."

The young groom whistled in amazement, "I would predict they won't open up to the public in that case."

Fraser added, "Or maybe can't. I imagine the entry fee would need to be huge to offset the costs."

"How long will it take to do the inventory Mr. Galbraith?" Beth asked as innocently as she could. She needed to assess how long it would be before she was forced to leave her job.

Galbraith gave her a subtle smile believing she was showing concern for him at being given the task. "I imagine quite a long time, so much work needs to be done first," he was pleased at least she appreciated the enormity of the task.

"I expect with the right help it wouldn't take too long, Thomas," Fraser suggested. He turned to Beth, "Remember me asking you if you knew anyone who was knowledgeable about clocks?" Beth nodded well aware of Sirus being set on to undertake the time piece inventory. "I believe the Laird has engaged someone….is that right?" he asked Galbraith.

"Yes, someone local who has a clock shop," Thomas replied.

*   *   *   *   *

It was much later when Beth retold the whole conversation to Bart that she gently warned, "I think we should be careful about showing we know each other after Fraser told them you were recommended by me."

He leaned over her kitchen table to pat the back of her hand, "Don't worry lass, you only admitted to having your clock mended," his reassuring words comforted her a little. "The March of Time *is* the only clock shop locally so it's going to be known." He could see she wasn't too reassured. "What's wrong, lass?"

He was used to seeing her nervousness believing it to be her 'natural' state, only this time there clearly was an issue.

"There's something not right about the place," she confided.

The whole encounter with the other staff reinforced her need to keep her distance from everyone, yet she wanted to be able to help

Sirus in any way she could to find out about the missing ghillie who so far they hadn't mentioned. Bart could see she was troubled.

"I still think there is something about Mr. Galbraith that isn't right. I don't think he would have sat down with us if I wasn't there at the table," she admitted.

"So he's attracted by you? Or he wanted to find out who you might be friendly with?"

Beth shivered visibly warning Sirus he was a little too close to her past, a subject neither of them totally revealed to each other. How could she tell him she wasn't allowed to have friends or even speak at length to anyone? She shrugged unable to articulate her concerns.

"Okay, so what are the dynamics of the people who were sat together when you joined them? Any close links or anyone dislike someone else?"

She smiled then. "Yes, I see what you mean," she said as if she'd realised something. "Okay." She paused to consider then revealed, "The gift shop woman, 'Joy'," at her name she made a face, "She likes Fraser. I could see I irritated her when I joined them especially as he was friendly towards me."

"She thinks you two are *really* friendly?"

"Err, no….*she* would like to be 'friendly' with him!" suddenly amazed by her own deduction it seemed to spur her on. "*He* on the other hand doesn't see her in the same way I'm sure…..for all I know he could be married," she added. "Anyway, if I can see how spiteful she can be……."

"Spiteful? Now there's a word I haven't heard since I was at school!"

Beth defended its use, "You didn't hear her making fun of Worsel, laughing at his expense."

"Sounds like they all were," Bart commented.

155

"True. The whole atmosphere changed when Galbraith joined us.....they all became guarded, more serious when the subject of opening to the public was discussed."

"What was your impression of Thomas Galbraith other than his interest in you?"

"I've always noticed, whenever I see him, he does seem a very anxious sort, whether he speaks or not. He got quite irritated when he talked about the inventory though," she said.

"Probably because it's his job to organise them all, hence hiring me to do the time pieces....I expect there will be others too for fine arts, paintings, books, weapons etc." Bart explained.

"No, I don't think it's that because when you were mentioned in respect of the clocks he seemed more angry than relieved which doesn't really fit with the enormity of the task does it?"

Bart became thoughtful not commenting. He changed the subject, "So do *you* think Fraser is sweet on you?" he teased.

Beth scowled, "No! I think he's a nice man everyone likes, who is happily married to a local girl and they have many children." Bart burst out laughing. "Actually, he did tell me later Morgan the young groom is!" Bart laughed again at the way she screwed up her face in distaste. This was the first time she seemed at ease and not perceiving the subject to be some kind of threat. She could see Bart was eager to hear what she felt about it. She shook her head.

"No way!" she chided.

"Ugly, eh?" Bart teased.

"Not at all," she admitted. "I'm not interested in getting involved with anyone," he could see her resigned determination.

As Bart drove home pondering on all the things Beth told him he realised he meant to mention Emily to her. He wanted to seek her advice on what he should do to try to stop her going to London.

He knew to do that would require him to fully update her on his past which, like her, he would rather it stay in the past.

Bart was old school in his views, once before he deliberated on inviting a fifteen year old girl to work with him in his shop. The world was a completely different place now to when he was fifteen. He knew he might invite criticism from some quarters. Even though he was a stickler for propriety, not everyone possessed his moral compass. He mourned the loss of innocence in the world.

One thing he did know he couldn't afford to invite criticism or draw attention to himself. He certainly couldn't have Emily staying with him. He may get away with employing someone her age if people thought she was local but no one would believe him if he claimed she was his niece. These days it was considered a joking matter to some, if a gentleman his age introduced a young girl as his niece. He even noticed at the Black-faced Sheep he'd drawn attention by eating in public with Beth, he would think twice about doing so on his own again. He did wonder how fathers got on being seen in the company of their own daughter without a female chaperone. Yet in society these days there were far more marriage break ups resulting in more single fathers. As to this general topic he had no one with whom to discuss it. Except perhaps for Beth but he left the subject alone for now given her own anxieties.

The other issue he needed to consider was speaking with Jayson Vingoe, pending Emily getting his telephone number. He remained reluctant to allow her to give Jay his mobile because he did, after all, work for the police.

CHAPTER 25

When Emily sent Jayson Vingoe's telephone number to Bart he was working alone in the Castle's 'Long Gallery' recording the few time pieces displayed there. He wanted to ease himself into his assignment by choosing the least daunting of rooms containing clocks. The gallery was vast yet held proportionately fewer horological exhibits. His mobile beeped loudly in the silence of the room making him start, he wasn't used to carrying such a device these days.

If left to him he wouldn't possess a mobile telephone at all, only buying this one to be available should Beth need him urgently. So far she hadn't. The number from Emily's phone on the screen he committed to his call register under 'Birdie' which doubled his number of contacts. His conscience pricked when he thought how sad Emily sounded the last time they spoke. The beep was a text from her with only Jay's telephone number, he felt concern there was no indication of her wellbeing. On impulse he pressed 'call' because he was perturbed leaving her with such a stressful life. The number was unobtainable confirming immediately she really did remove the sim card after contacting him.

He put the clipboard he was holding down on a side table walked over to one of the many alcove windows, sat down on the deep window ledge partially hidden by the heavy drapes, to decide how he could best deal with Jay's request to contact him. Any call he made would be taking a risk. Yet in his heart he knew Jayson Vingoe to be a fair minded person whom he held in high regard. He refused to believe Jay would jeopardise his safety. Of course, Jay was aware what was involved. He discussed some of the details briefly with him after D.C Braithwaite accidentally discovered his past.

He keyed in the number and called it. When Jay answered he felt the echo of their previous friendship on hearing his voice.

"Hello, my friend," Bart spoke tentatively almost in a whisper.

He heard, "Hold on, would you, whilst I look for a better signal," his voice was formal and professional. He then heard footsteps with some minor scuffling. After the sound of a door closing Jay finally greeted him, "Hello, how are you? Sorry, I needed to find some space."

"Indeed, I hope I find you both well," he deliberately withheld Agatha's name hoping they were still a couple, and he hadn't just committed a gross faux pas.

"We are," Jay acknowledged.

"You needed to speak to me?" Bart asked, cutting to the chase, not knowing how long he would remain alone in the Long Gallery. He bent forward to peer down the length of the room each way finding himself still alone.

"Indeed," Jay said. "I heard a chance conversation where your name was mentioned."

"With regard to?" Bart continued cautiously.

"There was someone asking questions about where you might have gone," Jay revealed.

"Did they seek you out?" Bart asked continuing in the vein of non-specific questions hoping Jay wasn't linked to his disappearance.

"No, only my police colleagues. The beauty of being seen as merely support staff these days, does give you a kind of invisibility…. you know?"

Bart thought the comment strange given Jay was once a police officer who had wanted to specialise in the forensic side of police investigation which was completely civilianised.

"There must still be people around who remember you from the time when you were one of them," Bart suggested.

"There are mixed feelings," he sounded rather sad. "Those who don't see me as deserting them by thinking I was looking for an easier working life may resent me for it. They do dismiss what I do as peripheral to 'real' investigation," he said. "Which of course, you don't, having the expert knowledge to know differently."

"Yes, indeed," the comment confirmed why he got along so well with this C.S.I. That and the fact he really liked him.

"I know we briefly discussed how I found myself living a different life by the seaside," Bart once told him a little about being in the Witness Protection programme. One day he would be called to give evidence against Toni Maola, because it mattered to him immensely Jay didn't think badly of him. "Do you have any idea why the person asking questions is looking for me? Has he told those people around you?"

"No, not really, I'm not privy to any of those kinds of conversations," he sounded sadly resigned. "I felt.....feel I should let you know......"

"It's okay. I'm not in any kind of trouble, at least not from the police. I'm key to providing some special information if they have managed to locate someone who is wanted by them. I can only assume he is no longer at large."

"Ah, I understand," Jay caught on.

"Seemingly, they are obviously in need of calling in my knowledge, giving me the problem there are some very bad people in this world who would also like to locate me. I moved away when your quiet seaside backwater suddenly erupted into mayhem. I also spotted someone from my past out running along the promenade with your colleague Braithwaite, which frankly quite alarmed me. I realised I needed to move on for self-preservation."

"Yes, I can understand that," Jay agreed.

"I would like to know, though, if my potential aggressor has been detained before I venture back there, to be able to make some kind of risk assessment."

"Hmm, I would need a name," Jay suggested. Bart took his request as an offer to try to find out if Maola had been arrested.

"The other thing is my young friend tells me someone called 'Steve' still has the same telephone contact number. The problem I have is I no longer have it."

"Difficult, yet so easy to lose a flimsy bit of paper," Jay was indicating he remembered the time they last met when Bart showed him the telephone number on a piece of paper which he destroyed severing the link with his past or rather his Witness Protection minder.

As the conversation was drawing to a natural conclusion, Bart suddenly thought of Emily.

"I'm concerned for my young friend," he spoke with great unease. "I understand things haven't gone too well down there since everything was unearthed by the investigating team. She could best tell you in her own words. However, I am greatly concerned about her intention to go alone to London to live. I really have no idea how to dissuade her from it. I wondered if your lady friend……"

"My wife," Jay interrupted.

Bart was delighted to hear it, "Many congratulations my friend, such wonderful news!" He gushed genuinely pleased they were now a married couple; he felt they were so well matched. "….if your *wife* would be able to have a word?" Bart hoped he didn't sound too presumptuous in asking. He remembered how Agatha McLeary (now Vingoe) was a uniquely sensible person with great skills in talking to most people and Emily in particular, "perhaps she could assert some influence on her?"

"Right," Jay interjected sounding guarded or no longer alone, "I have to go. Let me have a name if you would?"

"Will do," Bart agreed. "Thank you." It meant a lot to know he could rely on Jayson Vingoe. He didn't feel quite so alone.

When the conversation was over he resumed his inventory and was immediately joined in the Long Gallery by Duncan Munro who was smartly dressed in a formal business suit.

"Ah, Sirus, there you are," The Laird greeted him as he approached. "My apologies for not meeting with you sooner to see if you have everything you need. I'm actually on my way to Edinburgh for a few days on business....is there anything you need?"

It occurred to Bart to ask whether his role was merely to catalogue and value the timepieces or whether the intention was to test them to ensure they all worked well which required him to set them going. His inclination was to have them all functioning at the correct time if possible. He mentioned this to the Laird who stood contemplating as Bart added, "The issue is also who is responsible for keeping them wound up on a daily basis?"

"Ah," Duncan Munro exclaimed. "Yes I forgot this is one of my ghillie's tasks!" His sudden sadness Bart took for a deep affection for Mungo MacLeod. It also explained why he brought him the Grandmother clock for repair.

"Is there any news on him?" Bart asked gently not wishing to prolong any of his distress with him being missing. In normal circumstances Mungo MacLeod would be the significant person to go to for knowledge about the clocks. He realised he was working blind.

He shook his head, "The police have no leads. He has seemingly vanished. His personal belongings remain in his cottage as does his passport. Also apparently some medication he was known to use regularly."

"How strange," said Bart, "I take it the police have undertaken a thorough search of the estate as a matter of course?"

"As far as they are able, I understand." Duncan Munro scowled a little. "Our police force up here isn't overly equipped with resources, you understand. They cover a huge area of land. I also don't really think there is a consensus on whether he is actually missing or has merely gone away. They tell me over 30,000 people go missing each year in Scotland! It's a lot of people to find. Of course, some people don't wish to be found and the police see that as their choice."

Bart supposed the police became involved because of Duncan Munro's Laird status, otherwise probably would only do the basics. He didn't really want to discuss the merits of police procedures with him, after all he was only meant to be a clockmaker so he needed to be careful showing too much of what he knew from his previous vocations.

"I suppose depending on whether he needs the medication you mentioned, or being without, would put him in danger?"

The Laird considered this for a moment then looked at his wristwatch seeming not to want to comment. "Look I have to go now, if there's anything you think of you might need, perhaps you would speak with Thomas," he rushed off before Bart could say anything else.

Bart watched him go, leaving him with mixed feelings about their conversation. To him it raised other questions which he would have liked answers to. If Mungo MacLeod was responsible for the castle clocks in addition to his other duties as the Laird's ghillie, he would surely have delegated their daily maintenance to someone else if he intended to take some leave? After all he cared enough about them to bring a broken one to him for repair. Most of the clocks he'd observed so far had stopped.

Of course, he felt anyone going away for a holiday would take personal items with them, especially medication. No doubt they would also have sought permission from the Laird to be absent.

He did wonder if the Laird knew him at all well. If so, surely he would know about his lady friend, whom he didn't mention. He could only suppose either the Laird deemed talking about his staff's personal life improper or perhaps what Beth picked up from the idle gossip by some of the other staff about him having a lady friend was not true at all, merely idle gossip. If Bart remembered anything about the man who brought him the Grandmother clock, he was a mature man, maybe over fifty years of age, which would not negate him having a 'lady friend'. He made a mental note to find out and to see if he could identify her in order to speak with her.

The rest of Bart's day was spent alone. Thomas Galbraith was nowhere to be found when he tried unsuccessfully to seek him out. Likewise he saw nothing of Beth. The absence of her van parked anywhere suggested she was either not at work or else out on her delivery rounds.

By the time he arrived back at his shop the only welcome he received was from a chorus of chiming clocks when he pushed open the connecting door from the garage after putting his car away. He waited whilst the chimes moved through their inevitable sequence. The last sound of the five strikes told him the hour was exactly five o'clock. He moved into the shop where the setting sun caught the closed sign on the door underneath which he could see a small oblong card below the letterbox. He flicked on the lamp standing on his work table, before he moved over to pick up the business card. His thoughts immediately leapt to the ABC Detective Agency and the face of the gaunt albino-like Selwyn Jones PI. His stomach churned at the thought of him.

Why would he ever come back here?

When he got to the table he sat down, brought out his spectacles holding the card underneath the lamp he read: P.C Robbie Cowan, Police Constable, Police Scotland, below which were two telephone numbers, one of them a mobile. Bart knew immediately P.C Cowan called in connection with his meeting the missing Mungo MacLeod.

He left the card on the table where parts of a fob watch were spread neatly across the heavy candlewick table covering. He switched off the lamp having no desire to carry on with the repair to one of his own time pieces and therefore no urgency.

He felt extremely hungry having made do with a cheese sandwich he picked up from the gift shop café whilst looking to see if Beth was at work. One of the down sides to this contract with the castle was the upset to his normal routine. Briefly he wondered whether Alistair at The Moor Hen missed him at midday. He went in search of anything he could find to eat in the kitchen. He reprimanded himself for the poor choice of offerings.

This will not do, Bart, get yourself organised!

He put on his duffle coat, left the shop, to walk back up Main Street until he came to the café on the corner where Main Street met the A93 which he'd noticed was open as he drove past. He knew The Hungry Traveller was where a large number of bikers congregated during the summer when they toured around Scotland. He could smell the chips frying as he approached; his mouth began to water.

There was a small queue of people waiting to be served inside, whilst quite a number of adolescents hung around outside eating out of cardboard trays. *Needs must when you're hungry.* It was obvious to him the place dubbed as the local 'chippy', something he'd grown used to living by the seaside. From what he could see whilst watching the woman add the condiments she asked him about, the portions were massive. *That will do nicely,* he thought as he trudged back to his shop where he buttered a couple of slices of bread and made himself a cup of tea.

He was about to unwrap his fish and chips when he heard a loud knock on the shop door.

"Bugger!" he exclaimed out loud thinking the local police officer must have come back, he sounded a bit eager. He thought twice about answering the knock, but knew he left the connecting door open so the light would be visible from outside.

He went through to the shop switching on the main lights as he passed the switches. He saw immediately it was Beth peering in through the glass in the door.

"Come in, come in!" he greeted as he opened the door to her. She was smiling which cheered him up. "Just in time for tea if you haven't eaten yet," he invited her through to the back plunging the shop once more into darkness, adding, "And you don't mind fish and chips."

She beamed, "I don't want to take yours."

"There's enough to feed an army here," his comment was lost among the whirring of the microwave heating them up and he buttered more bread and made more tea. He served up their supper sitting at the table to eat it, whilst Bart described his first day at the Castle telling her how he looked for her at lunchtime and also couldn't find Thomas Galbraith after Duncan Munro left for Edinburgh.

"I wanted to ask him if he knew whether Mungo MacLeod has a lady friend. I wouldn't really know how to subtly bring the subject up in conversation."

Beth grinned, "No need," she said. "I've found her."

"Really? How?"

"You remember I told you about the situation with the hunting hounds?" Bart nodded mid-bite of a chip sandwich he had put together from the many chips. He nodded going for the bite whilst listening.

"Well, one of my calls is a woman who lives at Banchory, a Mary Macaulay. She has two of the castle's dogs," Beth began. "It was my first time delivering to her. Although she was friendly, she seemed uncomfortable with me. She wanted to know why Fraser wasn't delivering. I explained how he'd set me on to help out at the stables to do some of the deliveries." She explained. "She seemed keen to talk, offered me tea revealing sometimes Mungo MacLeod has done the same. I could tell by the way she spoke his name there was something there."

"You felt there was some connection between them?" Bart paused in his eating.

"She asked me how Fraser was, then added Mungo as if he was an afterthought. You could tell she was keen to hear about him."

"Do you think it's because he's gone missing?"

"No, I'm sure she doesn't know, she hinted she was expecting him to deliver the dog food this time instead of Fraser." Beth stopped momentarily before she carried on, "I thought she did know until she started to confide in me. She went on to tell me Mungo promised her he would come back because she was concerned about one of the dogs having fleas. The dog kept scratching his fur away causing sore patches. She told me Mungo assured her he needed to be given a bath in special medicated shampoo. He didn't have the time right then to help her, but would come back with flea powder and conditioning tablets next day."

Bart sat listening not able to see the significance of why she was so excited to tell him. She laughed realising she hadn't mentioned the important part, "Oh yes, the reason he couldn't stay was because he needed to go over to The March of Time to pick up one of the Laird's clocks left there for repair before the snows came."

Bart stared in amazement, "Did she tell you when that was? There must be a record of when the deliveries are made….?"

"Ah, I got excited so I went back to check the delivery book which is kept up to date in respect of feed distribution for both the dogs and the horses."

"The horses?" Bart queried.

"Yes, not all the horses belong to the laird. We stable others from around the area for those people who belong to the Hunt set.

Duncan Munro is the Hunt Master or rather used to be. The Hunt established quite a business for the castle back then, even down to breeding foxhounds for hunting. The law changed all that by prohibiting the chasing of wild mammals with dogs Act in 2004 after which it became illegal."

"Ah," Bart deduced, "I expect they still go out though....."

They fell silent whilst they carried on eating until Bart asked, "So did Mungo record when he made the delivery? He certainly didn't come to the shop to pick up the clock....."

"....which means something happened to stop him coming here," Beth realised now thinking out loud. "Or....he didn't intend to come here...."

"Strange though," Bart asserted, "Did she say whether he went back to help with the hound?" She shook her head, "She didn't elaborate. I did get the impression from her general mood she hasn't seen him since."

"And could be why the dog food delivery book didn't get made up by him delivering hers," she added. "There doesn't appear to be any gaps though."

"Does each person who delivers record their own deliveries?"

"Yes, there's a column for your initials after each entry is made," she pushed her plate to the side having eaten all she could manage.

Bart finished his own doing the same, "What would be mighty nice now would be a portion of one of your exceptional cakes! Unfortunately, I have nothing of the like to offer you."

"I couldn't eat another thing," she laughed. "Was this really a meal for one person?" "Apparently so, I'm sure I wouldn't have been able to eat any more than I have, if you hadn't arrived then."

They fell silent again until Bart asked, "Do you think we could get Mary Macaulay to open up about Mungo MacLeod or even to remember when she last saw him?"

Beth smiled, "I'd hoped you would say that because I did tell her I would go back to help her with the hound's skin problem and would bring a friend along who knew about these kinds of problems."

Bart pointed at himself as if to ask, "Me?" Beth nodded.

CHAPTER 26

The proposed trip to Banchory was arranged for Thursday when Beth wasn't working. She told Sirus she needed to see what medicines she could find in the medication cupboard at the kennels before they visited Mary Macaulay because she promised her she would help with her dog's skin infection. She knew she could be taking a risk if seen. She hoped she might do this early evening after work on Wednesday when no one was around. Bart entreated her to be careful otherwise she might be accused of stealing. The likelihood of if happening she explained was if Thomas Galbraith was hanging around watching her as he often did if he thought she was working late.

Bart promised to work at the castle on Wednesday, also to try to engage Galbraith's attention around five o'clock to stop him slipping over to the kennels where Beth would be. Beth giggled at their duplicity showing Bart she was enjoying every minute of her 'undercover' role as she liked to call it.

He was intrigued by the change in Beth since he first saw her outside his shop peering up at the picture of the March Hare on his shop sign. The timid fearful girl was slowly being replaced by a bright confident young woman whose laugh was delightful filling him with joy to hear it.

"I need you to play the 'animal' expert so she doesn't suspect we are there for an altogether different reason," Beth told him before she climbed into her van to head off home.

Next day Bart began his research on the clocks in the Long Gallery to begin his inventory. He brought his lap top into the shop to be on hand should he have any customers, his normal practice was to open up at ten o'clock in keeping with the opening hours of the other shops in the village. He only knew the post office in the Co-op store opened earlier, it being committed to the national nine o'clock opening which required the grocery shop to open early.

He was searching the internet for grandfather clocks when he heard the tinkling of the shop doorbell. He watched the very tall young uniformed police officer standing still listening whilst staring at his vast array of time pieces. Even having no particular reason to fear the law, the sight of this official figure made his heart skip a beat and his pulse to race a little faster.

He pulled himself together as he rose to his full five foot four inch height, "P.C Cowan I presume?" Bart asked. The constable twitched slightly as if he might have surprised him before he gained his composure to address Bart.

"Sirus Jeffries?" he enquired, his voice formal.

"Yes, indeed," Bart boomed back asserting himself, he felt like David addressing Goliath.

"I don't think I have ever seen so many clocks in one place before," P.C Cowan gaped at the vast collection.

"And doubtless not heard so much noise?" Bart suggested. "Now if you wait for the striking of the hour, you may have the desire to take cover – many people do!"

The police officer nodded before he announced, "I need to ask you a few questions about Mungo MacLeod?"

"Then in order to concentrate, perhaps you would slip the catch on the door, we can retire to the back room for a little peace and quiet," Bart turned to leave the shop expecting the policeman to follow him.

When he came through to the back Bart asked, "Tea, coffee?" as he flicked the kettle on to boil.

"Coffee would be grand, thank you," he said. Bart wondered how many drinks he must consume on a daily basis if he accepted every time. He knew he would never refuse a drink if one was offered to him. "So what do you want to know?" Bart asked as if he couldn't already guess.

The officer took out his note book consulting a page he began, "I understand Laird Munro's ghillie, Mungo MacLeod, brought one of the Laird's clocks to you for repair."

"He did, indeed," Bart confirmed, "At the time I didn't know his name. I thought he was actually the Laird," Bart walked over to the sideboard where he picked up his ledger in which he recorded all repairs, flicked back over one page. He put the book down on the table inviting the P.C to inspect it. Robbie Cowan sat down as Bart turned the ledger around for him to read the entry which filled the whole page with a substantial amount of information starting with the date.

"As you can see he brought me the clock on 22nd of November," under this Bart recorded Laird Munro with the castle's address followed by brief details about the clock, type, known make and the repair needed. Generally speaking with all of his repairs this entry was usually recorded as 'stopped' or 'won't wind up'.

"So he actually introduced himself as the Laird?" PC Cowan asked looking puzzled.

"You know, I have since given a great deal of thought to what he did say. I don't think he did say 'I am….' Rather he was more formal, merely meant the clock belonged to 'Laird Munro, address….etc.' Perhaps given my hearing is not perfect I assumed by his bearing he must be no less than the Laird himself."

"And how would you describe him Mr. Jeffries?"

"Tall, well made – not unlike yourself in stature – red hair and beard, perhaps a little wild looking, with a very mild genteel manner when he spoke." Bart finished thinking about the picture of

Seumus Grant in the castle library, "Not dissimilar to a painting I have since seen in the castle library of one of the previous Lairds, Seumus Grant? In fact, so similar they could be related."

P.C Cowan was scribbling quickly in his note book so Bart paused to allow him chance to catch up. When he finished he produced a three by two photograph from a pouch on his utility belt, which he handed to Bart. He was immediately reminded of the P.I Selwyn Jones; he pushed his rabbit-like image away. This was a black and white picture of Mungo MacLeod taken some years previously - he appeared to be in his thirties, his hair longer giving him a wilder appearance like Seumus Grant.

"It doesn't pick up his colouring," Bart teased somewhat deadpan. Robbie Cowan didn't laugh. "Probably taken some twenty years ago," he added. "I guess he isn't a man who likes to take selfies?"

This time the P.C did smile which changed his previously stern face making him seem more round-cheeked and boyish. "It is all I could get of him," he admitted apologetically.

"And his name is Mungo MacLeod you say?"

The Constable stared intensely at Bart as if trying to decide whether he was still being amusing. Bart continued, "Who you believe to have stolen the clock or perhaps impersonated Laird Munro?" Bart certainly wasn't trying to be amusing but was aware so far the Constable hadn't stated why he was making enquiries about Mungo MacLeod. The first time they met, Duncan Munro admitted he believed Mungo went off with an item (or items) belonging to the castle. This situation may still apply even though they knew one particular grandmother clock was returned by him.

Robbie Cowan fidgeted uncomfortably, "We have him registered as a MISPER," he admitted reluctantly. Bart made no comment about being a little premature given Mungo MacLeod was only reported to them recently.

173

"I see and you are here because I met him last November....." Bart's sarcasm wasn't missed on the constable who scowled at him.

"In these cases we have to start somewhere. Since 'you' can clear up any doubts about him not 'stealing' the clock, perhaps November isn't so random a place to begin." They locked eyes as Bart realised P.C Cowan was not the bumbling rural beat bobby he imagined him to be, he felt truly put in his place.

"Quite," he conceded. "I will say I was surprised I hadn't seen or heard from him again. I assumed the snow might have prevented a visit, but I expected him to telephone for a progress report, or at least to enquire whether I could mend it or not. There was some doubt about that which we did tentatively discuss at the time." Cowan made a note in his book. "I'm sure the people up at the castle would have many more contacts with him during the weeks after our meeting." Bart's curiosity having peaked was now aware he ought not to antagonise the constable. "What do the castle folk do at Christmas and the New Year?" Bart asked probingly.

"I believe the Laird was away over the holiday period, so I suppose nothing formal occurred, most of the staff have their own families to spend Christmas with," Robbie Cowan spoke as if he were reassessing what he already knew.

"Mungo MacLeod has a family?" Bart put in knowing already he lived alone in his ghillie's cottage on the estate.

The P.C shook his head, "Not as far as I know...other than the Laird. I'm not sure what the link is there, no one I've spoken to so far seems to know." He said which immediately intrigued Bart, obviously more staff gossip.

"Mungo MacLeod is a relative of Laird Munro you think?" he asked innocently.

Robbie shrugged, "Someone hinted as such, although I don't have confirmation."

Bart stored this piece of information away for future reference continuing with his probing of the officer by daring to ask, "What does someone like Thomas Galbraith do at Christmas when the Laird is away? I expect he gets an extended holiday with his family also?" He tried hard not to sound like he was being nosy. He could see he hadn't fooled Robbie Cowan, who laughed.

"I take it you've met him then?" he grinned.

"A proper little charmer isn't he?" Bart laughed with him. "I can't imagine him standing around the family piano singing Christmas carols with his wife and children or sitting tiny Tim on his knee in front of a flaming plum pudding."

Robbie Cowan laughed heartily, "No, I believe he isn't married," he admitted, "And more likely to get visited by three spirits at midnight on Christmas Eve!"

To his surprise Bart found himself liking this young police officer somewhat.

"You've met him also it seems," he commented. Whilst he was in such a convivial mood he slipped in, "Are you able to identify when he was last seen by anyone?"

Robbie Cowan showed his frustration, "Ah, now that's a difficult one. He is a bit of a solitary person. Of course, the laird himself would have more contact with him than anyone else. I understand he was away until early New Year. He seems to have kept himself to himself. He works mainly alone as you would expect a ghillie to do....," he shrugged his shoulders.

"I understand from Duncan Munro one of his jobs is to keep the time pieces wound up. I have only just begun to undertake the inventory of them......" he stopped when he saw the constable looking blank. "I have been taken on by the castle to do one as well as retained to maintain them or fix any of them needing my kind of expertise."

"I see," he said writing something in his note book.

"I only started on Monday last," Sirus added. "So it's early days. However I'm thinking if Mungo MacLeod intended to go away for a break, he might have asked someone else to undertake the task if he expected to be away for some time – say longer than eight days for example."

"Why eight days?" P.C. Cowan asked.

"Eight days is the length of time some of the grandfather clocks will run before needing to be wound up again, although generally more favourable every seven days."

"Ah, so if you have any still running….."

"Exactly," Bart interrupted realising he caught the significance, being one way to estimate when it was last wound up. "Unless, of course, someone else has actually wound them" Bart suggested.

"You say you've only just started the inventory?"

"Indeed, and yes I have found two in the Long Gallery are still running." Bart hadn't initially known Mungo MacLeod was the guardian of the clocks otherwise he would have come to the conclusion earlier.

Bart watched Robbie Cowan's face light up, "Perhaps we can leave them to run down to make a bit of a guess as to when they were last wound up, can we?" he requested.

Bart pointed a finger at him, "My thoughts exactly. I will do a quick walk through to check the others tomorrow," he offered. "I'll let you know what I find."

When Robbie Cowan left his shop Bart thought he seemed quite satisfied with the encounter. Bart certainly felt the interview was fruitful giving him a whole new perspective to take with him to talk to Mary Macaulay on Thursday. One of the other things Beth finding Mary made him consider was how the Castle (or rather Fraser in particular) picked out the people with whom to foster the Foxhounds, especially Mary Macaulay who lives at Banchory. Then, of course, there was Elizabeth Grant on the Balmoral Estate at

Aboyne. So far he hadn't discussed this with Beth which would keep until after he met Mary.

In the meantime he needed to speak with Thomas Galbraith whom he felt was a bit of an enigma, about what *he* saw as Bart's role in the huge task of identifying the castle's treasures with a view to opening its doors to the public. When Wednesday arrived Bart saw identifying the clocks still operational as his first priority of the day. He wanted to do this before he spoke with the Laird's secretary, certainly before Duncan Munro returned from Edinburgh. He couldn't determine what 'a few days' meant. Since he arrived early he decided to start with the reception rooms thinking he would be undisturbed.

The grand salon contained exquisite furniture with only a few timepieces apart from a mantle clock of considerable splendour which Bart found working. He decided to take a picture of each clock, what was the point of having a mobile with a camera if you weren't going to use it? Hence each clock he photographed he added to a list merely recording the type of clock, whether working or not, together with the position in the room where he found it. He moved swiftly in much less time than his initial inspection of those he found in the Long Gallery which he now discovered were all finally stopped. He made a note.

Eventually he found himself once again in the castle library. On entering he was again drawn by the picture at the top end of the Laird's ancestor Seumus Grant whose eyes fixed him in his icy stare, following him wherever he moved. He stood as if entranced by him and recognised for the first time in the picture the Laird was in fact standing in this very room, in front of the large fireplace. Bart shook himself to dispel the all empowering feeling he was being watched. When he glanced around the room with a view to finding any clocks, he was stunned by one particular fine clock over the very same large fireplace, although the clock was not reproduced within the painting.

He walked over to view it sitting on the stone mantle at its centre. Bart recognised this as a 'library clock'. He hadn't seen one before outside of a book of antique clocks, not even at the many auctions he attended over the past few years. Immediately he knew this to be a fine specimen. He stood in awe staring at it. He took a step backwards, got out his mobile, photographed both sides, then full on. He realised in order to examine this piece closely he would need step ladders, or else the help of some very tall people in order to inspect it.

At least this piece would be inaccessible to the public should they pass through the library.

On impulse he moved his mobile downwards to take a picture of the impressive fire place, being one of those you could actually walk into. In fact you would have needed to should anyone intend to light the logs lying in the fire basket at its centre. By the looks of the stone surround this particular fire surprisingly seemed never to have been lit as the stone was free from blackened markings.

When he observed two small alcoves one on each side of the fire, he noticed each contained a carriage clock though they weren't identical, he recognised one in particular was a fine piece probably worth a lot of money. He took a picture before he turned to its opposite fellow clock. He clicked his camera pulling up the resultant photograph he enlarged the clock with his thumb and index finger. He was quite shocked to discover how ordinarily plain it was. *How strange* he thought to have such an odd pairing. He was about to lean over to pick it up when he heard a voice.

"What are you doing in here?" the spiky voice behind him made him jump. He quickly slipped his mobile into his jacket pocket before he turned around to find the somewhat angry face of Thomas Galbraith. Bart was as much stunned by the sharp tone of the question as the question itself.

"Err, identifying the clocks in here," he felt like he'd been caught about to steal one, *what a ridiculous thought!* "Isn't that what I'm supposed to be doing?" he threw back standing his ground.

"The library is the Laird's working place, which won't be open to the public!" Galbraith retorted fiercely.

Bart stared at his open hostility towards him which he noted was extreme. He was reminded of Beth's comment about Galbraith getting very angry when his name was mentioned in conversation.

"I dare say that applies to a lot of the rooms here which has nothing to do with my inventory?" he couldn't help his rising irritation when he replied. "An inventory is about taking stock of 'all' the castle clocks otherwise how do you know what you own. How can you know if any are missing?" Bart stopped observing the rigid posture of the man in front of him. What he saw he found exceedingly weird being alarmed by his sudden strangeness.

He swivelled round to face the fireplace once again, his arms splayed looking up at the Library Clock on the mantel above him, "I'm sure a member of the public would have difficulty slipping this beautiful specimen into their pocket should they wander in here!" He swung back round again looking at Galbraith, "I would expect, however, an organised robbery by many people would want to remove this clock nonetheless," he smiled his most flamboyant smile hoping the expression spoke of friendliness. Galbraith wasn't looking at the library clock he was staring fixedly at the fireplace seeming enchanted by the made up fire basket. "Wouldn't you say?" Bart asked.

Galbraith's eyes moved up to Bart's grin which brought him back from wherever his mind had taken him. He didn't reply to the question Bart thought because he hadn't heard it. As the silence grew with Bart's increasing discomfort he decided to go, "Right, I'll leave you and press on." He walked away leaving Thomas Galbraith still standing transfixed in front of the library's fire place.

The encounter left Bart feeling alarmed, which he saw very much as a wake-up call. He now understood the concerns Beth raised about the man. The idea this strange man was hovering around Beth left him quite fearful. Neither of them used the word 'stalking' to describe his behaviour, however, what she described to him was nothing short of sinister.

When he glanced at his pocket watch he was surprised to see whilst being confronted by Galbraith in the library it was now past five o'clock. Quite unwittingly he'd engaged him like he intended whilst Beth 'hopefully' accomplished her task at the kennels.

He gathered his papers together, walked out to his car taking out his mobile he sent a text to Beth, "Where are you?" hoping he wouldn't draw anyone's attention by hearing the beep if she was still 'undercover' at the kennels. He stood at the side of his car which was now alone in the parking spaces in front of the castle. His telephone rang.

"Sirus, It's me," Beth greeted him little knowing she was only one of three people in his contacts list, now having included Jayson Vingoe's number. "I'm back home, mission accomplished," she laughed mischievously.

"Thank goodness!" He sounded so relieved Beth asked, "What's wrong?"

"No matter," he said. "I'll pick you up at eleven o'clock tomorrow, okay?"

"Okay," she replied.

CHAPTER 27

Bart woke next morning feeling uneasy, he was unable to shake off the mood since his encounter with Thomas Galbraith the day before. Drinking one or two glasses of his favourite Bell's whisky after he got home didn't relieve his disquiet; far from helping him to forget the exchange of words, he ended up with a mild hangover. His preoccupation with the secretary's hostility towards him prevented him from concentrating on the upcoming meeting with Mary Macaulay even though he knew he would have to tread carefully when they got there.

Conversely, Beth was in high spirits as she locked the cottage door she was smiling. For the first time that day Bart managed a smile seeing her grin mischievously when she jumped into his car. She was carrying a black holdall which she turned to place on the back seat before she put on her seat belt.

"Morning," Bart greeted her. "Is the bag your spoils from yesterday's raid?" He asked teasing her. Her giggle told him nothing was going to upset her mood today. He sank into speculative thoughts not mentioning Galbraith because he didn't want to burst her bubble.

As they drove off along the Aboyne 'old road' towards Banchory through Kincardine O'Neil, she told him how she waited for Fraser to leave before she dared search for what she needed.

"The dog shampoo was easy enough. They keep a good supply of Vet's allergy itch relief, so let's hope this will do the trick. The fleas and tick remedy was locked away in the drugs cupboard, it comes according to the dog's weight," she told him.

"You know how heavy her dog is?" Bart glanced over surprised.

Beth laughed, "Err, no, so I brought one of each.....we'll have to work out which to use when we get there!"

"Sounds to me like you're the animal expert," Bart suggested. "I may be superfluous to requirements."

They sat in silence whilst he drove being directed by Beth where to turn. The journey took about twenty-five minutes before they pulled up outside a small stone built chalet cottage.

"I'll let you take the lead," Bart proposed. "Since you know her, we'll try to keep the conversation light." He didn't want to confess he wasn't a great one with animals especially cats; he didn't like cats at all. They in turn certainly took an instant dislike to him. So he kept very much away from them.

His experience of dogs was also limited, not having any pets as a child. Since then he led a lifestyle not conducive to having one. He couldn't even remember a time when he actually considered owning a pet of any kind. He supposed this came quite naturally if you were a parent which, of course, he wasn't.

He was surprised when he pulled up outside the place, being on the edge of the countryside with a large garden ideal for having dogs. He could see two foxhounds chasing each other around the green space until they spotted his car which stopped them in their play and they began to bark at them through the picket fence.

"Nice," Bart commented. "Good choice for foxhounds."

"You sound just like an animal expert," Beth grinned at her cheek.

They got out with Beth carrying the black bag, approached the garden gate where the dogs were now standing behind yapping wildly at the visitors. Beth opened the gate talking in a low voice she began stroking the dogs. She imagined they could smell Sandy because she deliberately stroked him before she left to ensure they would recognise the scent to demonstrate she was dog friendly.

Bart on the other hand was treated with a great deal of caution together with a fresh bout of barking. This he thought was not going well for a supposed animal expert. The door of the house opened to reveal a small woman in her forties coming out to see what all the fuss was about. When she caught sight of Beth she recognised her and smiled.

The dogs meanwhile were sniffing nervously around Bart's ankles. He became seriously afraid they might attack him.

"Stop it!" Mary Macaulay shouted at them which they ignored by resuming their barking at Bart.

Not very well trained for hunting stock Bart thought.

"That's enough!" He boomed in his fiercest voice. "Sit!" He suddenly held up his arm over them. To everyone's amazement, especially Bart's, both dogs sat immediately side by side, obediently looking up at him as if awaiting further instructions.

He could see Beth stifling a laugh, "Hello Mary, this is Sirus I told you about, we've come to help with the dogs, how is the skin problem?"

"Still there I'm afraid. I'm hoping he doesn't infect the other one." She looked a little worried after asking them in.

"Let's leave them out there for a minute," Beth suggested. "Whilst we discuss what we aim to do."

Mary was obviously relieved to get their help with the dogs, she couldn't thank them enough. The apprehension she showed when they first arrived soon settled.

Bart had no problem convincing her of his 'animal expertise' as much to his astonishment when the dogs were let back inside after their discussions about the 'treatment' they immediately ran to him, sat in front of him then lay down at his feet waiting to be told what to do next. Neither of the women were more surprised than he was. He managed to hide it and even look like he expected such behaviour from them.

He was even more delighted when his contribution to their bathing only entailed calling each one to heel then lifting them into the bath tub for their medicated shampoo treatment which Beth instructed Mary to liberally apply then wash thoroughly away with the shower spray.

Bart sat drinking tea whilst the dogs lay at his feet in front of the fire drying off like it was normal practice to be there. Bart, having judged the weight of the dogs whilst lifting them into the bath decided each dog would be classified as large for the purpose of dispensing the flea and tick remedy, after he surreptitiously read the instructions whilst Mary made them tea.

Once again Mary repeated her gratitude, "I don't know what I would have done with Mungo not coming back....." She suddenly seemed so sad her former nervousness returned. Beth thought she might burst into tears.

"What's wrong, Mary?" Beth asked placing a hand on her arm to comfort her.

"I can't understand why he hasn't come back like he promised he would," her sorrowful eyes had lost their former emerald sparkle; they couldn't fail to recognise she was the person the staff referred to as Mungo's 'lady friend'. "I can only think he's annoyed with me for something."

"What could possibly have annoyed him?" Bart asked gently.

Mary's eyes filled with fear.

"Mary?" Beth coaxed.

"He might think badly of me thinking I have betrayed him," she began to sob quietly.

"Why would he think such a thing Mary, he seems a straight talking man, wouldn't he have asked you about anything bothering him?" Bart asked.

She recognised Bart spoke as if he knew Mungo MacLeod, "Yes, I suppose so, but why hasn't he been back?"

"What do you imagine he is cross about?" Bart asked ignoring her question; neither he nor Beth wanted to answer.

"I haven't told him about that man!" now she sounded really angry. "I have never encouraged his attentions," she snapped crossly. "In fact, when he turned up here at Christmas with flowers I told him to leave me alone as I didn't want his flowers or him!"

Beth glanced over at Bart to see how he was reacting to this sudden turn in the conversation.

"Who are you talking about Mary?" Bart asked having placed his tea cup down on the coffee table in between them he leaned towards her with some growing concern.

"Thomas Galbraith!"

Bart recoiled in alarm, "You know him?"

Mary nodded, "He's the reason I left the castle." She looked from one to the other of them as if she expected them to know.

"You worked at the castle?" Beth asked.

"We didn't realise," Bart added. "Is this how you ended up with two of the dogs?"

Mary nodded. "I worked in the gift shop then."

"So you know Joy?" Beth saw her eyes go wide realising there was another story to be told. "So you left because you couldn't work with Joy?" she dared to ask.

Mary shook her head, "No, she wasn't easy to work with, for some reason she didn't like me. I managed to get on with her though….no, my problem was the Laird's new secretary….he always seemed to be around which Joy didn't seem to like."

"What about you, how did you feel about him?" Bart probed.

Mary shivered which spoke volumes, "I thought his behaviour was a bit creepy."

"So you left?"

"Not because of that, more because it became impossible for me to take my break in the gift shop café with him keep coming in, sitting down with us. I could sense the others didn't like him there, which worried me they would get angry with me or even think I wanted him there. I heard the odd comment teasing me about him being sweet on me! I couldn't take it so I took my breaks outside, found little places to hide where he wouldn't find me; being summer outside was so nice with such lovely scenery." She stopped now embarrassed she was talking so much. Eventually she resumed obviously happy with her thoughts, "It was how I met Mungo, he was outside working, checking everything for a shoot or maybe a hunt," she realised she might have revealed, so she quickly corrected herself, "Not with the dogs you understand, but they still go out to exercise the horses."

Bart nodded acknowledging the significance, neither he nor Beth wanted to interrupt her now she was talking freely.

"I think he was a bit surprised when he spotted me watching him. He came over to say hello." She blushed with embarrassment telling them. "We got talking.......got along really well till eventually we would arrange to spend my break together."

"Did you tell him about Galbraith?" Bart asked.

Mary was aghast shaking her head again, "No because Mungo is the Laird's ghillie. I heard people talking about him being a relative through some ancestor, I never did understand it!"

"Did you not ask him about the rumours?" Bart asked trying not to sound critical.

"The thing is we don't talk much about other people. He certainly doesn't speak about the Laird, I think he's quite an honourable man."

"What about when you left, given your friendship with Mungo, what made you leave?" Bart thought this an excellent question from Beth.

She seemed uncomfortable now, both thinking she might stop talking and not answer the question. However, she went on, "This may sound a bit strange…..but everywhere I went at the castle I felt like I was being watched," she checked for their reaction. She went on encouraged by Beth who nodded to invite her to continue. "Except when I met Mungo it was the only time I felt free of the notion…..or perhaps our chats took my mind off it."

"I sense something changed?" Bart surmised.

Mary nodded, "Maybe I was a bit careless because I did try hard to make sure I wasn't being followed."

"Did you mention this to Mungo?" Beth asked. Bart could tell this whole conversation was upsetting her because she identified the same was happening to her.

"I didn't want him to think badly of me; you know, like some neurotic female, it's guaranteed to put some men off isn't it?"

"So how did you leaving come about?" Beth asked.

"It was late one night when I'd been helping Joy with a stocktake in the gift shop – or rather I got left behind to complete one –she hates doing them, they are particularly tedious to do."

"So you got lumbered," Beth already knew joy was capable of offloading work.

"Yes, it meant I was the last to leave. That particular night was dark and raining heavily when I got out to my car," she trembled again whilst she retold it. "He seemed to come out of nowhere up behind me. With my rain hood over my hair I didn't hear him approach me until he touched my arm….." Mary rubbed the top of her left arm with her right hand as if she could feel his touch once again. "I nearly jumped out of my skin."

"What did he say?" Bart asked remembering how Galbraith made him feel in the library yesterday, he felt real sympathy for her.

"My heart was still pounding from the shock, I know it's silly but the castle is meant to be haunted isn't it? My first thought was the ghost touched my arm." Mary could see by their faces neither of them knew about the ghost. "Anyway, it must have been a few minutes before I heard what he was saying to me because at first I couldn't understand him." She paused again as if trying to decide whether to reveal any more to them.

"What was he saying, Mary?" Bart asked.

Mary gave a huge sigh before she continued, "He told me he knew about me meeting with Mungo, he started to tell me the Laird wouldn't like that if he knew what we were doing in work time," she looked on the verge of tears again, clearly distressed. "He implied he'd seen us being....well intimate..!" Mary sobbed this time. "I swear it wasn't true, we only ever talked...."

Beth's anger was immediate and forceful, "What an evil man!"

Bart tried to calm them both by saying, "Some people have difficulty observing how comfortable some people can seem to be in each other's company especially if they themselves have difficulty communicating with people."

Mary smiled, "Yes, I see, even so he lied. Afterwards he kept asking me out implying if I didn't meet with him he would have to inform the Laird who would probably sack us both." Beth gasped as Mary went on, "I couldn't be responsible for Mungo losing his job, he's been at the Castle for years, so I decided to find another job nearer home after I left."

"What did you tell Mungo?" Beth was truly caught up in Mary's dilemma.

"Nothing at the time, I told everyone else I got a new job near to where I live hoping the message would get back to him."

"This is awful," Beth exclaimed. "But you obviously met up again later?"

Mary nodded, "Thanks to the dogs really. Before I left, Fraser asked me if I would take them since I would be working nearer home to be able to keep an eye on them."

"Ah," was Bart's only comment as this answered one of his outstanding questions regarding the fostering of the hounds.

"Then one day when Mungo, stood in for Fraser, he came to bring me the special dog food the hounds needed. After that he always brought it."

Beth caught Bart's eye as if to confirm the missing entries in the dog ledger.

"What about Galbraith, you say he turned up here at Christmas with flowers?" Bart reminded her.

"Yes, I thought I was well rid of him, even though I'm still worried about his obvious loathing of Mungo. I was just happy to be seeing Mungo again. We were getting on so well. The only thing was I kept getting some telephone calls late at night."

"From Galbraith?!" Beth sounded shocked.

Mary shrugged, "I could only assume so, whoever was there didn't speak."

Bart asked the question he wanted the answer to, "When was the last time you saw Mungo MacLeod?"

"Mungo?" she asked. They could see her thinking and she smiled remembering, "It was the day before Christmas Eve."

"Are you sure of the date?"

She got up after Bart's question, walked over to the sideboard, where she pulled open a draw taking out a small box covered in suede-effect material which she handed to Beth to open. The box contained a gold heart-shaped locket, "Lovely," Beth said showing Bart.

"It was my birthday, 23rd of December, Mungo gave me this," her eyes misted once again. "He was meant to come back to help me

189

with the dogs because he couldn't stay, he needed to go over to fetch the Laird's clock back before Christmas. I planned to invite him to come here for Christmas, but he didn't come back."

"And what about Thomas Galbraith when did he bring you flowers?" Bart asked.

"Next day, Christmas Eve.....I thought perhaps Mungo did come over, saw him here or as Galbraith was leaving and perhaps he misread the situation."

Beth handed back the locket. Bart made a few calculations regarding the clocks he knew were still working. He knew if he'd gone away on Christmas Eve the timing didn't fit with one or two of them still going. If Mungo MacLeod wound up the existing clocks, then perhaps Mary's theory he'd seen Galbraith over here on Christmas Eve was correct. He might have misconstrued his visit deciding to go away for Christmas. On the other hand something else could have happened to stop him coming back.

Nevertheless, this was something definite to add to Robbie Cowan's time line. The problem was how to add this information to it. He was aware Mary didn't know Mungo MacLeod was officially a missing person. Bart was very reluctant to tell her because he was now even more concerned about the seriousness of his sudden disappearance.

"You mentioned Mungo's potential kinship to the Laird, were you aware or did he ever mention having any family he might want to spend Christmas with?" Bart asked.

Mary seemed puzzled by the question, as if it hadn't occurred to her before. The more she thought, the more awkward she became not having considered there were other people he might want to spend time with. She stood up, turned away from them moving over to the dresser where she put the small box away. They couldn't see the sadness printed on her face.

CHAPTER 28

Beth sat deep in thought until they were driving along the A93 towards Aboyne when she asked, "Why didn't you tell her he was missing?" They both knew they came close, neither of them wanting to add more agony to her already miserable state, not sure whether it was better for her to believe he deserted her or to imagine something really bad happened to him.

"I don't think it's our place to tell her, after all we don't really know whether he is missing," Bart suggested. "I know Duncan Munro reported him missing more because of the missing clock. I suspect the Police are only investigating because of who he is – a laird. In any normal case I understand they only circulate a name with a description or if possible a photograph, unless there is a suspicion of vulnerability or foul play."

Beth reminded him, "Didn't you say his medication was still in his cottage?"

"It doesn't mean he hasn't got some with him or can't get some more if he forgot to take it with him."

"No I suppose not," she agreed.

"I think it's down to P.C Cowan to inform anyone of his absence including Mary," Bart was toying with the idea of telling Robbie Cowan about Mary because he didn't believe Galbraith would under the circumstances.

"Yes, has anyone mentioned Mary to P.C Cowan?" Beth's voice quivered. "I really do feel sorry for her, Sirus."

"Hmm," was all Bart would say.

They sank into their own thoughts until Bart asked, "On a different matter I would greatly appreciate your opinion on a little problem I have, if I might ask?"

He had given a lot of thought to telling her about Emily because he knew Beth was truly empathic, which he now did. The matter of her current situation came to a head when he received a text from her earlier that morning merely informing him: *The Silver Teapot has been sold subject to contract.* He was horrified to hear this knowing Emily was determined not to go with her mother to Grimsby threatening to seek her future alone in London. He hoped he would have more time to deliberate on the matter.

It took the rest of the drive back to Beth's cottage to explain succinctly the events leading up to him moving to Scotland, as well as how the aftermath of them impacted on Emily resulting in her parents splitting up. He was sure by now they would be close to being divorced.

"Does she believe you to be in London?" Beth asked having silently listened to his story whereby she picked up one or two hidden hints from it.

"Why do you ask?" he seemed surprised.

"I get the impression from what you say working in your clock shop was perhaps the highlight of her life so far, am I right?"

"I fear so," he said somewhat abashed.

Beth scowled at him. "You shouldn't underestimate the effect you have on people's lives. There are very few people in this world who are as kind or caring as you obviously are," she chastised which made him cough with embarrassment.

"Maybe I recognise how alone and sometimes wretched people can be who with a little help can change their life for the better."

"Has anyone ever done the same for you, Sirus?" she asked catching him off guard. He again felt the sharp pain deep inside he once felt as a child. This was before he toughened himself to become hardened against the rejections he received on many occasions. Before he knew and accepted he would spend his whole life on his own.

Beth was aware of how he helped the young Doyle couple who took her car away for her; they too were runaways.

"Could Emily not come to you?" She suggested gently watching the sadness appear on his face.

"It's not easy, is it?" he admitted. "This is not a liberal world we live in. I am an elderly bachelor whilst she is a young girl of sixteen or seventeen. It would be frowned upon. Society dictates a whole lot of unpleasant accusations coming out of such a situation," he looked across for her understanding. "I think you of all people know this very well."

She ignored his last comment. "So what would you do, or indeed did you do, when you took on a fifteen year old Emily as your assistant to help you in your shop?" she asked. "Let's face it, Sirus, you have the castle contract now and only this week so far you have been away from your shop three out of four days."

"Well yes, although I don't get many customers at this time of year." His argument sounded a little feeble even to him.

"So if you place an ad in the post office in the village for someone to help you in your shop and a local 'Emily' with the right passion for clocks applies for the job, what do you do?" Beth was now smiling at her own logical thinking knowing very well he would consider her. "If Emily's mother moved here I dare say you wouldn't have an issue, am I right?"

He nodded slowly, "Except I don't think her mother would necessarily enrich her life or her future!"

"That bad, eh?"

"Yes, she does have a point about not moving to Grimsby with her, by all accounts the woman barely registers her existence!"

"You know, Sirus, you really are a lovely man. Look what you've done for me. More than a parent would have done because you aren't tied by any false assumptions of what they ought to do for their offspring. You don't have to abide by the very rules you seem to be so afraid of being judged against." Beth went quiet for a moment. "I say the parent/child expectation is a lot of baloney; there are far too many appalling parents in the world!"

Bart laughed raucously because he couldn't deny thinking the same thing, "For someone so young you are very wise!"

"Wisdom comes from experience not only age; it's not always a good pill to swallow," she refused to dwell on those old experiences since she began to taste her newly found freedom.

He pondered for a moment on how tough childhood must have been for her. How desperate must she have felt to run away from it? She didn't disclose any details but he thought perhaps she found an even worse life. The idea made his melancholy much worse.

"I have no qualms whatsoever about having Emily to work with me in the shop. In lots of ways I confess she has more to offer horology than I ever could. Emily has never been young; she skipped the stage in her development. Even so she has managed to turn herself into one extremely fine human being...."

When he glanced over at Beth she was beaming, her face sparkled at his words in describing Emily. "Then there's no problem at all is there?" she enquired. He wasn't smiling, he scowled. "I'm teasing you," she laughed. "She must come to live with me and Sandy," *and whoever my spectral lodger happens to be!* Bart caught her face suddenly change to thoughtful.

"I will say one thing Beth," he said. "You will never have a problem with any of your time pieces if she does."

"There is always a bonus, uncle Sirus," Beth mocked, "Or whatever your name really is."

He watched her face light up at her own cheek.

"Bart.....my name is Bartholomew Bridges," he admitted, liking being able to say his name out loud for the first time in over two years.

"Well, uncle Sirus, your secret is safe with me."

*   *   *   *   *

Bart sat at a table in the Golf Club bar where he had ordered the chilli con carne special of the day for his lunch. He sat as close to the open fire as the table arrangements would allow in order to warm himself against the chill of the day. The Golf Club was situated on the flattest piece of land around the village and caught the full force of any arctic blast passing through. He marvelled at the few hardy golfers he observed out on the course as he got out of his car, not lingering too long before he rushed inside the clubhouse. Today wasn't a day for a casual stroll to get there.

Whilst he waited for his meal to arrive he took out his telephone, also the small business card which Robbie Cowan (Police Scotland) gave him. He turned it over between his fingers as if he was attempting a magic trick and was willing the card to stop to reveal the details of the local rural police officer's contact numbers. *No harm in entering them in my contacts list, you never know when you might need the police.*

Once done he pulled up the first number, pressed it, got a pre-recorded message informing him P.C Cowan wasn't there right now, then gave out the other number for his mobile. Bart spent the whole of the morning debating whether he should let Robbie Cowan know about Mary Macaulay. After hearing some of the worrying things she spoke about, the seemingly sinister side to Thomas Galbraith, worried him immensely in respect of Beth working at the castle. His worst fear was he might now have transferred his interest to Beth, seemed likely given she was experiencing some of the same behaviour from him.

On impulse he pressed Robbie Cowan's mobile number, sat listening to the ring tone in his ear. He was about to do disconnect when the police officer answered. He could hear a faint "Hello" which was almost drowned out by the sound of rushing wind. He caught "call you back" after which the line went dead.

Bart sat staring at his mobile screen waiting for the ring with the new name P.C Cowan displayed there. When it came, an out of breath Robbie Cowan announced, "P.C Cowan," just as Bart glanced up to see him coming in through the bar door with his mobile to his ear.

"Ah, you must be on a day off," Bart chirped. "Don't tell me you've been out there playing golf in this awful weather." He watched as his face turn from a frown to quizzical then glancing over towards the fire where Bart sat waving his mobile at him, he began to smile. He pressed his phone off and walked over.

Bart greeted him with, "Of all the bars in all the world….."

"How did you know I was here?" Robbie Cowan sounded intrigued.

"I didn't, I'm an associate member, here for lunch."

Robbie sat down in front of the fire to warm himself, "Do you play?" he asked.

"Good heavens, no!" Bart declared forcefully he couldn't abide the game. "I don't cook either, least ways not the kind of food I can get here and one of my main hobbies these days is eating." They both laughed. "I was telephoning you to meet for a chat about Mungo MacLeod, et voilà, here you are, like magic."

"Technically it's a rest day, although these days we are rarely ever 'off duty' if something crops up," Bart observed he didn't sound too concerned about it.

"I was about to eat, perhaps I could get you a drink or if you're staying for lunch maybe you would join me?" Bart invited affably.

P.C Cowan took off the jacket he was wearing over his golfing clothes to make himself comfortable. After the formalities of ordering more food and drinks they settled down with Bart politely enquiring after his golfing handicap, something he neither knew about nor understood the desire to possess, he just wanted to break the ice.

Eventually, Robbie asked, "So what do you want to talk about?"

"I was wondering how your enquiries were going in respect of Mungo MacLeod," he put in tentatively. "Is there any news of him?"

"No, very slowly, as a matter of fact, no further on than when I last saw you," the constable's disappointed was evident. "Why are you asking?"

"I expect it's true about most enquiries isn't it, people have a natural reluctance to getting involved, even where they might hold some vital piece of information however innocuous." Bart remembered the frustrations of being a private detective which was even worse with not having any formal legal right to make enquiries.

"True, we are largely mistrusted," Robbie agreed.

"Nothing much from his colleagues up at the castle then?"

"Not much at all," he admitted. "I can't even pin down who was the last person to see him around, which is odd when you consider he was there most of the time."

"Hmm, let me guess, most of them hardly knew him, no one claims to be his friend, he was a private sort of man who kept himself to himself?" Bart echoed half mocking.

It made Robbie Cowan laugh, "Pretty much the usual stance neighbours take when they are interviewed for TV news clips after discovering one of their neighbours is a murderer!"

"No one mention he might have a lady friend?" Bart asked knowing how forthcoming they were when Beth joined them for her break at the café.

Robbie's eyes widened with surprise, "They would know?"

"There are rumours. I have subsequently discovered who his lady friend is. She used to work in the Gift Shop up until last year, so yes most of them would know her," Bart revealed.

"You know this for certain?" he asked. "You've only just started there haven't you?"

"Let's say I know through a friend of an acquaintance," he was careful to keep Beth's name to himself otherwise Cowan might focus on her. So far she managed to avoid his attention because she never met Mungo MacLeod. Her desire to keep well away from anyone working for the police was entirely due to her understanding of how far her husband's influence stretched which she once mentioned to Bart, "They are all the same, they cover for each other, are like a club which can be quite sinister!" Beth didn't want any chance connections made to her past.

"As far as I know," Bart began by trying to distance himself a little from Mary Macaulay having asked her to keep their visit to herself by implying they could get into a great deal of trouble if the Castle knew what they did for her. He hoped that was sufficient to consign their visit to secrecy. "I understand she is unaware he is officially missing....."

"Oh, I thought she was meant to be his lady friend?" he interrupted.

"Yes, she saw him last on 23rd December expecting him to return. He didn't come back," Bart explained. "She believes, I think, he is upset with her and is deliberately staying away. I would rather you explain about the Laird reporting him missing."

"I see," he sounded cautious. "Where does she think he's gone?"

"Well, nowhere, he left her saying he needed to pick up the Laird's clock before Christmas Eve –the one I was mending. He didn't arrive at my shop, so I suspect this adds something at least to your time line. The only other curious thing is my quick inspection of the Castle's clocks suggests either he or someone else has wound them up or some of them since 23rd December because as of Wednesday they were still going. The question is if Mungo is missing and didn't, then who did?"

Robbie Cowan sat listening. He nodded once or twice before he asked, "Are you prepared to tell me who she is?"

"Indeed, that was the objective in meeting with you. Perhaps I might request you to handle her with some care, I think she is rather fond of Mungo MacLeod."

"Of course, that goes without saying," he seemed a little irritated that Bart would think otherwise. "With MISPERs we don't often have a happy ending I'm afraid," he sighed deeply at the memory of so many cases he'd dealt with. "We get about 30,000 people a year going missing in Scotland........of course, not all of them want to be found."

The figure confirmed what Duncan Munro told him. The amount amazed Bart, even with his knowledge of finding people he hadn't realised how big the problem was. He suspected there might even be more in England.

"The other thing I wanted to say was you might want to ask her why she left her job at the Castle which if handled carefully you will find interesting and could very well be tied up with his disappearance."

"How very cryptic, I may have to come to visit you more formally in that case," P.C Cowan got up to leave. As he watched him move across the bar to the door, Bart was put in mind of Jayson Vingoe when they used to meet for lunch at the links golf course in Wainthorpe where they were both members.

*   *   *   *   *

After his impromptu meeting with Robbie Cowan which evoked random memories of Jayson Vingoe, he was spurred on to make contact with Jay. Still a little embarrassed by his request for Agatha to speak with Emily about the dangers of going alone to London, he felt time was running out to stop her. The thought of her alone in the hostile city filled him full of horror.

Coincidentally, Bart caught Jay on a rest day. After apologising for intruding into his day off he explained about the sale of The Silver Teapot which urged him to call. Jay explained he already knew having seen the 'sold' sign over the shop and from a subsequent conversation Agatha encouraged Emily to text him to let him know.

Over the phone Bart heard a car door open and a female voice in greeting.

"I was sitting here waiting for Agatha to finish work," Bart heard him whisper his name to her. "We're going shopping." Bart immediately felt envious of the young couple's closeness. "I'll pass you over Cyrus," Jay added reminding him of his use of the other spelling of his first name when he met them both.

"Hello?" he heard the voice of Jay's wife say. He recalled the sweet trusting face of the young police officer.

"Hello, Agatha, how are you?" Bart enquired.

"We're fine thank you." He noted with envy the reference to the 'we'. "I imagine you are more concerned to learn how Emily is right now?"

"Indeed, I got a text from her about the café being sold, can you tell me anymore?" He asked, "I am most grateful for anything you can tell me."

"Well, not much I'm afraid. It's not good news really, nothing I could tell her about the pitfalls of going to London would dissuade her otherwise," she sounded abashed. "Having run the gauntlet of the woman who calls herself 'mother' to be honest I think I would rather take my chances in the 'big smoke'!"

It was a long time since Bart heard London referred to as the 'big smoke'. "Did you find out anything about her father?" Bart asked.

"I understand they are divorced now or as good as. Certainly he is no longer there. As far as I could find out from Emily he has fallen on hard times having lost his job."

Bart had a flash back of the dapper Insurance Salesman who would hold court at the bar of The Anchor, in Wainthorpe telling everyone who cared to listen what he knew about the murder of Arthur Claymore at The Art Gallery. He particularly recalled the brown suit with the tatty mackintosh he used to wear.

"So unlikely to be in a position to have Emily live with him, I take it?"

Agatha's answer wasn't encouraging, "I believe he has moved away from the coast and is living in a hostel somewhere."

How very sad thought Bart because as far as he knew he seemed to have nothing to do with Claymore's death whilst there was some suspicion Thelma Hobbs may have known about her sister's part in it even though nothing could be proven. There were tenuous links to her sister Elsie Draper and her husband's revenge fatal assault on him because of their son Peter being sexually abused by Claymore.

Bart didn't want to know how the case played out in the legal process. Rather his concern was for Emily whom he left in the thick of the aftermaths when he ran away for his own preservation.

"Thank you for trying Agatha," he knew she would feel as sad as he did. "Could I speak with Jay again please?" He heard the telephone being passed over to Jay. "Is there any news on the other matter we discussed?" Bart was referring to the Witness Protection minder 'Steve' who was trying to find him.

"It is as you suggested I believe. I'm not sure if a date has been fixed for the commencement of a trial. I believe the case is still being put together," Jay confirmed.

"Any likelihood of bail?" Bart held his breath even though he thought this extremely unlikely given Moala's previous abscondment.

"None whatsoever," came back after which he exhaled.

"Thank you my friend that is good to know at least."

"Do you have any plans to return?" Jay asked.

"Not at present," The truth was Bart hadn't given it any further thought. "On the matter of Emily I have a friend up here who will give her a home. With my commitments I am in need of someone to help me run my shop..."

"Ah, you do still have your fine collection I take it," Jay's pleasure at the news was evident. "Sadly there isn't much demand for hats around here," he laughed referring to his old shop now selling headwear and called The Mad Hatter.

"Likewise time keeping in the Highlands is a little slack, something to do with the pace of life I think since we are frozen in time for a good few months of the year!" This was Jay's first hint of where Bart was.

"Will you speak with Emily yourself?" Jay asked his voice now greatly relieved.

"Yes, I'll see if the proposition would be acceptable to her. Perhaps I'll get my friend 'Beth' to speak directly with her."

Bart heard a muffled interchange between Jay and Agatha his hand only partially covering the phone whilst Bart waited for him to speak again.

Eventually Jay went on to inform him, "The other thing you might be interested in is Agatha and I were planning on taking a little holiday – well actually we didn't have the chance of a honeymoon due to our work commitments. We were considering taking our new motor home, I think what the American's call a Winnebago, to explore some of the places in this country we have never seen." Bart listened with interest. "How is the weather where you are?"

Bart sighed with the relief at the silent proposal to help Emily to get up to him.

"Absolutely wonderful!" he boomed down the phone. "I'm sure you will both enjoy such a beautiful part of the world."

"We will speak again to make some definite arrangements," Jay confirmed.

Bart sat once again in front of his crackling log fire sipping a welcoming glass of whisky, going over in his mind all the things he needed to do to enable him to get Emily away from her mother and safely housed with Beth. He chuckled at the idea he did rather attract waifs and strays like moths around a naked flame. Even so it did please him to think his beloved collection of timepieces would once again be appreciated by someone who loved them as much as he did.

CHAPTER 29

Seldom was Bart excited by anything. After experiencing far too many disappointments in life he conditioned himself never to look forward to anything, tempting fate was just asking for things to go wrong. However, the prospect of meeting Jayson Vingoe again filled him with such bonhomie he felt sure he would not be disappointed. Needless to say Emily was absolutely elated when they spoke about her coming to Scotland; her only reservation being she was concerned she would be unable to pay her way if she came. She knew very well, she told him, his old shop didn't generate sufficient turnover to pay her enough wages to allow her to be self-sufficient.

He eased her fears by telling her about his new contract with the Castle, one aspect of which was a retainer for maintaining their clocks; his hope was she would play a big part in the repair side of the business as well as managing the shop in his absence.

"Cool!" her relief was great also reminding Bart she was still the young girl he once knew.

Jayson and Agatha organised Emily's removal from Wainthorpe-on-sea whilst trying as much as possible to keep away from the animosity generated by her mother when she announced her intention not to go with her to Grimsby. She confided in them later she thought her mother's concern was more about losing someone to help her in the new café she planned to open in Grimsby than in losing her only daughter. Emily assured her mother this was no different to if she had stayed on at school, got her exams, then gone off to University; the prospect of which her mother denied her.

Their parting wasn't much of a tearful one. Jay later described to Bart how Thelma Hobbs was aggressive towards him and Agatha, accusing them of abducting her against her will as they loaded her possessions into the camper. Thelma Hobbs blamed them both for 'turning' her daughter's head from doing what was right and proper in coming with her to Grimsby. Jayson's efforts were engaged mostly in keeping Agatha calm, her famous temper threatened to erupt wanting to confront Thelma Hobbs by telling her exactly what they were doing, saving Emily from a life of exploitation by her. However, they both didn't need a complaint against them being lodged with the police even though there was no case in law because of Emily's age. They knew the complaint would stay on their personnel files anyway, and worse perhaps even drawn unwanted attention towards the absent 'Cyrus Bartholomew's' whereabouts should anyone have investigated the move further.

There was no waving goodbye or hugs as they would have expected which only went to confirm what they were doing was right. The only doubt being during the first hour of the journey Emily remained quietly in the back of the traveller hugging a large misshapen parcel covered in brown paper and bubble wrap. Their concerns soon faded after their first stop at the motorway services for a break whilst refuelling. Emily was persuaded to relinquish hold of her parcel to join them for breakfast after which she stretched her legs walking round the gift shop where she purchased a packet of boiled sweets having announced herself to be a little car sick. She found the sweets always helped her with it. Jay told Bart afterwards she became livelier, inquisitive about their progress. They didn't see her hugging anything.

Bart's contribution to the 'move' was to book the newlyweds into the hotel making a secret arrangement with Phil Miller for them to have the 'honeymoon' suite which he knew about from a previous conversation. Phil once told him about a group of people who came to stay each year meeting up from their homes around Scotland. They would sit in the bar every evening where they sang either together or in random solos to the accompaniment of someone playing guitar, "they were like a group of wandering folk minstrels," he told Bart. At least on one occasion, the manager informed him, in order to get them to go to bed, so he could close the bar, he told them the bar was directly below Room 10, the Honeymoon suite, which was currently occupied and they were disturbing his guests. Bart was subsequently shown the room because he doubted there was a honeymoon suite, only to be surprised when he saw room 10 contained a four poster bed.

As his gift to Jay and Agatha he arranged for them to stay in the honeymoon suite after their long journey to Scotland. He also arranged a 'special' evening meal for all of them, including Beth, in the hotel restaurant on the evening they arrived.

Bart spent the morning on tenterhooks at the prospect of the arrival of his old friends. They were to split the journey up country by pre-arranging a stay overnight on a camp site. Sleeping in the camper was a bit of a squash with three of them, Emily's possessions, as well as their own luggage, however, they managed. Bart found himself many times walking over to the door of the shop to peer down towards Main Street, then up at the sky from where earlier he saw one or two lone flakes of snow drifting down. He prayed to the great Norse 'snow god' Ullr (also Patron Saint of Skiers, the son of Sif and stepson of Thor, the God of Thunder) to be patient for a little longer to allow his visitors time to get over the top at the Glenshee ski resort before letting the threatening clouds loose of their obvious heavy burden.

When they actually arrived, finding Bart's shop, he had vacated temporarily into the back as he often did for the noon chorus to be away from any untoward occurrences as was his habit. Since living in Scotland he hadn't once experienced one of his blackouts like before. But then he hadn't tempted fate even when the first chimes came, he would rush into the back room or outside into his small back yard to get away, to be on the safe side.

When the last of the chimes finished Bart came back into the shop to see the large traveller pulling to a stop outside. He rushed over to unlock the door as Jay, Agatha and Emily emerged wearily from it. They stood in a row looking up at the sign, The March of Time with the caricature of a white rabbit with bow tie and matching waist coat. Emily's hands clapped together at the sight as she jigged on the spot; her beaming smile left no doubt whatsoever of her approval. Jay and Agatha laughed at her show of delight.

Bart opened the shop door standing on the threshold with his hands on his hips, "Are you laughing at my caricature young lady?" he grinned broadly already knowing she would love the sign.

Emily bounded over to him, threw her arms around his stout frame declaring, "It's wonderful!"

Bart fought back his embarrassment at such a show of affection. When she released him he bellowed, "Come in, come in, you must be in need of a welcoming drink!"

Emily was the first through the door leaving Bart to greet his long lost friends. Jayson shook hands whilst Agatha kissed his cheek in greeting, "So good to see you again…..you look so well," she said.

Bart patted his Aran sweater where his belly was barely hidden beneath, "It's not all cable stitch," he laughed. The air and the food seem to suit me well enough."

The newlyweds followed him inside where they saw Emily standing absolutely still in the middle of the shop slowly turning on a 360 degree axis. Bart held up his arm to halt them where they were placing a finger over his lips to encourage their silence.

When Emily turned back towards him Bart asked, "Well?"

"There's a hint of one somewhere," she announced, "Which I shall bring back into the fold." She grinned.

"Excellent!" Bart boomed knowing Emily could detect any clock out of sync in his shop, even if the subtlety evaded him.

He turned dropping the catch on the door, "Come through," Bart led them through the shop to the back room. "Warm yourselves whilst I fix refreshments."

"You've set up very well Cyrus," Agatha's complimentary comment seemed to please him. "From what we've seen so far of the countryside this is such a beautiful place to live."

"Indeed, true and no matter what the season, there is always something wonderful to discover. I particularly love autumn, by October there are so many different colours to see when the trees change from green, to yellow, gold, orange, crimson, russet, they are quite breath taking."

"We saw a lot of deer coming through the mountain pass, they came right down near the road," Emily said excitedly.

"Looking for food left for them no doubt," Bart added.

Whilst he was making hot drinks he asked about their departure from Wainthorpe being particularly concerned to know if Emily suffered any regrets moving away from her family.

When he looked over to judge her reaction she was devouring a slice of cake from a selection he purchased especially for the occasion from The Black-faced Sheep in Aboyne where they were made. She certainly showed no sign of regret.

He could see she was enjoying the cakes anyway, "For your information the cakes are made at one of my favourite places to eat. The Black-faced Sheep you will love and is very close to where my friend Beth Grant has a cottage on the Balmoral Estate, where you will be living. I have to say Beth also makes the most amazing cakes which you will be pleased with no doubt," he saw her making short work of the slice going in for another.

"She doesn't mind me living there?" Emily asked pausing between bites.

"Indeed not and being young herself I'm sure the two of you will get along famously." Bart felt they both missed out on a normal early life and would discover a great deal together they both ought to have done sooner in their lives.

Later, after Jayson and Agatha booked into the hotel's honeymoon suite he arranged for them, they all convened in the hotel dining room where they met Beth. Bart noticed how both Beth and Emily retreated into their former shyness until the meal moved on a little making them gradually begin to feel more comfortable. He was very well aware Beth knew Agatha was a police officer and Jayson a CSI in the same force.

He found himself drawn to how much Emily seemed to have matured since he last saw her even though she was never really a child she appeared to have acquired more confidence. He tried not to dwell on attributing her maturity to the very stark experience she went through when they found her cousin Peter (her one time best friend) locked away in a drugs and alcohol clinic. After finding him, then helping him to escape, Emily sat with him through some of the worst stories he told the police about his sexual abuse at the hands of Arthur Claymore's paedophile ring. No girl of fifteen especially one as innocent as Emily was back then, should have been privy to hearing such things. However, Peter refused to let go of her hand during the telling.

He was pleased to note the change in her which he thought in part due to her mother forcing her to leave school which meant she was no longer subjected to the bullying she previously endured from other children. Even so, her physical appearance had also changed. The once spotty awkward young teenager was replaced by quite a stunning young woman. Her long auburn curls tamed by proper styling, were no longer allowing her to hide behind them in a shy manner. She seemed to ooze confidence. The pride with which she entertained them with her clock-mending stories made him realise how much she enjoyed interacting with those customers she came into contact with.

"You must appreciate," she directed at Bart, "How you feel when someone thinks you have miraculously mended their prized clock, when all you have done is taken it apart, released an overwound mechanism, then put it back together again?" she grinned broadly. "And no, I didn't feel ashamed letting them think I did much more," she laughed as if someone dared to criticise her. "Without me they wouldn't feel the pleasure they obviously did at hearing the clock tick again!"

Bart laughed but couldn't help thinking how he'd let Beth believe the same about her Grandfather clock. When he glanced furtively over at her he saw her face beaming back at him.

She was obviously directing her comments at him, "The point is, surely *they* couldn't get it going, but *you* could which to them is priceless!"

"Exactly," Emily agreed. "And I didn't charge exorbitant amounts for my skills!"

Bart found himself laughing loudly at the pair of them. "I think maybe we'll have to sort out a sliding scale of charges according to how 'difficult' the repair is as well as the time we spend on them." He hadn't charged Beth anything for his releasing the Grandfather clock's mechanism so his conscience was clear.

Bart was more than content to listen to the young people around him especially to see how comfortable the newlyweds seemed and as the evening wore on how Beth and Emily enjoyed opening up to each other. Beth entertained about the castle's horses and hounds much to Emily's delight whilst Beth enjoyed her stories about the clocks she'd rescued. He felt relieved by what he witnessed which reinforced his judgement for the part he played in taking Emily away from her mother.

When the evening came to an end with Jay and Agatha transferring all of Emily's things from the traveller into Beth's van, Emily hugged them both for bringing her to Scotland, they said their goodbyes. Jay and Agatha went back inside to their honeymoon suite whilst Bart stood watching Beth's van follow the A93 towards home. He stood alone watching until the tail lights disappeared around the bend out of sight. With a sigh he crossed over the road towards Main Street to walk the distance back home. One or two flakes of snow fluttered past his face as he progressed and he whispered, "Be patient Ullr, for a little longer."

CHAPTER 30

Bart lay in his bed having woken up to the realisation he retired to bed the night before without closing the heavy drapes at his bedroom windows. The room was, therefore, bright even though he could detect no sun. The brightness he knew could only come from a crisp snow filled day made more convincing by the very large snowflakes fluttering past his windows. He could feel the chill against his face. Moving from under his heavy winter duvet would be a challenge.

He glanced at the bedside clock establishing the fact he slept in after nine o'clock. He heard the church bells from the nearest of the churches across the way from his shop announcing the Sunday early morning service. He rose rather stiffly, his arthritic limbs no longer a mere hint, gave ample warning he must do something about registering with the village general practice doctors, something he kept putting off due to his status being 'et qui non est' – a person who doesn't exist or as he preferred to think of himself as 'et cavae hominem' – a hollow man.

The T. S. Elliot poem Hollow Men he once committed to memory sprang back into his mind:

"Is it like this

In death's other Kingdom

Walking alone

At the hour when we are

Trembling with tenderness

Lips that would kiss

Form prayers to broken stone."

He stopped his mind regurgitating the rest remembering more starkly lonely times when the words brought tears to his eyes. He didn't want to feel sad or sorry for himself, after all last night he was surrounded by friends, all of them good people, he wanted to count himself lucky.

His legs felt painful standing up as he put his weight on them. What would a doctor tell him anyway? You will improve if you lose weight, was the cure for almost every known illness these days, even though it might be true in his case. He walked jerkily over to the window, the one overlooking The Brae and part of Main Street. It was now covered in half a foot of untrodden white snow which gave him hope he would be able to take his Sunday papers those few yards to The Griddle Iron for his Sunday morning ritual.

Later he sat in his usual window seat looking out at the hillside of snow covered fir trees, with his pile of newspapers the young lad delivered earlier, whilst he waited for his morning coffee and snack. There was a tap on the window at the side of him. To his delight Jayson Vingoe stood beaming at him from outside, muffled up in a Gortex jacket and flat cap. He waved walking into the shop.

Bart's early melancholic mood dissolved at the sight of him. "Like old times," Bart declared. "Splendid." Then he realised he was alone. "Is Agatha okay?" he enquired a little concerned.

"She is, indeed," Jay took off his cap then removed his coat. "She's having a lie in. I thought I would take this opportunity to join you."

"How did you know....?" Bart began before he realised, "Am I so predictable?"

"Well, all I know is if I lived here, this is what I would be doing on a Sunday morning," he grinned knowing his old friend would not dispute it.

After he sat down and Max took his order for coffee only, he had just eaten his breakfast at the hotel, Bart pushed the pile of newspapers towards him to take one; for a while they sat comfortably in familiar silence, each reading the latest news.

When Max brought Bart's toasted tea cake he placed the paper he was reading aside and they began to catch up on the current situation in their lives. With nothing new to add to the Toni Maola arrest situation, Jay told him everything seemed to have gone really quiet. In the same way there was nothing to add concerning the policeman he called 'Steve' who was looking for him.

He didn't know why but Bart confided in Jay about the missing ghillie Mungo MacLeod from the castle whilst Jay quietly listened with interest.

"And you say there is nothing amiss at his cottage?"

"No…. nothing. Everything P.C Cowan told me looks like he still ought to be there – in fact, all his belongings are intact."

"How strange," was Jay's only comment.

"I get the impression if anyone other than the Laird, say his lady friend Mary, reported him missing, there wouldn't even be this level of investigation taking place. Normally only a general circulation of his details is done."

"What's the forensic set up like in Scotland?" Jay suddenly asked.

"I believe as good as anywhere else in the UK," Bart said remembering the conversation when he asked Robbie Cowan if any forensics would be undertaken at Mungo's cottage. "Although speaking to a police contact I've made it would be unlikely in the case of a MISPER unless foul play was suspected – they wouldn't be able to cope given the numbers of people going missing each year."

"Hmm," Jay replied.

"Why do you ask?"

"Oh, last night Agatha and I were talking hypothetically about living somewhere like Scotland," he revealed. "I think Agatha is rather taken by these parts, she likes the idea of a slower pace of life."

"It is different, though I must say it changes the whole of your wardrobe, certainly in the winter!" They both laughed. "Old bones are harder to keep warm I've discovered."

He watched Jay staring out towards the hills opposite as he quietly mulled things over.

"Are you serious about moving up here?" Bart asked.

"Well, I'm sure you are aware things these days are more dangerous, especially for a police officer," Jay looked a little furtive as if he were weighing up what to tell Bart next, "Especially for a pregnant Police Officer."

"My word! How lovely, Agatha is pregnant?" The delight on Bart's face spurred Jay on.

"I think what we unearthed at Wainthorpe made us think about the kind of world we are bringing a child into," he sounded most concerned. "We both want our children to be safe to be children as long as they can be."

"Yes, I can see that," Bart agreed. "One of the reasons I wanted Emily up here rather than on her own in London."

"Quite," Jay agreed. "She will be safe up here with your friend and you to look out for her."

The mention of Beth as his 'friend' made him realise he hadn't told Jay about how he met her or anything about her. Of course, it wasn't his place to divulge anything of a personal nature to him. He merely offered, "I do seem to have a way of attracting waifs and strays," which he hoped was sufficient to relay Beth's vulnerability without divulging any details.

Jay searched his face which revealed there was a whole different story contained in his words.

215

"I'm thinking perhaps even given the harshness of the weather up here this is a better place to be, am I right?"

"Well certainly perhaps easier to lose oneself in," Bart admitted half-heartedly. "Especially when the snows come and we get cut off. Even so we do have our fair share of passing strangers."

Bart took a few minutes to explain about meeting the very feral private investigator Selwyn Jones of the ABC Detective Agency.

"Now he is someone I'd like to know more about," he told Jay as his eyebrows rose in that 'if at all possible' inviting gesture.

"Any idea where he's based?" Jay asked casually.

"Yes, I believe he's from Newport in Wales," he said. "Caution is in order as he seems to work for police officers." Bart raised a finger to the side of his nose as if in warning.

Thereafter their chat was of a general nature with Bart enquiring about their holiday plans with the traveller discovering they intended to take in Aberdeen first before touring across the north coast then down the West coast. They wanted to visit John O'Groats and so many other places they didn't have enough days to take in.

Bart envied them the freedom, wishing them well on their adventure together. He knew wherever they went it was about being together that was the most important part.

*   *   *   *   *   *

Emily felt sad parting from Agatha and Jay whilst also very excited to begin her new life with Beth. It was almost too much to take in at first. She barely registered the drive to the cottage, being sure she couldn't describe how they got there especially as the one or two large flakes of snow she noticed outside the hotel multiplied by the time they reached it.

When she met Sandy the Foxhound he seemed inquisitive enough to meet them at the door to watch as Emily's luggage was brought inside, thereafter his interest waned. Her attempt to fuss him was shunned. He went back into the kitchen to lie in front of the dying embers of the fire.

Beth's first task was to place some logs on the fire to stop it from going out completely. Emily watched with interest as the logs caught alight and began to burn.

"I try not to let the fire go out in this kind of weather," Beth told Emily. "We have no other heating."

Emily was surprised, "It feels really warm," she searched around for any sign of central heating, detecting none.

"The stone building keeps the warmth inside," she sounded quite knowledgeable Emily thought.

"I don't think Sandy cares for me much," Emily admitted sadly watching the dog sleeping. Even without the experience of having a pet of her own she did expect a dog to be friendlier.

"He's the same with me," Beth told her. "Well actually with anyone other than Fraser from the castle, I think because he is a trained hunting dog so not used to being a pet. Fraser raised him and trained him so I expect there is a bond there."

Emily inspected the animal lying quietly in front of the fire where the flames began to take on new life. She was thinking he didn't look much like a hunting dog either, she couldn't imagine him chasing across the countryside after a fox. She found the thought somewhat pleasing.

During the course of their first conversation over a mug of hot chocolate before bed time, Emily raised the issue perhaps Sandy might be lonely on his own. She knew as an only child she was drawing a comparison with her own past life, after spending so much of her time on her own, without any real friends, other than her cousin Peter occasionally to talk to before he stopped altogether. That night she heard mention of Elizabeth Elspeth Grant and the 'other' dog running away after the old lady died.

Beth was reluctant to tell her more with it being so late. Emily yawned a lot looking like she needed her bed after such a long journey up to Scotland. She also didn't want to say too much about the strangeness of the cottage, this was something she felt Emily needed to discover for herself like she did. They parted on the landing with Emily retiring into the guest bedroom.

When Beth came downstairs next day, the kitchen fire was showing a healthy blaze with Sandy's place in front empty. After talk about his loneliness she briefly wondered if he too ran away during the night but this was dispelled when the outside door opened and Emily burst through, with a healthy flush to her cheeks. She was out of breath as if she had been running. Sandy rushed past her inside as if he too was being chased. He flopped down in front of the fire.

Emily grinned beckoning Beth over to the door, "It's snowed!" she declared gleefully.

When Beth peeked outside she saw the pathway cleared across the yard with a small patch indented into the garden, with access cleared all the way to the food store in the outbuildings.

"How did you know?" Beth asked surprised.

"Know what?" She asked. "When I came down Sandy walked over to the door so I assumed he needed to go outside."

"Yes but....." Beth pointed at where she could see the unmistakable yellow snow where Sandy left his mark.

"Ah, he's a strange one. He wouldn't come out even when I cleared this far. He sat patiently waiting, so I cleared a patch for him," she grinned remembering his antics. "You know the silly thing wouldn't do his business if I was watching him?!"

Beth knew all too well what he was like, "You cleared all the way to the food store," Beth pointed to the first stable.

"Food store?" Emily said mystified. "Err, actually....." she grinned, beckoned Beth further outside where around the corner of the cottage she could see where Emily built a large snowman in the place where she usually parked her van. "I needed the snow, so I took it from the pathway." She grinned sheepishly.

Beth could see where she managed to find sufficient stones for two eyes, a nose and a curved line for a grin.

"We'll have to see if we can find him a hat and scarf, it's pretty cold out here," Beth suggested.

They rushed back inside closing the kitchen door.

"What sort of food do you keep out there?" Emily asked as she ate her breakfast at the big table.

"I'll show you later," Beth promised. "So how did you sleep?"

"Best sleep I've ever had," was Emily's reply.

Beth merely nodded and smiled knowing the cottage was happy with the new family member.

CHAPTER 31

The sudden, though not severe, fall of snow that cast its white carpet over Bart's world would not last for long. It did, however, give him an excuse to stay at home for an extra couple of days due to the road conditions. Side roads especially were treacherous for his battered old Peugeot 208 which was ill equipped to battle through such conditions. He was reminded for future winters he would need to invest in a more suitable vehicle whilst he lived where he did. He pushed away the thought his current home might only be a temporary one. Advancing age convinced him the nomad life of a fugitive might not be for him.

At ten o'clock on Monday morning he brought his lap top through to the shop where he saw, by the steady snowfall through the shop door window pane, he might be a little optimistic in opening up. He left the door locked with the shop sign showing open. *If anyone is in urgent need of a time piece they can always knock.*

He sat down at his work table to begin to upload the photographs from his mobile phone of the many clocks he discovered during his 'walk through' of the rooms at the castle. He was surprised how many there were when he came to create his computer inventory grid. There were few he discovered still ticking, they were mostly the longer running ones needing less attention and mostly concentrated in what he described as 'family' rooms or those used most often by the Laird, like the library.

It occurred to Bart he knew nothing about Duncan Munro's immediate family circumstances. So far on his brief visits he hadn't encountered any evidence of them actually living at the castle. The thought diverted him away from his clock task in order to delve into some of the castle's history. He learnt the castle called Daingneach (meaning 'Stronghold') was originally built by the Grant clan, being described as a Tower House, which was further recorded as 'preserved, in use as a residence', currently owned by the Munro's. He marvelled at the Scots (certainly the nobility) who undoubtedly loved their history, particularly anything to do with clan rivalry and plenty to do with hard fought battles.

Not surprising really given this particular 'stronghold' with its evident fortification has a vast armoury collection displayed inside.

What surprised Bart more was the number of castles of all descriptions left in ruins over the centuries. He wondered in passing about their hidden stories of clan disputes that must have taken place. He read about so much fighting it left him feeling giddy.

He was surprised to find the current Laird's wife and children were recorded as living there. He sat pensively trying to remember whether he saw any evidence of a 'family' in any of the castle's rooms he'd been in so far. He couldn't recall even seeing any other members of staff other than the 'cheery' secretary Thomas Galbraith. Of course he hadn't ventured into the domestic parts of the castle, like the kitchen, where he expected the household staff would spend their time with domestic duties.

Strange though.

During his brief sojourn through the Scottish castles he came upon a link for 'Scottish nobility' reading about the title 'Laird' as reserved for owners of larger estates or pieces of land in Scotland. Eventually he found his way into the realms of 'who's who' which gave him Duncan Munro, his wife Anna (nee Muller) known to split their time between Scotland and Switzerland (where their children were at finishing school). Seemingly they spent most of the winter months away in sunnier climes.

"Ah!" Bart declared out loud as if solving a mystery, "And who could blame them!" He shivered suddenly feeling chilly and in need of yet another cup of hot coffee which he went to make bringing his antiquated fan heater through to the shop.

He deliberately hadn't installed a central heating radiator in the shop when he upgraded the old heating system in the original house because the excess heat he felt might cause shrinkage, warping or even swelling in the most highly-treated wood some of the clocks in his collection were made from. He preferred to keep them within cooler air flows, besides which having a radiator in the shop would limit the space, both wall and standing available to use. Certainly this amount of wasted space would inhibit him collecting any new clocks should he come across one he really wanted. No, he recalled thinking, he would continue with his old fan heater if he needed any additional heating in the shop. His minor regret soon drifted away after he plugged the fan heater and began to feel the benefit.

The next time he looked up to check on the weather, Bart could see the land rover defender/SP60 DFL pulling to a halt outside. The police markings left him in no doubt the vehicle belonged to P.C Robbie Cowan whom he assumed was here to see him. He stood to unlock the door whilst watching the police officer get out, gingerly treading the few steps up to his door.

"I did say I might come back," Robbie announced when Bart opened the door to let him in.

"Indeed, you did," Bart agreed. "Come inside out of the cold."

Once inside he walked him through to the back room where a warming blaze greeted them. Bart moved immediately over to the kettle, he knew the young officer would not refuse a brew. They settled in front of the fire, each taking an arm chair. Bart reached across throwing another log on the fire from the stacked basket on the hearth.

"How can I help you?" Bart asked. "Must be urgent to bring you out on a day like this."

"I would na'say 'urgent'," he replied. "It's just I can'na say how long Mungo MacLeod has been missing. After speaking with Mary Macaulay who as ye'know last saw him on 23rd December, I'm unable to narrow the time he's been missing down further. Either everyone is being difficult or they really don't remember."

"I see, so you didn't get anything from Mary then?" Bart asked looking a bit disappointed. He rather hoped she would open up in the same way she did to him and to Beth.

"I would na'say that," Robbie admitted. "Ma time line isn't much further on."

"Ah, well I've been doing a little research of my own in respect of Duncan Munro. From what I read, he does spend a considerable amount of time away from the castle with his family which might suggest there could be a limited number of staff around, certainly at Christmas or the New Year." Bart explained. "I imagine his absence would also be a sign, apart from the animal care needed at the stables, for the staff to take holidays. So there would be fewer people left there anyway."

Robbie's relief showed, "You mean he wouldn't be missed until Laird Munro returned?"

"Exactly so!" Bart declared. "He is after all his ghillie, so answerable to no one else."

They drifted into silence drinking their coffees, both gazing into the fire until Bart added, "Of course, none of which explains the clocks."

"The clocks?"

"Why some are, or at least were, working last week when I did a swift check of them. It does rather suppose either Mungo wound them up more recently in keeping with his duties or someone else did."

"Yes, I see, it does'na explain why he didn't return to see Mary Macaulay after promising he would," Robbie reminded him to Bart's relief, hearing at least she opened up a little about her relationship with Mungo.

"Or why he didn't come here on the 23rd of December to pick up the Laird's clock like he intended?"

P.C Cowan seemed surprised as if he'd forgotten, "Yes, of course, it does rather suggest 'something' happened to stop him. If I've picked up anything about the man, he's a very straight honest sort."

"Did you get anything else from Mary.......have you informed her he's officially missing?"

For one moment Bart thought Robbie Cowan might end the conversation there by pulling police confidentiality on him. "Did she, for example, mention why she left her job in the Castle gift shop?" Bart nudged him on without giving away anything confidential that Mary told them about Thomas Galbraith.

Their eyes locked searchingly for a moment before Robbie Cowan went on, each assessing whether they could trust the other.

"I did as you requested," Robbie disclosed. "It wasn't difficult to see how much he means to her. It's never easy to deliver bad news. She was shocked, there's na'doot. She was tearful until I mentioned missing items from the castle, then she got extremely angry at the implication he might have stolen anything from the Laird....she confirmed him to be an honest man." Bart was relieved. "She did open up about being harassed and stalked by Thomas Galbraith."

"Did she actually use those words?" Bart asked knowing Mary hadn't used them whilst talking to him or to Beth. In fact, she was quite reticent to do so, not knowing whether somehow she might have unknowingly courted his attention.

"Well no. What else would you call them, if not those things?"

"True," agreed Bart. "Look I need to tell you about my own experience with the Laird's secretary, particularly something strange which happened the last time I was there.....err, Wednesday last week." Bart filled him in about his seeming annoyance at Bart being brought in to undertake the inventory. Especially, how when he'd last spoken to Robbie agreeing to try to identify the clocks that were working, he resorted to photographing each clock in situ to enable a more rapid check. "I was in the Laird's library," here Bart pulled up the photograph of the fire place with the impressive library clock on the mantel, "I was taking pictures of a pair of carriage clocks," he showed him the alcoves with the fire basket in between, "You have to go into the fire place to take closer shots," he showed both pictures.

"They aren't an exact pair, are they?" Robbie observed.

"Quite," said Bart. "In fact, you don't have to be an expert to guess which one is the most valuable, it is quite obvious."

"Yes, I can see," Robbie agreed.

"I was taking the one of the inferior clock when I didn't hear Galbraith enter the library. He verbally accosted me wanting to know what I was doing........why I was even in the library at all! I can tell you he was extremely aggressive."

"I see," his reply didn't hold much conviction.

"Well actually that wasn't the strange part," Bart remembered the incident clearly prompting him to reconsider the man's equanimity.

"Strange, you say?"

"It was as if he'd gone into a trance. He stood staring at the fire basket like he expected the wood to suddenly spontaneously combust. He actually looked.......well, quite frightened."

"Not just angry to see you there?"

"Well, he'd already expressed anger, his argument being the library wouldn't be a room open to the public...."

"Sorry, what d'you mean open to the public?"

"The purpose of cataloguing all the contents of the Castle is for insurance purposes in the event of the Laird opening the castle to the public sometime in the future."

"Oh, so that's likely then?" he heard the same from one or two castle staff he spoken to. "So do you suppose Thomas Galbraith doesn't approve of opening the castle to the public?"

"I've not really considered that. I assumed his attitude was because he has been given the job of co-ordinating all of the inventories – all the artefacts, collections and furnishings –including cataloguing all those books in the library, some of which are possibly very rare books making them extremely valuable."

Robbie Cowan made a face, "Are there lots?"

Bart grinned, "Couldn't happen to a nicer fellow!"

"I can see you don't like the man much," the policeman laughed.

"I don't dislike people easily, though you meet a fair mixture working in a shop," Bart's reply held some conviction though most of his experience with strange people was during his P.I days. "I don't respond too well to openly hostile folk."

Robbie Cowan was once again studying Bart intensely whilst he thought about Galbraith's behaviour towards Beth. Personally, Bart found Galbraith rather sinister preferring not to mention this to the police officer, he knew she wouldn't like herself brought to his attention even though he feared for her safety.

"I have asked Mary Macaulay to contact me should Galbraith resume pressing his attentions on her," Robbie informed him thinking perhaps Bart's obvious concerns about the man were about Mary. He took Bart's smile as indicative of his approval. "Even so, you can'nae arrest someone for buying flowers for a lady, can you?"

"No, of course not……then you were the one who used the word 'stalking'….."

"You think I should have a word with Galbraith….?"

"No, no of course not," Bart interrupted quickly, the last thing he wanted was to antagonise Thomas Galbraith who might think Beth complained about him to the police putting her visibly in his sight which wasn't what she needed. He suddenly felt a little more comfortable now Beth wasn't living alone in her remote cottage. He tried to forget Emily was only a child, even though she was mature beyond her years. "It's best to keep a 'watching' brief under the circumstances. You being 'around' making enquiries about Mungo MacLeod should also help curb any odd tendencies he might have."

Just then he heard the tinkle of the shop bell making him realise he hadn't relocked the door after letting his visitor in.

"A customer!" Bart muttered getting up to serve them. When he moved out into the shop he found Emily standing going quietly through her usual ritual of listening for any anomalies amongst the ticking clocks.

"Heck, child, I didn't expect you to turn out on a day like today!" Bart's surprise at seeing her there just as he was thinking about her and Beth alone in the cottage made him forget not to call her 'child' as he knew this irritated her. On this occasion she didn't respond or perhaps it didn't register with her.

She smiled broadly, "The main roads aren't too bad, mostly clear now. Beth has gone up to the castle to help Fraser as he's short staffed." This also surprised Bart making him feel nervous in respect of Galbraith being there. "She dropped me off at the bus stop in Crathie which brought me all the way nearly to your door. How cool is that?"

Once again Bart observed Emily's transformation from the gawky teenager he first met. She was positively radiant in her newly found confidence. "When I saw the police car outside I did wonder.....it reminded me of....." she stopped as her face revealed the déjà vu experiences back in Wainthorpe.

Robbie Cowan appeared out of the back room, his police hat in his hand. He was smiling, "I'll let you get on," he told Bart. "We'll catch up again soon."

He moved over to the door putting on his hat, nodded at Emily whom he took for a customer before he left.

"Who was he?" Emily asked flushing slightly on seeing the young constable.

"He's our local beat officer, P.C Cowan," Bart refrained from offering any further explanation.

Emily laughed, "My Mum used to say they'll go anywhere for a free cuppa!" She didn't add she also warned her never to allow them a free one if they came into The Silver Teapot or she also added *bloody parasites* with her warning.

"You'll want a hot drink yourself after your journey," Bart suggested.

Emily moved towards the inner door, "I'll do it!" She said eagerly feeling the comfortable sensation like old times. Bart moved to the door to lock up once again and went into the back to update Emily on a few things she needed to know about living up in the Highlands.

CHAPTER 32

Bart was reminded about their previous tea drinking sessions when Emily presented him with the old Willow patterned tea cup, noticing she also found the Crown Derby hand painted floral one she used back in Wainthorpe. He remembered she supplied both of them which she purchased from a car boot sale, they both had chipped saucers. In fact, he'd forgotten he kept them when he moved here. Even hidden behind other things in the cupboard she managed to find them. He was comforted by the feeling of familiarity.

Bart began to show her his new computer inventory whilst she sifted through the pictures of the clocks he collected on his mobile phone camera.

"I've only just begun to research them to estimate their value," he told her.

He could see the excitement register on Emily's face, "Is this something I could help with?" she asked enthusiastically. "I could learn a lot about clocks."

"Yes, of course," Bart pulled up the photograph of the carriage clocks in the fireplace alcoves in the castle library. "To start with see what you can find out about these. I think the fine looking one might be French, it's not much to go on I know." Emily merely smiled, took the lap top into the shop where she could also attend to any customers wandering in.

Bart sat quietly, his thoughts straying once again to Thomas Galbraith. The strange look he observed on his face disturbed him more than he so far admitted to himself. He felt sure knowing Beth turned out on a day like today to help Fraser would leave her exposed to this strangely nervous man. He worried because there would be few people around at the castle which made matters worse.

On impulse he sent her a text: "You okay up there?" in the hopes she was in a position to telephone him back. She rang him after some fifteen minutes of fretting coming straight in with, "Did Emily arrive okay?"

"Yes, she's fine, the bus comes all the way down to the terminus outside The Griddle Iron, no problem," he replied. "What about you?"

"I'm okay, it was a bit slippery on some side roads but the main route is clear. It's a little quiet here though. 'Joyless' Joy didn't turn in so I'm covering for her in the gift shop this morning until after lunch when we close." Bart didn't know whether to be pleased or not as he knew Galbraith wouldn't fail to see her working in the gift shop if the café was also open.

He didn't want to express his concerns in case he unnerved her, so he quickly updated her about his morning visit from Robbie Cowan.

"It's good Mary raised the issue of our friend," Beth replied. "Oh!" he heard her whisper.

"What is it?" he asked knowing Galbraith must have come into the shop.

"Got to go, he's coming over."

"Okay, phone me back when you can!" Bart ordered sharply as the line disconnected.

When he looked up a worried expression on his face, his eyes met Emily's as she stood in the doorway from the shop.

She appeared embarrassed being caught watching him, "I wasn't eavesdropping – are you okay Mr. Bartholomew?"

He beckoned her in, "I'm fine Emily," he was a little shocked at hearing her address him using his previous name. "I think I ought to update you," he told her. "You need to call me Sirus, I am Sirus Jeffries now," he began to explain a little about his circumstances and why he moved away from Wainthorpe-on-Sea.

"Ah, I did see the name outside on your sign, I assumed perhaps this was the previous owner," she said. Bart once again recognised how astute she was for her age. "Thank you for telling me, I wouldn't want to make a mistake. I know the man back in Wainthorpe is looking for you."

"Yes, I am wanted to give evidence against a really bad man they have now managed to capture, which is why I went into the Witness Protection programme in Wainthorpe setting up my clock shop."

She smiled, "I'm pleased you did, though I wouldn't want anything bad to happen to you. Is this how you know Beth?"

He shook his head, "Err, no, I met her up here...she's.....￼" he suddenly found himself lost for words or what to tell her about Lily Frances.

She shocked him by saying, "She's also a runaway isn't she?"

"She's told you her story?" Bart asked surprised.

Emily's head moved from side to side, "Only, I should tell her if I see anyone hanging around the cottage....so I assumed.....we were both hiding from our pasts."

"You know sometimes I think you are extremely intuitive," Bart stopped himself adding *for a child*.

"Is this why you sounded so worried just now? You were talking to Beth weren't you?"

Again Bart smiled at her, "Yes, I was. No, not about her past, but I do need to update you about why the Policeman was here," he decided Emily needed to know about Mungo MacLeod being missing. "Put the kettle on," he told her, "I'll get the biscuits."

For the next hour he told her everything he knew about the missing ghillie. He mentioned his concerns about the Laird's secretary Thomas Galbraith. They drank tea with the remains of the cake from the Black-faced Sheep which Emily ate whilst she listened. There was a point at which she looked intrigued saying, "This is like one of those TV detective dramas!" She grinned gleefully reminding him she was after all only a child.

He was more or less at the end of his tale when his mobile rang giving a sigh of relief when he heard Beth's voice once again. She assured him Galbraith didn't stay too long and she couldn't really say why he came over other than she thought he might be quite lonely.

"He seems so nervous all the while, I sometimes feel really sorry for him," she admitted. "Perhaps I've misjudged him?"

Bart couldn't help comparing this sentiment to Mary Macaulay's when she implied she might somehow have inadvertently encouraged him by being too friendly. He didn't provoke the same kind of sympathy from him.

"Well, keep your wits about you," Bart warned her. "I do think there is something....not quite right about him."

"I will," Beth promised. "I'm closing up here soon to go back to the stables to help Fraser with mucking out before I leave. Tell Emily I'll pick her up later as agreed."

"Okay, take care," he finished the call. "Beth will pick you up here later," he reminded Emily. She nodded at him looking thoughtful, "What's the matter, Emily?"

"You'll think I'm being silly," he could see the slight flush begin across her cheeks.

"Of course I won't."

"It's just.....knowing Beth is coming over from the castle to pick me up made me wonder about the missing man you told me about."

"In what way?"

"Well, if the man went from the castle to see the dog lady, didn't you say she lives in Banchory?" Whilst she was talking she opened the laptop, flicked through a few pages until she brought up a map of the area around Banchory, she zoomed out on the map, "It's not on a direct route like Aboyne is to here, there's probably not a bus route from the castle," she stopped to see if he was following her. Bart leaned over to look at what she meant, "So how did he get there?"

"Well I expect he used the jeep he came here in to drop off the clock...."

"He must have because he was on his way to pick it up from here when he disappeared?" Emily waited for his reaction; saw his puzzled face, "You didn't mention his jeep was missing also."

Bart's mouth opened in realisation Robbie Cowan didn't mentioned an estate vehicle was missing, or the Laird thought Mungo MacLeod stole one, *only* about the clock being missing.

Bart picked up his mobile phone again, pulled up Robbie Cowan's number. She listened to him greeting the local Policeman. "I wanted to ask whether there was a castle vehicle missing, one perhaps Mungo would use to get about in?"

Emily obviously couldn't hear his reply. She waited whilst Bart listened to him, making a few 'uh-huh' noises followed by, "I see." When he finished he switched the mobile off.

"It would seem his own vehicle is the jeep which was parked at his cottage and I believe was why they initially searched the estate expecting him to still be there," Bart revealed.

"So how did he get to Banchory from the castle?"

It was then Bart's face lit up, "I remember now, he was delivering the dog food from the kennels, so would be in one of their vehicles, like the one Beth is now driving."

Emily nodded. "We can ask her when she comes over to pick you up." Bart suggested.

She went on to explain she emailed the clock pictures to herself so she could do some work at the cottage when she wasn't covering the shop or if they got snowed in again.

"I've put my email in your contacts so we can work on them together, it's easier to communicate that way with each other," she saw Bart staring at her. At first she mistook his look for one of disapproval thinking she'd overstepped her role. She quickly added, "It is okay I hope?"

"Of course, lass," he boomed his voice disguising the fact she seem so much more confident than the young school girl he knew before. "I can see you are going to be absolutely indispensable to this contract I have." He saw the pleasure evident on her face.

"I've had a little experience with mending clocks now, so I hope I will," she sounded eager. "I found some really useful websites when I was looking for information about the clocks I was given to mend," realising she might sound a bit grand she blushed quickly adding, "Not that they were real antiques or worth very much. I did find myself accessing sites with some incredible clocks; ones I know I will never actually ever see....."

"I don't know, some of those up at the castle look quite special at first glance, who knows what we might find, eh?"

Emily moved back into the shop where she carried on with her research until Bart appeared before the noon chorus to announce he was going up to the Moor Hen for his lunch if she would like to join him. She explained she was in the middle of something so would like to finish up first. She would come along in fifteen minutes.

Despite being surrounded by clocks Bart heard a 'ping' from his alarm setting, took out his pocket watch, saw the time was five minutes to midday which filled him with his age-old anxiety about the noon chimes bringing on his previous history of losing consciousness. To Emily's surprise he quickly explained where the Moor Hen was, told her he would wait for her there and speedily rushed out the door.

Emily seemed bemused by his behaviour. She sat staring at the closed shop door as the midday chimes began. If anyone was passing by just then or even if they came into the shop because the door remained unlocked, they would have seen a young girl sitting absolutely still behind the counter listening to the very noisy chimes, clicks and cuckoos. They might even have thought her a statue, until she smiled first then nodded her head slightly as she resumed her work on the computer.

Twenty minutes passed before Bart saw Emily enter the open plan bar at the Moor Hen. She stopped to look around the assembled people at their individual tables, some were eating, others only drinking; most of them were staring her way. Bart spotted her from his corner, where he stood up to wave her over pleased to see her there. Her flushed face indicated she was still the blushing girl he'd known before; public recognition always embarrassed her. His sense of propriety made him feel guilty having abandoned her by rushing away without waiting for her knowing she wouldn't be used to entering this kind of place alone. This was one of those moments when she actually did look her age.

"Sorry Emily," he apologised. "I shouldn't have left you." What could he say that would sound remotely reasonable to account for his behaviour?

Emily was aware she was blushing from being stared at, "I'm being silly.....I'm not used to......" he could see she was uncomfortable which increased the guilt he felt.

"I ought to explain," he went on to tell her. "Do you remember when I asked you once before to stay in the Time and Tide over lunch time?"

She nodded. "Yes, when I found the bird with no beak."

"Aye, you did lass, I didn't really explain why I got you to stay there, did I?" she shook her head.

"Wasn't it because you knew there was one of the clocks out of time with the others? You told me about the snooty woman journalist, the one who died, didn't she tell you all the clocks chimed at different times."

On that occasion Bart found the local journalist, Poppy Fields inside his shop listening to the noon chorus after he rushed outside into his back garden to avoid them. He didn't really believe her anyway. He remembered her as wanting to be spiteful because he wouldn't talk about Arthur Claymore being murdered at the Art Gallery next door.

"Indeed, she did," he recalled she was a particularly obnoxious person. "She wasn't really why I got you to stay there. More because I knew you had such a good ear for clock mechanisms." He really didn't want to explain how if he stayed there when they chimed he would find himself waking up on the floor from passing out which scared him at the time. He also felt a huge amount of guilt not knowing whether the same thing might happen to her. Despite that he subjected her to the possibility. He still felt guilt about that part even though nothing did happen to her. Since she suffered no ill effects, he left the cuckoo clock with the bird with no beak with her when he left Wainthorpe.

It was only at this moment he felt curious about the clock. When he caught her glance and their eyes met, she was staring at him curiously.

"You didn't believe her did you?" she asked.

"Well, no I didn't." he said firmly then added, "I did feel there was something wrong...."

"There was, or should I say there still is?" she admitted.

"You couldn't fix it I take it?"

She shook her head, "No I tried so many times though." She gave a dejected shrug of acceptance.

"Ah," Bart held back on the one question he wanted to ask.

As if she knew instinctively, she said, "I still have the clock," she watched Bart give an involuntary jerk, "It's at the cottage.....I haven't even opened the packaging I wrapped it in for travelling here or even set it going....it not being my home." She didn't explain how she sensed she shouldn't even in the room she slept in. There was just a feeling, nothing tangible, so she left it unwrapped inside the big wardrobe in her bedroom.

"No perhaps you're right," Bart agreed but for reasons he felt he couldn't explain to her.

"Although I have thought about something we could try....." she began.

At that moment Alistair the Landlord of The Moor Hen approached their table bringing Bart a shot of Bell's whisky and to take their lunch orders. Introductions were made first with Bart explaining Emily was his new Horology Associate (he saw Emily grin at the description) who would be managing the shop when he was absent.

"Well, I hope young Emily you have as keen an appetite as Sirus here and will frequent The Moor Hen in his absence......even though I don't expect to be serving you with the whisky!"

Emily blushed again as Bart chuckled, "He's only teasing."

It was much later when Beth arrived to pick Emily up they were able once again to raise the issue of Mungo MacLeod's vehicle. Beth agreed he would have been driving the delivery van or at least one of the two similar vehicles used by the stables and the kennels. They were quite old vehicles and certainly both were still functional.

"Mungo would have been driving one of them on the last day he visited Mary?" Bart asked.

"Yes, he would be delivering the bags of dog food. She gets two like we used to have until the other dog ran away."

"He must have returned to the castle in the van....." Bart said thinking aloud. ".....otherwise you wouldn't still have two."

"Yes, or for that matter, gone in for repairs later. Fraser told me mine suffered some damage to the front and been left with the garage where they have the castle's vehicle maintenance contract."

"Do you know how the van got damaged?"

Beth shook her head, "No, he made a passing comment when we discussed me having use of the kennels' van."

"Do you know the garage they use?"

"Somewhere close to Aboyne, at Dinnet I think; there is only the one in the area." Beth heard this from the other castle staff. "Why don't I go there to see what I can find out?"

Bart suddenly felt a stir of unease. He could see Beth looking at him enquiringly, "I can't see how there would be a problem asking."

"I'm not sure," Bart began.

Emily looked from one to the other, "Maybe we could play the dizzy females, tell them we can hear a noise in the engine, we're not sure if the van has been serviced lately."

Bart burst out laughing, "When did you get so devious?"

"I saw it on a cop programme once, seemed to work fine," she was grinning from ear to ear.

"Worth a try," Beth smiled quietly and Bart could see there would be no stopping her.

He told himself later as he sat worrying about Beth, he must stop fussing like a doting father; he was way too inexperienced in such matters.

CHAPTER 33

On the way back home Beth concentrated on the road conditions whilst Emily did all the talking, chattering about the clocks she found on the internet. She became aware of Beth pulling into the side of the road before stopping, leaving the engine running to maintain the warmth from the heater.

"What's wrong?" Emily asked.

"I think I can hear a strange knocking sound coming from the engine," she turned to catch Emily's concerned face.

"Really?"

"Can't you hear it?" Beth stared ahead through the car windscreen. She nodded her head sideways. Emily followed the gesture which directed her attention to a building attached to a disused unit with a faded sign for a bus company, where she could see the equally washed out 'For Sale' sign outside. The weathered sign was ancient; the wooden stake in the ground was rotting and waved precariously in the wind. The garage attached showed dim lights even though the time was now past five o'clock and dark outside.

"Is this the garage?" Emily enquired. "It looks closed down."

"Yes, the old bus company is long gone by the looks of it. The unit next door is a car workshop." Emily peered closer at the dimly lit unit. "What say we go there to check out this noise, are you up for it?" Emily grinned whilst she nodded mischievously.

Beth engaged the idling engine to drive over the road slowly, parking outside on the garage's forecourt. She pressed her horn once before she got out with Emily following. She made her way to the small side door next to the closed roll-down unit door.

On entering she called, "Hello?"

There was a radio blaring pop music with no sign of life until she spotted the saloon car at the centre underneath which two overall clad legs protruded. She shouted even louder, "Hello! I wonder if you can help us?"

The legs began to move slowly forward as the car mechanic's heels dug into the concrete floor, slid forward from under the car with their mid-torso lying on a mechanic's car creeper which Emily thought resembled a skateboard, revealing the owner of the legs, a young woman. They were both surprised into silence as she emerged.

The girl brushed back a heavy dark fringe of hair covering her eyes causing more oil smudges to the ones already on her face, her hands being heavily engrained with engine oil. The rest of the hair was pulled back into a ponytail. She stood up waiting for either of them to speak whilst the radio moved on to a heavy metal rock song 'Bad to the Bone', she scowled at them. She walked over to a side bench to switch the radio off.

Turning back she asked, "How can I help you?" The voice, gentle sweet, seemed out of place coming from such a stern face.

Beth was speechless, she seemed transfixed by the mechanic leaving Emily to begin, "We were passing by when we heard this awful noise coming from the van's engine."

"A noise, what kind of noise?" the girl reluctantly asked having heard this one too many times before. Emily glanced at Beth for support, she didn't look like she was about to reply, so she carried on, "Err, like a knocking sound? We thought we might break down so we stopped then we saw you were still open," she sounded nervous now because she couldn't remember if she saw a sign for the garage outside or any indication they were still open other than the light.

Beth stirred back into life, "I remembered you have the contract for Castle Daingneach vehicles? I wondered if the Kennel's van has been serviced recently? Or maybe even due to come in soon?"

The girl's face brightened a little at the news, "Yes we do," she confirmed walking over to a small paper laden desk in the corner. "Dad does have the Castle contract, let me check," she turned over a pile of loose papers until she found a greasy looking dog-eared ledger which she opened making even more stains appear. She skimmed back a few pages, ran a finger down the page leaving some smudges, "What's the registration number?"

Beth glanced at the bunch of keys in her hand with the registration number written on a tag attached stepping over to show her. Her finger continued down the page stopping at an entry.

"Ah, yes, I do remember this one," she glanced at Beth with renewed interest. "It came in at Christmas, though it wasn't for a service. There was a smashed in front grill with a dented bonnet." She looked enquiringly at Beth for some recognition of it, "An accident involving a Stag if I remember rightly?"

A shocked Beth said, "Are you sure?"

The girl seemed bemused, "Are you new?"

Beth nodded, "A bit before I started working there."

"Ah, thought so, just a minute," she walked over to an old yellow metal filing cabinet, ran her hands down each side of her overalls to get off some of the grease, then opened one of the draws pulling out a flimsy piece of yellow paper. She read through the sheet, "Yes, I thought I was right. I remember there was a lot of blood. I worked on the van myself because Dad took Mom away for New Year."

"Can I have a look," Beth asked which didn't seem to faze the girl. She handed the invoice to Beth. "Can't say I remember a noise in the engine when I test drove it. I could have a look for you," she took the keys out of Beth's hand looking at her smiling and left the garage.

Emily leaned over to read the invoice with Beth, there wasn't much more than the girl already told them. Emily took her mobile out to photograph the page as they heard the van's engine start up easily outside.

"Hit by a stag," Beth whispered pointing at the date, the 23rd of December. "Well this is the reason he didn't get to pick up the clock at any rate."

The van went silent outside then the girl reappeared.

"It sounds okay to me, I could take a closer look or you could wait to see if you hear the noise again."

"Right," Beth was now eager to get away beginning to edge away. "If you think we aren't going to break down?"

"Did anyone get hurt," Emily asked ignoring them as they stood staring at each other. "What happened to the stag?"

The girl laughed at Emily's worried face, "It's not so unusual an accident around here. They often jump out across the roads. If you kill a deer you can keep the carcass for the meat and if the police are called they will issue you with a 'possession permit'. If I recall in this case he mentioned the deer ran off, so must only have been stunned." She could see the relief on Emily's face. "Does'nae affect your insurance which is all *he* was worried about," the girl gave a disapproving grimace. "I da'na like the man anyway!"

Beth was surprised because most people spoke really well of Mungo MacLeod, "You sound like you disapprove of Mungo MacLeod?"

The mechanic frowned, "Mungo? No, not him, the man who is Duncan Munro's new secretary, he brought the vehicle in, *he* did'na look injured at any rate," she told Emily. "I did'na ask!" Her distaste for the man was unmistakeable.

Beth handed her the job sheet which she swopped for the van keys. "At least you've put our minds at ease, maybe we just panicked or ran over a pothole in the road," Beth elaborated. "Thank you for looking at it......"

"Nessa," the girl offered her name, smiling sweetly at Beth. "It's na'bother, I'll look forward to seeing you again when the van comes in for its service."

When they got outside Emily burst out laughing.

"What?!" Beth asked feeling self-conscious.

"Nessa? Like the monster?" Beth didn't look amused. Emily added, "She's sweet on you!" she giggled watching the shock appear on Beth's face.

"Silly girl!" she muttered. For once Emily wasn't the one who was blushing.

They drove away from Dinnet to Aboyne without another word, each thinking their own thoughts. When they reached home Beth immediately contacted Sirus to update him about the van.

"It doesn't make any sense at all," Bart acknowledged, puzzled now. "So where did Mungo go? His jeep was at the cottage. Now you say Galbraith was driving the van."

"Well, only when he took it in for repair. Nessa assumed he must have been driving otherwise...."

"Who is Nessa?" Bart asked.

"She's the daughter of the owner of the garage at Dinnet. She worked on the van whilst her parents went away for New Year."

"You say there was blood?" Bart felt uneasy at the thought of it.

"Yes, she told us there was a lot, but she thought the stag was unhurt it ran away apparently."

"Hmm, a bit late for forensics, probably been washed a few times since being in the garage." Bart was mystified by the new development. He was sure Robbie Cowan didn't know about the kennel van. This raised all kinds of doubts about Mungo's mode of transport on that day.

"Do you know Mary Macaulay's telephone number?" he asked Beth. "I'm wondering if she noticed what vehicle he was driving the last time she saw him."

Fortunately, Beth brought the Kennel's feed book home with her to plan her next delivery rota. She told him she would get back to him as soon as she found out. When she called him after speaking to Mary, she was certain Mungo delivered the dog feed in a van because she helped him unload the two sacks from the back.

"I even asked her if he mentioned the run in with a stag on his way there but she was certain everything had been fine," Beth lowered her voice as if she didn't want Emily to hear. "It's strange isn't it? Whatever happened to the van must have been after he left Mary only he took the van back to the castle for Galbraith to use," she suggested. "Could Galbraith have meant to go to visit Mary on 23rd like he did the next day, only having the accident stopped him, so he returned maybe in another vehicle when he took her the flowers on Christmas Eve?"

Bart didn't reply straight away, he'd gone really quiet.

"What do you think, Sirus?" she prompted.

"All that is possible," he reluctantly agreed. "But it doesn't explain anything about Mungo going missing does it?"

Bart needed to speak to Robbie Cowan again, either he didn't know about the damaged van or else he wasn't revealing everything he knew. Sadly Bart thought the latter. Why would he tell him anything about his investigation anyway?

After they finished their conversation Bart heard a 'ping' on his mobile. Emily sent him the picture of the van's job sheet for the 23rd of December. Whoever this Nessa was, she recorded quite clearly the presence of blood on the van's damaged grill. Bart's forensic experience prompted him to think even if the van had since been cleaned, providing they didn't use a high pressure hose or go through one of the drive-through car washers, there could be some residual blood left sufficient to determine whether it was from an animal or a human source.

He rang P.C Cowan, got a recorded message asking him to leave a name, number with brief details of the issue. So he did. He was sparing with the 'detail' only mentioning if he knew about Mungo using the Kennel's van to visit Mary Macaulay on the 23rd. He told him about the van being in some kind of accident after he left her, which needed repairing. He heard nothing that evening in response to his message so he went off to his bed deeply puzzled.

Bart spent a restless night, his mind dwelling on the image of a blood soaked grill. He was taken back to other times particularly like the more recent blood splattered wall behind where Arthur Claymore's bed would have been, mere bricks and mortar away from the one he slept in next door. Claymore's blood was days old having dried to a brown sepia hue, it nonetheless frightened him thinking, as he did at the time, the blood was meant to be his. He really believed Toni Maola's hired killer came for him at last mistaking the Art Gallery for his clock shop.

CHAPTER 34

He woke up with feelings of great unease, no amount of imposing other images, like the sea of white snow drifts he often found when opening his curtains, could dispel the images. Those only reminded him of the time more recently whilst out walking up The Brae when he heard the high pitched screaming of a creature's death throes. He came upon the mauled wild rabbit still twitching and screeching, left by some other creature to die. With the mangled body oozing blood stark red against the whiteness of the snow, the rabbit writhed around in pain fighting against an inevitable death.

Red blood, white snow with the crushed jaw exposing jutting rabbit teeth reminded him of the other feral predator, Selwyn Jones, the Private Detective searching for Beth. He used his heavy walking boot to stamp on the rabbit's neck silencing the miserable cries. He left the steaming red mass of guts there, stark against the whiteness of the snow, callously walking away, knowing another animal would claim it as 'road kill' to dispose of the body as Nature intended.

He lay awake with this stark image in his mind worrying about Beth's safety. For the first time he wondered how persistent her husband might be in trying to find her. He would hate to see her newly found confidence crushed in one moment if he found her.

Road kill.

The anomaly for him was if there was as much blood as the garage mechanic told Beth, how could a deer survive to leap away? Perhaps, the stag died on the spot for someone else to come along to claim the carcass as 'road kill'? None of which explained what happened to Mungo MacLeod.

All these thoughts slowed Bart's morning routine. He was like a ghost gliding about in slow motion. Even the sight of a thawed out world outside as he opened his curtains to green rather than white, couldn't cheer him or dissipate the blood drenched pictures in his mind.

Normally he was eager for his breakfast. Today he ate half-heartedly, uncharacteristically leaving one or two abandoned mouthfuls of his bacon sandwich on his plate, interrupted as he was by the sharp rap on the shop door. He didn't even get the chance for his normal second cup of coffee before he was ushering the policeman through to the back room.

Clearly Robbie Cowan was a man who preferred to deal directly with people because here he was bright and early, at least an hour before the shop opened.

"Heavy night?" Cowan asked as he eyed Bart's scowling appearance.

Bart automatically filled the kettle again, "You will take a drink?" he asked ignoring his comment, he knew what he looked like after a sleepless night, his bathroom mirror never lied.

"Aye," Robbie sat down next to the newly laid fire which was crackling away whilst fighting to catch alight. "Now what's this message about a van?"

Bart tried to assess if he might be deliberately holding back admitting he knew. He saw nothing to indicate divergence tactics. "It's how Mungo got from the castle to Banchory to visit Mary Macaulay on the day before Christmas Eve."

"We assumed he used his own Jeep which we found at his cottage," Robbie disclosed.

"And why you searched the Castle Estate?"

"Aye," Robbie sensed a bit of criticism in Bart's tone so he added, "And why we did a forensic examination of the Jeep."

Bart's head came up sharply, "Did you find anything?"

He shook his head, "Not much, only a few feathers with spots of pheasant blood, nothing of any significance."

Bart stopped spooning coffee granules into the two mugs in front of him thinking *Mungo is a ghillie so you would expect any vehicle he drove to be spattered with animal blood be it pheasant, mallard, rabbit, or even fish.*

But not human.

He finished spooning coffee, poured in hot water bringing the mugs over to the crackling fire.

"So?" Robbie asked.

"He was delivering dog food to Mary Macaulay that day.....according to her he drove the white van." Robbie was about to ask a question when Bart put up his hand to stop him. "The same van was later booked into McKinley's garage at Dinnet, with a bent grill, a dented bonnet having been hit by a stag and....." Bart paused for effect, "....was covered in blood."

P.C Cowan stopped in mid sip of his coffee at the news.

"You're sure of this?"

Bart hesitated for a moment thinking about how he might avoid involving Beth, but justified doing so on the basis this was actual evidence, therefore should not be withheld, before he picked up his mobile to show Robbie the picture of the job sheet.

"How....?"

He knew the question that would be coming as he heard the shop doorbell tinkle followed by Emily's voice shouting, "Halloo!"

"My assistant on cue, I'll let her tell you for herself." Bart waited until she came through to the back. When she caught sight of the young policeman, true to form, Bart saw her redden. "Just in time Emily," Bart began. "I've shown P.C Cowan here the job sheet you photographed yesterday when you discovered Beth's van was brought in for repair at Christmas," he turned to the constable to explain. "Emily got a ride from her landlady when they had a bit of a problem with it, as they passed McKinley's Auto they took the opportunity to get the vehicle checked over, turns out it was booked in on the 23rd of December having been hit by a stag...."

Not to be left out of telling the story, Emily added dramatically, "....covered in blood...."

"So let me get this straight," Robbie appeared a bit confused. "Your van....."

"No the castle kennel's van," Emily corrected.

"....was booked in on the 23rd of December," he examined the image on Bart's mobile phone.

"Yes," Emily confirmed with a sigh of impatience.

"Which is the same van Mungo MacLeod drove over to Mary Macaulay's...." Bart said.

"Nessa confirmed the registration number as the same as the one outside when she went to check for us," Bart could see Emily was thoroughly enjoying herself.

".....Nessa can confirm Mungo MacLeod took the van to McKinley's after his accident?"

"No, that's the point," Bart interrupted. "Not Mungo.......Thomas Galbraith took it in." He couldn't quite read Robbie Cowan's face as he now adopted a more neutral expression. "Did he not tell you when you interviewed him?"

Emily moved over to the kettle to make herself a cup of tea as Bart watched Robbie's eyes follow her all the way.

"Why did you take this picture?" he asked her back.

She turned to face him, "Nessa showed us the job sheet because we asked if the van was recently serviced or might even be due one." Bart saw Robbie's lips move as he fought to hold back a smile. She could see she didn't fool him. "It isn't the weather to be breaking down is it? There shouldn't be a problem with a newly serviced vehicle....my Dad sold insurance for a living. I was weaned on Insurance Companies trying to evade paying out!" Bart burst out laughing at her impertinence. Robbie joined in. Emily pointed at the mobile picture of the job sheet. "That is evidence," she finished sternly.

"Thomas Galbraith," Bart nudged gently. "Must have told you about taking the van in for repair?"

Robbie was aware of both Bart and Emily staring at him. "No, he assured me he took advantage of the Laird being away, did the same as everyone else leaving to take a festive holiday. He told me he didn't see Mungo MacLeod after he got back from his break."

"Hmm," was Bart's muttered comment.

"I wonder how they got the van back from the garage?" Emily asked.

"I do think it might be worth a forensic going over even after all this time," Bart suggested.

"I might take a run over to Dinnet, speak with Nessa," Robbie offered. "Where is the van now?"

"It's over at our place, Beth hasn't gone in today on account of working yesterday on her day off," Emily informed him.

"Do you know Nessa?" Bart asked wondering about her reliability as a witness.

"Yes, we were at the same school together," he revealed as he watched Emily smile. "She's a straight sort of lass, reliable," he confirmed in her defence trying to avoid Emily's probing stare. She turned her back to finish making her tea concealing the broad grin on her face.

Robbie, slightly embarrassed, got up to leave, "I don't suppose," he addressed Bart, "you might come with me to Dinnet, I want to drive the route Mungo would have taken if he was heading over here to pick up the Laird's clock. I could do with another pair of eyes to see if we can pinpoint where the stag might have run out in front of the van?"

Bart's face brightened, "Will you be okay in the shop on your own?" he asked Emily.

"Of course," she said. "I've got plenty to do," she pointed at the lap top on the table. She would have preferred to go along with them.

They left her seated at the work table in the shop as she watched them drive away.

CHAPTER 35

They took the A93 towards Ballater before Bart began to have doubts about the exercise. He knew the accident could have happened at any point along the way from Banchory where mid-afternoon the van was observed to be intact. This exercise seemed like looking for a needle in a haystack.

"Are you aware of any particular areas where there might be deer?" he asked the policeman.

"Aye, the wooded areas are best suited to herd habits," Robbie confirmed. "They do tend to stay together. You may think the odd stag might wander off, though it's likely there's a herd somewhere nearby." Bart was far from convinced they would be successful and his face showed it. "I'll indicate the likely places," Cowan promised. When they passed such places he slowed the Land Rover Defender so they could each scan their side of the road.

However, when they reached Dinnet Robbie Cowan stopped the car close to McKinley's Auto. The roll-up unit door stood open. They could see a saloon car next to a battered jeep parked inside. There were no signs of life. Bart noticed Robbie's expression become tense, his face invaded by a deep scowl.

Intuitively Bart asked, "Do you know the owner?"

He nodded sighing deeply. "There's no love lost," the policeman admitted.

"May I ask why?"

"Ah, that goes back to school days, mine and Nessa's."

"You dated her?" Bart thought his question a bit presumptuous, the constable didn't seem deterred.

"In a manner of speaking," he replied. "We were friends, knocked about together for a while, mostly to keep McKinley off his daughter's back......I covered for her if she was out with another lass," he eyed Bart for his understanding.

"Ah," Bart caught on.

"The only problem being I think he expected more from us or rather from me," he smiled. "Which was never going to happen, d'y ken? Though his biggest disappointment came when I joined the police as a cadet."

"I would have thought taking up with a policeman would be every father's dream for his daughter," was Bart's assumption.

"Not McKinley," he scoffed. "It got a bit embarrassing if he was pulled in for some trivial stuff. McKinley had 'expectations' from someone he might consider 'almost' family," he saw Bart frown. "There's a good deal of poaching goes on up here. McKinley wasn't quite the upright citizen he seems to be with his castle vehicle contract."

"What about the contract?" Bart asked. "Duncan Munro's must be one of the estates to suffer from poachers, surely?"

"Aye, then there's not many auto-repair places across this part of the world is there? Quid pro quo, as long as the poaching does'na exceed a tolerable level, all's well with a blind eye being taken."

"Any dodgy 'auto' fiddles?" Bart knew not all garages were reputable.

"Ah, now that's never been put to the test - Duncan Munro can always be assured of getting preferential service," his eyes widened in a knowing way.

"So are you expecting this van business might be a bit of a test?"

Robbie shrugged, "I hope not if Nessa is involved."

"Well I can't see how, she was very clear about there being blood when she spoke to Beth and Emily. She made sure to include the fact on the job sheet."

"Like I told you, she's a very straight up lass, so let's see shall we?" He opened his car door to get out. Bart followed behind him as they walked over to the open garage doors where Robbie shouted, "Anyone about?"

Bart watched the girl Nessa rise from behind the far side of the saloon car. When she spotted Robbie Cowan she smiled, then glanced sharply over to a closed door at the back of the garage.

"Morning Nessa," Robbie sounded official rather than friendly given their history, which surprised Bart. "Is your father about?"

They heard the flushing of a toilet from behind the closed door. They could tell she was feeling edgy.

"What can we do for you Robbie?" Nessa asked. She lowered her voice to a mere whisper, "Da's not in the best of moods," she managed as the door at the back opened to reveal a rather sour-faced Jock McKinley emerging.

McKinley's face became even darker when he spotted the uniformed Robbie Cowan, "What do *you* want?" he growled glaring at him across the garage.

"That's enough, Dad!" Nessa spat a warning his way which surprisingly seemed to calm him down a little.

"Won't keep you long," Robbie announced. "I'm here about one of the castle's vehicles – a white van I believe you booked in before Christmas after an accident involving a stag?"

Nessa peered over at her father, "Aye," she agreed.

"Don't know 'owt about it," was McKinley instant retort.

Robbie was about to become more officious when Nessa answered, "Yes, that's right," she glanced again at her father willing him to keep quiet. "Dad was away for Christmas, I worked on it," she admitted. "What's the problem?"

"Are you sure it was accident damage Nessa?"

They both could see McKinley getting angrier by taking the question as an insinuation, "If my lass says so, then it's right!"

Robbie put up his hand to stop him, "I don't doubt her," he assured him. "I was asking for her opinion of the damage." He turned back to Nessa for her assessment.

"Had to be something as heavy as a stag because of the extent of the damage. There was a lot of blood," she added. "I've seen a few with similar damage. On the basis of the amount of blood on the grill, I'm sure the stag must have been quite injured even though he said only stunned."

"Who brought it in Nessa?" Robbie continued.

"The Laird's secretary," she didn't say his name as if the words would be distasteful spoken out loud, she was none too pleased.

"Is that normal?" Robbie queried.

She shook her head, "No, usually the Estate Manager or at least the main user brings the vehicles in."

"So if it's the stable's vehicle who would usually bring it in?" Bart asked stepping forward from behind Robbie Cowan. They both stared his way as if he'd materialised from thin air. Neither of them noticed him before he spoke. Bart was used to being invisible even with his distinctive looks.

"Who the hell are you!?" McKinley demanded fiercely.

Robbie interceded, "Mr. Jeffries is helping us with our investigation."

Bart was a little put out at the introduction, sounding like he might be a suspect in a crime case.

Nessa ignored her father again, "Fraser would usually bring in the stable or kennel's vans. He would need to know how long they would be out of action as well as how much the repairs would be. Fraser isn't too pushy. The Estate Manager used to get a bit tetchy."

"So were you surprised when Galbraith brought it in?" Robbie asked.

Nessa shrugged, "Not really, he brings his own car here for the annual service or when his car needs some attention. I assumed he was using the van when he had the accident. The blood looked fresh to me, as if it just happened."

"Is that all?!" McKinley clearly didn't want the police around his business for too long.

"No, Mr McKinley I'd like to see the job sheet, please. I need to establish a few things."

"Sounds to me you don't believe ma lassie here...." He accused.

"Of course I believe her. It's not as simple as you might think.....so please let me do ma job and see the job sheet." Bart watched him having no problem standing up to McKinley.

"Dad, please let me deal with this, you weren't even here at the time!" Nessa glared over at her father with frustration.

She saw him relent. He walked over to the battered jeep muttering, "I'll take this for a test drive." He got in, started the engine first time and backed it out of the garage space.

"Never mind him," Nessa urged walking over to a filing cabinet she retrieved the job sheet handing it over for Robbie to look at, "You know what he's like." She glanced at Bart apologetically, "Like I said he's not in the best of moods."

He didn't comment, glanced at the sheet before he asked, "What time did Galbraith arrive?"

She moved over to the desk to look in the booking in ledger, found the entry, "Yes, I remember....quite late...we would usually be closed at six o'clock. I was trying to finish up for the holidays," she grimaced. "Turned out I didn't get to have one."

"How long did you work on it, Ness?" he asked sounding friendlier now her father wasn't around.

"Until the New Year because I needed to get a new front grill…..which took a bit of time because of the holiday. I did manage to get the dent in the bonnet fixed myself."

Bart's heart sank at the news. He hoped the battered grill was repairable and might have retained some blood samples for analysis. "What did you do with the old grill?" he asked not expecting much joy. He knew if the old grill was beyond repair garages' usual practice would be to sell it on as scrap metal.

Nessa came back immediately with, "It's out back." She walked off expecting them to follow her out, around the side of the garage, into the back compound which was full of junk, a mass of scrap parts, old cars and assorted rubbish.

"Heck!" Bart declared seeing the shambles.

Nessa laughed, "Quite a mess, eh?" she went straight over to the nearest pile, picked up a heavy polythene bag containing the grill from the van. They could see where the blood oozed a good deal against the transparent sides of the bag. "I put it in here because there was rather a lot…….it would have gone over everything." She watched as Bart's face lit up. Neither he nor Robbie asked why she hadn't hosed the van's front down to get rid of the blood before she removed the grill.

"So you weren't really sure, eh?" Robbie asked knowingly.

She merely stared at him without expression handing the bag over. "This amount of blood usually means more than 'stunned' and to 'run off' immediately after, well unlikely." She made no comment about not believing Thomas Galbraith's version of events or wanting to cover her own back which her silence implied.

Robbie was tempted to ask why she didn't phone the police if she had doubts, but he let it ride. They followed her back around to the front of the garage. He held up the job sheet, she waved her hand, "You'll be wanting the invoice," she said simply.

Bart asked, "How, or rather who, fetched the van back?"

"No one, I drove it back to the kennels," she laughed. "I got a lift back here from Worsel."

She saw Robbie grin as he began to ask, "Is he....?" Nessa merely nodded raising her eyes skywards.

Bart didn't need an explanation he'd heard enough hints from Beth to know Worsel lived in hopes. He smiled at her, admitting to himself she was yet another very astute woman.

PC Cowan carried the grill back to his Defender, opened the back to place it inside.

"You'd better double bag," Bart suggested. "Fingerprints – just to be on the safe side." He remembered enough about his old SOCO days when he meticulously collected the evidence at the scene of a crime.

The young officer gave him a searching look as he reached inside his car for a large evidence bag, which he handed to Bart to open out to receive the bagged grill. Cowan took it off him, secured it, then put it in the back of his car. "I'll need a statement from you at some point," he moved around the car to the driver's side. Bart climbed in beside him, "Old habits," he told Cowan knowing he'd given himself away. He always found it difficult to pretend he had no past.

"I thought so," was his passing comment only the satisfied expression on his face confirmed his suspicions about Bart. Over at the garage, they saw Nessa had resumed repairing the saloon car, they could see her lying underneath it.

"She's a canny lass," Bart told him.

"Aye, she's worth more than this," Robbie remarked sadly as he nodded towards the building. "She won't leave McKinley and that awful temper of his."

"What about her mother, what's she like?"

"She deserves better too, but doesn't have great health. I think she struggles making it hard for Nessa to leave Mckinley to do it all," Bart could tell Robbie's concern was genuine. "She's a damn good mechanic though."

They set off again in the direction of Banchory, after a while Cowan said, "This next stretch of woodland has many deer, although you can seldom see them through the trees from the road. I'll go as slowly as I can, we'll let anyone over take us."

Bart remained pessimistic about finding anything with such a time gap. The weather conditions since Christmas were also against them.

"I'm trying to remember what the weather was like around Christmas....." Bart mentioned as he scanned the roadside on the passenger side. Before Cowan could attempt a reply he heard Bart suddenly yell, "Stop! Back up," as he thought he saw a broken young sampling on the edge of the wood.

P.C. Cowan stopped, backed up a little immediately hearing the angry horn of a speeding car overtaking them, making them jump in their seats. Bart's hand shot up to his chest where he could feel his heart racing.

"Sorry," Cowan whispered, he failed to notice the approaching car concentrating as he was on what Bart had seen. This time he checked the driver's side mirror before he got out. He fetched a police warning cone out of his boot to place at the back of the car to warn approaching vehicles, then joined Bart who stood beside the car.

Bart stared at the splintered young sapling standing tall above a low stone wall.

"Well something or someone broke that...." He pointed at Bart's find. "Well spotted." He checked both ways before he crossed towards the opposite side of the road where more trees grew. They were more spaced out than on the other side of the road where the denseness of the trees made it difficult to penetrate with the eye.

"The wall," he pointed back to where Bart stood before he moved away to follow him. "Is nothing for a deer to jump, they can reach great heights. In this case the trees would stop this one having much of a run before leaping." He sounded as if he was speaking his thoughts out loud. "Mungo would have been coming from Banchory...he would have been over on this side of the road." Cowan was nodding as he continued.

On the other side there was no stone wall, the trees began further in from a shallow ditch filled with an assortment of tangled weeds. Robbie turned back, "The wall would have shortened the stag's leap, so likely why the stag hit the bonnet. The forward momentum of the van would cause quite an impact even if Mungo took his foot off the accelerator when the stag hit." He turned away to the direction of travel walking along the edge of the ditch. Bart could see him assuming the van wouldn't have stopped straight away; he followed behind him, his short legs not pacing the constable's huge stride.

Cowan stopped, pointed at the ditch, "There!" he exclaimed. Bart followed the direction of his arm to the ditch where something heavy must have flattened the plant life leaving some dark residue now brown in colour.

He crouched down to examine the ditch, prodded the residue with a finger, then sniffed it, "I believe this is blood and where the stag must have been thrown by the van's momentum. He stood looking for signs of blood on the road. Watched by Bart he said, "Perhaps all the snow has washed everything into the ditch."

He walked back to the Defender, opened up the back again, leaned inside to retrieve a pair of binoculars which he raised to his eyes to penetrate the depth of the wood.

"Ah, yes a herd. I can see their white rumps," he began to move the binoculars back towards where they now stood examining the ground between until he suddenly stopped. He handed them to Bart, "Work back from the herd, tell me what you see."

Bart obeyed eventually stopping in the same way, "Could be a deer, it's not moving."

"Exactly," Robbie searched around further on from where the brown residue covered the crushed vegetation. He moved over to descend into the ditch to avoid it. Bart remained where he was following his progress into the woods as he walked a parallel line to avoid stepping on any evidence. He stopped when he was alongside the obstacle. Bart raised the binoculars to see the herd standing motionless having turned their white rumps, sensing danger. Robbie raised his thumb in affirmation, then began to walk back covering the same ground already trampled.

Bart extended a hand to help him up out of the ditch, "You found the stunned deer?"

"I do believe it is the same stag, yes," Robbie took his radio in his hand and called the Control Room , beginning to walk away from Bart who turned back to have another look through the binoculars. The herd of deer were no longer there. He moved his view backwards till he found the stag again, spotted the antlers were at a strange angle to the rest of the carcass.

When P.C Cowan came back to his side he confirmed, "Yes, it's got extensive injuries with a broken neck," he told Bart. "How many animals do you know can walk with a broken neck?"

"Oh," Bart was shocked at the implication. "So someone moved its carcass from the ditch?"

"I suspect much easier to do if there was a lot of snow, I need to look up the weather conditions for the 23rd of December.....I've called out forensics and CID," he informed him.

"CID?"

"I still have a missing ghillie who was meant to be driving the van that killed the stag," Cowan explained. "And when they get here I think we need to go over to secure the white van."

Bart's stomach gave a lurch as the implications of the police turning up at Beth's cottage hit him. She was going to be devastated especially since she would need to give her own fingerprints for elimination purposes. The question was should he warn her? If he did she might get spooked so much she could bolt taking the van with her, which wouldn't do at all.

"Look, can we go sit in your car I have to tell you something?" He requested. Robbie Cowan could sense the seriousness of Bart's question, he nodded and they moved over to the Defender to sit inside.

CHAPTER 36

On hearing the bell tinkle above the shop door Emily glanced up to see a man whose face seemed familiar although she couldn't place him. For one moment she even considered he might be someone she once saw back in The Silver Teapot in Wainthorpe-on-Sea. She hadn't been in Scotland long enough to meet many people, maybe at the pub yesterday?

"Hello, Emily," the man greeted her by name. It immediately brought puzzlement to her face, which he recognised, "Philip Miller, from the hotel?"

She remembered being introduced to someone when they all ate there after they arrived although she was way too tired to take it all in. He hovered fussily around their table giving orders to the Spanish waiter who stared blankly back at him. She stood up to move over to the counter, this was her very first customer.

Philip Miller asked, "Is Sirus in, I need to speak with him?"

"Sorry, he went out, I'm not sure when he'll be back," she thought he had a worried look about him, so she added, "Can I take a message, get him to ring you?"

He seemed to hesitate before saying, "No, I'll give him a call myself." He turned quickly hurrying off leaving Emily standing silently in the shop. She moved back to the work table to resume her research and was tempted to call Sirus. She knew his involvement in the missing man case was important, so she decided to leave it.

Towards lunch time she felt the pangs of hunger. She went in search of food in the kitchen. There was always the hope there might be some of the delicious cake Sirus kept in the cake tin left. Much to her disappointment apart from crumbs the tin was empty and her further search of the fridge even more so. As the cupboards also drew a blank her stomach gave a resounding growl.

She even began to think about the Landlord's words to her to come back to The Moor Hen for her lunch; the idea of being there on her own gave her goose bumps. A further tinkle of the bell drew her back into the shop; much to her delight she saw Beth standing there. She brought a huge grin to her face.

"I wondered if anyone wanted to join me for lunch?" Beth could see Emily was delighted with the idea.

"Yippee! I can't find anything to eat! Sirus isn't here to go with to the pub." It reminded her, "He's just like my Dad when he didn't have my Mum to look after him – I think they would starve." She pushed away the image of her father in a hostel without her Mum. She didn't want to think about how she also abandoned him.

"Good. So how about I take you out of the village a little way to a place I know, The Ostail, for a bite to eat?"

"Okay, sounds good, I'm starving. I don't think he'll mind me shutting up the shop for lunch. He does most days anyway."

They vacated the shop as the noon chimes began heading out of the village to the tiny roadside Inn Beth visited on her arrival all those weeks ago. This time she wasn't so weary so she parked the van in the car park at the back where one or two cars were already parked. Briefly Beth wondered if the place was now open to residents. When they walked around to the front entering the bar, they saw a large group of people sitting at the big wooden table in front of the log fire. The 'reserved' sign on the table indicated the cars must belong to this party of people.

They sat inside near the door at an empty table, the only other one available being on the other side of the room. Emily searched the menu chalked up on a blackboard, "What are you going to have?" she whispered to Beth.

"I'll ask him what the soup of the day is first."

The party of people were sombrely chattering to each other occasionally smiling at some amusing anecdote. Beth thought perhaps they were related in some way given they were all of different ages. She could make out no actual resemblance between any of them. The noise calmed down when a woman appeared through the bar hatch carrying a large tray with plates of food. It interested Emily to match their meals with those on the blackboard. They appeared to have some different meals not displayed there. She whispered this to Beth hoping the burger was the special of the day.

After they were all served the woman came over to them, "What can I get you?" Her English accent was similar to that of the chef she already met.

Beth explained, "My friend was wondering if the burger and chips was available?"

The woman lowered her voice, "It's a party of people from a nearby estate, come for a funeral of one of their old ghillies. I'm afraid they pre-ordered." She could spot the disappointment on Emily's face, "I'll see what my husband can do." She turned to Beth, "Do you want the same?"

"Beth shook her head, "No, can I ask what the soup of the day is?"

"It's cream of celery," replied the chef's wife.

"Oh good, I'll have some please; then the local smoked salmon to follow."

They ordered drinks, Emily a coke while Beth asked for black coffee.

When she went back through the bar, Emily declared, "This is a nice place."

"I came here when I first arrived in Scotland. I was too late and missed lunch, but the Chef made me a sandwich and found me a bowl of soup, after my long drive."

Emily's thoughts strayed to The Silver Teapot where her mother hadn't been as obliging to her customers.

"What are you thinking?" she asked. "You look troubled."

Emily shook her head, "Not really, you reminded me of....of....back home."

"Any regrets?"

She shook her head again without answering.

When the woman returned with their meals Emily was ecstatic with the huge homemade burger in a bun surrounded by chunky chips, she grinned with pleasure. Beth asked the woman to thank the chef for her.

They took their time, eavesdropped on the funeral party who seemed quite a jolly band of people all reminiscing about the man they all once knew. The bar filled up even more after they heard a motor bike pull up outside. Two leather clad bikers entered the bar carrying their helmets speaking to each other in German. They took the one vacant table over the far side where they began to strip off their biker leathers piling them up with their helmets on the floor. The bar was now full to capacity.

The youngest member from the large table walked past them leaving the bar as the Chef's wife took over a tray of shot glasses with a measure of amber liquid which one of the older members distributed around the group. The man wearing a green oilskin coat with a weathered face placed the last one in the girl's vacant place at the table. She reappeared carrying a violin case to re-join the group.

They heard her say, "This is a song I wrote for Fergus." She opened the case took out a bright blue fiddle, began to sing the most melodic song with beautiful words as a tribute to him, accompanying herself on the fiddle. The whole of the bar was

stunned into silence, the Chef's wife stood at the open hatch door of the bar listening. Beth's eyes were full of tears whilst the German bikers gawped in amazement both reaching for their mobile phones to take photographs of the scene.

Everyone sat quietly until the last strain of the song faded to everyone's applause. The older man stood raised the glass of whisky to give a toast, "RIP Fergus!"

Emily's face was a picture never having seen such a thing before. "This is awesome!" she whispered to Beth who was using her fingers to clear her eyes.

It was later Beth read in the local paper about the ghillie Fergus who was laid to rest that day having worked on the same estate all his life.

"The funeral was attended by people who had known him for many years travelling from far away to be there."

CHAPTER 37

They sat in the Land Rover Defender where Bart began tentatively to broach the subject of Beth's arrival in Scotland. He was hardly in a position to supply any of the specifics that led her to flee her previous life, only to fill Robbie in on how he met her, leaving out any reference to her old car the young couple, also runaways, helped him to dispose of. Some of which he was sure hadn't been quite legal. He made sure he mentioned creepy Private Detective, Selwyn Jones who came looking for her. He referred to her change of name being an inevitable attempt on her part to evade being found, which Bart thought was absolutely necessary.

Robbie Cowan didn't comment until Bart finished speaking, "I'm not certain why you're telling me all this."

"The police going mob-handed to Beth's cottage to fetch the van will likely have an extremely adverse affect on her."

Robbie's puzzlement necessitated Bart to reveal her husband to be a police officer, as well as some kind of 'monster', which forced her to run. "It has nothing at all to do with your missing person case, constable," Bart said. "I'm not even certain she has been herself declared as 'missing', otherwise why would he pay a private investigator to find her? However, this is the reason why I'm not warning her we're coming to fetch the van....in case she might....."

"Bolt with the van?" Cowan suggested.

"I do know the thought of him finding her terrorises her so much flight might seem to be her only option. Rationalising it as a potential crime would not occur to her. She would disappear as fast as she could."

"What on earth did he do to her?" the police officer asked.

Bart shrugged, "Whatever he did was severe. She has confided no details. What I do know is any contact with the police she sees as a potential threat to being discovered. She believes 'they all stick together, protect their own' so I can only deduce she has tried to seek help in the past which failed. Any police contact she now sees as dangerous."

They sat in the Defender near to where they found the stag, for the moment in total silence, neither of them knowing how to resolve the issue of the van. Eventually Robbie Cowan offered, "Well, there's no doubt now we need the van as evidence...."

Bart interrupted in Beth's defence, "She would agree with you. She is well aware Mungo MacLeod is missing. Beth was the one who discovered his relationship with Mary Macaulay. She would want to find out what happened to him as much as we do. In fact, *she* discovered the van was involved in an accident when she went with Emily to the garage as you well know."

He saw a smile appear on Robbie's face, "She's quite a lass."

Bart couldn't make up his mind whether he was referring to Beth or Emily, so he ignored the comment. "Look, I'll take you over to the cottage if you allow *me* to explain about needing the van for forensics. I'll need a moment with her first to assure her you aren't in any way linked to her husband."

"I have very few contacts outside Police Scotland and no desire to subject her to any further contact with her husband. You will realise I haven't even got a name for him," he reminded him, ensuring Bart understood her false identity was noted. "If she wants my help in relation to her problems in her previous life.....I'm here....I can'na abide domestic violence of any kind!" This at least gave Bart encouragement as he scrutinised him for his sincerity. He saw he showed real concern with no objection to the idea.

"Okay! Let's at least try!" Bart boomed.

They set off for Aboyne leaving the police forensic team looking for evidence at the scene, having handed over the van grill to take back for analysis. Bart thought the CID officer who eventually showed up seemed less enthusiastic about the relevance of the accident. He determined he would wait for the forensic results before declaring the missing ghillie the subject of suspected foul play. At this point in time Robbie Cowan was still the lead officer in a missing person case.

Bart passed a caustic comment about the detective, "He's a bit laid back, isn't he?" He found his attitude a little too cautious under the circumstances.

"Maybe a bit lazy," is all the comment Cowan made of him. "I'm not so bothered, we do need to find Mungo don't we?"

As it turned out Bart's worries were shelved when they didn't find Beth at the cottage. There was also no sign of the van. "Maybe she went into work after all," he suggested.

As they stood in the yard at the back of the cottage Bart's mobile began to ring. He was surprised to see Philip Miller's name on the screen as he'd only just added his number to his call list. He pressed the cancel call, this wasn't the right time to take a private call, priority was in locating Beth whom he thought must be out somewhere in the van. "Shall we drive over to the castle to see if she's there?"

"She could be anywhere, that might be one huge waste of our time." Cowan remarked. "I'd rather not go back there until we see what the forensics come up with. Are you sure you can't telephone her, arrange to meet her somewhere."

Bart shook his head thinking meeting her in a marked police car wouldn't be such a good idea. "Maybe we could get Emily to ask her over to the shop to give her a lift back here."

Bart noticed how much keener the constable was with this new idea, "Good thinking," he grinned encouragingly. They got back into the Defender.

They were both surprised to find the white van parked outside the March of Time when they arrived back there. Bart was disconcerted when he found the door locked with the 'closed' sign showing. He reached into his pocket hoping he'd remembered to pick up his key then found them in his pocket. *Old habits die hard.* He let them both inside discovering his lap top open on the work table, with no sign of Emily.

In the back room they found Emily sitting with Beth in silence. Bart knew immediately something was very wrong. Beth's distressed face was patchy, her eyes were red rimmed, whilst her cheeks were wet from crying. Emily glanced his way with those wide eyes declaring herself to be out of her depth.

Bart's phone buzzed with an incoming message which he quickly read. The text was Philip Miller again: *Need to speak urgently!*

"I've got to take this," he apologised moving back into the shop leaving them together.

After five minutes he returned. Emily was making tea, her fall-back position in times of crisis or when she was out of her depth. Robbie Cowan was seated close to Beth softly talking to her trying to discover why she was so distraught, clearly he was failing to engage her.

"Beth?" Bart spoke gently controlling his booming voice. All she could manage was to shake her head, she was unable to speak. He looked over to Emily for some kind of explanation.

She turned, tried to find the words, "She was okay when we were driving back from lunch at the Ostail. We got some petrol at the Esso garage outside the village.....I heard her cry out as we were passing the hotel ......she looked really scared," Emily waved her hand in front of her own face, "Then the colour went from her face.....I thought she was sick, she could barely drive the rest of the way. When we got here.....” words failed her because she had been unable to comfort Beth or get her to talk since.

Bart said, “That’s okay Emily, I know, what’s wrong.”

Beth’s soulful eyes turned towards him, he could see the same haunted look he first saw when she stopped outside his shop on the day she arrived in Scotland. She searched Bart’s face, “How did he find me?” her plaintive whisper was barely audible.

“Did you see him?” Bart asked fearful she’d come face to face with her husband who had booked into the hotel two hours before. He asked Philip Miller if he’d seen her by showing him the very same picture of her as an eighteen year old Lily Johns.

She shook her head, “I saw his car outside the hotel when we drove past....how did you know?”

“Philip Miller, the Manager, recognised you from that same old grainy picture the P.I was showing everyone.”

By the shock on her face she thought the worst, “Did he tell him?”

“Absolutely not!” Bart raised his voice forcefully. “He’s been trying to get hold of me to warn you.”

Robbie Cowan sat quietly listening until he affirmed, “If you din’na want to be found, that’s your right.” He chose to ignore any echoing thoughts he may have about false names or driving licences, in favour of pacifying someone who was obviously frightened.

Beth stared at him in amazement, “He’ll make me go back. I can’t.....he’s....he’s.....” She broke down again.

Cowan held up his hand to stop her, “No, he can’na make you do anything you don’t want to do, we’ll make sure okay?”

Emily, ever practical, said, “Maybe we should go back to the cottage, hide there. He won’t find her there. We need to wait for him to leave.”

"The only thing is we need the van, Beth," Robbie Cowan urged gently.

"I can take you both back in my car, then we'll take it from there," Bart suggested. "Okay with you Constable?"

"Aye, I'll take the van keys, arrange for forensics to pick it up. I'll come over to see you tomorrow." He slid a furtive glance towards Emily then back to Beth who was nodding her consent.

"What if he sees me when we drive past?" The fear in her voice made her quake.

"He won't," Bart spoke with great confidence. "We'll play safe, I'll smuggle you out....it won't be like I haven't done it before!" He grinned sheepishly making Emily laugh. P.C Cowan frowned at his admission. Beth was stunned into silence once more.

When Bart thought about it later he considered himself a master of stealth. Spying on people, watching and following them was once his mainstay business and hard for him to forget those kinds of skills. He covered them both in a blanket in the back of his old Peugeot 208 before he drove out of his garage. He took them both home, promising Beth he would pick her up to take her to the castle until the van was returned to her. They left Robbie Cowan to arrange the police truck to get the van in for forensic examination.

Bart told none of them about arranging to have a meal at the hotel that evening. He wanted to check out the man whose name he knew was Martin Frances. A brief telephone call to his old friend Jay conveyed the name and set him off finding out all he could about him. It almost seemed like old times. Even though he found he already detested this man he didn't even know because of his devastating effect on Beth, there was a little part of him that still felt the thrill of a new case. He had, after all, dealt with some of the vilest people in the past. He did have to admit rarely were they in law enforcement.

The March of Time

For some reason this time his ripple of excitement was short lived, soon turning to dread. Whether because of Phil's initial expression when he arrived at the hotel later for his lone meal or his first glimpse of Beth's husband, Martin Frances that caused it, he didn't know. When he watched him enter the hotel restaurant to be shown to his allocated table by Philip Miller, who gave him a slight nod to indicate who he was, there was something about his bearing that prompted dreadful memories of another man he knew briefly as a 'hired killer', Damien Nance.

He was pleasant to look at, of course, showed consummate charm, the kind meant to attract the ladies or to beguile anyone he needed to do business with (or in Nance's case to kill). Bart tried to picture him in a police uniform which would only reinforce his air of authority Bart knew to be a false face; knowing he could turn on a sixpence into something darkly sinister.

He watched from his vantage point across the room. Phil placed him facing Bart to ensure he got a good view of him. Martin Frances didn't smile at Philip Miller, his face was set in a confident pose showing no interest in those who were there only to serve him. He quite blatantly scanned the tables of other guests already seated or eating. His attention didn't stray too far from his iPhone which he left at the side of his place setting.

There was not a flicker of doubt about his features, he was confident in his appearance as a well-groomed immaculately turned out individual who in no way felt self-conscious sitting alone in a room filled with couples – except for Bart. Bart knew how such a man would rationalise *his* solitary presence there. He was thankful his looks gave him the reason to be alone. Also, of course, to have a certain degree of invisibility as no one really ever wanted to look at him for long. Martin Frances' eyes hadn't lingered on him either; they passed over him briefly without settling. Like him Bart was playing with his mobile phone.

He held the phone up in front of him, screwed up his eyes as if trying to read a message. With the sound turned down and a light brush of a finger, he took a picture of Martin Frances.

He watched his flirtatious behaviour with the plump vivacious waitress who approached him to take his order. Unlike the other foreign staff she also appeared confident. They chattered briefly, whilst Frances gave a friendly amiable performance he kept up for the entire three course meal. She came over to Bart's table, her pen poised over her pad.

"You seem to be in favour over there," he nodded towards Martin Frances.

She only shrugged. Bart wondered about her nationality, whether like Phil indicated, she was with the newly arrived Spanish set.

She surprised Bart with perfect English yet with a slight accent he couldn't place. "Mr Charm offensive is trying very hard," she grimaced wearily.

Bart took in the grin she presented him with, "It's okay my manager has briefed me."

"Ah, I see," he replied. "You have perfect English, you must live over here."

She shook her head, "No, I'm new. I came here from South Africa."

Bart realised there was the subtle hint of Afrikaans, "Your friend over there likes it anyway."

"Maybe," she said without looking back over at him knowing who he meant.

"Most of the young staff come here to learn the language. You don't need it, so why are you here?"

"I wanted the freedom to see more of the world," she didn't sound too convinced shrugging her shoulders. "I had to choose

Scotland, which is like learning a new language," she laughed at her own impertinence. "And it's strange waiting on tables. I'm used to having servants!"

Bart's laughter boomed, "And what have you learnt so far?"

"It is hard work!" her eyes swept around the room at the guests seated at their tables. "And there are a lot of people who are rude!" She turned back towards Bart, "It makes me see how we ought to treat the people who wait on us."

"Now that is a lesson worth learning," Bart noticed her name badge, she was called Bonita.

Bonita took his order rushing off back into the kitchen leaving Bart wondering what 'brief' Philip gave her. If it was just to engage Martin Frances in conversation she certainly didn't have a problem as he saw her once again talking to him each time she served part of his meal. Bart watched Frances reach into his jacket pocket to produce what he knew would be the photograph of Lily Johns (his wife as a young girl). He handed the photo to Bonita which she spent time scrutinising, drawing it closer to her face for a better look. One of her hands went to her head, she scratched and tentatively nodded her head looking thoughtful.

Bart was horrified. He desperately tried to remember if she was on duty the night they all ate together when Emily arrived. He remembered Phil served them himself, he couldn't recall who else was serving at tables. He silently chastised himself for being so lax. He knew if she remembered Beth then she was sure to realise he was with her as well as Jay, Agatha and Emily. Bonita gave him back the picture, clearing away the remaining dishes before going back into the kitchen. Martin Frances smirked, pleased with himself, he stood to leave the restaurant.

He sat finishing his coffee, wanting to speak with Philip, as his waitress came out of the kitchen directly over to him.

"Can I get you anything else?" she asked politely.

Bart shook his head, his meal was now sitting heavily inside him, "What did your friend just show you?" he dared to enquire.

"Oh, a photograph of a girl, he asked if I'd seen her around here," she said.

"And did you recognise her?"

She leaned in conspiratorially, "I told him what Mr Miller asked me to say," she grinned sheepishly. "That I thought she looked like someone I worked with over at Fort William before I came here."

"Oh, I see, what else did he tell you about her?"

"Well, he says she's a runaway. The police are looking for her because she stole a car?" she frowned angrily. "I know that isn't true, he works for immigration chasing up illegals."

"Ah, right," Bart's relief was great. "So you used to work at Fort William?"

She shook her head again, "No, I've only just arrived in the country." She leaned in again to whisper, "I don't like immigration!" She moved away to clear more tables leaving Bart alone enormously relieved. When he got up to leave he left a rather large tip on the table.

On the way past the hotel bar Bart popped in for a nightcap, a tot of Bell's whisky. The room was crowded. There were no seats available anywhere. Further along the corridor a traditional Scottish refrain filtering down from the evening's entertainment didn't seem to tempt any of these people. He stood to one side of the bar with his scotch watching Martin Frances being sociable with a group of people as if he hadn't a care in the world.

As he watched him, Bart speculated briefly on his determination to find his wife. On what might drive him to seek someone who clearly didn't want to be with him. He settled on 'possession', knowing how important it was to those who saw human beings as possessions. Often it came down to 'power'. He knew Frances' type could only acquire self-worth through the power they hold over others which is why they take jobs specifically for that reason. The longer he watched him entertaining the young people he sat with the more he detested the man.

He gulped his drink in one mouthful and left the bar. He didn't know how much longer he could control the urge to do the man some harm. He took himself home without seeking out Philip Miller, tomorrow would be soon enough.

CHAPTER 38

Bart drove over to Aboyne next day to pick Beth up already having received the good news about her husband checking out of the hotel. Philip Miller was convinced he fell for Bonita's story. Neither of them voiced the fear of his returning once he exhausted all enquiries over at their sister hotel at Fort William.

After dropping Emily at the bus stop in Crathie they drove most of the way to the castle in silence. Bart could feel Beth's subdued mood because her husband turning up already destroyed much of her newly found confidence. He told her nothing about his evening meal at the hotel observing Martin Frances. He didn't want to make matters worse.

"Will P.C Cowan interview Thomas Galbraith again now we know about the van?" Beth asked as they began the journey up the long approach road to the castle.

"Maybe, we'll find out later when he calls round to speak to you again," Bart suggested. "I expect he might wait to see what forensics there are first." Bart hadn't told her about Galbraith's lie he was away over the Christmas break or failing to mention he took the van to McKinley's after the accident with the stag. All this he thought was suspicious.

They parted in the car park, Beth going to deliver the news about the kennel's van to Fraser whilst Bart resumed his inventory of the clocks. He hoped to avoid any further contact with Galbraith. He went back to the long gallery to finish off.

Emily telephoned shortly after eleven thirty asking him if he could take some more shots of the library clocks. "I'm pretty sure

I've found something similar for the large mantel clock, if it's an eight day striking with Rosewood casing, could be a George IV which is valued at around £10,500," she said. "I'll show you later. I'm intrigued by the strange carriage clock in the fireplace alcove, could you check to see if there are any markings underneath as I can't find anything remotely similar? "

"I'll try, however if Duncan Munro is working in there today, then I won't be able to," he didn't add his apprehension about bumping into Galbraith or receiving further hostility if he were to find him there. He would need to tread softly. "Is everything okay at the shop?"

"Yes, made my first sale today," she didn't sound overly enthusiastic. "If you can call a watch strap a sale."

"Never mind, lass, one day someone will want to buy one of the grandfather clocks," he wanted to add *don't hold your breath*. He always thought of his collection more his hobby than a business. He often wondered how he would feel about someone wanting to buy any of those he held most precious or whether he could ever part with one of them. So far there had been no challenge which suited him.

An hour later Bart knocked on the library door, the intension being to ask Duncan Munro about the keys to the clocks, he wanted to begin to wind them in order to judge whether they were in working order or needed repair, to add the information to his chart. He felt self-conscious waiting outside the library but chose to knock again in case someone was in there. With no reply he let himself inside.

It didn't look like anyone had worked there since his last visit, when Galbraith accosted him whilst he took photographs. He found himself looking up at what might be a George IV library clock now no longer ticking. He calculated someone previously wound it about eight days ago. As far as he knew the timing didn't fit with the timeline for Mungo going missing; a mystery in itself.

280

He found a wooden three-tread library steps strong enough to hold his weight which he climbed to take a few close-up pictures. He couldn't move the clock to examine the back because the mantel was too narrow to take the turn; instead he did one close-up of each side.

After placing the steps back where he found them, he went over to examine the plain carriage clock inside the fireplace. He could tell immediately it wasn't silver even though first impressions told him otherwise. There was a small amount of tarnishing in places suggesting this was made of some other metal alloy. Silver he knew would tarnish all over unless polished. When he reached to examine the back and the base, he couldn't move or lift the casing which was somehow secured in place. He thought perhaps it was slotted into groves to prevent anyone stealing it. *Why would anyone want to steal such an ugly clock?* He tried to slide it forward. To his surprise the casing moved very stiffly in his hand. Behind him he heard a grating noise which, when he turned round, he saw was the large fire basket moving forward to reveal a hole at the base of the fireplace.

He thought he heard a further sound of voices somewhere out in the corridor leading to the library, he quickly pushed the carriage clock back into place. The fire basket moved back to its original position covering the hole. He went quickly over to the large oak desk in the centre of the library, picked up a pen from its holder, ripped a sheet of note paper from the note pad standing on the desk then he began to write quickly as the door opened. Duncan Munro entered with Thomas Galbraith in tow.

"Good!" Bart boomed across at them in his loudest voice. "I was just writing you a note."

Laird Munro greeted him with a smile, "Ah, Mr Jeffries, Sirus, how's the inventory going?"

He could see the dark expression appear on Galbraith's face reminding him of their last encounter when he caught him alone in there.

"Good," he exclaimed. "Which is why I wondered about the keys to wind up the clocks, do you have them? Now would seem expedient to test them whilst I'm doing this.....to identify any needing attention?"

The Laird looked round at his secretary, "Thomas, would you sort this for Sirus please?" Bart noted for the first time there was very little in the way of affability from the laird towards his secretary. Bart could only assume by the instruction they must be available otherwise they would have been reported missing along with Mungo MacLeod.

"Excellent!" Bart chirped as he walked away from the desk having placed the pen back in its holder. "I'll get back to my inventory," without looking back he left the library. He knew if he could see through the door Galbraith would walk over to where he'd left the note he was scribbling when they came in. What he would see: *Do you have the keys to all the time....,* was as far as he could manage before they entered.

Instead of returning to the long gallery he walked around the outside of the castle to the gift shop having arranged to meet Beth during her lunch break in the café. He found her sitting at a quiet corner table eating a sandwich; she was reading a book. He got himself a beef with horseradish sandwich and cup of coffee before he joined her. The café was almost empty, with no residual noise they resorted to whispering so they wouldn't be overheard.

"How did Fraser take the news about the police taking the kennels' van?" he asked. "You told me he already knew about the accident?"

"He didn't say very much at all other than mentioning he was away over Christmas," he could tell she was far from pleased with his reply.

"Did you tell him you knew when the accident happened?"

She shook her head, "No, I only told him the police took the van because of being involved in an accident," she seemed a little upset by Fraser's response, thought he sounded a bit guarded. "He did say I can use the stable's van when it's free until we get the other one back." Nevertheless, she still appeared a little worried, adding, "Do you think he meant the accident must have happened when he was away on holiday?"

"I expect so," Bart agreed half-heartedly. He guessed she didn't like the idea he might have something to do with the incident. "Look, I've discovered something....." He began intending to tell her about the fireplace as a group of staff burst noisily through the café door to prevent him. Most of them Bart didn't recognise except he saw Galbraith lurking behind them.

Beth bent her head to examine her sandwich, whispered, "Fraser, Joy, Worsel and Morgan the groom."

"Okay, I'll leave when you're ready around five o'clock. I'll telephone Emily to meet us at Crathie....speak later," he left as the group carried on seemingly poking fun once again at Worsel. Galbraith caught sight of Beth sitting alone, the book she was reading before Bart joined her lay on the table in front of her. She got up moving towards the door. Galbraith manoeuvred himself to cut her off.

"Come and join us," his invitation coming before she got the chance to escape.

"I've finished," she told him, "I've got to get back." Before he could say another word she moved around him and left.

She spent the rest of the day in a restless mood with thoughts resurfacing about leaving her job at the castle. She no longer felt comfortable with the place or the people she worked with. Mostly she felt too exposed to enable her husband to find her. Her text to Bart later was to the point, "Need a lift." When he walked out to his car she was already waiting for him beside the Peugeot.

Bart's earlier call to Emily set her off researching the castle Daingneach's history. He asked her specifically to find out as much as she could about the castle itself and the previous owners. She didn't even ask him why, he went on to tell her not to become too engrossed she might miss her bus back to Crathie. Once in the car he handed Beth his mobile as they left the castle asking her to text Emily to remind her they were on their way. He hoped she wasn't still at the shop because she should be on the bus back to Crathie.

Beth heard the beep reading Emily's reply to Bart, "She's already there she wants us to meet her at the Information Centre opposite Crathie Church." He smiled nodding, once again impressed by her. The phone beeped with a second message. Beth relayed, "She says to bring money or a credit card!" Bart burst out laughing at her cheek.

They parked in Crathie's public car park walking the short distance to the Information Centre which they found dimly lit with the closed sign on the door.

"Oh!" Beth checked her watch, "Half past five, they're closed." She searched the shadows for any sign of Emily in case she was waiting somewhere outside. "Maybe she started walking back to the cottage," she speculated despite knowing how far away the cottage was.

Bart shook his head, tried the door which opened, "Emily wouldn't go without telling us."

The shop was empty. What light there was came from a frosted window in a door behind the counter. He was about to reassess his comment when the door opened spilling out bright light across the shop revealing a middle-aged woman smiling at them.

"Have you seen a young girl....?" Beth began.

The woman grinned broadly, "You're here for Amelia?"

Beth and Bart exchanged glances, "Do you mean Emily?" Bart asked her.

The woman beckoned them opening the office door wider where they could see Emily sitting behind a desk surrounded by piles of books, "In here, we're doing some research," clearly from her smile the lady appeared to be enjoying it.

Emily spotted them, closed the note pad in front of her, picked it up with two of the books from beside her. "This is Mrs Buchanan...." She began.

"Grace, please," she prompted Emily.

"Grace," Emily announced. "Who has been helping me with my research on Scottish castles." Emily shot a look at Bart which demanded his discretion, "These are my friends Beth and Sirus," she politely introduced them to each other. She turned to Grace handing her the two books, "I would like to buy these two I think." She swept a hand above the books left on the table. "Shall I put the others back?" she asked Grace Buchanan.

"No need, I'll put them back, only too pleased to be able to help you with your assignment."

"Thank you," Emily smiled graciously. "And you have been such a help too." She gushed seeing how pleased the woman was.

Out in the shop Bart paid for the two books with cash leaving Grace Buchanan to finish up. Once in the car, Emily ripped open the package Grace so carefully wrapped, and handed the books to Beth to look at. Bart flicked on the dim overhead light so they could examine their titles.

"Sorry about buying these books, I felt I ought to because she was so helpful. I got such a lot of information out of her," Bart could tell she was excited. "Those two were about the most useful of the ones she showed me.....it was her contribution whilst showing me them which was really good. The Scottish castles one does include Daingneach though – it means 'Stronghold' did you know?" Beth shook her head whilst Bart nodded he did. "The other one is about myths and legends, more to do with witchcraft than anything else.

285

There is quite a bit of history to it." They could see how animated she was. "Grace seems to know more about our castle than even the history books reveal but then she is from an Aberdeenshire family where these kinds of stories seem to be handed down."

"Is there anything about the castle being haunted?" Bart asked.

"There's nothing in any of the history books about Daingneach, not even the ones about famous Scottish ghosts...there's plenty of those," Emily went on, "Mostly, it's about some lost treasure belonging to Seumus Grant which no one has ever been able to find so people think it's a myth."

"Did Grace confirm the legend?" Bart asked.

"She did mention it," Emily was disappointed she couldn't elaborate further.

Beth asked Bart, "Didn't Mary Macaulay tell us something about the castle being haunted?"

"Yes, she did, when Galbraith frightened her in the car park one night after she stayed late," Bart pointed at the books, "And there's nothing in any of those books?"

Emily shook her head, "I'll do some more searching on the internet, see what I can find."

Beth checked her wrist watch, "We better get back, P.C Cowan is meant to be coming round."

When Bart turned his car into the cottage gates they could see the police defender already parked there. Robbie Cowan climbed out when he saw the Peugeot, "Ah, I was about to call you," holding his mobile ready in his hand.

Emily scurried off to open the back door. Bart caught a glimpse of the blush spreading across her cheeks confirming what he suspected about her liking the young police officer. "Sorry to keep you waiting, constable," Bart said formally, "I needed to pick Emily up along the way."

"It's na'bother," he followed them into the cottage where Emily was already busying herself having put new logs on the fire. Sandy the Foxhound as usual was fully stretched in front of the range, he barely moved let alone made any attempt to greet anyone.

"What a strange dog you have and no mistake," Robbie Cowan commented.

Whilst Beth went with Robbie to the front room so he could ask her questions about the van, Bart sat with Emily around the big table in the kitchen drinking tea.

"What's all this about your assignment young Amelia?" Bart teased.

She didn't appear one bit self-conscious, "I told her I was researching for a paper on castles, wanting to include any local ones. She assumed I was still at school, I didn't see any point in correcting her. She did say she used to be a teacher and liked to help children wherever she could." Emily shrugged in the way teenagers often do. "Amelia is my actual name……. everyone has always called me Emily. My Dad did say I would grow into my real name one day."

"Well I think Amelia is a delightful name, it suits you," Bart replied thinking it did sound quite a grown-up name reflecting her maturity, which he didn't mention to her.

Emily searched his face for sincerity, "I shall use Amelia as my 'sleuth' name when I'm undercover searching for information," she sounded so serious but caught the reproving look on his face before she burst out laughing. "Just kidding!" she said, only Bart knew she wasn't really.

He went on to show her the pictures he'd taken of the library clock as he handed his phone to her to upload them onto their computers.

"What about the silver one?" she asked flicking the screen to find any new pictures of it. Bart paused momentarily wondering whether to wait for Robbie to finish interviewing Beth in the front room to update them. Emily sensed his reluctance quickly asking, "What is it?"

He gave in, "It isn't really a clock at all." He lowered his voice as if he might be overheard by someone who shouldn't be there as Emily hung on his words her mouth forming the 'W' of 'What'. "It opens a secret passage in the fireplace under the fire basket." He knew he sounded implausible so he wasn't surprised when Emily laughed.

"Come on!" she exclaimed. "You've got to be kidding me, right?" His face remained deadly serious as the full realisation hit him of what he'd found. He shook his head. "You found..." she gasped too loudly then lowered her voice, "You really have found a secret passage?"

"Yes.....I'm not sure what kind because the laird came in with his secretary..."

"They caught you!"

"No, I managed to move the clock back which moved the basket back into place," he breathed deeply. "In fact, I only caught a quick glimpse of a hole.....my impression is it's quite large......could be one of those 'priest's holes' they sometimes used to hide contraband in," he explained. The idea came to him perhaps this was the reason Galbraith was so angry when he discovered him alone in the library. "I have reason to think Galbraith might know about it because of his attitude towards finding me in there. I don't know about Duncan Munro he seems too friendly, he wasn't bothered about finding me in the library today."

"So this Galbraith person does you think?"

"Why else is he so hostile towards me?" Bart asked as if he was talking aloud to himself.

Emily sat up straight looking contemplative.

"What?" Bart asked watching her thinking.

"Do you think he's found Seumus Grant's lost treasure?" her face was so serious Bart burst out laughing.

"We don't really know if there is any treasure, do we?"

"Well no…"

"You would think after all these years someone would have at least found this hole by now, wouldn't you?" he asked.

"I definitely need to do more research, maybe go back to talk to Grace again, see if she knows anyone else who can help me with my assignment," Emily winked conspiratorially. Then her face grew furtive, "Do you think we could go to look where the hole leads to?"

"Whoa, there young lady!" Bart held up his hand to stop her. "Don't let us get carried away."

They heard voices outside in the hallway. Bart quickly put a finger over his lips, "Let's hold fast on telling P.C Cowan about this for now."

Before Emily could say anything more the kitchen door opened and Beth came back from the front room, "Robbie wants a word Emily," she sounded really serious.

CHAPTER 39

Emily found herself tapping on the lounge door forgetting for one moment it was she who lived in the cottage not him. She hated when she blushed every time she saw him. So far she hadn't grown out of this uncontrollable reflex action making her face redden and her to feel so damned self-conscious. She caught a glimpse of Sirus behind Beth's back as she was making the officer a cup of tea; he slipped his finger across his lips to warn her to be careful what she told the young police officer.

She opened the door pretending she caught her hand because she was holding the mug of tea.

"I didn't know if you took sugar," she stammered in embarrassment. "I'll fetch you some if you want."

He stood up, feeling as awkward as she did, took the proffered tea from her hand and put the mug down on the coffee table.

"No, err thank you," he said. "Sit down, this won't take long. Beth's already told me most of what happened at McKinley's garage. I need your version." He also seemed nervous.

She sat down in the arm chair opposite the couch where he perched sideways, his long legs restricted by the coffee table in between them. She waited watching him pick up the tea to take a sip before he began.

"Nice brew," he muttered. "Now, I understand you were having problems with the van...."

"Well actually we heard a noise in the engine," Emily lied hoping Beth kept to the story. She hated to have to tell him the noise was her idea as an excuse to go into McKinley's to ask about any previous servicing of the van.

He showed no signs he disbelieved either of them or doubted it was by mere chance they discovered the van was thought to have hit a deer. He merely accepted everything she told him.

"Were you driving?" he suddenly asked her.

She was shocked by the question, "No! Beth was, I've only just got my provisional licence." She suddenly felt confused as if he was accusing her of something. "I haven't had any lessons yet." She sounded apologetic, her old habit of lowering her head to hide behind her hair returned.

He recognised he'd upset her, "I'm sorry I didn't mean to...." he began.

"No, it's okay," she felt embarrassed by her reaction. She felt she needed to explain, "I was meant to have lessons...... my Dad was going to teach me before my parents split up and......well I haven't seen him since." Her voice trailed off, she suddenly felt like weeping because of everything that happened back in Wainthorpe. She wasn't going to let him see her cry. "I expect I will do when I've a bit more money....."

"I shouldn't have asked. I was thinking about how loud the noise must have been if you both heard it before you stopped the van in Dinnet?" Emily immediately thought he was suspicious about there not being anything wrong with the van.

"I think Beth heard the noise first, she drew my attention to it," she said. "When I listened hard, not being used to the sound of the engine, I did think I heard something."

She watched him scribble some more in his note book, then he shocked her with, "According to the vehicle examiner's initial look at the engine, it looks like someone has tampered with the brakes," he heard her gasp as the shock appeared on her face. "I'll know more when he's finished the examination."

291

Puzzled Emily asked, "Surely the lady at the garage would have checked for damage after the accident?"

"Yes, Nessa did a thorough service and test drive," he confirmed.

Emily was stunned, "Are you saying someone did this *after* the van went back to the castle?"

Robbie Cowan closed his note book, put his pen away then glanced searchingly at Emily who sat waiting for an answer. "I'll wait for the results before I comment," his face showed all the signs he was taking the matter very seriously.

More questions formed in her head, she could see their interview was over and as the silence grew longer she missed her chance.

Eventually he said, "I could take you out." Emily was stunned into silence. She didn't know what he meant or how to reply. "I mean for a driving lesson," he added to her amazement.

"Pardon?" she queried.

"If you really want to learn, I mean."

"I don't have a car," she pointed out confused by his sudden offer.

"I do," he smiled now a little embarrassed by his forthrightness.

"Don't you need insurance for teaching a learner driver in your car?"

He laughed and couldn't help saying, "Said the Insurance man's daughter." They found themselves laughing together, unable to stop. When their laughter subsided he added, "I'm fully comp," which set them off giggling, again the ice well and truly broken.

They were still chuckling when they came back into the kitchen to find Bart and Beth both staring at them which made them laugh even more. Before he left he turned to Emily saying, "I'll be in touch," she nodded showing him out of the back door watching him all the way until he climbed into the Defender she waved and closed the door.

When she turned Beth and Bart were staring at her expectantly which made Emily blush. She moved over to Beth's new kettle, tested the weight for water, finding it full she flicked it on once again to make more tea. Bart recognised this as her contingency in a crisis, knew despite the laughter she was feeling anxious.

Bart tapped the chair at the side of him, "Sit down, Emily" Bart insisted. "What did P.C Cowan tell you?" She could see by the fear in Beth's face they knew already.

"Did he tell you about the van?" she asked Beth who nodded.

"We've been talking while you were in the front room," Bart told her. "Certainly looks like a good thing the police took the van away."

"It's like judgement on us for pretending about the noise," Emily suggested. "How could this happen?"

Beth trembled slightly, "We discussed the possibility Martin, my husband, tried to….." she left the words unspoken shaking her head in resignation.

"I can't see how," Bart interceded. "I really don't believe he knows for definite you are here. I saw him showing your picture to Bonita at the hotel. He was still asking people if they'd seen you right up to when he checked out……"

"Why would he want me dead?" Beth asked shaking uncontrollably. Bart reached across the table to put a hand over her arm to comfort her.

"I don't for one minute believe he does," he patted her arm. "Anyway, there was no time to do anything to the van since he arrived as the police had taken it by then. I am convinced he's over at Fort William after Bonita misled him; he's still searching for you. Anyway, he sounds very much like a control freak to me. No he wants to take you back, I am certain."

Emily asked, "Who else would want to cause an accident or to….?" she stopped herself from saying 'kill Beth' the thought was too much for her.

"Now, we don't know or even if it was actually intended for Beth."

"Not me!?" Emily exclaimed.

"Stop, will you," Bart shouted. "The van belongs to the castle, is one of two. Could have been meant for any one of several people who have use of either of them?"

Beth stared at him in amazement, "Are you saying someone could have mistaken my van for the stable's van, they are after all identical apart from the registration numbers?"

She could tell Bart hadn't thought if through, "Yes, I suppose so. They are often parked together at the castle," he remembered seeing them. "Who outside of the castle would realise there were two identical vans?"

"It could even be someone who knows someone who works there." Emily suggested.

"Or even used to work there, someone who might still have an axe to grind?" Bart silently reprimanded himself for an unfortunate use of terminology. "Wouldn't they know which van was which in that case?"

Emily frowned muttering, "This is all a bit far-fetched if you ask me."

"You're not suggesting someone like Mary Macaulay are you?" Beth asked. "Why would she? You saw how distressed she was about Mungo MacLeod not coming back on Christmas Eve....." All this speculation was unnerving her. "Let's wait to see what Robbie comes up with."

They both saw Emily's face flush again at the mention of his name and made a face at each other in recognition of it.

Bart got up to leave, "Are you coming over tomorrow Emily?"

She nodded, "Yes, we need to look over the information I've found about the library clocks, don't we?" She stared hard at Bart wondering what his intentions were regarding the secret passage which she hoped might be to explore it. He bid them good night before he left.

CHAPTER 40

Robbie Cowan sat in the Defender opposite McKinley's Auto; he was on an early shift. He was in two minds whether he really needed all the agro he knew Jock McKinley would give him. He also knew he could have telephoned to speak with Nessa and likely would still have got the old goat answering the phone. Nessa did most of the work these days leaving her old man with the admin if he could be bothered even to do that.

He watched the roll-up garage door rise, saw McKinley yell something across the cars parked inside he couldn't hear at that distance. He came out moving across the forecourt to the next door deserted lot where he got into a battered open backed truck and drove away.

Robbie Cowan heaved a huge sigh of relief, got out of the car to cross over the road. He could hear radio Northsound blaring but couldn't spot Nessa anywhere inside. When the music faded he caught a voice speaking in anger. He approached the sound catching sight of her talking to someone on her mobile as she sat at the small desk in the corner.

Nessa was yelling into the phone, "Stop phoning me! Leave me alone!" She pressed the mobile off, threw it down in anger on top of a pile of papers strewn over the desk. When she spotted Robbie standing still a few paces away he noted her red face was fierce which slipped away into a smile.

"Nessa?" he greeted. "You okay?"

"Aye, Robbie," she stood up as her mobile began to ring again and he could see her patience once again ebbing away. She picked up the phone cancelled the call then switched the phone off completely. "What can I do for yer Robbie?"

He pulled out a copy of the original invoice she gave him for the kennel's van. "Thought you might need a copy for your records," he held it out to her. "We need the original as evidence."

"Aye," she took it off him, went over to the filing cabinet where she dropped the copy inside the first draw she came to.

"Can I ask you something else?" She stood waiting after nodding a yes. "When Galbraith brought the van here on 23ʳᵈ December, can ye remember how he got home?"

She stood scratching her head thinking. "I'm not sure, I was a bit preoccupied wi'the van....it was losing blood all over the forecourt, d'ye ken?"

He nodded. "You didn't give him a lift back t'the castle then?"

She shook her head, "I was on ma own, Da was away with Mam. I needed to get the grill off quick like. As far as I can remember he walked away....." She closed her eyes for a second trying to remember, "Wait!" she said. "I was underneath the van getting the grill off....it was rusted, hard to shift.... I did hear someone pull up and a car door slam."

"How soon after he left? Did you see who?"

She shook her head, "No idea, I was too busy wi'the van. I d'na see who, I only heard the motor was diesel.....the timing was off, probably needed a service, wasn't sparking properly, that's all I can tell ye."

Robbie felt all the frustration of knowing how close she came to seeing who helped Galbraith.

"Anything else?" she asked sounding a little bit irritated. "I've got to get on, this motor needs to be done for this afternoon," she pointed at the car she was working on.

"I wonder if you might have a spare pair of learner driver plates to lend me?" He looked a little embarrassed.

"Oh aye, have you got a lassie?" she teased like she used to in the old days.

He flushed whilst saying, "No, I'm doing someone a favour."

"That right?" she walked over to a standing fitment, picked off a set of new L-plates in a packet to throw across to him.

The garage phone began to ring. He saw the scowl creep over Nessa's face. She walked across picked up the phone tentatively saying, "McKinley's Auto," then he watched her slam it down her anger once more returning.

"So how is Shona?" he asked intuitively now wondering if Nessa broke up with her long-term girlfriend.

"She's persistent! Actually, bloody annoying!" she spat.

"Ah, sorry, did you two have a row? Bet your old man is pleased," his hint of sarcasm didn't go unnoticed.

"He'll never accept anyone I'm with will he?"

"What happened with you two, I thought you were fine," he asked.

She shook her head, "Not really. I thought her bein' possessive was cute....at first," she grimaced, "Which, eventually turned into something sinister 'n' very stifling. She was jealous if I spoke to anyone, even if a customer wanted ta book in their car if she took the call......especially a woman..... she could be bloody rude!" She shook her head again. "I've had enough, told her I couldn't take any more....."

The phone started up again. She pointed at it, "See? Now she won't give up pestering me. She got all irate, asked me if I was seeing someone else. It's my fault. For spite as well as to get her off my back I told her I'd met someone, she was young, beautiful and if I wanted to see someone else I would!"

Robbie grinned at Nessa's determination, "And are you?"

"No – well there's always someone who comes along to catch your eye isn't there Robbie Cowan?" she grinned at him, knew only too well every expression of her old friend's face. "Like the lassie with the van! Now there's someone I would like to get to know." She winked at him saw his alarmed face, "What is it?"

"You mean Emily?"

"I'm not sure what her name is, she works up at the castle......drives the van you're interested in," she was looking worried now.

"Ah, Beth Grant, I thought you meant...." He left Emily's name unspoken, not before she could see how relieved he was. "You think she might be interested?"

She shrugged pointing at the L-plates in his hand, "Always someone you want to do a favour, eh?"

They both laughed. He walked away held up the plates to her, "Thank you, see you around Nessa, you take care now."

"You too Robbie."

*　　*　　*　　*　　*

It was a fine morning, just short of nine o'clock, when Emily got off the bus at the turning circle and walked up The Brae to The March of Time, she never failed to smile at the caricature of the rabbit who resembled Sirus. She expected the door to be locked with the 'closed' sign up because he'd dropped her at the bus stop in Crathie to take Beth with him to the castle. He already gave her instructions about today's priority. Her first task when she opened up with the new key cut especially for her was to stand still when she met with the mass chiming of the clocks. This was her ritual, one she learnt at his old shop back home. She turned in a full circle listening intently for anything amiss. She smiled. Nothing wrong here so she walked through to the back.

There was a newish aroma of bacon with a subtle hint of something spicy in the background. The computer sat on the kitchen table ready for her with a note he'd written hurriedly before he left, *'Emily, I think you are quite correct it is a George IV library clock. Don't forget to search for the ghost of Daingneach, see what you can learn about Seumus Grant especially how he made his money – he owned rather a large collection of weaponry so he must have had some, see you later, Bart.'*

Of course he'd already told her this when he picked Beth up and gave her a lift to Crathie.

Her first port of call was the kettle even though she'd not long eaten breakfast, tea being a continuous requirement for her. She took the lap top along with the cup of tea through to the shop, turned over the open sign leaving the door unlocked before she set about searching for anything she could find about Seumus Grant's time at Daingneach. Her first sight of him was the same image as the painting currently hanging in the castle library. Sirus told her Mungo MacLeod resembled him which was why he believed him to be the Laird when he brought the clock in for repair. This was initially reinforced when he saw the portrait of Seumus Grant hanging in the library at the castle.

When her mobile began to ring she could see Robbie Cowan's name which set her heart racing a little faster. She was thankful he couldn't see her face flush when she answered him.

"Hello?"

He was up tempo with his "Hi, Emily, I called because I have a day off tomorrow if you're serious about a driving lesson?" There was too long a pause so he added, "I would offer you Friday only I have to get Thomas Galbraith in for CID, it required me to cancel my second rest day."

"Tomorrow is good," she said suddenly feeling nervous. "Look you do know I've never even had one lesson don't you?"

She heard him chuckle, "That's okay we'll start somewhere safe so you aren't a threat to the public." For one moment she believed him until he laughed again. "Don't worry! I've done my advanced driving course, we'll start from basics?" The sigh showed her relief.

"Okay, what time?"

"We'll let the roads settle down after the rush, how does eleven suit you?"

He arranged to pick her up from the cottage next day. He left her staring at her mobile trying not to worry about letting herself down. Eventually, she got lost in her research.

She was surprised when the shop door opened to find Sirus back from the castle so soon. He locked the door leaving the 'open' up to indicate they were there, "Let's go through to the back, if anyone wants us they can knock." Neither of them expected too much, this was after all Wednesday. The hotel guests in on tours would be away on trips around the Highlands rather than shopping locally. Today the village would be like a ghost town.

"Is there anything wrong?" Emily asked once she'd filled the kettle again.

"No, lass," he'd dropped Beth off then after making an enquiry about Duncan Munro, discovered he was away on business for the rest of the week. "The Laird is away so I thought if I could keep his secretary busy one day this week, I might be able to have another look at the fire place in the library."

Emily grinned, "What if I told you he's going to be taken to the police station on Friday?"

Bart's face brightened, "How do you know?"

She grinned back impishly, "Because P.C Cowan is giving me a driving lesson on his day off tomorrow. He couldn't offer me Friday because he has to take Thomas Galbraith in for questioning by CID!" Bart's mouth dropped open. "So I reckon we can safely explore the hidden passage whilst he's away helping the police with their enquiries."

"We?" Bart laughed.

"Well I am your assistant researcher so I should accompany you to examine the library clocks."

Bart's sudden laugh gave way to a frown, "Are you sure about Galbraith....?"

"I'm sure I can find out tomorrow from Robbie," she grinned again.

"Where did the timid schoolgirl go?" he asked joining in. He could see she enjoyed the intrigue.

"It's the company I'm keeping!"

It took some time to update him on the story of Seumus Grant's extensive collection of weaponry reputed to be the largest single collection. Bart saw the portrait picture at the side of the article Emily found.

"It's an uncanny likeness to Mungo MacLeod they have to be related," he said. "What have you discovered about him?"

She pulled up another screen from her bookmarked list leaving him to read up on the reputation of the once Laird of Daingneach.

"It's possible Mungo could be related somewhere along the line, otherwise as doppelgangers go he must be the closest I have ever seen to another person," Bart suggested.

"I wonder?" Emily asked.

"What?"

"What do we know about Mungo MacLeod? Maybe we could work back, try to set him a family tree, you never know there could be a vital link." Emily never ceased to amaze Bart these days. "People do have secrets, don't they?" She eyed Bart curiously then retrieved the note he left her, she pushed the paper over towards him.

He read his own handwriting again even though he only wrote the note a few hours ago. He sat up shocked, "Oh!" He saw he signed 'Bart' in his haste to get out to pick up Beth, "I see."

"There's no problem leaving it for me. You need to be careful otherwise you might do the same in the wrong circumstances," she said rather shrewdly for someone so young.

"Let me explain," he began to tell her the story of his journey through so many name changes. After half an hour of reflecting he stopped to wait for her comments or any questions.

"Will you go back to give evidence?" The question surprised him.

"I always intended to, I didn't think they would catch Toni Maola. I assumed he'd gone back to Italy. I understand he is in line for a large fortune in the event of his father's demise."

His comment brought her back to her current research, "I wonder who inherited Seumus Grant's stuff," she declared out of the blue. "In those days the eldest son always inherited; history wasn't very kind to women back then was it?"

Bart sat reflecting as Emily thought about him having to give evidence against Toni Maola, which left her feeling fearful. "For what it's worth I didn't like the cop Steve who came looking for you."

It took Bart by surprise, "Why not?"

She tried to formulate her thoughts to explain how she felt an instant dislike for the man. "I know most police officers are determined, you know to catch....say murderers or very bad people," she knew because of their reaction to her cousin Peter being abused which flashed through her mind. Bart nodded to encourage her. "This time he was....well quite different."

"How do you mean?" he tried to remember all he could from his own limited contact with him; only a couple of superficial meetings so not much to judge him on.

"I thought he was weird. I mean it's not like *you* are the criminal is it? You're a witness and don't forget I already knew you. This time he was kind of keener – no – it's hard to explain. More like his life depended on finding you. He seemed much more desperate, like he was searching for someone to donate their kidney to save someone's life," she apologised for not explaining very well. She couldn't do justice to how he made her feel. "One thing's for sure. I didn't like him at all."

Bart fell silent, moved by what she told him, knowing whatever she meant he trusted her judgement on the matter. He suddenly felt quite afraid, influenced, no doubt partly because Beth was being pursued by a ruthless man who also happened to be a police officer. His own feelings on seeing him operating in the dining room at the hotel produced a similar dislike. It was instinctive, so he knew how she felt.

"Did he show you his I.D or to anyone you saw him speak to in the café?"

"No, he didn't even say he was a police officer, only that he was looking for the clock maker Cyrus Bartholomew."

"Did he give you his full name?"

She shook her head, "Not to me, I overheard him say Steve to someone else. I think he dismissed me being a child but he did try to intimidate me by telling me it was my duty to tell anyone who knew where you were to contact him. I saw him give someone a card. To be honest I felt bullied like I did at school only he scared me. There was something not right about him."

"I believe you, Emily. I think Jay felt the same," Bart began to feel even more worried.

CHAPTER 41

Next day Emily woke up feeling nauseous, unsure whether the thought of driving for the first time or meeting Robbie Cowan again, was giving her the shakes. Beth recognised her own nervous reaction when she drove for the first time assuring her if she could do it, Emily would have no problems. In her case she had Martin to contend with which would have been a challenge to anyone to learn. She was amazed she ever passed her test.

Emily's stomach churned when she saw the silver Vauxhall with L plates pull up in the yard. Climbing into the passenger seat she felt a surge of excitement as Robbie Cowan grinned at her.

"Okay?" he asked realising by her paleness how she must be feeling. "Don't be nervous I'm going to take you to my flying club where there's a bit of space."

"You fly?!" she sounded shocked.

He laughed at her reaction, "Only microlights, not jumbo jets!"

"Wow!" she stared at him agog, noticed how young he looked in faded denims with a grey sweatshirt. She could feel herself begin to flush never having seen him without his uniform before, she thought him 'hot' as the girls back at school often used to say if they liked a boy. She couldn't think of another word to best describe him.

"Don't worry I'll teach you to drive today, the only obstacles will be a few small microlights which we'll try to keep away from."

She tapped him lightly on the arm with a bunched up fist but the ice was very much broken, the conversation moved on with her asking many questions about his flying hobby, so by the time they arrived at the airfield she was already relaxed for her first lesson.

He was business-like first asking to see her provisional licence before he let her sit at the wheel.

"Amelia, eh?" he saw her real name on her licence. "Now there's a very grown-up name." For which he got another thump on the arm. "I meant pretty name, honest." He sat rubbing his arm as if she really hurt him.

The day turned out to be the best she ever had, with a lot of fun because he was such a patient instructor. He made her feel confident, whilst driving for the first time gave her a feeling of freedom. At one point when she drove really smoothly around the airfield she let out a cry of pure joy, her face alive with it. He sat laughing at her reaction. He knew how she felt because he felt the same way about flying his microlights.

The only down side was Emily's guilt at subtly bringing up the subject of his cancelled day off the next day which indirectly confirmed his intention to take Galbraith in for questioning. Her guilt was more to do with deceiving him about what she intended doing with Sirus in Galbraith's absence which she kept from him. Even so, she felt nothing could spoil the excitement she felt at having her first driving lesson or the anticipation of next day's inspection of the moving library clock's hidden passageway which intrigued her.

*   *   *   *   *

The following morning she travelled to the castle with Beth in the Stable's white van where she waited for Bart in the gift shop café. During his telephone call the night before he told her he wanted to make sure Thomas Galbraith would definitely not be around to see her or to discover what they were doing.

He positioned himself in the grand salon overlooking the castle's front car park to watch for P.C Cowan's Defender approaching to take Galbraith away. He looked mightily annoyed, Bart thought, as he was invited to sit in the back seat. There was one moment as he watched them drive away when Galbraith turned round to stare out of the back window directly up to where Bart stood, making him duck out of sight. He felt silly after because there was no secret he was in the castle today, his Peugeot was after all parked out front, then he was officially meant to be there.

Bart sent an all clear text to Emily to meet him at the front door of the castle. She was overawed stepping inside her very first castle. As she followed Bart she took in as much of the interior as she could whilst moving swiftly behind him. He stopped once or twice to hurry her along to the library where to his dismay he found the door locked.

"Blast!" he cried alarming Emily who looked extremely disappointed. "Wait there," he ordered. He rushed off leaving her standing in the dimly lit corridor. The dimness of the lights together with the silence of the castle made her think about the stories of the ghost reputed to be of Seumus Grant she'd heard about.

Bart returned carrying his Gladstone bag of tools which he placed on the floor, bent down to rummage inside. Emily saw him take out a small black case containing a set of lock picks he'd managed to keep from his sleuthing days.

"Let's see if I've still got the old skills," he muttered selecting two he moved nearer the door, inserted one feeling around inside the lock until he was satisfied. Then he introduced the other at an angle, whilst Emily watched fascinated. She had seen enough TV crime dramas to recognise what he was doing. The tiniest of clicks brought a smile to his face. He extracted the picks and turned the handle. The door opened with him saying, "Eh, voila!"

Emily took the picks out of his hand, returned them to the case, then into the Gladstone bag which she carried entering the room behind him and closed the door.

"Wow!" she exclaimed seeing all the books arranged from floor to ceiling, "This is awesome!" She curiously sniffed the air, "I love the smell of old books!"

Bart wasn't sure the smell of mildew appealed to him. He smiled anyway walking over to the open fire place he pointed at the mantel, "Meet your first George IV library clock." She put the bag down on the floor, moved closer to view it above her. "It's stopped," she declared.

"Yes, but it was going about ten days ago," Bart informed her. "I've asked for the clock keys which Galbraith is meant to be giving me, now I'm wondering whether he actually has them."

Emily looked around the room, "Could they be somewhere in here?"

"I expect Duncan Munro would have known if they were. He would have given me them when I asked him for them. He didn't, he told Galbraith to deal with it."

He stepped up into the fire place where he pointed at the strange carriage clock, "Watch this," he said. He took hold of each side, pulling the clock forward which started the grating sound from the fire basket. Once again it moved forward arching to one side exposing what they both believed to be the start of a passageway. When they peered inside, the hole was completely dark with an unpleasant odour rising from it, a smell of stale earth. They couldn't see very far into the blackness.

Bart went over once more to rummage in his bag. He took out a couple of torches, one larger than the other which made Emily laugh.

He countered with, "Standard clock mending tools, you always need plenty of light to see inside the mechanisms of the bigger ones. He handed the small torch to Emily whilst he pressed the large one into life giving an intense beam he directed down the opening in the floor, "There's a ladder attached to the wall, I wonder how far down it goes?"

Emily peered over the hole, "Let me go first," she offered. "I'm….." She stopped herself from using 'smaller' or 'thinner' in case she hurt his feelings. She opted for, "…younger."

Bart had no illusions about his physical shape. He didn't think the size of the tunnel would impede him. He could see Emily was enthusiastic about exploring, "Okay, but be careful, make sure you test those ladder rungs before you put your whole weight on them. I expect they've been there many years so they could have rusted some."

She pushed the slider on the torch which gave off quite a beam considering its size, took the end into her mouth before she positioned herself over the hole ready to step on to the ladder. She gave a mighty stomp on the first rung to test its stability taking a jolt to her foot.

Bart stood at the top aiming the full beam of his torch down the hole. He watched the top of Emily's head move slowly downwards until all he could see was a small dot of light bobbing about as she went lower. The stale air wafted upwards with the motion of her descent.

"You okay?" he shouted down, then realised she wouldn't be able to answer with the torch in her mouth. Minutes passed silently until below a brighter flickering light came on illuminating Emily standing on firm ground at the bottom.

"It's not too far down, a bit dusty and I found a light. Yes, it's a passageway alright......I can't see where it goes to!" she shouted up, her voice echoing.

He watched her begin to climb back up the ladder until her head appeared at the top. She made no attempt to get out.

"There has to be a way of opening this from the inside," she suggested as she began to run her hand around the wall at the top of the hole. "Ah!" she cried finding an indent with an iron ring embedded. She held the ring twisting gently anti-clockwise. They saw the fire basket begin to move back into place. She stopped, twisted back clockwise to open it fully again.

"Clever!" Bart declared. "So you can come and go without being seen, excellent."

"Shall we explore?" Emily invited. Bart turned to look behind him as if someone had entered the library. "Get the bag, I'll take it down," she told him as he picked up the Gladstone bag to hand to her. "Put your torch in," she told him before slipping the small one inside. She hooked her arm through the handles pulling the bag over her shoulder before she began to climb back down, "Make sure you close up completely after."

After closing up the hole Bart gingerly climbed down the metal rungs. Although his body mass didn't prevent a smooth descent he vowed to himself he would try to lose a bit of weight if he was going to spend time playing Indiana Jones.

When he reached the bottom setting foot on firm ground he could see the light came from an old lamp inside which the naked flame burnt steadily.

"How did you light the lamp?" he asked her.

"Some kind person left matches?" she shook a long box of matches in front of him. He could see they were specifically for lighting candles or log fires.

"So there has to be someone who knows this passageway exits." He thought immediately of Thomas Galbraith remembering him staring trance-like at the fireplace when he moved away from where he was examining the carriage clock, *I wonder.* "Did the match strike okay?" he asked. "They could get quite damp I imagine if they're left down here for too long."

"No problem with these," she left the matches where she found them, held up the lamp towards the passage leading away from the entrance, "Shall we?"

"Lead on MacDuff," Bart said which amused Emily. She handed him the Gladstone bag to carry when she started along the tunnel illuminating the stone walls as she went. The floor, which was roughly hewn, slanted downwards in places, was covered in a fine sand-like layer that must be the residue from cutting away the stone tunnel. The sandy surface was slippery making standing difficult in places.

"Must have taken a long time to create this," Bart's legs were already beginning to ache from the sheer effort of staying upright. After walking for ten minutes the passage levelled out where another tunnel met at right angles. They stopped to reassess, spotting a half burnt candle in a tarnished brass candle holder on a ledge where the tunnels met.

"Which way?" Emily asked.

Bart pointed ahead the way they were already going, "Let's leave this one for later. I think this will lead to the end." So they carried on. Eventually the floor began to rise slowly until they came to a dead end with another iron ladder up a wall like the one leading from the library fireplace.

"This has to be the way out, don't you think?" Emily asked. She put the lamp down on the floor below the ladder, took the bag from Bart to retrieve the small torch which she put on aiming the beam upwards. Not far above them they could see a round covering.

"I expect this one won't have a matching carriage clock," Bart suggested. "Off you go lass, see if it's easy to open," he told her as she placed the torch in her mouth she began to climb.

Bart watched her progress again testing each rung like she did before. She took no time at all before he saw natural light appear at the top following a heavy clunk, after which she disappeared completely. Bart waited patiently until her head appeared over the hole. She was grinning, "You aren't going to believe this. Blow out the lamp, come up!"

He left the lamp in the passage, away from the base of it, being a shorter ladder this time his climb was easier made slower due to him carrying his Gladstone bag which Emily took out of his hand when he got to the top. When he peered over the edge he could see they were inside some kind of enclosed wooden structure. He climbed out letting the round wooden cover drop back into place. A coarsely woven piece of rush matting pulled back across to conceal the cover. The mat was covered in mud suggesting a lot of feet must have trodden the soil tightly into the weave over time.

"What is this place?" she asked.

Bart examined the narrow interior, nodding his head slightly when he found what he was looking for down the length of one side. The structure was oblong in shape and when he released a couple of wooden pegs on the wall, lifted part of a side panel they held in place, it opened upwards to reveal a window through which they could see an abundance of trees.

"This is a hide," he declared knowledgably. "I expect when we go outside the structure will be camouflaged in some way to blend into the surroundings," he could see Emily was no wiser. "This is where people observe wildlife at close quarters without disturbing them. In the past, given the architecture of Daingneach castle with its vast array of armoury, I imagine it may also have been used to spy on any attacking army threatening the castle."

He could see Emily agog at his knowledge. "I wouldn't be at all surprised Mungo MacLeod used the hide to inspect the pheasants around shooting season."

Emily scowled her disapproval at shooting defenceless creatures. He kept quiet about the other kinds of shoots or culling of deer herds. She watched the puzzlement appear on Bart's face.

"You know, thinking about it, if Mungo MacLeod used this hide for years it would be inconceivable he wouldn't know this was the start of the tunnel."

CHAPTER 42

The missing person enquiry on Mungo MacLeod moved swiftly to a suspected murder investigation after the discovery of the van grill and the stag's body. The forensic examination found two kinds of blood. The stag's being on the grill, whilst inside the van a smattering of blood on the windscreen was human, thought to be from the driver's head colliding after impact of the van hitting the stag or vice versa. A further sample of the same match blood, type O positive as that inside the van was discovered on a tree branch at the side of the stag's body.

Partial fingerprints were lifted from the tree branch which only matched some found on the inside trunk of the van. It appeared as if the driver's side of the van had been wiped clean at some point. Only those of Nessa McKinley, Beth Grant and Emily Hobbs were found inside the van. No others were found except a partial believed to be Sirus Jeffries, yet to be confirmed. Given her evidence, recording Thomas Galbraith as bringing the van to McKinley's Auto after the accident you would have expected his to be somewhere. The case was now transferred over to a CID investigation. For continuity PC Robbie Cowan joined the CID team and was asked to escort Thomas Galbraith in for questioning.

He deposited the Laird's secretary in an interview room in the custody suite before he went up to the CID unit to report. D.I Leslie Morris, the appointed SIO in the case, stood in front of a white board and was in the middle of updating his team when the constable joined them. He stood at the back of the room listening to the forensic evidence report. The discussion taking place being whether the driver or drivers of the van were wearing gloves, hence the lack of fingerprints other than those identified for elimination purposes.

"Chances are there should be other prints around the steering wheel and gears or even on the hand brake," the DI was saying. "Other than the mechanic's at the garage who drove the van into the unit at Dinnet and days later when she took it back to the Castle. No surprises, they were where you'd expect them to be. The van was subsequently used only by Beth Grant when she started working at the castle and those of Emily Hobbs whom she gave a lift to and a few partials on the passenger door belonging, we think, to Sirus Jeffries, the Clockmaker. There were no other fingerprints, although there is evidence someone used something to clean down these areas before it was taken to McKinley's Auto."

"Like a duster?" someone asked.

"More like some kind of wet wipe, they're working on possible types, none were found in the van."

"So at some point the whole van was cleaned?" the same D.C asked.

"No, not in the back of the van where there was a certain amount of spotting of blood believed to be pheasant in origin....." he looked over at his D.C who was about to speak again, "...with a small quantity of pheasant feathers as well."

Most of those present laughed as the D.C closed his mouth.

P.C Cowan asked, "What about the grill, sir, was the mess all stag blood."

Les Morris nodded, "Aye, and matched exactly the blood of the dead stag," he said. "In addition, there was a small splatter of blood on the windscreen inside the van. This was believed to have been missed when the screen was wiped leaving this small quantity over to one side. There was sufficient to establish the type of human blood to be, O Positive, which 44% of people have and matched the blood found on the branch at the side of the stag's body."

"Careless," the D.C commented.

"Except, if you consider the stag was dragged away from the ditch where it fell after impact, the site wasn't expected to be found because the van was repaired over Christmas, then was back in use at the castle by the New Year, no questions asked."

"Except for Mungo MacLeod going missing," P.C Cowan reminded them. Everyone stared his way.

Morris went on, "I understand he was thought to be either away on holiday over the festive period or to have absconded with some of the castle's artefacts."

Robbie confirmed, "One clock was identified as missing, aye. We now know he took that to be repaired in November."

The assembled detectives stared over at him with some curiosity. He ignored them, "I understand he's been a ghillie at the castle for a considerable number of years, he's rumoured to be some distant relative of the Laird."

"So, unlikely to be a thief?" DI Morris asked.

Robbie nodded, "And as far as anyone with any kind of service at the castle reports, has never taken a day's leave in years."

"What about this secretary chap, Galbraith, how long has he been there?" Les Morris asked.

"He's fairly new, not even a year yet, he was taken on I believe because the Laird is thinking of opening the whole castle to the public which requires a substantial inventory of all the castle treasures for insurance purposes in order to be able to."

"Right P.C Cowan can I have a word please?" The D.I walked away into his office followed by Robbie Cowan. Once inside Les Morris said, "Close the door would you?" He pointed to a chair for him to sit down and asked him if he already spoke to Thomas Galbraith in respect of Mungo MacLeod being missing.

He nodded filling him in on how he appeared vague about when he last saw Mungo MacLeod. He explained all the staff claimed to be away on leave for Christmas, the whole place having closed down for a couple of weeks with the Laird away for Christmas until the New Year.

"They can't all have gone, aren't there animals at the castle?" the D.I asked knowing how the castle used to be the centre for the hunt in those parts.

"Horses, yes, they stable other people's as well as their own......some dogs though most of the foxhounds are fostered out to a variety of local people I understand."

"What I need to know is who didn't go away. I need a tighter time frame of holiday dates now we have a potential murder enquiry on our hands. I would like you to do that because they know you and can you take D.C Ambrose with you – he's the mouthy one out there, as you might realise - asks a lot of pertinent questions?"

"Right, sir," Robbie replied.

"First I want you to sit in with me when I interview this Galbraith chap because you will have a lot more insight than I do right now to know if he is contradicting anything he's already told you. You okay with it?"

"Yes, sir."

*   *   *   *   *   *

Thomas Galbraith sat alone in the interview room. He only looked mildly curious when D.I Morris came in with P.C Cowan. On the journey into the station he remained silent showing no emotion whatsoever.

"Good morning Mr. Galbraith, I am Detective Inspector Morris and this is Police Constable Cowan who you already know I believe?" Les Morris was surprised at such a lack of response. He was used to interviewees in these circumstances being aggressive from the start, demanding to know why they were there. Galbraith waited patiently for them to sit down, his face lacked any emotion. The D.I pressed the recording machine on the table before commencing the interview.

"Thomas Galbraith has been brought here for questioning in relation to the disappearance of Mungo MacLeod," a slight frown passed across the man's face briefly; he remained quiet. "Present in the room is DI Morris and PC Cowan. Have you been given the opportunity to have a solicitor present Mr Galbraith?"

The frown appeared again, this time Thomas Galbraith asked, "Why do I need a solicitor?"

"It is your right to have one present whilst being questioned," Morris replied.

Galbraith caught P.C Cowan's eye, "You already asked me questions about the Laird's ghillie going missing. You didn't offer me the choice of a solicitor being present then," he accused.

Robbie Cowan and D.I. Morris exchanged glances, "I was making general enquiries about the background of a missing person......there was no requirement."

"And I haven't got anything more to add to what I told you on that occasion," Galbraith added.

DI Morris interrupted, "The general enquiry has moved on now Mr Galbraith, I have been given the case because of a suspicion of foul play." Galbraith remained silent. "Given the formality of this new enquiry I ask you again if you wish to have a solicitor present?" Galbraith shook his head. "Could you speak for the tape as well as shaking your head Mr. Galbraith?"

"No!" his voice came out loud and irritated.

"First can I ask what role you are employed in at the castle?"

"I am Laird Munro's Secretary," he replied.

"How long have you been the laird's secretary?"

"Since June last year," he offered.

"Who did you replace?"

"Replace?" Galbraith asked puzzled by the question.

"Yes, who was the Laird's secretary before you?"

"As far as I know he didn't have one," Galbraith said. "I'm sure if you speak to Duncan Munro he would be able to answer that question for you."

"You seem incredibly calm for someone being questioned in a possible murder enquiry Mr. Galbraith," DI Morris commented.

"Murder? You think the ghillie has been murdered?" He looked from one to the other for an explanation.

"We thought you might be able to help us with that one," Morris pushed wanting to see if he could knock him out of his stoical state.

Galbraith pointed at himself, "Are you saying you think I have killed Mungo MacLeod?" The shock was clearly evident on his face.

"Perhaps we should begin with where you were on 23rd of December last," Morris asked.

The man sat thinking for a moment before saying, "It was the day of the beginning of the Christmas holidays."

P.C Cowan said, "You told me you went away for Christmas."

Galbraith nodded, "Yes, the Laird was away in Switzerland with his family and most of the staff at the castle broke up or went away."

"So when did you leave and where did you take your holiday?" Morris asked.

"I didn't go anywhere. I finished at the castle on 23rd," he now displayed a smirk which gave the impression he was merely tolerating the repetitive questions.

D.I Morris took out a sheet of paper from the folder he brought with him into the interview, which he pushed over so Galbraith could read it.

"I draw your attention to this invoice of 23rd December when you took one of the castle's vans into McKinley's Auto for repair after being in an accident." D.I Morris watched as Thomas Galbraith read the details then looked up showing no surprise whatsoever.

"Yes," he said. "I did."

"You are confirming you took the van in for repair after having an accident in it?"

"Yes, to taking it in for repair, no to having an accident," Galbraith stated. Robbie Cowan couldn't help thinking he seemed to be enjoying himself.

"Please explain if you would," Morris asked.

Galbraith took a deep breath seeming to find the whole line of questioning tiresome.

"I was travelling home towards Dinnet from the castle. I came across the van at the side of the road. I was driving slowly because conditions were treacherous, at least a few inches of snow and snowing heavily. When I got closer I saw a lot of blood covering the snow on the road near the white van so I slowed down even more, then realised the van was one of the castle's……"

"How - were you familiar with it?" PC Cowan asked.

"Not really, I recognised the sticker in the back window, all the castle vehicles have them including mine – it's a silhouette of a castle with Daingneach, the company logo."

"What did you think happened?" DI Morris asked.

"When I realised the van was one of ours I stopped. I could see lots more blood all over the van so I followed the trail into the trees until I could see there was a stag carcass lying a distance away. I assumed the stag got that far before dying….."

P.C Cowan asked, "Did you go to check?"

He shook his head, "No, I couldn't see it moving."

"What about the van driver?" Les Morris asked.

"There was no one there," he seemed really calm, not a sign of all the nervousness everyone previously referred to. "When I checked the van, it was empty; the driver's door was unlocked with the keys in the ignition."

"Why did you take the van in for repair? Why didn't you phone for help or report the accident to the police?" P.C Cowan asked.

"Do you have to report hitting a deer? My understanding is you only have to if someone is hurt. There was no sign of anyone injured."

"Don't they? How would you know that?" Morris sounded doubtful.

Robbie Cowan was also surprised he would know. "Most people do," he assured him.

"The reason I was taken on by Duncan Munro was because of my extensive knowledge of insurance issues. I now specialise in large artefact collections and public liability. I have worked my way up through other types of claims," Galbraith sounded really pompous for one moment. Robbie nearly laughed out loud he reminded him of Emily's reference to her father, the insurance salesman.

"Still you might have called for help to the castle....."

Galbraith cut Morris short, "No signal. I did later after I drove the van to McKinley's. I phoned then, got the groundsman for a lift back to my car....then I went on leave for a couple of weeks."

"Were you wearing gloves when you drove the van to McKinley's?" Cowan asked.

"Of course, it was freezing cold outside, snowing heavily, I told you that already."

"What about the windscreen?" Cowan scrutinised him closely.

"What are you asking me? The wipers worked, I used them to clear the snow off the windscreen so I could drive......" Galbraith sighed.

"I meant inside the van."

"When I got the van started, the heater was on, misted up the inside, so I wiped the windscreen with my hand to be able to see out." There was not a flicker of emotion again.

The two police officers exchanged glances.

"So you know McKinley's have the castle contract....." Les Morris began stopping when he caught Galbraith's frown.

"Of course, I may be engaged to produce the castle collection care plan, but I have to know about other castle business – apart from which I have a castle vehicle myself. I have taken mine in for a service to McKinley's." He seemed to be getting a little irritated now which was the first emotion he'd shown so far. "What is this anyway? You seem to be implying an awful lot!"

P.C Cowan couldn't help but say, "You seem to have withheld a lot when I asked you questions about Mungo MacLeod."

"Not really, I've hardly spoken to the man since I started work at the castle – in fact, I can't recall one conversation with him – our jobs don't cross."

"What can you tell me about Mary Macaulay?" Cowan felt irritated with him now.

"Who?" Galbraith asked looking him straight in the eye.

"She's the woman who used to work in the gift shop, left because you were pestering her!" Robbie's anger got the better of him. Galbraith reacted for the first time by standing up as his temper flared, "Lies!" he yelled.

Les Morris stood up in anticipation of him going for the PC. He towered above him even with a table in between them he was a formidable threat by his sheer bulk.

"Sit down, please Mr Galbraith!" he commanded.

Galbraith flopped back onto his chair after which P.C Cowan continued, "I understand you kept on asking her out, you threatened to tell the laird she was having an improper relationship with Mungo MacLeod during working hours which they would lose their jobs over if she didn't meet you for a drink after work. I believe you carried this on even after she left."

They both could see him seething.

"Well did you tell her or not?" Les Morris asked.

Galbraith bowed his head muttering, "No, I did not!"

"Where were you on the 24th December at six o'clock in the evening?" Robbie asked.

"Can't remember," he replied sulkily.

"Okay, were you at Mary Macaulay's house taking her a bunch of flowers?"

Galbraith's guilt was obvious, "They were only to say sorry because I thought I'd spooked her in the car park at the castle – I think she thought I was the ghost of Seumus Grant."

"I thought that was only a myth, a story to make the castle more attractive to the public?" Robbie clearly didn't believe there was a ghost.

"It's not open to the public..... yet...... and no it's not a story, I've....." he suddenly stopped realising what he was about to say.

"Were you about to say you've seen the ghost of Seumus Grant?" Robbie asked.

"I was about to say I felt sorry for scaring Mary, I wanted to apologise."

The officers both knew he was lying.

"So when you got a lift back to your own car did you see anyone else about?" Morris asked changing the subject back to the accident.

"Like who?" Galbraith asked puzzled.

"Like Mungo MacLeod who was driving the van you took in for repair?"

"I saw no one. I got into my car, went home for Christmas." He sat with his arms folded as if that was the end of the interview.

D.I Morris leaned over towards the tape, "Interview terminated," he glanced at his watch, "Ten fifty five." He flicked the tape off.

When they let him go and returned to the CID office Morris gave instructions to one of his D.C's to do a thorough background check on Thomas Galbraith.

"There's something not quite right about him," he told this team. "I want no stone unturned!"

CHAPTER 43

After a long surreptitious process Bart dropped Emily back at the cottage. They left the hide as they found it making sure the trap door was well concealed. It hadn't been easy to leave the castle without either re-navigating their route through the passageway with the risk of being discovered in the library or as they chose, by making their way across open parkland back to the castle. In order to pick up his car Bart was obliged to leave the wood to walk across in the open as if he were taking a lunchtime stroll to take in the air.

Emily took a different route, carrying Bart's Gladstone bag with her she was concealed by the trees most of the way, she cut across in the direction of the Castle's gatehouse, there to wait until Bart could pick her up on his way out. The timing was tight as Bart saw in his rear view mirror once he was clear of the grounds, the marked police car turning in at the castle gate he was sure must be Thomas Galbraith returning from the police station. He left with the thought he needed to find out what happened at his interview.

Before he drove home he left her at the cottage with the task of researching all she could find out about Castle Daingneach's history. A substantial excavation like the one they discovered would have taken years and certainly would have been hard to keep a secret. He'd heard of other similar constructions across the world mentioned in history books down the centuries, many of them related to warfare as the basis for creating them.

The strain of the day left Bart feeling exhausted as well as emotionally drained, something he often experienced as an active Private Investigator in his past life; on this occasion, as in times past, he was left with the fear of repercussions. He was unable to throw off the nervousness he felt when Emily explained her reaction to his witness protection minder 'Steve'. She was a shrewd young woman and he knew she wouldn't over react. Didn't Jayson Vingoe also feel something similar about the man?

Thoughts of Jay urged him to make the call to update him about Martin Frances' visit, which had been a close call. Jay needed to know if he was making enquiries on Bart's behalf about the man. He wondered if they were still on their trip around Scotland, he'd forgotten how long they were meant to be honeymooning or when they were due to resume their jobs again. Rather than telephone him, not wishing to intrude on their holiday, he sent a text: "Could we speak soon there have been developments?"

The call from Jay came not quite an hour later waking Bart from a nap he was taking in front of the fire.

"Sounds like I woke you," Jay was apologetic when a sleepy-voiced Bart answered his mobile.

"At my age any form of exercise has to be pacified with a snooze," Bart said in his defence. "I wondered where you were because I have had the unfortunate 'pleasure' of seeing Martin Frances in the flesh."

"Oh! Really? That isn't good news is it?"

"Indeed not," Bart agreed. "I wondered if you were still on your travels?"

"We are on our way back down the West Coast. We return home in a couple of days," Jay informed him.

"I trust you are having an enjoyable trip?"

"Yes, quite an epiphany for us both," Jay laughed to show he was being strictly serious.

"Oh? How so?"

"I believe we have definitely decided we would like to live in Scotland, it is an amazing country, so we have been making plans which I will tell you about on another occasion. For now.....what news?"

"Martin Frances turned up here at the hotel where he began to show the same photograph of his wife as our detective friend did previously. How or why either of them have come to this part of the world I have no idea. I did witness him for myself having been tipped off by my friend Philip the manager at the hotel. At first glance he appears to be quite a charmer. Phil enrolled the help of one of his waitresses to misdirect him to Fort William where she fabricated a previous job over there. She told him she thought she recognised the picture as one of the other waitresses whom she worked with there; she resembled the photograph only she was a bit older now."

"Ah, Fort William is our next stop over. I'm sure Agatha wouldn't take much persuading to take a one night break in a hotel – complete with bathing facilities!" Bart heard him laugh. "Text me the hotel name and a bit of a description of the man......"

"I can do better, I took his picture." Bart coughed nervously before he went on, "Jay, on another matter, I'm a little concerned about the policeman who was my minder for Witness Protection. I think you have seen him. I only know him as 'Steve'. Something Emily admitted to me is quite worrying. She tells me he seems to have changed in attitude from when he first began looking for me after I left Wainthorpe, to how he seems after they caught Maola."

"How is he different?"

"She actually used words like 'bullying' and 'scary' which isn't how I remember him."

"Oh?" Jay sounded surprised. "I'll certainly make some enquiries when I get back about the trial or if anyone else has encountered him recently."

"You might want to speak with a DC Barney Johnson who was also subject to Maola's attention – well actually Maola put a contract out on him at the time he disappeared. I believe Johnson may have transferred forces since to join yours down there. I'm not sure whether 'Steve' was his minder when he also went into Witness Protection for a while."

"Okay, leave it with me, I'll be in touch next week, meanwhile let me know if this cop Frances turns up again."

After his call with Jay, Bart felt a little easier. He always gave him a great deal of confidence. He knew he felt better because he was suddenly very hungry which was always a good sign.

CHAPTER 44

Jay, in his report back to Bart, didn't tell him they were disappointed with the hotel when they arrived in Fort William. They felt it lacked the history and the impressive façade of the many other splendid hotels they saw in Scotland. Certainly the hotel didn't match the one he so graciously gift to them for their first night in the honeymoon suite. He doubted any could, given how spacious the room was with the four poster bed. He knew they wouldn't have booked in to the Fort William hotel at all even with its proximity to the iconic Ben Nevis if not for their mission to seek out information about Martin Frances.

There were compensations for the lack of a castle-like appearance, as all the rooms especially the dining room gave panoramic views of Loch Linnhe which added a certain romantic touch to their stay and at least Agatha could relax in a hot bath whilst he favoured the soft bed, which Jay did mention to Bart.

"How is she?" Bart asked tentatively not wanting to mention her condition, after all he knew nothing about such things as women's childbearing, an alien world he never wished to enter.

"Fine," Jay didn't want to detail any of her early morning sickness bouts, he felt instinctively the subject would embarrass Bart. "I'm sure sleeping in a comfortable bed overnight will be most welcomed." Jay changed the subject with, "I intend to recce the bar facilities pre-dinner tonight to look for our friend there, if not then later in the restaurant, before I make any actual enquiries about him."

"Indeed," Bart agreed. "Go carefully, don't reveal yourself to this man, I fear he may be quite dangerous – softly, softly, catchee monkey!" Bart quoted the old English proverb as a warning.

"I will," Jay assured him. "I'll give you an update later."

In some ways the whole exercise of being there was somewhat disappointing, even though they ate a wonderful evening meal overlooking the Linnhe, one which she could actually enjoy. Breakfast on the other hand she now preferred to miss; she would wait until much later to attempt anything to eat.

With a no show of Martin Frances the evening before and at breakfast, Jay assumed he was no longer there. After taking some food from the breakfast buffet for Agatha by the kindly ministrations of the waiter, he left Agatha to take her time to settle her morning sickness whilst he went in search of the manager or someone with whom he could make some enquiries about Frances.

The young man he cornered was, by the badge he wore, the deputy manager who Jay thought was far too young to hold such a position. He didn't look to Jay long out of school by first impressions. At first he seemed quite suspicious when Jay showed him the picture of Martin Frances on his mobile. Whether he thought the question might be a trap to catch him divulging something which he shouldn't, he fell back on reciting the 'confidentiality' reason for not meeting Jay's enquiry. Until Jay hinted he was making semi-official enquiries about him believing he was claiming to be either a policeman or from immigration. As Jay pointed out, he could hardly be from both.

The deputy manager looked stunned, "You mean neither?" he asked. Jay made no comment. He indicated by his disapproving face it was a possibility, the shrug left him in no doubt.

"He was asking about a girl he believed was working here as a waitress," Jay told the deputy manager who became quite alarmed that he may have breached the very rules he just quoted.

"You have to understand immigration is doing a tight trawl of potential illegals, most of our hotels use foreign attachments." Jay nodded he understood. "We keep a very tight ship," he reiterated the learnt company line easily. "There's a process done at head office to recruit them. I assure you their papers are scrutinised closely." Jay confirmed he understood. "We get sent who they allocate. We only take a few locals, necessary backup because these foreign ones don't always stay very long."

"Oh, why?" Jay asked genuinely interested.

"Too much like hard work as some of them are extremely lazy, they think it's a paid holiday abroad!" He laughed cynically. "Fortunately, not all of them."

"I believe the girl he's looking for was a national," Jay explained.

"Really? That's not what he suggested," he said irritably. "He said she *was* an illegal he believed worked here recently as a waitress. In fact, he expected her to still be here."

"Did he show you a picture of her?"

"Yes, the photograph was very grainy, kind of old; she was about the right age for the ones we set on. I would have remembered her if she worked here, she was very pretty in a solemn kind of way."

"Solemn?"

"Well actually she did look rather frightened if you ask me – like someone taken whilst acting in a horror movie – like Jamie Lee Curtis in Halloween when she was younger. Now she was a 'screamer'," his enthusiasm and the way he laughed set Jay's nerves on edge. He felt he was enjoying the image far too much.

"So what did he say when you told him she didn't work here?"

The deputy manager winced, "Never saw anyone move so fast from pleasant to angry," he stressed. "Well outside of a horror film when the psycho turns from an ordinary person into an axe-wielding monster." He laughed strangely. Jay could see where his interests lay.

He was beginning to think he might be talking to a very sick individual. "Did he say anything?"

He stopped laughing to think, his face became puzzled.

"Yeah. That was also weird because he suddenly became quite calm. He was creepy, he smiled, leaned over towards me, you know, like intimidating me saying something like 'she thinks I can be fobbed off easily does she? Big mistake'."

"Are you sure?"

He shrugged his shoulders like the insolent teenager he still appeared to be, "Hell, I wasn't taking notes, but pretty much."

"Is he still here?" Jay rather hoped he wasn't because he knew he couldn't trust this man to keep quiet about his enquiry; he didn't want to subject Agatha to Martin Frances' temper or reprisals.

He walked over to the computer on the desk behind the reception counter, pressed a few keys, "He checked out last night before dinner," he announced.

Jay muttered a thank you and started to walk away, turned back to ask, "What name was he using?"

The deputy manager glanced down at the screen again, "Michael Johns."

Jay raised his hand in thanks before he walked away.

* * * * *

After Jay's second call Bart went in search of Philip Miller at the hotel only to find him on a day off. Bart's urgency took him around the perimeter of the hotel where he could see the Manager's car parked outside his bungalow. Ordinarily he wouldn't dream of disturbing him during his time off, however, the tone of Jay's voice raised his concerns. He wasn't sure whether Martin Frances' reference to 'she' meant Beth or Bonita who sent him on a wild goose chase across Scotland to Fort William; either way he was convinced the man now knew this was a deliberate ploy to divert him. It would also confirm Beth was known up in the highlands which ensured the likelihood of his return to the village, perhaps even the hotel.

Philip Miller was surprised to see Bart standing at his door when he answered the knock. His face showed his relief the caller wasn't a member of staff there to report on some problem or other at the hotel was clear. He greeted him warmly asking him in. Bart was pleasantly surprised to find the inside of the bungalow was neat. Whether he expected Philip Miller, the recovering alcoholic, would struggle to resist a drink at times of crisis, he felt guilty even considering he might have a problem with his domestic chores, he now found himself apologising profusely for disturbing his day off. Phil asked him to sit down, if he wanted a drink which, because of his controversial thoughts about him, Bart found himself flushing with embarrassment.

"Tea, coffee?" he asked watching Bart struggling. "As you know I don't keep anything stronger here, it wouldn't be wise."

"I would love a coffee if you're having one," Bart needed the time to rid himself of his wayward thoughts before he said something he really would regret. He took the time Phil was away to look about him as anyone might left alone to intrude on someone else's private space. He spotted a couple of photographs of children on the mantelpiece over a gas fire. He knew Phil caught his glance when he returned with the coffees.

"My children," Phil told him as he sat down putting the cups on the coffee table between them. "I think I may have mentioned I was once married?" Bart nodded. "Of course, my son and daughter are much older now, these are the last pictures I have of them."

Bart didn't know what to say. Here was Phil Miller who always managed to put him at his ease, which for a troubled man he found remarkably resilient. He inspected Bart with a penetrating stare, "I'm sensing all is not well with you Sirus and this isn't a social visit because you needed some company."

Bart once again felt awkward, "Indeed not," he began. "You remember my friends Jay and Agatha who brought Emily up here whilst touring on their honeymoon?"

Phil nodded regarding him briefly with some concern, "I hope they are well?"

"Yes, indeed. They have passed through Fort William on their way back home to make some enquiries about the man who stayed here."

"Ah yes, and...?"

"I have reason to think he might return here," Bart divulged. He updated him on what happened at the hotel in Fort William. "Needless to say he will come back here looking for Beth, also I fear he may target your young waitress Bonita.....his comment certainly suggests he recognised she spun a deliberate story to misdirect him. I really think the man is quite dangerous. He's certainly very angry by all accounts."

"Yes, I have some misgivings myself since I made the suggestion to her. I also thought perhaps I shouldn't have done what I did. At the time I wanted to divert his attention away from here. I didn't think I might inadvertently confirm your young friend was definitely up here somewhere."

"Of course," Bart tried to pacify him with, "It might also have got rid of him altogether. I have to say I can't see why he or the P.I he engaged even suspect she came this way. She says she was careful not to draw attention to herself."

They sat for a moment in silence until Philip Miller spoke again, "Like you I did consider he might return to seek out Bonita again which is why I have dealt with the likelihood of him finding her."

Bart looked surprised, "How so?"

"I took advantage of the fact Bonita found our particular part of the world a little dull. I think she was used to a much livelier social life so I've sent her away to the South where, as she would say, they speak proper English. The night life better suits her.... I won't say where she is. I have told no one here, so there can be no accidental slips or betrayals." Phil could see Bart's smile return to his face. "I do think it might help to get some kind of protection for your young friend though...."

Bart held up his hand, "Yes I already alerted at least one police officer who is aware of her situation. Given her mistrust of the police in general this is quite a step in the right direction....so we shall see as if Martin Frances shows his face here again."

When Bart took his leave of Philip Miller he agreed to alert Bart to any new developments. Of course, there was no saying he would book into his hotel again but likely because it was the only one open in the village. There were plenty of other places around Aberdeen where he could stay, knowing he was a loose cannon Bart felt he ought to warn Beth and Emily. He feared he might have to call upon Robbie Cowan as well, certainly to update him on the circumstances.

CHAPTER 45

Bart drove Emily home on the pretext he wanted to buy some of his favourite cakes from the Black-faced Sheep at Aboyne when in fact he didn't want her travelling alone by bus. Only when they arrived at the cottage to find Robbie Cowan's Defender already parked up in the yard as previously arranged by Bart, did Emily begin to think something wasn't quite right. For one thing, she saw Bart was not one bit surprised Robbie was there; also stopping to buy cake seemed to have slipped his mind completely. The café would have closed by now anyway.

When they entered the kitchen Beth sat with Robbie already drinking tea. Emily was pleased as well as surprised to see a quantity of Beth's own cakes laid out waiting for them. The passing thought, wondering how Beth could have managed to bake whilst working all day at the castle, skittered across her mind before the lure of them took over. The thought slipped easily away as she immediately sat down, took a scone, split the cake in half to fill with the waiting jam and cream. She took a bite whilst pouring herself a cup of tea from the waiting teapot.

Robbie Cowan laughed at her. Instead of blushing as she normally would in his presence she whispered, "So, I'm hungry!" in her defence.

Emily could sense he was there officially being in uniform, so she waited expecting something quite significant to have brought him there. "I wanted to update you on the findings of the forensic examination of Beth's van," he began. "I can definitely confirm the van was tampered with *after* it left Nessa's garage. She did, in fact, thoroughly examine the engine in case the impact from the stag hitting the front might have caused damage, which is why she checked."

"So are you saying Martin may have sabotaged the van later?" Beth looked suddenly frightened.

Robbie said, "That I don't know."

"Well unlikely to be him because he didn't stay long enough at the hotel," Bart pointed out. "There's been insufficient time for him to find you and of course he was still asking staff if they recognised you. I saw him do that myself. Philip Miller got one of his waitresses to decoy him over to Fort William pretending she worked with someone there who looked like your old photograph he showed her."

He could see Beth was surprised but not convinced.

"He left pretty quickly to go over to Fort William," Bart confirmed. "Now would he do that if he'd managed to find out where you worked or to mess with the van's brakes?"

Robbie asked, "How do you know he went over there, we can't be sure......"

"I am certain because my friends Jay and Agatha booked into the Fort William hotel to check if he was there."

"Oh!" Beth cried. She seemed surprised until she saw Bart's face showing no signs of relief.

He didn't want to cause her even more concern but felt there was no choice. "Unfortunately, he spoke with a rather immature deputy manager who.....well, managed to convince him you have never worked there. In fact, he admitted to Jay, Martin was not well pleased at being duped."

He watched as Robbie Cowan quickly caught on about the repercussions, "So he'll be back here looking for whoever told him the lie?"

"I fear so. The only good part is he won't find the lassie who did misinform him, she is no longer working at our hotel in the village."

Beth sat quietly stunned whilst Emily caught the significance of her departure. "He will know she deliberately misled him won't he?"

"It will tell him I am living up here somewhere?" Beth's voice quaked.

"Or you *were* here but not necessarily still in the area," Robbie offered weakly.

"He'll know!" Beth's forceful reply chilled them. "He has a sixth sense, he always managed to know everything about me or what I did….it was like I was being followed."

"I dare say you were. Then you were living with him which makes following you easier," Bart said quite confidently. "Now he has no idea where you are, he's fishing around. Don't forget how we led his P.I away when we got rid of your car," Bart cast a sheepish glance at Robbie as he knew nothing of their initial attempts to fool Selwyn Jones which weren't quite legal.

"It's only a matter of time, he's got spies everywhere," Beth tried to hold back the tears.

"It doesn't mean he has up here," Robbie replied assertively, they could see he didn't much like the implication. "I believe the fact of the sabotaged van together with you wishing him to stay away from you, would constitute this becoming a criminal case which means my police force would take the matter very seriously. In any case you can take out an injunction against him to prevent him coming anywhere near you. If he doesn't stop harassing you after the court has made the injunction it becomes a criminal offence. He would be prosecuted in a criminal court."

Beth's head bowed as she trembled at the thought of him coming anywhere near her. "He's a police officer. I know they won't believe me," she stated with great conviction.

"The point is, the van would be evidence to convince the court you are in danger," Robbie pushed.

"Yes, but didn't Sirus just say he couldn't have been the person who messed with the van?"

Robbie asked whilst Beth slipped back into being the victim again.

Emily asked, "If it wasn't him, then who could it possibly be?"

Everyone stared at her as if they hadn't noticed she was still there, each now wondering who would.

"I think he would have to do something really bad to me to convince a court," Beth's tiny voice invaded the silence. "You have no idea how persuasive he can be."

The shock on Emily's face showed she suddenly realised she was also in the line of fire if Martin Frances found out where they lived. She lost all interest in the scone now and her eyes moved over towards the sleeping foxhound lying in front of the fire. Three other pairs of eyes followed her gaze. No one said what she was thinking, *some guard dog you would be!*

*   *   *   *   *

Robbie Cowan left the cottage deep in thought taking the A93 towards Dinnet, he was greatly perturbed by their discussion. He also realised if Beth Grant was exposed to this dangerous man Emily could also receive some of his reprisals. He realised how much she meant to him. He didn't want anything to happen to Emily, he was certain. *They live together, what if Martin Frances believed they were an item?* He knew the irrationality of some people's thought processes, hadn't he been on the receiving end of those from Jock McKinley for many years?

These thoughts made him stop as he drove through Dinnet. He needed to think logically about Beth's white van especially what happened after leaving McKinley's Auto until the police took it in for forensic examination. He couldn't let his long standing distaste of Nessa's father stop him doing his job.

To his great relief he saw Nessa was alone in the garage, finding her in good spirits unlike the last time he saw her. Two old friends sitting drinking coffee together and chatting was like old times. After catching up a little about her father then asking after her mother, he broached the subject of the van.

"I need to ask some more questions Ness about the white van."

"Oh, aye, what more can'na tell ye?" She asked.

"Before you took the van back to the castle did you keep it locked up inside here or in the compound out back?"

She didn't hesitate with, "Inside while I worked on it. It was ma only job, so there was th'room." She glanced across at him trying to guess what he was thinking. "Except when I took it home wi' me on New Year's Eve, I was taking it back to the Castle next day, it's closer to the castle. I was'na going in to work after."

Robbie suddenly appeared interested, "You took the van to your flat?" He knew where she lived with Shona in Aberdeen, there was only on street parking.

She shook her head, "No. I moved back to Tarland to stay at the folks," she didn't look too pleased at the thought. "I'd split from Shona by then, tha' was'na pleasant, I could'na spend another day with her. Dad'n'Mam were away so I got some peace. I was to take the van back next day and already sorted a lift back to Tarland with Worsel," she grinned as they both knew he would jump at the chance, always pestering her for a date even though he knew she liked girls.

"He still thinks he's got a chance then?" Robbie chuckled.

"I think he sees me as a bit of a challenge, ye'know he can convert me," she winced at the thought. "Well they don't call him Worsel because he's applied to Mensa, do they?"

Robbie got serious again, "So the van was parked outside the bungalow over night?"

"Yes, of course, have you seen the rubbish Da keeps in his garage?" Robbie knew it was as bad as the compound out back, full of auto parts he'd collected over the years.

He watched as Nessa's face grew sad, "I was to have a quiet New Year's Eve on ma own," she explained. "Until Shona turned up. She'd been drinking......she's na pleasant when she's bladdered!"

"So she would have seen the van parked outside?"

"Aye, funny you should say that...... she went off on one when she saw it, thinking I'd someone wi'me. Proper rampaging she was. She pushed past me to search the place." Nessa laughed cynically. "I even pointed out the sticker, you know, with the castle logo, told her I was taking it back next day."

"Was she happy with that?"

"Well as happy as she could under the circumstances," He could tell by her face that was far from the truth.

"Did she stay...?" Robbie began.

"Hell no!" Nessa almost shouted. "Shona, in a dark mood is'na pleasant."

"You took her back to Aberdeen?" he asked. "Don't tell me she was driving in that state."

She shook her head again, "Shona doesn't drive. I've no idea how she got to Tarland. Actually, I got her a taxi back – cost me a bloody fortune!"

"How are things with her now?" he dared to ask.

"A bit better d'ye ken," she sat sadly drinking her coffee. "Until she goes off on a bout and you've seen how she keeps calling me? She'll get the message eventually...." She became thoughtful. "I do wish I had'na told her I like someone else......bloody stupid of me."

"Why?"

"She kept on asking me who....she wouldn't leave it alone for ages," she sighed deeply. "Then, gradually it got less......now it's been quiet for a while."

"Do you regret splitting up with her?"

She glared at him sharply, "No! I would sooner be on ma'own than have someone so overbearing. God, having Da is bad enough!"

"Are you still living at home?" Robbie thought how confining that must be. He knew how Jock McKinley would take advantage of her living there.

She nodded, "I'm looking at getting a flat. There's one coming up in Ballater, over the hairdressers," she glanced to see if he knew where she meant. He nodded. "It's okay if you can stand the smell of ammonia waftin' up every wee while. They both laughed.

CHAPTER 46

Emily's misgivings about being discovered by Beth's husband were short lived. Her outlook on life was *why worry about something that might never happen.* She was certainly not going to live in fear or change her way of life just in case he might. She was now intrigued to find out everything she could about Castle Daingneach. She decided to go back to ask Grace Buchanan in the information centre at Crathie if she knew anyone else who might know more about its history. Ghosts, treasure and family feuds were more on her mind than sitting around waiting for Martin Frances to get lucky in finding out where they lived.

What she failed to do was warn Bart she might be late arriving at the shop, so when she finally got there he was quite agitated. She completely dismissed any thoughts he would wonder where she was or check with Beth to enquire after her, only to discover she was coming over by bus having been dropped off at the bus stop at the usual time.

When she didn't arrive Bart began to worry especially after failing to raise her on her mobile which seemed to be switched off. He was close to contacting Robbie Cowan to report her missing. He was stopped by her bursting excitedly through the shop door where she found him pacing in front of the counter. She was hot in the face and slightly out of breath as if she'd been running or to Bart's mind possibly having been chased. He rushed to the door, moving out onto the step he searched for anyone lurking about in the street. He went back inside where Emily stood looking excited as well as a little mystified by his behaviour.

"What's wrong?" he demanded.

She scowled at his agitation, "Nothing's wrong. I've found a new contact for my research on Daingneach Castle."

He ignored her, put the catch on the door then stomped through to the back room with Emily following behind. She could see he was upset.

"I thought something had happened to you, I was about to call the police!"

At the mention of the police Emily blushed when Robbie Cowan sprang into her mind.

"I didn't think I would be very long. I went to see Grace Buchanan again. You know how she can talk, so I missed my bus, I caught the next one."

She watched him sulkily fill the kettle for their morning tea, knew she was out of favour because this was always her job. She moved to the cupboard to get out their cups allowing him time to calm down.

"Sorry, I couldn't ring you, my phone is dead, I forgot to charge it last night," she didn't let on it hadn't occurred to her to telephone him.

"Okay, it's not a good idea to be without your phone."

She shook her head now feeling quite ashamed as he did have a point.

"I won't let Martin Frances change my life!" she defiantly stood her ground, after all she hadn't let her mother take over her life.

"Okay, lass, but be sensible, please."

"I am sensible," she countered a little sulkily.

"I know you are," he agreed as he poured boiling water onto the teabags in each of their cups.

They sat quietly drinking their tea and dunking biscuits until Emily apologised again, "Sorry.... I'll make sure I call you in future........ thank you for caring."

"So what have you found out?" he finally asked seeing by her face there was something significant.

"I've been trying to find out more about the castle's history. Grace Buchanan at Crathie has given me a contact for someone who knows more about the castle than anyone else she knows."

"Who? Do you have an address?"

She shook her head, "Only she called him 'old Jim'.....she told me he spends most of his time in a pub at Ballater."

Bart tried to think of the pubs he'd seen in Ballater, could only picture the one on the corner on Bridge Street, only he couldn't remember the name.

"Apparently there is only the one real pub, she says he always goes there every Friday for the fish and chips," she grinned, licking her lips.

"Yes, I know it. They do really good fish and chips," he laughed having tried them himself when he first came to Scotland.

She was smiling at him profusely as she searched his face expectantly willing him to make the offer that followed, "Looks like we might be eating out this Friday," he said as Emily clapped her hands together enthusiastically. "But you'll have to keep off the beer," he teased.

"Done!"

*   *   *   *   *

Jay's telephone call to Bart on Thursday evening came out of the blue. They were barely back home from their holiday, let alone able to make any enquiries about anyone on his behalf. Straight back onto 'afters', Jay was called out to a suspicious death, where he met the detective Bart knew from his former life. Assessing the scene Barney Johnson confided to Jay it reminded him of one he came across once back in his old force which unnerved him a little given the main criminal link from the time was Toni Maola, who was now awaiting trial, although the whole process wasn't going at all well he heard.

"He admitted to having certain knowledge in the case. Apparently, two police officers, bent cops by all accounts, were now dead, while another key witness has slipped out of Witness Protection. They have no idea where he is," Jay coughed knowing the latter to be Bart himself.

"Oh my, I hope you didn't admit to knowing my whereabouts."

"Absolutely not," Jay said forcefully. "Then he went on to tell me how one of the Witness Protection minders was currently suspended pending investigation for suspected witness intimidation!"

Shocked Bart asked, "Do you know who he is?"

"He wouldn't say......I did ask. He did go on to tell me he was suspected of visiting Maola in prison a few times pretending to be a relative. Maola sent him a visiting order under a fictitious name."

"How do they know this, was he being watched?"

"He believes one of the warders recognised him as a police officer, raised the alarm internally. Police officers usually seek permission when visiting prisoners, so they used CCTV to try to identify him. They could tell by the way he acted to avoid the cameras there was something suspicious about him," Jay explained. "It was after one of the other witnesses reported they were being threatened and another died suddenly in a random car accident, something this Barney Johnson admitted was a typical Maola M.O, resulted in them opening an official enquiry."

"Have they got this cop locked up?" Bart asked, his fear now rising, reminding him of how ruthless Maola could be.

"Apparently not even arrested, there's still the internal enquiry going on whilst they look for evidence."

"What is the link between him and Maola, could they actually be related? What makes a straight cop turn bad?" Bart could barely believe this was the same Steve he'd known back when he entered Witness Protection, he seemed such a decent police officer.

"They think it could be financial?" Jay admitted.

"Surely not worth losing your job, reputation and pension over is it?"

"Depends, according to Barney Johnson Toni Maola comes from a very aristocratic Italian family, the very richest. He is first in line to inherit from a father who is apparently terminally ill."

"Oh my!" Bart declared. "That does sound worthwhile then if Maola gets off with everything he's done. Even his hired assassin is dead, so the case against him looks a little thin now."

"His point exactly. You do know what this means?" Jay asked. Bart went quiet not daring to voice his thoughts. "It means your evidence becomes even more vital to the prosecution."

"It also means finding and eliminating me becomes more urgent, as well as crucial, to Maola who will be willing to pay even more to achieve it." Bart reluctantly admitted. "And there's one corrupt cop out on the loose willing to earn some easy cash from my disposal, no doubt."

"At least he has no idea where you are," Jay tried to assure him.

Bart said nothing, hearing the plaintive voice of Beth in his head telling him how they all stick together like an old boys club. He seriously altered any plans he may have regarding going back to testify against Maola should he actually come to trial. Who could he trust if Maola could command a copper's help from the confines of a prison cell?

Unlike Beth who did have some room for manoeuvre in changing her appearance, he couldn't alter much about what Nature gave him in the looks department. He was sure a growth of beard wouldn't make him taller or change his unfortunate facial features which only surgery could. His only claim to invisibility was the knowledge people didn't care to look at him for very long. Inversely, if someone wanted to find him, then his physical appearance would give him away immediately.

As a private investigator skilled in following people he relied entirely on his instincts; avoiding CCTV cameras was his speciality as too was his reliance heavily on pre-planning, *know your surroundings* was always a motto.

Jay signed off by advising him not to worry he would endeavour to find out all he could about Martin Frances to keep him posted. They both knew he would show up again at the hotel. When he did Bart knew Phil Miller would alert him to the fact.

CHAPTER 47

Bart found the last space in the car park at Ballater then walked around to the green in front of the church where he arranged to meet Emily. She could tell by the way he looked he was in a sombre mood, he walked with his head bowed as if scrutinising his every foot step. This visit to find 'old Jim' excited her so much, she felt like she was doing proper research work. If her research cast any light on the whereabouts of the missing ghillie, Mungo MacLeod all the better, it made her feel like the sleuth she imagined Bart used to be.

When he eventually raised his head spotting her she noticed his tentative smile was far from his usual one and could tell immediately something was wrong. *Surely he wasn't still annoyed with her for not letting him know she would be late yesterday?* Today she made an extra effort to ensure she was there on time by catching the bus before the one she needed to which meant she hung around the shops waiting for him.

"What's wrong?" she asked when he drew close.

"Nothing for you to worry about, lass," he said which to Emily at least confirmed there was something troubling him. "How's Beth?" he asked changing the subject which also suggested there must be something seriously wrong.

"She's okay," she wasn't about to tell him Beth was driving alone to Banchory for the shops because he didn't need anything else to worry about.

The night before, when Bart was thinking about his appearance, coincidentally Emily was discussing with Beth the possibility of changing their own appearances. Beth was well aware her hair and clothes were those styles Martin Frances demanded of her which she hated because they made her feel dowdy and unattractive. She assumed was why he demanded it. He hated anyone looking at her or admiring her. In defiance she wanted to change them dramatically vowing to make herself look as much like someone she knew he disliked. Emily hadn't seen her this passionate about anything before, she laughed hard at her expressions. Beth, spurred on by earning her own money, set off for Banchory leaving Emily at the bus stop.

Emily wasn't about to make Bart's day or mood worse by divulging this to him, so she also changed the subject, "Since this is a mission, I am Amelia, your assistant, today," she told him.

Bart guffawed for the first time in two days, "Well then….Amelia….let's go find 'old Jim'!"

They walked the short distance to the pub. Bart was immediately reminded about his fear of being seen in public with someone as young as Emily after pushing open the door of The Balmoral pub. The room went silent as they walked in together. Everyone stopped to stare at them making him feel very conspicuous.

"What do you want to drink?" he asked Emily whilst spotting an empty table. He pointed for her to sit down. He barely heard the word 'coke' as she walked away, knew even with her back towards him she was blushing with all the eyes on her.

The tables were set with menus. As the noise level grew back to normal with everyone getting on with their own business, she was pleased to have something to hide behind whilst she surveyed the room for any likely old Jims.

"Spot anyone old enough to be 'old Jim'?" Bart asked joining her. He nodded at the menu in her hands, "What do you want to eat?" he asked with only a cursory glance at the menu himself.

"Fish, chips with mushy peas, please," she ordered without hesitation.

He laughed, got to his feet to return to the bar where a spotty youth took his order whilst blatantly staring at Emily across the room, seemingly entranced. There was a moment when the youth stalled, his pencil poised over his pad as if someone turned him off. Bart repeated loudly, "That is TWO rounds of bread and butter!"

Bart waved a hand in front of the youth's face which startled him, "Are you receiving me, young man?"

He realised he wasn't paying attention, "Sorry," he mumbled writing +2 at the side of each entry. "Is she your wain?" he asked Bart having been staring at Emily ever since they came into the bar.

"No! Amelia is my research assistant," Bart replied grandly. He watched the spotty face form an 'Oh!' "Did you ask for a reason?" Bart asked. He shook his head resuming taking the money for the order. Bart went back to Emily.

"Did you ask him about 'old Jim'?"

"Let's wait a while, the lad's with the fairies, communicating isn't one of his fortés," he said. He searched the room, couldn't see anyone who might fit the title, then realised the hour was still quite early.

When their meals arrived the large oval plates could barely contain the massive fish resting on top of the chips, they hung over each end whilst the mushy peas with tartare sauce came in small pots either side. "My word!" Bart declared, "I'm thinking this might be a wee bit much for someone called 'old Jim', perhaps they do OAP portions." He could see the meal wasn't too much for Emily who was already setting about the condiments, trying to rip open the plastic packets of vinegar and tomato ketchup. She sprinkled vinegar all over whilst dolloping the ketchup in a blob to dip her chips into.

More customers arrived, showing the popularity of the food. When Bart saw a young barmaid serving behind the bar, with a promise of fetching a cup of tea, he excused himself to move over to speak to her. She was serving twice the number of customers to the barman as Emily watched him chatting to her. He turned towards her, pointed to the end of the room where a large crowd of non-eaters were congregated, drinking and laughing merrily.

Bart indicated Emily should follow him as he moved in the direction of the barmaid's pointing finger. They found 'old Jim' sitting alone at a solitary table nursing a half pint of Guinness. He looked ancient; as if someone carved him out of a piece of old drift wood, his face marked with deep lines. His age Bart placed at ninety but could have been older. He sat wrapped up in a well-worn top coat despite the warmth inside the bar, his flat cap perched on his head.

Bart approached him first, "Hello? Are you Jim?"

The old man eyed him suspiciously until he caught sight of Emily who added, "The lady at the Information Centre at Crathie, Grace Buchanan told me you could help me with my research about Scottish castles?"

Jim smiled making his face crease even more, his watery eyes disappearing amongst them, "Lovely lady, 'er." he said in a dry croaky voice.

Emily squeezed in beside him, "She's been very kind to me....."

"Aye, that's 'er," Jim agreed nodding.

"We were wondering if you could tell us the history of Daingneach castle, if you know it."

Someone standing close by in a group who obviously overheard their conversation shouted, "He'll bore you stupid with his memories!"

Jim ignored him, whilst Emily looked over, saw a group of workmen laughing together at Jim; she scowled her disapproval at them. They could both see by his face the memories were coming alive.

Before he could say anything Bart asked, "First, could I buy you something to eat, Jim?" Jim's old eyes sparkled. "We just ate the fish and chips, they are very good."

Jim shook his head, "I like the beef pie, neaps wi' tatties," he said pointing at his mouth where they noticed he had only a few remaining teeth.

"Okay, Jim I'll leave Amelia with you," Bart pointed at Jim's nearly empty glass offering him another, he nodded vigorously as Bart walked away to the bar.

"So lassie, what do you want to know?" Old Jim asked.

*   *   *   *   *

Once Jim started talking he only paused every so often to put a forkful of his dinner into his mouth or to wash it down with a sip of his drink. Even entreaties by Bart to not let his meal go cold couldn't halt him once he started. They could see he relished being able to talk to someone about a life he once led or to recall other generations of his family. His father and grandfather both worked at Daingneach like he did all his life until he was forced to retire.

Emily and Bart discovered the Laird replaced Jim with Mungo MacLeod after he retired. Most of his time spent being ghillie to the previous Laird, Donald Munro, the first Munro at the castle. Apparently, between his grandfather's time when Seumus Grant was Laird and his father's service to Donald Munro, there had been some talk of non-entitlement when Daingneach passed from Seumus Grant to settle a dispute with the Munro Clan; for what reason he did not specify.

"So who should have inherited the castle?" Bart asked.

"Talk was Seumus Grant 'ad many bastards scattered about an' no child wi' 'is wife," Jim said.

"So no one was legally entitled to the castle?"

Jim shook his head, "It wor different in them days, there were rumours he was canny wi' his wealth and though the castle passed....."

Emily interrupted, "Seumus Grant had hidden treasure?!" Her excitement made Jim laugh until he began to cough then fight for breath.

When the coughing spell subsided he managed, "Aye, as maybe, none can say."

"Has anyone tried to find it?" Emily persisted.

"'Spect so, no one 'as though." Bart noticed he seemed quite sure of himself. Jim picked up on his scowl. "If Donald Munro 'ad found Seumus Grant's treasure you'd expect he wouldn't 'ave been so strapped for cash. When he passed on and Duncan took it on, there was too much owed, he was al'ays trying to raise money for something or n'other."

"I thought he was quite well off, doesn't he own property in Switzerland?" Bart asked.

Jim shook his head, "He married money, yes, his missus won't waste any on a crumbling Scottish Castle she hates, so word 'as it, Duncan Munro wants rid."

"The contents alone must be worth a lot," Bart suggested.

"Mebbe more than the bricks 'n' mortar pr'aps," here Jim winked. Bart thought for the first time perhaps the 'collection plan' Galbraith was drawing up for opening to the public was a ruse to asset strip the castle.

Bart could see Emily was eager to get on to the topic of the ghost so he broached the question of a rumour about the ghost of Seumus Grant.

"Aye, I've heard that too, though no one I know 'as seen a ghost and we g'back to the time of Seumus's death," Jim reported.

"How did he die?" Emily asked.

"Well, given he was allus off in some battle or t'other you'd expect him to die in one, he were a fierce sort," Bart nodded thinking of his portrait in the library together with his armoury collection. "It were gout 'n' too much drinking, took him off with the pneumoni' at the end," he asserted as if he'd seen it himself. "My grandpa was his ghillie at the end. He 'eard a lot of goings on when he were took to bed."

"Was it about who got the castle?" Emily asked.

Jim nodded, "Aye, I reckon. I 'eard as 'ow there were all kinds of claims to birth right, none succeeded. So Donald Munro became Laird."

"Did you ever hear any rumours Mungo MacLeod might be a relative of Duncan Munro?" Jim's face grew concerned, he shook his head. "There are rumours it's why he got the ghillie's job," Bart persisted.

Jim suddenly seemed reluctant to speak on the subject only quietly muttered, "He d'unt look like a Munro, do'ee?" His eyes locked on Bart's for a second before he smiled knowingly.

Whether the result of having hot food or all the reminiscing he did, the old man suddenly seemed to tire very quickly. He began to visibly slow with his narrative. Bart insisted he give him a lift back home mainly because it would give him the means to contact him again. He readily accepted, Bart finding he only lived a few streets away from the pub.

Bart saw him inside his small terraced house, settled him in the one old easy arm chair in the small front room. The place felt cold and damp to Bart. There was a hint of a smell of furniture polish with an underlying mustiness as though the house hadn't felt any kind of heat for some time. Otherwise the house was remarkably tidy. Jim began to nod off to sleep even before Bart asked if he might come again to hear more of his experiences. Jim muttered, "I reckon."

Bart covered him with a colourful crocheted blanket from the back of his chair, slipped a twenty pound note sticking out from under a candlestick on the sideboard before he saw himself out the front door, dropping the catch as he left.

Back in the car where Emily sat waiting for him Bart seemed to be deep in thought. He was thinking about how he might cope if he lived to be in his nineties as he was sure the old man must be. Clearly he lived alone, *like you do*, there was no evidence of anyone else present in the house. The prospect of having no one who would care to look in on him was a daunting thought.

Emily waited for Bart to say something about what Jim told them. Eventually she asked, "I wonder if he knows anything about the tunnel?" This was something neither of them dared to mention.

Bart said, "It's hard to believe his relatives didn't know….. hard to hide with such a huge excavation, that must have taken a very long time to finish."

"Maybe it was before Seumus Grant's time?" She suggested.

"He did seem rather reluctant to talk about Seumus's treasure. I don't know…… there was something about the way he looked as he spoke about the treasure when you asked him if anyone ever tried to find it. How could he have been so certain no one did?" *Only if he had himself, then he would be certain.*

"Do you think he would see us again?" Emily asked.

"'I reckon'," Bart did a passable mimic of 'Old Jim' which made Emily giggle.

He started the car, driving away towards Aboyne to take Emily home.

CHAPTER 48

Déjà vu. Visions of another place caught hold of her as she walked past the hairdressing salon in Banchory. The picture of the girl with short blonde hair caught her eye, arrested her progress along the shopping precinct. She took a step closer to the window, gazed at the picture knowing instinctively Martin would hate her to look like this.

It brought back the other time, when she'd gone for a restyle because she hated looking so old. She was only eighteen then, too frightened to go through with it. Fear made her whisper, "Just a trim," to the hairdresser who asked her what she wanted. The picture of the girl was an old one; the same one in both salons, years apart.

She stared hard remembering how the slight trim she settled for instead put her in the hospital's emergency room with a dislocated shoulder. She would never forget the lesson his anger taught her; the ferocious temper that could do so much damage.

The young girl sweeping the salon floor at Banchory waved cheerily at her; her smile infectious, she waved back opening the door to step inside. One wave with a smile was all it took to give her the courage to answer the question differently this time.

*   *   *   *   *

Emily was relieved to see Beth's white van parked in the yard when they pulled in beside it. At least Bart would be none the wiser about her trip to Banchory. He advised her not to go out alone after hearing Martin Frances checked out of the Fort William hotel now being aware Bonita's story was false. However, her relief didn't last very long. When they entered the kitchen, their noses twitching at the sweet spicy smells of fresh baking, they found Beth seated at the large kitchen table laden with the spoils of her endeavours, hot tea and coffee pots already waiting.

They both did a double take barely able to recognise her. Bart was clearly taken aback at the pixie cut blonde hair. She was wearing denim dungarees, grinning broadly at their shocked faces. Emily clapped her hands delighting at the vision, whilst Bart declared. "Oh my!" Sandy the foxhound stood beside Beth. He moved closer in to her presenting himself to be fussed and to have his ears stroked.

Beth raised both hands, palms upwards, "Well?"

Bart glanced Emily's way, "Did you know about this?"

With a shake of her head she explained, "Last night we discussed the possibility of changing how we look," she grinned at Beth. "You sure did it!"

There was no doubt the new style made her look much younger. You couldn't dispute differently. Bart was less convinced Martin Frances would be fooled.

"Why so extreme?" he asked sitting down at the table. Beth began to pour drinks for them,

"It's not really meant as a disguise," Beth confessed. "It's more defiance. When he finds me – and I know he will – he'll hate the way I look! He will say I look like a tart because if I ever admired any other woman's appearance, their clothes or their hairstyles, he would criticise them. He only let me wear the things *he* chose for me to wear. They made me look old, dowdy and unattractive. I wasn't allowed to go shopping without him, he was so controlling about every aspect of my life." She shook her head sadly. "If anyone told me I looked nice he stopped me wearing those clothes by ripping then to pieces." They gaped at her in disbelief.

"How awful," Emily's face twisted in pain.

In voicing this for the first time Beth's sadness turned to anger, "It didn't stop him from looking at other more attractive women though! He ogled them all the time; I could tell he liked them!"

"Well you are attractive whichever way you look," Bart assured her.

"It's how you feel about yourself, isn't it?" She countered angrily unable to explain how she really felt about her new look. To Bart she seemed far from happy, anger bubbling under the surface.

"Yes, lass, you are quite right. I can't understand how anyone can be so possessive." Clearly Bart was ill equipped to wipe out all the years she suffered. "Well, certainly looks like Sandy approves," he watched amazed how the dog nudged her hand until she placed it back on his head to rub his ears.

Beth burst out laughing at his antics, "And we all know how strange he is." She grew serious again, "I may not have chosen quite such an extreme change of hair style if I didn't have a real need make a statement, to be myself. The only problem is I don't really know who I am.... I never got the chance to find out. When you grow up in Care you have to conform to their rules. There is no room for self-expression, you do what they ask or you have a difficult time. I suppose I thought it would be different when I met Martin. He was kind to me at first, paid me lots of attention. In care, I was used to doing what was expected of me, I was conditioned to comply. So more of the same really, except I suppose at first I wanted to please him. It didn't occur to me what was happening until I showed an interest in something I wanted. Then I discovered his disapproval and his insistence I do exactly what *he* wanted me to do. The first time was when I wanted to get myself a job. He didn't want me to go out to work, just to stay at home."

"Did you ever rebel?" Emily asked knowing how she could be rebellious herself.

Beth nodded her head slowly, "Yes, I did. That was how I learnt the hard way not to try."

Bart's anger flared, "Did he hurt you?"

She nodded slowly, "He was careful not to let anything show to outsiders. He had a very sadistic streak which didn't take much provocation. I came to realise he actually enjoyed hurting me," An involuntary shiver ran through her body. "Over time you learn to anticipate the mood swings, watch for the signs - like after a bad day at work, I'd try not to trigger the anger, except...." She gulped as if forcing back a sob. "There were times when I couldn't influence what I knew was about to happen," she looked up into their horrified faces. In a smaller milder voice she continued, "You have to give yourself up to it, take yourself off in your head to another place, lose a little focus on reality so you can minimise the noise you want to make.....it's like screaming internally so no one can hear you. He hated if I reacted loudly, me crying made him worse....he would kick me until I stopped screaming." She bowed her head as if she were praying to an unknown God, she really didn't want to see their reactions or see if they thought her weak.

"How long did you put up with it, Beth?" Bart asked.

Still looking down she immediately replied, "Five years, four months, three days," as if she plucked the numbers randomly out of nowhere.

"You were very brave to stay so long," Emily knew as a child you have no choice, even so she was grateful to both of them for making it possible for her to leave home.

"Not really, otherwise I might have left when he began," she stared into space recollecting the past. "Only he told me if I ever left him he would hunt me down....kill me."

Bart felt a shiver of fear run down his spine. The face of Martin Frances came back to him as he remembered him sitting in the hotel restaurant, assured, confident, charming, talking to Bonita the waitress and he realised someone who could do those things to a young girl was definitely psychotic.

"Well we must endeavour not to let him find you," Bart said emphatically.

"Do you think he's like he is because he's a policeman who sees too many awful things?" Emily asked with the innocence of a child.

"I'm sure the majority of police officers have seen as much real life horror as Martin Frances," Bart surmised. "And I'm more than certain they would want to change the world for the better." He studied Emily for a moment, could tell she was agonising over something, so he went on, "Think about Jay, who once was a policeman. Then there's Agatha who works to make the streets safe for all of us," he said, then as if he suddenly knew what she was thinking he added, "What I know about Robbie Cowan, whom I haven't known for very long, is he is a thoroughly decent copper."

He watched her smile gently and knew instinctively she was smitten by the young Scottish police officer. *Well I do declare!*

CHAPTER 49

Saturday morning dawned with the 'new' Beth preparing herself to venture out in public for the first time. She was expected over at McKinley's Auto to take the stable's van in for a service. She wore the dungarees with a blue striped t-shirt and after using the new make-up she purchased in Banchory, applied the plum eye shadow, black mascara with a smattering of pink lipstick to her face. She eyed herself in the mirror, felt a sudden pang of uncertainty about her image, never having used makeup before she could hear Martin's voice in her head screeching at her, "You look like a tart!" The echo nearly made her wipe her face clean until that new reserve of rare confidence she found returned. She yelled at herself in the quiet place inside her head, "No you don't! You look good!" Instead of cleaning her face of the makeup she took out a bright multi-coloured chiffon scarf which she arranged decoratively in her hair around her head.

"Come on girl, go strut your stuff!" she ordered herself out loud. Sandy lifted his head lying where he usually was in front of the fire, made a subdued chuffing noise as if he agreed.

Wrapped in her white coat to keep out the chill, she left the cottage, for Dinnet a few miles up the road. It was a sunny start on an otherwise cold day. She thought she might drop off the van then walk back on such a pleasant day. If the weather changed she intended to get the bus; the one that detoured down the old Aboyne road dropping off at the bottom of the hill leading to the cottage.

When she got to McKinley's Auto the roll down garage door was firmly in place, the small side door stood ajar with the 'open' sign up. She left the van in front of the roll down doors. When she went inside, Radio Northsound was playing popular music on their Saturday morning slot. She walked over to the unit's desk in the corner, which as usual was piled high with papers, no one was sitting there.

There must be someone in otherwise there wouldn't be music playing. She could also feel the intense heat wafting over from a small fan heater. She slipped her coat off, threw it over the chair where it briefly made contact before sliding down onto the floor under the desk. Just as she was about to bend down, a door at the back opened and Nessa McKinley walked out wearing the same oil-stained overalls Beth remembered her in, her dark ponytail swinging.

All thoughts of her coat disappeared as their eyes met briefly; she saw Nessa's face turn to surprise, "Wow!" she exclaimed at the sight of her new look. "You look amazing." She openly stared at Beth's dramatic new look, there was no doubt whatsoever she approved.

The blush appeared on Beth's face giving away her embarrassment. She tried to lighten the exchange with, "You approve of my disguise?"

It took Nessa a moment to realise she was joking, "Well I would recognise you anywhere," she was smiling as she walked over. "Then I admit I was expecting you since you are booked in for a service." They both laughed as Radionorth slipped into an advertising jingle. Nessa switch the radio off as she passed. "I hate these adverts."

At that moment they heard the outer door open and a male voice behind Beth shout, "Morning ladies!" Beth froze. Her face remained fixed on Nessa's, turning instantly into a horrified mask of terror which the mechanic could see was a reaction to the man's voice. Almost as a reflex Nessa pointed behind her to the door she'd come through moments ago, in a low voice as she walked past Beth, she whispered, "In there," now moving towards the man who'd just entered the garage.

"Morning, how can I help you?" she asked pleasantly hoping Beth responded to her hint.

The stranger met Nessa half way across the unit, his charming smile leading him forward she could tell was well practiced, which he held a little too long to be quite normal.

"I believe McKinley's are the only auto shop around here?" He asked as he seemed to peer around her. When Nessa half-turned she felt thankful Beth was no longer there. "Your friend isn't very friendly," he commented.

"Oh, she's deaf, so wouldn't have heard you," she hoped it would serve as a deflection away from Beth, adding quickly, "Yes, we are the only auto shop locally. We're usually very busy if you were looking for a mechanic. I'm up to my eyes in bookings today I'm afraid," she observed the slight sneer momentarily cross his lips.

"You are the mechanic here?" confirmed her suspicion here was yet another man who didn't readily accept the job could possibly be done by a woman.

"I am," she waited for some kind of excuse to leave or at its very worst a mouthful of abuse – she had been on the receiving end of both.

He gave a dismissive shrug, reached inside his jacket bringing out a couple of photographs. Nessa stiffened when his hand disappeared inside his jacket then relaxed when she saw he didn't pull out a weapon of any kind.

"I wondered if you have seen either this car – maybe brought in for repair or service by this girl." He handed over the photographs which she took to scrutinise, not shocked to recognise Beth given her reaction to his voice.

Of course, she saw she was much younger when the picture was taken. She turned the picture slightly in her hand to pick up the name Lily Johns with 'at 18 years' written on the back. The car was an old dark red Vauxhall Astra she hadn't seen before. She shook her head, "No, haven't seen either here," she gave them back to him. "I'm pretty sure a car this old would end up here if it were to be driven on the roads out there."

"Yes, it's a cranky old thing," he sneered scornfully.

Nessa stood her ground hands on her hips waiting for him to leave. There weren't many men she actually liked, this one she instantly disliked. He put the photographs back in his inside jacket pocket, unzipped the front pocket to take out a small business card, "Perhaps if it is brought in you could telephone me...?"

She took it, frowned trying hard not to sneer, "I'm sorry, you haven't told me why you're looking for the car?" She read the card showing 'Michael Johns' together with the word 'immigration'.

"We aren't looking for the car it's the girl we're interested in, she is believed to be an illegal." The sickly smile returned to his face taking Nessa all of her concentration not to show contempt for him. She slipped the card into the pocket of her overalls nodded back saying nothing. "You can get me on the number on there," he turned to leave.

Rather than follow him to the door which she wanted to do, she walked over to the radio to put it back on. When she turned back he was gone so she walked quickly over to peer out of the door to see him driving away in his Audi Saloon. She immediately locked the door putting the closed sign up.

When Nessa opened the door to the back room she found Beth sitting rigidly on one of the wooden chairs, she was deathly pale with wild staring eyes, she was shaking uncontrollably.

"He's gone," Nessa assured her quietly she could see the state she was in. She moved over to a small filing cabinet with a kettle which she flicked on to boil, made a cup of tea stirring in two spoons of sugar which she took over to Beth. Her hands were shaking too violently to hold it, so Nessa placed the mug down at the side of her. "He really has gone, I watched him drive away. I've locked the door, put the closed sign up."

She sat down at the side of her until the fear subsided a little, "Drink some tea," Nessa urged. "He really didn't recognise you, so that is some disguise, yes?"

Beth found herself laughing a little. "I didn't think he would find me," Nessa heard her say. "Or...or..... hearing his voice again would make me react so badly."

"I take it Michael Johns is your husband? You are the Lily Johns in the photograph?"

Beth face became instantly puzzled, "He is Martin Frances, a police officer. Yes, he is my husband. I once used to be Lily Johns.....is that the name he told you?"

Nessa took his business card out of her overall pocket, handed it to Beth. She saw her face crease into a frown.

"He's a police officer?" Beth said making Nessa frown.

"The bastard!" Nessa spat letting her contempt show. "I think you need to speak to my friend Robbie Cowan......"

"You know Robbie?" Beth asked surprised.

"Aye, we were at school together, my Da hoped he would become his son-in-law," Nessa giggled softly. Beth couldn't see the joke. "Robbie used to be my cover, when I was out with ma girlfriend, d'ye ken?" Nessa winked making Beth laugh again.

They both suddenly froze hearing a loud thump on the outer door.

"He's come back!" Beth exclaimed in terror.

Nessa jumped up, "Stay in here," she ordered. She left her closing the door. Beth could hear voices out in the garage; she began searching around wildly for anything she could find to serve as a weapon. All she could see was the kettle standing on the cabinet which she picked up finding it almost empty, having no weight at all. The voices drew closer. When the door handle began to move down and the door to open slowly, she raised the kettle ready to strike if necessary.

Robbie Cowan in his police uniform came in with Nessa following behind him holding a monkey wrench she took with her to answer the door. When Robbie saw Beth with her new look he grinned.

"I doubt Martin Frances would recognise you now," he said cheerily. He gently took the kettle out of her raised hand; he didn't care for the way she was holding it.

"Nessa sent for you?"

"Err, no. I was here to see, Ness," he replied. "She also greeted me with a blunt instrument," he nodded at the monkey wrench she was still holding. "Ness tells me he didn't recognise you from seeing your back."

She shook her head, "He didn't see my face though."

"Well that's good. I'm glad you're here Beth, I have some news to impart," he said. "Sit down Nessa," he instructed. He made a huge gesture to take the wrench away from her.

Beth and Nessa sat on the only two chairs in the small office, whilst Robbie perched on the end of the desk a twin of the one out in the garage. "It's about the sabotage of the other white van," he began making Nessa frown again.

"It was definitely tampered with?"

Robbie nodded looking solemn. Beth visibly sank in her chair, "Not Martin?" she asked now resigned to hearing he'd already tried to kill her.

Robbie shook his head, "I think if it was him he might have wondered about the one parked outside at the moment, perhaps asked Nessa or even have guessed you might be here?" Beth looked to Nessa for confirmation.

"No, he certainly didn't mention it.....I watched him leave here so fast there was na'time to even look at the van." She became puzzled then, "So who did Robbie?" Nessa asked as something dawned on her at the same time as Robbie began to speak.

"Shona did," there was no easy way to lessen the blow. "Whether it was meant for you or for Beth is uncertain," he surmised. "What is certain is she has admitted to tampering with the van, we have cautioned her. She claims she didn't intend to harm anyone, she was angry and took it out on the van believing it belongs to someone you're seeing."

He could see Nessa was shattered at the news, "Oh no! It's my fault for telling her I liked someone else. I should have more sense knowing how possessive she is." She looked at Beth, "I'm so sorry to put you in such danger."

Beth was overcome with relief it wasn't Martin and therefore intentionally meant to kill her. It would also have confirmed he did know she lived somewhere close by.

"To be quite clear Ness, the damage she tried to do to the van was a poor attempt, obviously done by someone who knows nothing whatsoever about car engines."

"Praise be!" Nessa declared sarcastically. "Since there was no intention meant to harm anyone driving it does she have to be charged?"

"The fact of not causing harm is mitigation....with there being no intention to....depends on what you both want to do about her being charged," he agreed. "And of course, The Crown Office and Procurator Fiscal Service get the last say."

Nessa caught Beth's eye, saw her raise her shoulders, "I can't see how she meant to harm either of us really," Beth said. "I would like to forget it ever happened."

"I wouldn't want to see Shona go to prison....all I want is for her to leave me be."

"Okay points taken." Robbie Cowan left it there adding. "Now what are we going to do about Martin Frances?"

CHAPTER 50

Emily didn't see Beth leave on Saturday morning because she already left to meet Bart for another recce of the secret passageway at the castle. Their visit was prompted after meeting 'old Jim' the day before, both of them leaving him with the impression he was keeping some of what he knew to himself. Emily was convinced his reluctance was something to do with Seumus Grant's 'treasure' whilst Bart wasn't as sure about it. He wanted to explore the other tunnel they found under the castle first.

They left early to avoid any of the castle staff arriving. Instead of driving up the long meandering approach road to the castle, Bart drove past the gatehouse in search of another way in. When he found the entrance he was surprised to see, although gated, it stood wide open for anyone to drive through. He thought at first perhaps this wasn't part of the castle estate at all, only hesitated slightly as he made the turn into the narrow roughly made up access road. The trees on either side cast a gloomy shadow over the track.

"This must be part of the wooded area," he said.

"Except weren't they mostly fir trees?" she pointed out, "These are different."

"Ah, yes," he agreed.

After driving a short distance they came to a small cottage set back amongst the trees with a jeep parked outside.

"Isn't this….."? Bart began.

"…where Mungo MacLeod lives…..err, lived?" she corrected herself then regretted inferring he was dead.

"I know he does live within the castle estate. I recall Robbie Cowan saying they did forensics on his jeep which they must have brought back here afterwards."

He parked the Peugeot in a clearing opposite the cottage between the trees out of the way.

"Let's have a look inside," Emily suggested. Bart chuckled at her eagerness.

"I can't imagine what we could possibly find if the police have already done a search," he said, however, seeing her pleading face he gave in, "Okay, no harm looking."

They got out, approached the cottage which appeared as if it were deserted. Emily led the way, her hand already over the door handle when he caught her up. He placed his hand over hers to stop her, "Knock first," he whispered. "It's someone's home."

She frowned, "Yes, he's probably......" she couldn't bring herself to say 'dead'.

Bart shook his head, "Maybe the laird has given the cottage to someone else to live in?" he offered. "The entrance gate being open might suggest as much." He actually thought, *more likely the police not bothering to shut it when they left.*

Emily knocked lightly, waiting impatiently. There was no answering noise or signs of life from inside, so she pressed the door handle, which she was about to say was probably locked when to her surprise she felt the movement inwards.

"They are prone to leave their doors unlocked up here," Bart explained.

Once inside they felt the chill of an empty place, the old curtains at the one window were closed making the room dark. Emily moved over, pulled them back to give some light. Bart momentarily gave thought to the idea the CSI's must have closed them after they were finished. They would certainly have needed the extra light the window would give. He must have been frowning because Emily asked, "What?" when she saw his face.

"Nothing," he said looking around at a very basic set up which was incredibly orderly given he knew from personal experience how forensics could leave quite a mess. His mind challenged whether they were actually here at all.

Emily began to look through the draws in an old sideboard whilst Bart silently took in the room's contents.

"It doesn't look at all disturbed," he muttered almost to himself, *maybe they cleared all Mungo's things out.*

Emily opened the bottom cupboard in the sideboard having rummaged through the contents in the draws. "There's someone's stuff still here," she whispered suddenly feeling like an intruder.

Bart joined her as she leaned in, her arm searched into the farthest corner of the cupboard, pulled out an album. She stood up flicking through the dark pages set with photographs, in between each one a flimsy tissue paper page to protect the pictures.

There was no mistaking the album belonged to Mungo MacLeod, even as a youngster his flaming ginger hair was a giveaway, even in the black and white photos. The later ones confirmed it, when a beard appeared he began to resemble the man Bart met last year.

"Whoa!" He put his hand over Emily's as she flicked through. "Go back two pages!"

She flipped back, stopping at a picture of Mungo MacLeod as a younger man walking at the side of another man holding a shot gun broken open in the safety position over his arm. Bart tapped the old photo, "Remind you of any one?"

"Isn't it Mungo MacLeod?" she queried never having met him like Bart.

Bart realised it was definitely his photographic memories through his life. "The man he's with?"

She squinted at the picture then up at Bart, "That's...."

"Old Jim?" he said. "You can see there's a likeness. Do we know what Jim's name is?"

She shook her head, "Damn! I should have asked him – some sleuth I am!"

"*We* should have asked him," he corrected.

He flicked the rest of the pages, moved towards the end where he found what he was looking for, a colour picture of 'old Jim' closer to the age he was now.

"I think there's another ghillie in this family tree which Jim didn't mention," Bart declared. "Mungo MacLeod is Jim's son."

Emily was shocked, "Didn't he say he didn't know Mungo?"

Bart tried hard to recall what he actually did say. "No he didn't, he only mentioned the laird appointed Mungo as his replacement after Jim retired, which implies he didn't meet him." *The cunning old bugger.*

"Wouldn't he have been upset when I mentioned his name though?"

"Why?" Bart smiled. At this point he realised Jim didn't know Mungo was reported missing.

They put the photograph album back inside the sideboard, left the cottage stopping only briefly at the Peugeot to pick up Bart's Gladstone bag before they walked into the trees towards where they thought the castle was beyond the wood. When the selection of trees changed to fir trees they knew for certain they were moving in the right direction. They feared they would be unable to spot the camouflaged hide amongst all the trees.

After a ten minute brisk hike they stopped to rest near an old tree stump, took a sip of water from the bottle Bart packed in his bag. As they sat silently getting their breath's back they heard the snap of a twig to the left of where they sat. The antlers gave the deer away first. The sudden flight of a pheasant spooked the deer making it bark before springing into life to flee. As their eyes tried to penetrate the depth of the trees searching for the rest of the herd, Emily pointed excitedly, "Isn't that the hide over there?"

She indicated beyond the place where the deer had been. Bart tried to follow the direction of her arm. He relented letting Emily lead him closer, his eyes poorer by many more clock mending jobs, than Emily's younger vision. When they drew closer he praised her, "Nicely done young Amelia, at least it's a hide, let's hope it's the only one."

On entering the hide they found the false floor under the rush matting.

"Okay, let's see what we can find." Bart let Emily go down into the tunnel first, handing her the bag before he went himself. Try as he might he couldn't pull the mat over the entrance so he left the floor exposed hoping no one would use the hide until they came back up later.

When he reached the bottom of the ladder Emily said, "Someone's been down here since we last came."

Bart was surprised, "How do you know?"

She held up the lamp which she lit as Bart descended, "I found this on the shelf in the wall," she pointed to her right where someone had roughly hewn an indentation in the wall big enough to take the lamp. "I left it at the base of the ladder when we found the way out."

"Oh! That means whoever did, will know we've been down here."

She nodded moving away along the passage with Bart following behind. As before, they found nothing unusual about the tunnel until they reached the one leading off at right angles to it.

"I wonder if this is also a way out." She stood holding the lamp up high to no avail; the light hardly penetrated the darkness along the side tunnel.

"Only one way to find out," he said holding out his hand for her to proceed. She saw he already held the large flash light which he used to sweep the beam ahead down the tunnel.

"Let's conserve at least one of the lights," she blew out the lamp letting Bart take the lead.

In some ways the tunnel was a huge disappointment to them when they reached the end of the short passageway, which as suspected was indeed a dead end, finding nothing upwards leading out. The end opened out into a large cavern and when Bart swept the area along the floor with the flash light he found signs someone was here at some time using the cave to sleep in. There was a sleeping bag at one side with various items of half-consumed food including the bones of either chicken or pheasant from the size of them.

Emily bent down to examine the sleeping bag for any indication of who it might belong to. She knelt beside it, cried, "Ouch!" She picked up a large bunch of keys concealed by part of the sleeping bag, consisting of an old iron ring with many keys on it. They were all shapes and sizes, some old, some new, others quite strange. She handed them to Bart who began to smile which she caught in the dimness of the back light from the torch as he aimed the flash light at the bunch of keys.

"These are mostly clock keys unless I am very much mistaken."

"Why would Thomas Galbraith sleep down here?" Emily asked remembering he was asked by Duncan Munro to give Bart the keys to the clocks.

"Why would Galbraith put the keys down here is the question?" Bart posed. "I suspect he might have given them to someone to keep all the clocks wound up, don't you?"

She nodded, stood up saying, "I don't much like being down here, the airs a bit stale. I can't see why they would create this tunnel in the first place as it doesn't lead anywhere."

They left the tunnel moving back to the main passage.

"It could be where Seumus Grant put all his valuables – it's not far off being a priest hole, maybe where they brought their spoils from all those battles they liked to get involved in. What they called 'plunder' in those days," Bart surmised.

"Well it's certainly not here now is it?" she sounded disappointed as she looked one way, then the other. "Which way?"

Bart pointed the way they came, "Let's go get the car, go back to the main entrance," he held up the bunch of keys. "I have a mind to try out a few of these before we leave today."

CHAPTER 51

Out of the darkness, came shadowy faces behind the piercing bright light, disturbing the impenetrable blackness. Once or twice the head of a stag appeared its horrible barking screech of a creature in torment. The neck at the wrong angle to the prone body oozed deep red stickiness across the white snow.

A human voice, not the stag's, was light and feminine, "Hello? Can you hear me?" It faded into the solid blackness with the light.

Another time now a deeper voice, a silhouette of a man close to his face holding up a hand, "How many fingers?" He started to count, knew there were too many for one hand, yet he heard his own croaky voice reply, "Six".

The endless sea of undulating waves brought him back to the surface. He could feel the cold air in his nostrils before he saw the pretty face looking at him closely. Green sparkling eyes with long dark lashes had no business being this close, "Hello?" The rosy red lips asked, "How do you feel?" He tried hard to fix on the face, thinking this must be an angel come to save him from the waves. "Can you tell me your name?" the angel asked, but a name wouldn't come. He shook his head making giddiness surge. The waves grew stronger pulling him back down, where he sank once again to rest just under the surface.

Next time he opened his eyes the place was semi-dark, with a bright strip of light under a door. Yes, he could see a door. As his eyes adjusted to the gloom he saw he was lying in a bed, in a room with a window covered in drapes. He lifted his hand, the one with a dull ache, focussing on the blue plastic cap sticking out of the back, taped over with something to keep it in place.

He lay awake for a long time remembering the stag with the wonky head, large sadly startled eyes, looking at him, crying with pain and pleading for it to stop.

*   *   *   *   *

The man in the hospital bed sat propped against the pile of pillows. He knew he was in hospital because the nurse with the green eyes told him. His name was 'John Doe', which was written on a board behind his bed. Everyone who came to see him called him 'John'.

"How are you today, John?" the ward receptionist would ask him.

"What do you want to eat today, John?" the ward orderly asked every morning helping him to fill out a menu card.

An endless stream of people who knew his name; a name that didn't seem quite right to him yet he couldn't say why. The ward consultant told him he was suffering from amnesia which often followed from the kind of trauma he suffered to his head. He couldn't remember how he got the injury, every time he thought really hard he could see the stag, its breath coming out in steam whilst he held a tree branch hitting the animal to stop it from making those screaming noises. The eyes no longer pleading with him were still and fixed in its wonky head. This was all he could remember at first.

*   *   *   *   *

The cheerful nurse with the green eyes called Maggie showed him how to raise and lower himself in the bed using the control box. She told him he'd lost his memory, "These things take time, John, don't try to force it."

So he didn't. How could you when there was a complete void? Another doctor, a psychologist told him with his kind of injury you needed to wait until the brain was fully healed, then his memory would only come back a bit at a time but he may never remember the point at which he received the injury.

When the process began he found himself feeling anxious. It began with Maggie, the 'angel' nurse taking his temperature by

377

putting a gun into his ear. She leaned over him, the upside down clock pinned to her chest gave him a flash of a large ornate clock that chimed loudly in his head. He was holding a heavy bunch of keys. The clock began to chime, boom, boom. He knew instinctively if he didn't attend to it the clock would die. Only he could save it, unlike the stag.

CHAPTER 52

The walk back to Bart's car seemed to take much longer than when they came. He felt worn out from the uneven terrain by the time they found it again. Bart's legs felt weak when he backed the car out of the clearing to jerkily crawl down the bumpy track away from Mungo's cottage. His knees made him stop in the open gate for a moment to ease the ache in his legs.

"Do you want me to get out to close the gate after us?" Emily asked, a reasonable question given where they were.

"No, lass, I need a moment to let my legs rest, we'll leave things as we found them."

They both stared ahead out of the car windscreen as a navy saloon car cruised by on the road ahead. Bart recognised the unmistakeable image of Thomas Galbraith at the wheel. "Oh dear," he said. "Looks like Galbraith is going in to work today, that was him driving past."

"Did he see us!?" Emily asked alarmed.

"No he didn't look this way, thank goodness. I think I would have difficulty explaining being here."

Emily studied him intently, "What do we do now?"

"I think if there's even the remotest chance he's around I wouldn't want to cross paths with him again," Bart's voice held an edge to it. "We'll leave going to try the keys today, let him think I'm still waiting for him to give me them." He grinned at the idea of Galbraith being put under pressure to find them. "Change of plan, let's go have another chat with Jim to ask him directly about his son Mungo."

"That might upset him," Emily suggested, "if we have to tell him he's missing."

"I don't think so because he didn't strike me as someone whose son has disappeared." Bart remembered how Jim's house was extremely tidy. Even though there was no sign of anyone else living there, he was sure Jim didn't tend to his own domestic arrangements. He didn't say anything to Emily, merely started the car aiming for Ballater. He expected Jim to be at home, being too early for eating out at the pub. He was sure Jim would use the £20 note he left under the candlestick to treat himself to a Saturday trip to the Balmoral.

After there was no response to their knocking Bart insisted they walk to the pub. Even if Jim wasn't there they might be able to find someone who knew him or could tell them his name.

It was still quite early even for a Saturday. Only the heavy drinkers were already in residence. Bart was pleased to find the amiable barmaid from the day before behind the bar. The lack of customers made looking for Jim easier, they could see he wasn't there. He approached the barmaid once again explaining he stopped off in order to give 'old' Jim a lift to the pub only he found he wasn't at home. He stopped talking when he saw her face become distressed and she retold what one of the customer's minutes before imparted.

"Apparently one of the community nurses from the health centre visited him this morning, she found him dead, sitting in his armchair, still wearing his old top coat and flat cap from yesterday. They say he must have fallen asleep when he got back home from here, he died peacefully sometime later." She looked genuinely sad, "I know he's had a good innings but he was one of our regulars......we'll miss him."

Bart and Emily's eyes met in shock as Emily asked, "I'm right in thinking his last name is MacLeod?" she directed to the girl. "We hadn't known him very long but we would like to pay our respects." Bart did a double take at her presence of mind as she spoke.

"Yes, that's right," the barmaid confirmed. "I think they will announce the funeral details more likely in the Aberdeen Evening Express. The Eagle will probably do something about him later; he was a well-respected character around here."

Emily felt a stir of anger when she recalled the group of men at the bar yesterday making fun of Jim as he began to tell them about his life.

She told the barmaid "Thank you," before she walked away, not wanting them to see the tears in her eyes. Emily stood outside on the pavement at the corner thinking how sad to hear Jim died alone. She felt Bart's hand on her shoulder give a gentle squeeze, "I know lass," he sighed as they began the walk back to the car.

They sat side by side for a moment in the car outside Jim's house, Emily finally spoke, "No one should have to die alone."

"I know," he agreed. "There is something comforting about knowing he went peacefully in his sleep. I think if I had a choice, when the time comes, I would choose his way, after a visit to my favourite pub, a meal with a beer, being able to talk to someone about my own life and ancestors." The sad thing for Bart was he hadn't ever been able to do the same because his identity kept changing. He daren't risk telling anyone about himself, not that there'd ever been a real friend to tell anything to. Emily raised sad eyes nodding.

*   *   *   *   *

When they got back to the cottage Robbie Cowan's Defender was parked in the yard. There was no sign of the white van.

"Something's happened!" Emily exclaimed throwing open the car door she rushed off inside.

Bart found all three of them in the kitchen where he could see immediately Beth looking anguished.

"Martin Frances turned up at McKinley's when Beth took the van for Nessa to service," Robbie explained.

Emily gasped with shock, "What did he do?"

"He only caught a glimpse of her back. Ness managed to distract him whilst Beth found refuge in the back office," he continued.

"Thanks to Nessa, she was incredible," Beth's gratitude shone through her distress.

Robbie went on to update them about the forensic findings on the kennel's van explaining how they knew for certain the saboteur wasn't Martin Frances.

Robbie asked, "So he's back here looking for her after his abortive visit to Fort William?" What little hope Bart held that Martin Frances would give up his search for Beth faded. "We also have news," Bart cast a glance at Emily with a warning frown as he updated them about Jim MacLeod's untimely passing. Emily took the cue noticing he deliberately omitted anything related to the secret passage, the castle library or the Hide in the woods. Later he explained to her he needed to test the clock keys before the police got involved. Emily accepted his explanation. Bart didn't want to tell her he hoped to flush out the person who was sleeping in the tunnel.

He set Emily back on to researching the castle clocks because he began to have a germ of an idea what was behind the disappearance of Mungo MacLeod. The sooner he finished his inventory the sooner would his theory be proven.

In the meantime he was more concerned about keeping Beth safe from Martin Frances for which he needed Robbie Cowan's help; he would rather he wasn't distracted by investigating false leads in the Mungo MacLeod case.

When he got Robbie Cowan alone he asked him about the possibility of police protection for Beth which he discovered would be easier if the courts granted her a protective order, a breach of which would allow the police to prosecute him. Bart didn't like the sound of that.

It seemed to him the law had a long way to go before someone could be protected in a domestic violence situation. In Beth's position this could only be achieved if Frances was to violently assault her. Of course, Frances being a policeman he would be aware of all the mechanisms in law related to domestic violence which he probably used to keep Beth with him. Bart didn't doubt when Martin found her he would force her to go back home; in his eyes she was his possession which gave him the right.

He also explored the possibility of Beth divorcing him. In Scotland to do so without his consent required her to be separated from her spouse for two years. He imagined Martin Frances would never agree to a quick divorce which meant Beth needed to be separated from him for the full two years proving they lived apart all that time. He suggested to Beth she should get herself a solicitor in order to register her separation from her husband. This would enable her to fully document her reasons including the domestic abuse she suffered during their marriage, to eventually provide the divorce court with what they would require for her to divorce without his consent. The threat of divorce would probably not stop his obsession with her. However, it would be a start.

"That sounds very expensive," she replied. "I don't have the money to undertake the process….especially if I have to give up having a job to be able to hide from him."

Bart knew she was right and to seek legal aid required an in depth assessment of her financial status, income, assets or valuables which would be complicated whilst she was living in a cottage she didn't technically own. She may even be called upon to divulge how she came to be living there; even Bart wasn't sure about that.

"At least it would show you no longer want to be with him or married to him," Bart suggested.

She nodded reluctantly agreeing to seek out a solicitor who could better tell her about her rights.

CHAPTER 53

When Jay's text came a few days later, Bart felt torn between complying with his wishes and not telling Emily. He was coming up to Scotland for an interview with Police Scotland the following Monday, staying overnight at the hotel. He merely finished by saying, "Perhaps we could get together for a meal in the evening – the two of us?" Bart read the message a couple of times before he was sure there was something Jay needed to talk to him about which he inferred was meant for no one else's ears.

It put Bart in a tricky position because he knew Emily would be upset if she felt she was being excluded. For a while he toyed with the idea of not telling her at all. He already felt guilty withholding certain thoughts he was having regarding Mungo MacLeod which he wanted to keep to himself until he was certain about his 'facts', so he kept his theories to himself.

As to Jay that was a different matter. By the time Saturday came around and he confirmed his stay over on Monday evening, Bart relented deciding to tell Emily about their proposed meeting.

"I need to tell you something about next week," he began when they were together in the shop on Saturday morning. He was getting ready to show her his clock winding regime which was prompted by them finding the bunch of keys to the castle's clocks.

"Ah, me too. I want to talk to you about Monday afternoon," she said much to Bart's surprise; *could she know about Jay arriving on Monday afternoon?*

"Go on, you first," he urged hoping to give himself time to think of a plausible excuse to meet Jay on his own.

"I was wondering if you minded me taking the afternoon off as Robbie is giving me another driving lesson?" She expected to be teased about it. "In fact, he wants to give me a driving lesson every week so I can put in for my tests as soon as possible."

"Well how splendid! I'm sure you won't take long to learn, Robbie says you're a natural!"

He could see Emily hugely pleased at hearing it.

"What were you going to say?" She asked the smile still lingering.

"I was going to tell you Jay is coming up on Monday for an interview for a job with Police Scotland. He will more than likely be staying overnight at the hotel." It occurred to Bart he could very well have invited Jay to stay with him; he vowed he would clean out his spare room which was still cluttered with junk including his moving boxes, to be able to get another bed for this very purpose. Emily was clearly delighted at the prospect of seeing him again.

"Will I get to see him before he goes back on Tuesday?"

Bart smiled, "Of course you will. I'm not sure when he'll be leaving but I know he'll want to pop in here to see you before he does.

"Cool!" Emily grinned making Bart smile back relieved at how easy it was after all.

"Now then, Emily let me explain how we keep the clocks going here," she was encouraged at hearing the 'we' he could tell she was eager for this to be a two-person process.

When they began Emily noticed he kept the keys to the wind up clocks together with the clock they belonged to. Some were taped to the back or placed conveniently underneath the shelf standing ones or maybe on a ledge as with the Grandfather or Grandmother clocks.

As they progressed Emily asked, "How come the castle keys are on a bunch altogether? Surely it's harder to identify which clock they belong to?"

Bart was pleased she recognised what already occurred to him, "Exactly so!" he declared. "In fact, my biggest problem will be to identify them throughout the castle. I suspect the bunch does not contain them all," he surmised. "I know the one Mungo brought me came with the key taped to the back of the clock. That key will be missing from the bunch."

"Maybe he took it off the bunch to give to you," Emily suggested.

"He could have. Don't forget he also wound up every other clock in the castle, he must have known which clock each key belonged to."

"Are they marked in some way? There must be a lot of rooms with clocks up at the castle." Bart was once again impressed by her common sense.

"My thoughts entirely, that's something we are going to have to deduce," he touched a finger to the side of his nose.

She laughed saying, "Bartholomew and Hobbs Private Detectives!"

He stared at her for using his Witness Protection name realising Bartholomew was the name she first knew him by. He must have appeared shocked as she placed a hand over her mouth mumbling, "Sorry!"

"No harm done," he replied. "It does have a ring to it," he laughed again loudly.

Bart produced the keys so they could examine them closely. He found no specific labels with which to identify them. Emily took them, examined them, moving each one in turn until she stopped with them split leaving the keys hanging across the bottom of the curve of the metal ring, each side of equal amounts.

"There," she handed them back to Bart asking, "Have you got a magnifying glass in with your tools?"

Bart nodded, went to search his Gladstone bag which sat on the floor beside his work table, coming back with a large magnifying glass. She picked up his spectacles from the table, gave them to him to put on, "Someone has scratched a number on each of the keys. I suspect they will all be in order starting with number one," she pointed to one side for him to check.

After using the magnifying glass, he said, "Well I do declare! That means whoever...."

"I imagine Mungo MacLeod would have marked them if he was responsible for keeping them wound up," she said. "He would know which number went with each clock."

Bart screwed up his face, shaking his head doubtfully, "Now that would be some memory!"

"Not if you wrote a list," she grinned. "Like number one might be the library clock, two the carriage clock in the fireplace and so on."

"The Grandmother clock you repaired would be missing from the bunch. You could identify where it's numbered key sits on the bunch, start there if it's been replaced in its original place."

"What an excellent idea! At least that would give us a start," Bart felt daunted at the massive task ahead.

"He would have known them all, whether they were eight day clocks and such like," Bart was beginning to get a feel for Mungo's ingenuity. He frowned again, "It's a bit long winded though, would be easier keeping each key with its clock. Why would he deliberately make it hard for himself?"

Emily shook her head, "I have no idea unless he didn't want anyone else to know."

"Ah, now that makes more sense and fits in with something I've begun to suspect." Emily sat expectantly waiting to be let into the know. "It was something 'Old Jim' implied about the state of the castle not being good whilst the contents were worth more. I think his actual words were, 'more than the bricks and mortar'! I began to wonder if these inventories were perhaps not really meant for insurance purposes at all." Emily sat pondering. Bart could see her

388

struggling so he explained, "There are a large number of castles in Scotland that have been left to fall into ruins, aren't there?"

"Yes, I saw them when I researched the history. There are more than 1,500 castle ruins in Scotland. Some castles were purchased by the National Trust for Scotland, some by private owners to renovate to live in...."

"I imagine those in the poorest state wouldn't get far in any of those property deals or attract much of a price," he said.

"Well they might if they contained a lot of valuable treasures whether of historical significance or valuable antiques......ah!" She suddenly caught on to Bart's way to thinking, "The Laird could sell the contents make a lot of money leaving the castle to either be sold at a low price or to become yet another ruin!"

Bart was nodding vigorously, "Well it's not illegal is it?" she asked. "Not if you own the castle?"

"That's the point isn't it?" Emily said. "The castle belonged to Seumus Grant, built by his ancestors. On his death it moved to the Munro's. The question is, why not to his own line?"

"Because he and his wife didn't have any children," Emily reiterated Jim's words.

"According to Jim he was reputed to have many outside of wedlock," Bart interjected.

"Couldn't it be easily proved if the Munro's gained the castle legally?" Emily asked.

"How? Are there any Deeds of Entitlement? I believe there is a statute of Limitations after which you have no claim. I'm not sure if there ever has been a test case after the reclamation of land. Scotland has complex issues," Bart was very well aware of his lack of knowledge about property laws in Scotland, he wasn't at all sure about subsequent generational claims in the lineage.

The subject came to a natural end after which they continued with the task in hand as Emily took on more of the clock's maintenance.

CHAPTER 54

Beth's deliveries took her on a wide route around the area leaving her on an unscheduled call to Mary Macaulay in Banchory on her way back to the castle. She took another bottle of medicated dog shampoo from the kennels before she left because she wanted to check up on the dogs' progress. At least that's what she told herself when in reality she wanted to see how Mary was coping knowing there was no progress in finding Mungo MacLeod. The last time she saw Mary she was extremely distressed even before she was told he was missing.

Arriving at the cottage there was no sign of the dogs in the garden or any kind of life when she knocked on the door. She knew Mary worked somewhere in Banchory but was surprised not to hear the dogs bark. She made her way back up the path, got as far as her van when she saw Mary walking towards her from the direction of Banchory High Road. Mary beamed at seeing Beth. She greeted her warmly.

"I was driving by so thought I would check on the dogs and bring you some more shampoo if you need it," Beth said.

"They are doing really well," Mary walked past her up the path, "Come and see."

"Are they here?" Beth was clearly surprised which elicited an odd look from Mary.

Beth laughed, "Have they been getting some training? They didn't even respond to me knocking."

Mary led her inside where they found both dogs in their respective beds in the kitchen. Beth was reminded of Sandy who rarely acknowledged people, but this was a huge contrast to the last time she called. She recalled them responding to Bart's instructions at the time which they instinctively obeyed.

Mary showed Beth how the dog's flea bites were nearly fully healed, his chewed fur was now beginning to grow back.

"Excellent," Beth handed her the new bottle of the shampoo from her bag. "And how are you, Mary?" she asked wondering if she might open up like she did the last time. The least she expected was for her to ask if Beth had any news about Mungo, however, she didn't.

Instead she asked if she wanted a cup of tea which Beth thought sounded rather forced as if she was obliged to offer her one.

"Err, better not," Beth took the hint to leave. "I'm sure you don't get very long for your lunch break and you'll need to sort the dogs." Mary didn't reply she merely followed Beth as she made for the door to see her off.

Beth walked slowly back up the path to the gate deep in thought. She noticed when Mary bent down to show her the dog's skin she was wearing the locket Mungo gave her for her birthday when she last saw him. She wondered if perhaps the locket gave her comfort, hadn't she sensed a difference in Mary to the last time they met?

When she turned to lean over to secure the gate, she glanced up to the first floor dormer window, saw the net curtain move. She moved away towards the van. She heard the kitchen door open and Mary shoo the dogs out into the garden. She drove away.

CHAPTER 55

On Monday evening Bart arrived at the hotel to meet Jay at eight o'clock as arranged. He went straight to the dining room where he found Jay already seated at a quiet table near one of the dining room's windows. They greeted each other warmly, shaking hands like the old friends they were.

"How was your interview?" Bart asked immediately he sat down opposite him.

Jay shrugged his shoulders nonchalantly, "You can never tell, it's all rather serious with police interviews, they never give anything away. I'm hoping I did okay, there are precious few openings in our kind of work," he told Bart who appreciated how he included him as a fellow professional even though his stint as a Scene's of Crime Officer was many years ago. "Agatha has put in for a transfer to Police Scotland," Jay continued. "It would prove difficult if she got hers and I couldn't find a CSI post especially with her being pregnant." He appeared rather glum at the prospect.

Bart secretly relished the idea of them moving up there to live. "What *will* you do if she gets hers but you don't?" Put this way it sounded really brutal even though he wanted very much to have Jay back in his life.

"Of course, we've talked about all the possibilities," Jay admitted, "Including me having to get other work until another opening for a CSI comes up."

"Do the options include joining the police again?" He knew Jay resigned as a regular police officer because of his love for forensics when they civilianised crime scene work. His leaving the police was one of the factors in the breakup of Jay's previous marriage which he wouldn't want to happen again. His first wife favoured the idea of being married to a high flying career police officer and was against the move entirely. Bart never enquired if she moved on in search of some other police officer, he let sleeping dogs lie.

Jay shook his head, "Agatha understands where my true vocation lies." He smiled as he thought about her, "What she actually said was she wanted me to be happy so would go anywhere as long as she was with me."

Bart turned his head away inspecting the dining room full of people thinking how lucky Jay was to have found his soul mate. The tear in his eye might be misconstrued as him feeling self-pity, when in fact he was pleased to know such good people. He scanned the couples eating together. They were mostly elderly making him ponder on how many of them had experienced such a feeling. When his eyes stopped searching his head turned sharply back locking with Jays.

Jay could see he was upset, "What's wrong?"

For a moment he continued to stare at Jay as if transfixed before he found his voice, "Two tables down from the door," he managed to say.

Jay moved his body slightly to be able to look over Bart's shoulder at the man sitting eating alone. "Isn't that Martin Frances, you sent me his picture," Jay watched him as he ate his dinner.

"Yes, also known as Michael Johns, like he used at Fort William. And the name he told the mechanic at McKinley's Auto in Dinnet a few days ago, whilst pretending once again to be from Immigration asking about Beth, the illegal immigrant."

"So that's him.....he's back again."

"I expect he's here looking for Bonita who misled him about Fort William," Bart suggested. "Beth was at McKinley's Auto when he walked in on her!"

Jay's face became horrified, "What happened? Is she okay?"

Bart laughed, "Beth's back was turned towards him when he walked in and she recognised his voice. Nessa on seeing her shocked face had the presence of mind to direct her into the back office. Fortunately, the day before Beth changed her appearance....somewhat! I doubt whether you would recognise her now."

"Thank goodness," Jay exclaimed. "So why come back here?"

"Unfortunately, he smelt a rat when he realised he was duped by Bonita," Bart didn't look round again at Martin Frances, he leaned into Jay, "I'm trying to get her to go to a solicitor, take out a protection order to stop him pestering her or at least register her separation with someone legal in order to commence the two year separation needed to divorce him."

"How is he able to be away from his force all this time?"

Jay ever the practical one, Bart thought, was right of course.

"Hmm, interesting thought, we could check," then he cheekily added, "Or maybe Agatha could?"

Jay laughed at him," I'll be talking to her later..... I'll ask her if there is any way she can find out." Bart could tell by his reaction she would try to help if she could.

"If you don't get the CSI post, maybe you could join the Bartholomew and Hobbs Detective Agency when you come up here to live," he suggested.

"The what....?"

"It's Emily, the amateur sleuth's idea....we have been trying to find out what happened to the ghillie Mungo MacLeod I told you about, who disappeared before last Christmas..... it's a long story nonetheless intriguing."

"Hmm, maybe disappearing is catching eh?" Jay commented cryptically. "And brings me to why I need to talk to you." Bart could tell by his face the matter was very serious.

It was at this point their waiter appeared to take their orders.

*   *   *   *   *

After ordering their first two courses Jay began by telling Bart Agatha discovered his Witness Protection handler was a Sergeant Steve Paterson who according to his force's internal weekly orders was recorded as being suspended from duty pending enquiries into serious misconduct. After making enquiries she learnt he was suspected of tampering with witnesses in the Toni Maola prosecution case of which Bart was already aware.

He went on to inform Bart, Steve Paterson had also disappeared. His previous contact with Maola in prison having ceased, the Prison officials believe they may have found some other means to contact each other than face to face prison visits. Unfortunately, Jay conceded, mobile phone smuggling into prisons was more commonplace than previously thought.

Agatha discovered Steve Paterson returned to Wainthorpe-on-sea again before going to ground completely. He discovered the Silver Teapot café has changed hands. He was seen once again talking to locals there only this time making enquiries about the whereabouts of the Hobbs, especially asking after Emily.

"It wasn't exactly a secret thanks to Thelma Hobbs who believed Emily was spirited away against her mother's wishes!" Jay suddenly became angry, he remembered the woman's accusations against himself and particularly vicious when directed at Agatha, "She took great pains to tell anyone who would listen, seemingly declaring herself aggrieved at losing her only daughter who was meant to go with her to Grimsby to begin a new life with another little tea shop."

"So Steve Paterson will know Thelma Hobbs has moved to Grimsby?"

Jay nodded, "How easy would it be to find someone running a café in Grimsby?"

"I imagine that awful woman will still be aggrieved enough to blab again, should she be asked directly by Paterson," Bart suspected. "Do we know if Emily imparted any details to her about where she was going to live?"

"We deliberately withheld everything from her when we helped Emily to come up here," Jay assured him. "I don't know if Emily has told her mother anything since. I suspect very little which is why she is so annoyed," he said. "You need to ask Emily about any contact she has had with her mother."

Bart nodded taking the hint, he felt mightily sick with this latest news. He was worried once again he might be in danger from Maola. "Jay, perhaps you could be there when I speak to Emily before you leave us tomorrow?" He sounded a little pleading, "She did ask me to tell you she would like the chance to see you before you go back."

"Of course, Agatha and I are really concerned about you both," Bart saw a flicker of fear pass over his face.

"What is it?" Bart asked.

"I'm also a little concerned for Agatha, if Paterson does catch up with Thelma Hobbs. She is sure to remember her involvement in the Arthur Claymore's murder case isn't she?" He didn't voice his thoughts about Agatha being pregnant or the dangers to their unborn child if Paterson got rough with her.

"I take it there's a circulation out to find Steve Paterson?"

Jay nodded, "Yes, he's a bit of a loose cannon, isn't he?"

Bart thought about the man sitting not too far away from them, "He's not the only one!"

*   *   *   *   *

Next day Jayson Vingoe parked his camper outside The March of Time at about half past nine as the local bus came down Main Street, turned into the turning circle outside The Griddle Iron café at

397

the bottom of The Brae, letting off a few passengers. When he got out he saw Emily making her way up the hill having got off the bus. When she saw Jay she waved enthusiastically.

"Hey, there!" Jay greeted her returning the wave, "Just the person I've come to see, how are you Emily?"

She came level with him, they hugged shyly before they turned to the shop doorway as Bart opened up to meet them. He'd settled at his work table with the lap top earlier to wait for Jay's camper to pull up. He was too preoccupied to try to work on the pocket watch spread out in front of him.

"I'm surprised you came in the camper," he told Jay. "It must be a petrol guzzler I imagine."

"Yes, it is, also very handy if you break down in some out of the way place."

They trooped through to the back of the shop after Bart closed up again. He left the closed sign up to deter anyone, their conversation was more important than selling someone a watch strap.

Emily made tea whilst listening to Jay's small talk about his interview. Astute as usual she caught one or two pertinent glances between the two of them warning her something important was occurring.

She deflected with, "Has Bart told you about Martin Frances turning up, nearly discovering Beth right in front of him?" Jay could see she was quite shaken by such an incredible near miss.

"Yes, he did, and I did see him last night at the hotel having dinner only feet away from our table."

Her face turned to shock, "No!" she gasped. "He's here in the village?" It reinforced her sixth sense that morning by refusing a lift over from Beth. "Thank goodness Beth didn't come with me," she glanced at Bart, "She's phoned in sick this morning, doesn't think she should go into work whilst *he's* around. She was really scared by him yesterday!"

Bart agreed, pleased to hear she was taking the threat seriously. He changed the subject with, "We need to speak to you about your mother, Emily."

Jay asked, "Have you contacted her since you came here?"

Emily asked anxiously, "She's okay isn't she?"

"As far as we know," Bart assured her.

"The thing is, that man Steve has been back to The Silver Teapot. He's discovered your mother has sold up and moved on," Jay filled in. "We think he may go to Grimsby looking for her or rather you...."

"Why? What does he want with me?" she asked nervously.

"He believes you to be a link to find me," Bart confided.

"We don't want to alarm you, Emily, we have found out that Steve Paterson is suspected of tampering with witnesses in the criminal prosecution of a man called Toni Maola," Jay could see she was uneasy.

"Was he the one you were put in Witness Protection for?" she obviously worked some of it out for herself.

"Yes, he is," Bart was trying to decide how much he ought to tell her so as not to frighten her too much. "The police are investigating the possibility he is now working for Maola to get rid of as many witnesses as possible....."

"That man's in prison, right?" she asked.

"Maola is.....Paterson isn't...." Jay said.

"Why.... if he's doing bad things?"

She was quite right of course. Bart thought he would feel safer if he was.

"Asking questions isn't against the law. They don't have any actual evidence about the other things to be able to arrest him," Jay explained, "That sort of thing takes time to get."

"Does it mean my mother is in danger?" They could see Emily's concern for her mother was now heightened.

"No, we don't think so. If she knows where you are I'm...." Bart glanced over at Jay, "....*we* believe she wouldn't hesitate to tell him, she's still very angry about you leaving her."

Emily appeared pensive, "I know she is." Bart exchanged glances with Jay. Emily shook her head, "No I haven't contacted her....my father told me." The news didn't seem to cheer either of them much. "She contacted him about me asking my Dad if he knew where I was living."

"Do you know when that was?" Jay asked. Bart nodded at the importance of the timing.

"It was when I first came here," she sounded definite.

"Does your father know where you are?" Bart held his breath waiting for the inevitable confirmation.

She shook her head, "No, I only made the one telephone call, because I was worried about him. I doubt he would tell my mother we have spoken, I rather got the impression he was pleased I contacted him instead of her."

"Can I ask how you phoned him?" Jay tried not to force the issue even though he held fears about the call being traced, after all Paterson was a police officer with friends in all kinds of places. Bart, who knew the issues, also waited, hardly daring to breathe.

"The call was from the untraceable sim card I used when I tried to contact Bart for you. You told me the shop and our home were both likely being bugged," she reminded him. "My Dad doesn't have a mobile now, so I called the hostel where I knew he was living at the time – it took me some effort to get the person who answered to go find him," she laughed at the memory of the partially deaf man she spoke to. "Not the brightest person....after ages I did get my Dad on the line. I expect he has moved on now, he was going to try his luck somewhere else, and probably the last time we'll have contact." She watched their faces brightened a little. "Apart from which I got rid of the sim card." She grinned broadly at her own ingenuity, watched the tension ease out of them. "I did tell you Steve – you say Paterson is his name, scared me when I met him for the second time. I knew something about him wasn't right."

Jay smiled contentedly. Bart said, "Better make it Hobbs and Bartholomew Detective Agency!" He guffawed loudly.

After a silence she asked, "Now, what are we going to do about Martin Frances?"

CHAPTER 56

The young police woman with her male police partner walked to the end of the corridor as directed by the ward receptionist at the nursing station. They were at the end of a very long shift consisting of numerous episodes of public disorder; latterly an elderly woman shop lifter at Tesco who was being held awaiting their attendance by an irate shop manager. They spent time trying to persuade him not to put in a complaint as clearly the woman was desperate, suffering from Alzheimer's and probably mistook her shopping bag for the small basket she held in the other hand.

The item in question was a packet of tea, not the crown jewels, they told him. Her other purchases were at the bottom of her basket. By the time they could get to the hospital it was past the end of their shift. They considered leaving the call for the next shift to do. John Doe wasn't going anywhere if he couldn't remember who he was or why he was in the hospital.

They went anyway. When they found his bed empty they were back at the nurse's station asking where he was. Later he was recorded as a 'self-discharge'.

*   *   *   *   *

He found a staff locker room having gone down to the ground floor in the lift. The room was empty of people. There was a vast amount of outside clothing scattered around having been abandoned by late arrivals with barely sufficient time to put on their uniforms to rush off to make the handover for their shifts. He picked through the mess. By the time he left the hospital through a staff exit with his mismatched appearance, he resembled a vagrant with nowhere to go.

He walked away warily out into the countryside; his heavy pair of too-tight purloined Doc Martens were almost too heavy to lift one foot in front of the other in his current fatigued state. As he tramped along, seemingly for miles, his mind drifted aimlessly over the only bit of his life he could hold on to – a hospital bed and a pair of angelic green eyes that wanted to prompt another memory to the surface which wouldn't come.

The woods either side of the road were monotonously similar as he trudged along. It was cold with a great deal of snow covering the ground, the chill making his breath puff out in visible mist sprays. He heard an engine in the distance, pulled the hood of the parka further forward to hide his face, he was certain he didn't want to go back to the hospital. He angled his eyes towards his feet stepping closer to the verge with the shallow ditch. The car sped past sending up a spray of wetness from the road surface hitting him with an icy spray.

When he looked up again the vehicle was disappearing around a distant bend in the road leaving an eerie quiet which only the clomp of his boots disturbed. He stopped to listen. There was something comforting about the silence that made him smile. He heard a thump from the trees to his right making him picture a falling pine cone not knowing how he knew the sound. A twig snapped drawing his eyes to penetrate the trees. He saw the slight movement, a white patch appeared as the animal turned round to show its face instead of its white rump. They locked gazes momentarily before the deer leapt away enticing the man to step off the road to follow.

The deer herd moved deeper into the wood as he trailed them. John Doe felt a moment of familiarity creeping over him like a gentle hug. Even the deer seemed unafraid of the tall vagrant stalking them. Eventually they stopped to stare his way, continued to graze, they searched for whatever they could find to eat in the woods – leaves, twigs, grass with the odd tasty lichen or fungi.

When he got close they didn't bother to turn their white rumps in warning, just kept a wary eye on their visitor. John moved past them, his instinct pushing him forward until he found it. The remaining snow emphasised the shape even with the camouflage, instinctively he knew this was somewhere safe, a dry place to take refuge in.

*   *   *   *   *

With an early start on Wednesday, Bart and Emily began the task of identifying the clock keys. They both needed a diversion from the pending threat they felt after their goodbyes to Jay when he left for home. They did a quick survey of the inventory photographs Bart took of the clocks in their current positions deciding they would start with the one he knew, the Grandmother clock he previously repaired. Someone replaced the clock in its original position on the wall in the passageway between one of the Laird's day rooms and the library. They found the key still where Bart taped it under the pendulum for safety when he transported the clock in the boot of his car. No one thought to wind it up, probably because they didn't think to look for the key. Just like the others on the bunch someone had scratched a number on it.

It was a starting point. They began their task by searching for the clock keys beginning with the day room. They would leave the library alone for the moment. Each room they came to on their journey through the castle led numerically on from the previous room making their task less daunting than expected. It wasn't very long before the majority of the keys were accounted for, their numbers entered on the inventory against their position. Those remaining included the library clocks which they chose to leave when they found once again the door to be locked. They had no idea of the whereabouts of either Galbraith or the Laird, so left this task for another day. They went home, Emily was anxious to get back to Beth, not wanting to leave her alone for too long.

On the drive back to the cottage Bart took the opportunity to ask her how she liked living with Beth at the cottage. He was surprised when she failed to respond immediately. He chanced a glance her way noticing her troubled face.

She immediately felt self-conscious, "I like Beth enormously," she put in quickly in case he thought otherwise.

"What's wrong?" he was now familiar with her give-away expressions.

"You'll think me crazy if I even begin to explain."

"My impression of you is you are an extremely rational, sensible young lady who is way too perceptive for your tender years," he countered.

That blew her away, "Really?" She grinned in appreciation never before having heard anything positive from someone about what they thought of her as a person. She tried hard to forget the gibes from her bullying contemporises.

He nodded, "So if you have something to say I can only think there must be a reason for you thinking it."

"Okay," she made up her mind to come clean, "I think the cottage is haunted."

This declaration took him by surprise, not being what he expected, "I'm assuming there is a reason for saying that?"

She nodded knowing merely saying so was the easy part, explaining *why* was going to be more difficult. The silence between them lengthened whilst she assessed examples to best illustrate what she thought.

"Okay, what have you seen?" he asked breaking the silence, expecting something like the stories of the sightings at the castle of Seumus Grant's spirit.

"To be honest I haven't seen anyone or rather anything to suggest there is someone else other than Beth and me living there......but I think there is." She frowned at the lameness of her answer. "I am convinced we aren't the only occupants."

Bart caught her serious face, "You mean other than Sandy?" He expected her to at least smile at the comment.

She didn't. "Ah, now there's a thing," pleased he mentioned the Foxhound to prompt her. "He knows too. I catch him staring as if he's listening to someone standing right in front of him. He's fully attentive, his ears standing pricked, then they flop downwards and he runs off into the front room, jumps up on the couch, his tail wagging, he looks out of the window as if he's expecting someone."

"I've only ever seen him flat out in front of the fire. I assumed he did that most of the time."

Emily shook her head, "Not all the time."

"Okay, what else?"

"How can I explain? It's like time passes differently to anywhere else......there doesn't seem to be sufficient time to accomplish everything that happens there," she scowled at her own inability to explain clearly, she could tell Bart didn't understand what she meant, so she tried to think of an example.

"Don't you think it's strange how Beth can be working all day at the castle yet produce an amazing amount of baking, newly baked still warm from the oven, when she didn't have the time to do it?"

Bart tried to pull up a memory that once perplexed him only he couldn't quite remember what it was. Then one did occur to him, "I have to say I was surprised once how there was fresh tea and coffee ready even though she wasn't expecting us to arrive," he admitted. "I assumed you sent her a text to tell her we were on our way."

Emily shook her head, "No I didn't."

"Oh! Okay," surprised, he now doubted his own memory.

After another silence she went on, "Sometimes I do feel something is there," she tried to assess his reaction but couldn't tell what he was thinking. "At first I felt like the cottage didn't much care for me moving in....."

"Isn't that part of changing from living in a familiar place to moving to a strange one?" Bart felt the same, certainly in more recent times since he began to move so often. He thought that was more to do with his being in danger than the whole uprooting process.

"Possibly you do get a feel for places, I know. I didn't really feel comfortable at my Aunty Elsie and Uncle Mark's house. I think that could be more to do with the people though." She still felt sad at the loss of her cousin Peter who was her best friend. "I mean look at who they turned out to be. I would never have suspected Uncle Mark was a murderer!"

"You felt these same feelings at their house?" Bart asked alarmed.

She shook her head again, "No, I'm saying houses can make you feel happy or sad depending on who lives there. This is different," she said. "I'm sure Beth feels the same."

"Have you discussed this with her?"

"No, I haven't. I do think she 'knows'," she sounded mysterious and a little frustrated with her inability to explain it. "I hear her talking to someone when there's no one there."

"Maybe she's talking to Sandy."

"Not when she's upstairs in her bedroom, Sandy doesn't come upstairs," she said.

"Can you hear what she's saying? People do talk to themselves. I do all the time living on my own!" He laughed. "I always thought older people did and I was declining into my dotage!"

She wasn't about to tell him she once deliberately listened at Beth's bedroom door where she could hear her having a conversation, though she couldn't hear anyone else speaking. He would only say she must have been talking to someone on the telephone. She knew she wasn't. The gist of the conversation was about the cottage. Beth was asking what she should do about it, after a pause she heard her say, "Ah, yes of course!" as if someone replied.

Emily shrugged in resignation. She would have gone on to tell him about the small bedroom with the icy patch of air she felt one day when she went in to the room to look out of the window. She felt someone's presence in the room so hasn't been in there again. Now he *would* think her crazy if he knew that.

Instead she suggested, "Maybe it's the Cuckoo Clock I have in my wardrobe?"

It surprised Bart because he forgot all about the clock even though he knew Emily brought it with her. However, he was reminded about the strange things to happen to him when he lived in Wainthorpe which he kept mostly to himself in case, like Emily mentioned, people might think him crazy.

"Ah, yes the Cuckoo Clock," he felt a sudden sense of unease reminding him there were strange inexplicable things in the world. "I forgot about the clock." He suddenly recalled their previous conversation about the clock, with the bird with no beak, especially its habit of missing a half beat in time. "Wasn't there something you were going to tell me we could do to make the clock right?"

She nodded, "Yes, we got interrupted," she said. "I thought perhaps we should give him a new beak!"

Bart burst out laughing. When he stopped he gave it some serious though, "Do you think that would correct the tick?"

"It might because perhaps he's upset or off balance, could be a subtle weight issue?"

Her face was so expectant he couldn't bring himself to dispute it, "We could try, no harm in trying," he conceded. "I'll give some thought to how we might do that."

"Okay," she said as he turned the Peugeot into the yard at the cottage, Emily was surprised to be home already.

When they walked into the kitchen Beth began to pour the tea and coffee into their cups already set on the table. Emily exchanged looks with Bart, both knowing they hadn't telephoned her to tell her they were on their way back.

CHAPTER 57

Lily Frances (née Johns, also known as Beth Grant) sat in the echoing panelled hallway of the Advocate's offices amongst much coming and going of clients, their footfalls rebounding off the high walls. She took in the far from plush ex-municipal building, now leased to a range of advocates after local politics went up market to new premises. The bustling building didn't make her feel hopeful for her future she was just one of the many desperate people seeking help. The outside door opened revealing Nessa McKinley, her new friend, who recommended this particular lawyer she was here to see today.

"Did you find a space?" Beth asked Nessa as she sat down beside her to wait with her.

"Aye, eventually," Nessa was pleased Beth (or Lily) was still waiting. She half expected her to chicken out before she could join her. "She'll be running late, she tries to see as many women as she can." Beth shivered. A reflex action at the prospect of having to relive the things she was trying so hard to forget.

Beth's new hairstyle, the almost white blonde colour enhanced her frail form, making her resemble the little girl her husband wanted her to be. The colouring merged with the wanness of her face emphasising her emotional distress. Nessa picked up on her despair. She knew how it felt having seen far too many abused women over time not to recognise the signs. Nessa McKinley knew all the women's advocate services, her involvement in a local women's refuge went back many years.

The plaintive voice of her latest victim of domestic violence eased its way through the clatter of shoes on wooden stairs and far off raised voices, "You shouldn't have to miss a day's pay for me," Beth's words were tiny against the background noises.

Nessa saw the concern in the large sad eyes set in the most appealing face she'd seen in a long time. She felt the pull of attraction which she pushed away, "It's na bother. It's about time my old man got his hands dirty for a change." She laughed at the image of Jock McKinley's language as he swore at the car's engine she left for him to service.

"Your mother needs him though......" Beth began to protest remembering what she heard from Robbie Cowan about her illness resulting in the need for so much help.

"Och, no!" she interrupted. "You've done me a favour, or rather my Ma! She has lots of friends my Dad resents. I've arranged a day's treat for them with him out of the way." Nessa grinned broadly, "She'll be having the time of her life."

"I sometimes think it's the men who are the neediest," Beth sighed.

"You can say that again!"

A young smartly dressed girl appeared in front of them. She didn't look old enough to be working there, "Ms Lily Frances?" she enquired.

Beth sat up straight at hearing her married name. She scowled, "At the moment, yes, soon to be Lily Johns again." She sounded defiant. Nessa nodded to the young girl smiling approval.

"Well, Ms Johns, if you could follow me, we're ready for you now," the young girl turned walking slowly away.

Beth passed a doubtful glance at Nessa, "Will you come in with me?"

Nessa stood, "Of course, let's do it!"

So began the first day of Beth's new life in which she allowed a sneaky hope to enter which would enable her to discover who 'Lily Johns' really was.

*   *   *   *   *

As Beth Grant climbed the wooden stairs with Nessa McKinley at the Advocates office, Robbie Cowan parked the Defender outside the hotel, walked in to the reception to ask for Michael Johns, the Immigration Officer who was staying there. He was directed to the dining room where the late arrival for breakfast, the man he sought, was only one of a handful of fellow guests still eating. Those doing so watched fascinated, as the young police officer approached the man sitting alone, unable to hear the conversation taking place.

Robbie Cowan asked, "Michael Johns?"

The man sat up, a slight flash of fear crossed his face before a practiced smile took its place.

"What can I do for you, officer?" He could barely keep the inflection of mockery out of his voice, he imagined this young copper was well out of his depth.

"I am right in thinking you are the Michael Johns I just confirmed is booked into Room 66?" Robbie continued.

"And you are?" was the challenging reply.

"Police Constable Cowan, Police Scotland," Robbie informed him, his collar number was prominently displayed on the epaulettes on his shoulders. Robbie could see the few diners eying them so he added, "Perhaps we could go somewhere more private, sir?"

'Michael Johns' was holding a last piece of toast which he threw onto his plate before he stood up; his face now held a contemptible sneer.

Robbie led the way to the foyer where there were two areas with easy chairs. He chose the side nearest the blazing fire leading him to it. He indicated for him to sit down.

"I will ask you once again – are you the Michael Johns booked into room 66?" What came back was a nod of his head, the smile failed to materialise this time. "It has been reported you are identifying yourself as an Immigration Officer, not only here, also in other places. Could I see your official identification please, sir?"

The shrug of his shoulders was followed by him putting a hand inside his pocket and withdrawing a card the size of a driving licence which he handed to Robbie who inspected it closely. As forgeries went, Robbie thought, this was certainly a good one; if he didn't know differently he would have believed it was real.

Robbie opened up one of the pouches on his utility belt, took out a piece of paper which was a photocopy of Martin Frances' driving licence which contained the same photograph as the one displayed on the I.D card.

Martin Frances didn't bat an eye, "An uncanny likeness," he said meeting his bluff.

"Spot on I would say Mr. Frances," Robbie stood his ground. "Or should I call you Sergeant?"

Martin Frances frowned this time, "What exactly do you want?"

Robbie sat down in the chair opposite him. "I have a proposition for you," he announced unexpectedly. His confidence caught Martin Frances off guard a little.

"Oh?" he asked. "What is it?"

"I think it's a question of how much you care about your role in the Welsh police," the reference to his home force left him in no doubt this police officer knew a great deal about him. "For example, if I was to arrest you for using a false name to impersonate an Immigration Officer, in addition to travelling across Scotland presenting yourself as such, seeking the whereabouts of illegal immigrants, I am sure when you were charged it would have an adverse effect on your police career, would you agree?"

Martin Frances' slow smile led to him reluctantly nodding in agreement. Robbie Cowan gave him back the false immigration I.D. "It would be advisable for you to return to Wales to get on with your life," he left a pause whilst he took it in. "Of course, if you, or anyone else on your behalf, were to return here falsely accusing anyone of being an illegal immigrant *or* a thief, you will not be given this opportunity a second time. Are we clear on that?"

Martin Frances' face turned thunderous, reluctantly he nodded his agreement.

Robbie stood up, "I have arranged with the hotel Manager for your bill to be ready for you to check out immediately," he walked off back to the reception desk where Philip Miller was finalising the bill for the man in room 66.

Robbie Cowan sat outside in the Defender waiting for Martin Frances to check out. Twenty minutes later he followed him all the way to the Ski resort at the summit of Glenshee where he watched as his car disappeared down the steep road from the top. When he was gone he turned in the large empty car park and made his way back down to the village. He couldn't resist stopping off at The March of Time to tell Sirus, and of course, to see Emily again to arrange for her next driving lesson.

CHAPTER 58

The face of the hotel manager with the oh so professional 'yes, Sir', 'no, Sir' infuriated him as he settled his bill. He knew under his false smile and practised etiquette he was relishing every minute of seeing him leave. He half expected him to say something they all usually did, 'I hope we'll see you back again soon'. Not this one. He could tell he was pleased to see the back of him. He knew he was there looking for his wife because he was sure the manager knew where she lived. It took him a lot of self-control to walk away hearing him say, "Drive carefully," the two-faced smug bastard!

The cop was outside sitting in his car watching him leave. He made a point of following him all the way to Glenshee. Martin Frances drove slowly away from the ski resort. He could see the cop's Defender stop at the car park behind him in his rear-view mirror. He could feel his blood boiling, his anger spilling over, nearly to an uncontrollable level. He knew once he lost control he wouldn't be able to stop himself from pulverising the smugness he saw behind his eyes. No wet behind the ears novice cop was going to tell him what he could or couldn't do. There was no way he was going home without her, he was sure of that.

Out of sight now he stopped his car to fetch a map book from the boot to find a route, to double back without using the same road. The plan formulating in his head was made difficult by the lack of major roads up there. He cut across country, aimed for Aberdeen knowing you could get lost in a large city. If he needed to he would change his car to make sure his registration wouldn't get caught on any cameras. It was about time he upgraded anyway, he couldn't have her spotting his car or reporting him to the police.

His anger was fuelled by the fact she seemed already to have made friends up here; certainly she'd found people who were prepared to help her which wouldn't do at all.

*   *   *   *   *

He booked into a small hotel in the centre of Aberdeen, one of the many cheap chain ones which were adequate, clean and somewhere to sleep until he decided what to do next. He needed a drink badly having driven out of his way to get there, but more specifically to calm his anger. He chose a more traditional pub because he hated gimmicky places which he found irksome. They were usually full of posers which would make his anger worse. Only a pint with some food would soothe him, he wasn't at all fussed about the deadbeat customers he saw around the place, he wasn't in the mood for company anyway.

The one he chose allowed him to sit quietly until the people sitting close by began to irritate him by their loudness. The Scottish girl amongst them was particularly irritating. By the looks of her she'd been out drinking early doors and was well lashed. He sunk further into himself listening to her moaning on about her girlfriend who dumped her for someone new. This was all he needed to hear, he certainly had no sympathy with a hard done-by lesbian. By the looks of the company with her they were also sick of hearing her moan probably because this wasn't the first time.

"Give it a rest, Shona!" one of the men yelled, "We know you and Nessa are done."

"Aye, 'n' for what? Some common English bitch with peroxide hair who looks like a laddie wearing dungarees – I'd have thought Nessa McKinley 'ad better taste, the bitch!"

Martin Frances's ears pricked up, as he remembered calling at McKinley's garage where he saw the 'mechanic' with someone who fit the same description.

It didn't take long for the men sitting with the girl Shona to leave. He saw her sink further into her self-pity as he watched her empty her purse onto the table to count the loose change to see if she could afford another drink.

He shuffled along the seat to get a bit closer until he could ask, "Can I get you another?"

Shona looked up sharply, he could see she was tempted despite toying with the obvious problem – he was a man, she was a woman, he would expect something in return.

She shook her head, "Ya not ma type!" she snapped rudely.

"And you're not mine!" he threw back at her. "I thought you could use another drink." He made himself sound suitably insulted. He could see her giving in.

"Sorry, didn'a mean to be rude," she slurred, "I'm angry wi' losing the love of m'life!"

It was worth paying for a drink or two whilst he listened to her recount the sorry tale of Nessa's new girlfriend from the castle who suddenly changed from a drab brunette overnight into a sexy attractive lesbian with short spikey blonde hair. He was left intrigued by the girl who didn't turn round or whose face he didn't see when he spoke to them because she was supposed to be deaf. Of course, when he suggested this to Shona she laughed hysterically at the idea.

One thing was certain, Martin Frances knew he'd found his wife Lily even before he presented Shona with her picture to look at. Blurry eyed she glared at her girlfriend's new love, spat at the picture before she passed out completely her head hitting the table hard.

It's a small world, Martin thought as he got up leaving her there.

CHAPTER 59

Two days later, leaving Emily to cover the shop, Bart set off for the castle. He got as far as the end of Main Street, the junction with the A93, whilst waiting to pull out he glanced over at the hotel. Briefly he thought he must find the time to have lunch with his friend Philip Miller to catch up with him on the Martin Frances business. The thought slipped away when he caught sight of the flashing police lights, an array of liveried police vehicles outside the front of the hotel as well as at the back where the spill-over car park gave patrons somewhere to park their cars.

The other side of the hotel, a road he knew led to Philip Miller's bungalow, was also jammed solid with unmarked cars and a waiting ambulance.

Bart's guilt hit him forcibly as he tried to remember how Phil seemed the last time they met. He knew the man possessed demons but a flash of fear he may have succumbed to them, stirred his other old friend, his stomach ulcer, to life. He found himself unable to drive past without first checking on him. He did a U-turn to park near the Co-op on Main Street before he walked back to the hotel.

There was a small crowd of local people standing in front of the yellow police barrier tape, they were speculating about what was happening at the hotel. Bart heard someone denouncing the young police officer with a clip board for not being forthcoming when asked about it.

Bart saw Robbie Cowan come out of the main door to the hotel, glance at the people assembled; recognising Bart he walked over. First he addressed those gathered, "Best to go about your business, there's nothing to see here." He lifted the tape nodding to Bart he beckoned him to duck under it. Bart took the cue following him inside the front door of the hotel.

Robbie could see Bart was anxious, "Tell me it's not Philip Miller?"

"I believe you were friends," Robbie replied leading him to the chairs nearest to another blazing fire.

Bart felt the life drain out of his legs at the reference to the 'were' past tense. "Oh Lord!" he exclaimed sitting down heavily on the nearest chair. "He seemed okay the last time we met. He's been sober a long time even though he did have some bad days..... he seemed to cope remarkably well," Bart realised he was jabbering and Robbie wouldn't necessarily know this private stuff about Philip Miller, he was merely speaking his thoughts out loud.

Robbie held up his hand to halt him, "It's not suicide," he said. Bart could see how pale he appeared.

Bart looked puzzled, "What....?"

Robbie glanced away, swallowed hard as if he was trying to keep control of himself. "One of the young Spanish waiters went to see where he was this morning when he didn't show up for work.... he wanted to switch his shift so needed Mr Miller's permission," now Robbie was rambling. "He found him at his bungalow, the front door was ajar. Getting no answer he walked in....." He stopped took out his handkerchief to dab his face.

"What are you saying?" Bart managed.

"When I found him.....they called us.....I was first here," he explained. Bart could see him struggling. He got up, went round to the reception desk where the receptionist, an older woman, was sitting in front of a computer terminal seemingly staring at the screen as though transfixed by the glow.

"Excuse me," Despite Bart speaking softly he still made her jump. "Could I have a glass of water for PC Cowan, I fear he needs it?"

She merely nodded, got up as if she was only too pleased to have something to do. Bart walked back to Robbie Cowan to sit silently with him to wait for the rest of his narrative. After a few gulps of water when it came, he continued, "Someone....someone beat him so badly....." Robbie's voice broke as he went on, "He was barely recognisable." Bart's gasp was stifled by his placing his fist against his mouth. "The anger of the person who delivered this.....must have been ferocious to do that amount of damage," he was now relatively calmer than before.

"Who would do such a dreadful thing?" Bart tried to think of anything Philip Miller told him about having enemies. "He used to be married once. He has.....had....children that he no longer saw."

Robbie's face appeared grim as he shook his head, "There is only one person I can think of who might do this to him.... And I believe I am to blame."

"If it's Martin Frances you're thinking about, then I hardly think it's your fault," Bart said sternly. "Phil played a part by asking Bonita to lie for him about working with Lily Johns at Fort William. I think we may have underestimated how dangerous he is."

"Beth did tell us he threatened to kill her if she ever left him," Robbie reminded him. "What kind of sick person puts someone through ....it was horrific!"

"Perhaps it's time to come clean with your colleagues," Bart suggested. "I have many fears about further reprisals after Beth's recent visit to a solicitor who I'm sure will have served Martin Frances with Beth's Protection order and also notified him of her intention to divorce him by now." Bart's face appeared grim. "I certainly don't believe we've heard the last of him."

Robbie Cowan was devastated, "I did rather give him my assurance he would hear nothing from us if he left and never came back."

"It doesn't look like he kept *his* word does it?"

"I suspect he will have a rock solid alibi for the time Philip Miller was being beaten to death, he is after all a police officer. I even doubt he would do it himself." Robbie Cowan was beyond being comforted.

"No, I don't agree. I think he would relish doing it himself. He was obviously after information about Beth's whereabouts," Bart surmised. "The man does seem rather obsessed where she is concerned, he certainly does see her as his property."

Robbie knew he would be in deep trouble once the enquiry team discovered what he did letting him go rather than reporting him. He felt he had no choice at the time. He merely wanted to warn him off; now he would have to own up to it.

"Will you come with me to the station to explain what's happened so far?" he asked Bart. "I think Beth needs all the protection we can give her. No one is going to disbelieve her after what's happened to Philip Miller."

Bart nodded his agreement and the two of them left for the station to give what evidence they could.

*   *   *   *   *

At about midday Emily closed the shop to walk to the Co-op on Main Street having found Bart with few groceries in the kitchen, there was nothing whatever she could find to eat. She toyed with the idea of taking up Alistair's invitation to go to the Moor Hen for lunch; her inbuilt self-consciousness won in favour of getting a snack at the Co-op. When she saw Bart's car parked outside she assumed he was back from the Castle having stopped off to buy the badly needed groceries missing from his cupboards. She knew he wouldn't buy Pepsi, so she went inside to buy herself some.

The small shop was busier than usual with a number of people standing around in front of the counters in conversation. After a search of the aisles she couldn't find Bart anywhere, so she picked up a sandwich, crisps and a drink joining the queues of people she thought were waiting. She couldn't detect anyone being served. A young girl behind one of the tills beckoned her forward. Feeling self-conscious in case people thought she was jumping the queue she moved hesitantly forward to allow the girl to check out her purchases.

Emily indicated the others waiting, "It's okay they've been served," the girl said. She could see Emily was still uncertain. "They've heard about the murder at the hotel," she confided, saw Emily looking blank she added, "Haven't you heard? Someone murdered the manager."

"The shock on Emily's face spoke for itself, "Philip Miller is dead!?"

The cashier nodded, "Yes," then lowering her voice to a whisper, "He was badly beaten, it's awful apparently."

Emily took the change offered her, picked up her bag of purchases rushing outside. She stood at the side of Bart's car, took out her mobile she rang him getting the answer service immediately. She waited to leave a message, "Where are you? I've just found your car outside the Co-op. You must be here somewhere – are you okay?" The message was rushed sounding frantic, she didn't know what else to do.

She pulled up his details again to send a swift text: "Are you OK? I've just heard. Where are you?"

She walked quickly back to the clock shop, sat in front of the laptop waiting, got even more worried by the lack of response because she knew he always kept his mobile on, hadn't he even chastised her recently when she allowed her battery to run down?

She telephoned Robbie Cowan who she knew always kept his personal mobile with him even when he was on duty. This too was unresponsive. She now began to fret. Even though she thought she shouldn't, she called Robbie's work mobile which he gave her to keep for emergencies only. *Wasn't this an emergency?*

It rang several times before being answered. She knew immediately it wasn't him when a female voice answered, "P.C Cowan's phone, can I take a message?"

Emily began to panic. She was torn between hanging up immediately at this stranger's voice, a woman answering his phone made her feel like she might be intruding on something private but the need to speak to him about Bart made her swallow any personal doubts she may be having, "Hello, I was trying to get hold of P.C Cowan," she mumbled.

The female voice was charming, "He can't come to the phone right now," she sounded like a pre-recorded message.

Emily's mouth suddenly went dry, her voice cracked, "Look, I really need to speak to him. I'm very worried about my boss, Sirus Jeffries. I think he might be missing."

"Who's calling?" the woman persisted in the same robotic tone.

"I'm Emily Hobbs," she felt like she might cry at any moment.

"Ah, yes, Emily," the woman sounded like she was familiar with her name. "I can tell you both P.C Cowan and Mr. Jeffries are here giving statements to the enquiry team."

Emily gasped with relief but still felt like crying, "Thank goodness!"

"I will get them to telephone you as soon as they're free," she promised. "So don't worry."

When she cut the call Emily felt not much better at the thought of Philip Miller, the man she only met a couple of times, being dead. Before she tried to continue her research or even attempt to eat anything she telephoned Beth who she knew had resumed her job at the castle, since Martin Frances went back to Wales, meant she felt much safer. She restricted the days to when she knew Bart would also be there or as she now knew was supposed to be there.

Beth answered, she seemed a little surprised at the call, she could hear immediately something wasn't right by the tone of Emily's enquiry asking after her.

"You don't sound right, Emily, what's wrong?" Beth was sitting in the café having her lunch. Emily could hear a lot of people noises and the chinking of crockery.

"Something bad has happened," she began.

"Is it Sirus, he was meant to join me for lunch, he hasn't turned up?"

"I think you should go home," Emily continued not wanting to spook Beth unnecessarily if she was in a public place or with her work colleagues.

"Hold on, I'll go somewhere quieter. I'll phone you back," Beth cut the call leaving Emily to decide, without really knowing what actually happened, what she ought to tell her.

Her phone rang, this time she could see the number was a withheld one. She was in two minds whether to answer, after all she had very few contacts in her list, this wasn't one of them. Her phone kept ringing until she answered it.

Robbie came straight in with, "Thank goodness I was worried there for a minute!"

"Sorry, you came up as a 'withheld' number, I don't usually answer those. What's going on? I saw Sirus' car outside the Co-op...people are talking about….."

"I know, don't worry he's here with me, I'm bringing him back now, so we'll be with you shortly to explain. Close the shop and keep the door locked, okay?"

"Yes," she agreed knowing she sounded feeble.

When he cut the call her phone rang again immediately. This time it was Beth.

"Where are you?" Emily asked.

"I'm sitting in the van, what's going on, Emily?"

She explained finding Bart's car then being unable to find him. "I heard from Robbie they are at the police station having given statements, they are now on their way back here."

Beth was silent for a moment, "I don't understand….."

"Something really bad has happened," Emily tried to keep her voice normal, "Someone has been killed at the hotel. I think it might be Philip Miller, the Manager."

She heard the shock settle over Beth, "I still don't understand."

"Neither do I, but I think you should go home and stay there."

Another pause from Beth was followed by, "I don't see why," she said, "You say they are leaving the police station coming to you?"

Emily knew instantly what Beth wanted to do.

"Don't come here!" she warned not really knowing why she felt so alarmed. "I think you will be safer at the cottage."

The problem for Emily was a feeling she couldn't substantiate with any evidence; just a deep seated unease this latest development affected them all, especially Beth.

She heard the small voice of Beth, "I don't really want to be on my own in the middle of nowhere," she confided. This was the first time since she arrived in Scotland she felt unsafe. The voice of Martin from somewhere behind her at McKinley's played in her head, "*Hello, ladies!*" She shivered uncontrollably. "I'll see if Nessa is around, I'll get back to you." She was off the line before Emily could say anything else.

CHAPTER 60

John suddenly kicked his feet out; the movement woke him from a deeply troubled sleep. He was having a chilling nightmare where the screaming barks of a deer with a twisted head rang loudly in his head. He sat bolt upright crying out, "Noooo!" gasping for what air there was in the confines of the small space. When he looked around him he found he was sitting on the floor in a wooden hut with only a door and the pile of blankets he fell onto exhausted after his long walk. That much he could remember.

He didn't know why this place seemed familiar in the semi-light. He got up to stand on wobbling legs, saw the closed hatch in front of him knowing when he moved the pegs holding it closed he could raise the long wooden panel to reveal the early dawn light with the sun rising between the trees. He sucked in the fresh air like this might be the last breath he took.

An image of birds flashed across his mind, he thought they were 'pheasants' reminding him of something that wouldn't come to him. A baleful bark from a nearby deer giving warning was followed by several other alarmed barks in reply. He dropped the flap to close out the cold and the cries of waking animals.

When he turned away he saw his feet had push the dirty rush matting into a heap on the floor and was now covered in the mud and dead leaves from his boots. He picked it up to carry to the door where he shook the debris off. When he took it back he found the trap door with the iron ring sunk into a hollow. He pulled it lifting the hatch, not at all surprised to find the steps leading down. This was like finding the door to his memory.

*   *   *   *   *

Jay sat with Agatha on the couch, having eaten their evening meal they were now watching the news. The picture switched to an outside broadcast covering the horrific murder at a Scottish Hotel in the Highlands. They both recognised the familiar facade with the twin towers of the hotel they stayed in thanks to Cyrus's generous gift. They both instantly sat forward as the news journalist reporting live from in front of the hotel gave brief details about a nameless man who was found fatally beaten in his home at the rear of the hotel. His name would not be released until his next of kin were informed. Agatha and Jay stared at each other, both frozen in shock.

Agatha spoke first, "It has to be Philip Miller, the manager, isn't the bungalow where he lives?"

Jay nodded his head. The first thought he didn't want to voice was of Steve Paterson whom he knew was searching for Bart Bridges also known as Cyrus Bartholomew. He stood up, crossed to the dresser where his mobile was on charge; he detached it before he went to the kitchen to fill the kettle with water ready to make an evening drink. He pulled up Bart's number, called him hoping he was still awake at this time of the night.

A rather subdued voice answered, "Hello Jay, have you just caught the news?"

"Lord, what on earth is going on?" Jay asked. "This is shocking."

"Yes, shocking indeed."

"Do they have any idea what it's about?" Jay asked not daring to voice his own thoughts.

"Robbie and I are convinced it's Martin Frances taking revenge on Phil for getting Bonita to send him over to Fort William," Bart filled in. "He would be sure after the diversion Beth is somewhere in this area. You saw for yourself he was back again pretending to be from Immigration because he booked back into the hotel, started

426

asking questions again." He went on to tell Jay how Robbie Cowan warned Frances off, even escorted him out of the area.

"Are you sure it's him?" Jay sounded doubtful.

"Not a hundred percent, but very likely," Bart suddenly realised what Jay was thinking. "You think it might be Steve?"

"It did cross my mind. He is missing," Jay clammed up.

"What?"

"You do have the misfortune everywhere you go something bad seems to happen!" Jay tried to laugh only he sounded strangely cynical.

"It did occur to me although the last place was hardly my fault, was it?"

Jay did laugh this time, "No I can see how an outsider might view you as a disruptive influence!"

"Thank you for that!" Bart managed a faint chortle. "Agatha will be wondering if this perhaps isn't the place to bring new life into," he volunteered.

"I think you could say the same applies to everywhere." After a pause he asked, "Are the police taking Beth's story seriously? I hope she's getting some protection now."

"Yes, they've been out to the cottage to put in security alarms since Phil was found," he said. "Beth is staying overnight with Nessa McKinley who is helping her through the legal stuff."

"What about Emily?" Jay didn't want to elaborate on how vulnerable he thought she was or touch on any of the Steve Paterson issues. He knew if Steve Paterson has killed Philip Miller looking for information about Bart, then Emily could also be in danger from him. Both men didn't want to name Paterson, least of all Bart whose fears of being discovered had accelerated with the murder of his friend. He didn't want to think he was in any way responsible for it.

"Emily is well covered by the new safety installations which include a panic button. She also has Robbie Cowan fighting her corner," Bart confided. "I do believe they are what you might call 'an item'? Robbie is loathed to have them put a marked police presence out at the cottage because that would be like putting up a sign saying 'we are here' don't you think?"

"I think having a serving police officer trying to hunt you down puts you at a disadvantage straight away," Jay didn't elaborate on which serving police officer he was referring to which didn't escape Bart's notice.

"I expect the murder team will be in touch with Martin Frances' force in Wales, if only to try to eliminate him from their enquiries," Bart suggested.

"Well, I'll see what we can find out here in the next couple of days," Jay didn't sound too hopeful. "To keep you updated, Agatha's transfer has been confirmed, she's waiting for a start date from Police Scotland."

"Well some good news at least," Bart felt the delight of knowing they would definitely be moving up to Scotland, his elation only clouded by Jay's potential jobless state. He ventured, "And what about you?"

"I have been called for a second interview. I am coming up in a couple of days, so there is something more positive on the horizon. I shall also start the process of looking around estate agents for somewhere for us to live."

"You may not be aware of the hotel being closed after...."

"Yes, I imagine so. I will be coming up in the camper and I'll find a camp site somewhere I'm sure," Jay's vagueness was tempered with some sadness at the prospect. "I'm feeling a little concerned at having to leave Agatha here alone."

"Ah, I see, does she have to serve notice?"

"Yes, some.......she does have time owed with holidays accrued, so it isn't as much as you would think." He didn't mention they were negotiating the possibility of her taking unpaid leave for her remaining notice.

Bart's thoughts homed in on a possible solution to Jay's camp site issue which he needed to explore first, so he raised it, "Perhaps you could call here before you book into a camp site, I may have the ideal solution which I need to check out first."

Jay agreed leaving Bart with much to think about. Jay's reference to 'serving police officers' took his mind to the conundrum of how someone might find a person they sought. After all Bart Bridges, P.I spent much of his time looking for people who disappeared and way before the internet era which laid wide open the issue of finding people.

*   *   *   *   *

Whether because she found herself alone in the cottage, which seemed strangely quiet without Beth, or she suddenly suffered a pang of homesickness, Emily felt the need to make contact with her mother. She knew it could be dangerous for Bart if she let her mother have her telephone number, reluctantly she felt she ought to warn her about the man 'Steve' who visited The Silver Teapot café. She was relieved that at least her Mom was away from there, now living in Grimsby. She had no idea whether she was still angry about her not going with her. When Thelma Hobbs answered her call to her daughter, Emily felt the chilly reception down the line.

"Emily?" Thelma was surprised at the call. "Not going well, eh?" Her assumption Emily would *live to regret it* as she threw at her on their last day together did nothing to warm Emily to her. In fact, the comment reinforced what an uncaring person she really was whilst emphasising once again Thelma Hobbs' world was all about herself.

"Not at all, really good," she couldn't help throw back at her.

"So why are you telephoning if it's so great, what do you want?"

Emily was tempted to hang up immediately, any homesickness she might have felt dissolved with her mother's spiteful tone.

"I'm phoning to warn you about the police officer Steve if you remember him who visited us a couple of times at the Silver Teapot….." Emily began not knowing how much she should divulge about him.

"Yes, of course I do……at least he cares about what's happened to me…."

"What are you talking about?" Emily got really angry. "You were lucky to avoid any comeback over Aunty Elsie and Uncle Mark's crimes!"

"Not about that!" she yelled down the phone. "I'm talking about the female copper who took you away!"

Emily's shock sent a chill down her spine, "You've seen him since I left Wainthorpe?"

"Yes, he came here looking for you again," she said angrily. "Of course, like any normal person he expected a child to be with her mother!"

Emily felt sick, "Oh my God, what have you done now?" she wanted to add *you stupid woman* but couldn't bring herself to say this to her own mother.

"I'll tell you what I've done – I've made a complaint to him about them…. that's what…."

"Stop!" Emily shouted down the phone. "Listen to me! He's a suspended police officer who is currently being investigated for seriously tampering with witnesses in a murder trial. He may even have killed someone himself!" Emily tried to breathe through her panic. "What exactly did you tell him?"

Thelma Hobbs went quiet; furious as she was at her daughter speaking to her like that she couldn't in all honesty remember exactly what she did tell him because at the time her temper made her ramble on pitiably about Emily's departure in their camper van.

Emily cut the silence with, "Did you tell him their names?" her question was strained as she waited for the reply.

"Of course I did, how else can a complaint be registered against them? I'm not stupid!" Thelma Hobbs yelled at her daughter.

"Mother, that is exactly what you are! I can tell you, you have put them in real danger!" Emily couldn't remember this person she called 'mother' whom she could now hear fuming at the other end of the line. "I'm sorry to tell you I'll not be having any more contact with you after this!"

"That's typical of you, you ungrateful brat!" Thelma raged. "You haven't even contacted your Aunty Elsie since you left....."

"You expect me to keep in touch with them after they murdered someone – well more than one person?!"

"That was Mark not my sister!" Thelma clearly convinced herself of a different version of the truth.

"She killed the man at the Gallery *with* Uncle Mark, forensics don't lie! Now you may be responsible for some deaths yourself," angrily Emily cut the call. She switched her mobile off.

Her venting anger at her mother quickly turned to fear for Jay and Agatha. Her anger eventually turned to tears. Her raking sobs were a blessed release making her incapable of rational thought. She was interrupted in her anxiety by a flash of headlights which partly lit up the kitchen. Only a vehicle pulling into the yard could do that. In her confusion she grew frightened Martin Frances discovered where Beth now lived. She was thankful Beth went to stay with Nessa.

She walked over towards the fire where she expected Sandy the Foxhound to be stretched out in front of the range. When she glanced back she saw he was standing close by alert, watching her. She noticed the fire was burning low, so she placed two more logs in the embers then prodded them with the poker from the set at the side of the log basket.

She heard Sandy's low growl in his throat, saw he was now looking towards the door as a shadowy figure moved around outside. There was a loud knock on the door. Emily's heart raced in her chest whilst Sandy's growls turned to low barks, something she hadn't heard from him before and which chilled her even more. She moved towards the door with Sandy matching each of her steps beside her.

"Who's there?" she shouted knowing she couldn't pretend there was no one home because of the lights being on, they would also see the smoke from the chimney.

"It's me, Robbie," Robbie Cowan shouted back.

She rushed to open the door. When she did she could see he was shocked at the sight of her red swollen eyes, "What on earth….are you okay?" he asked walking inside gently taking the poker she still held in her hand away from her. "I tried to call you, why have you switched your mobile off?"

Once he was inside, she shut the door quickly, pushing the bolts into place behind him. There was no mistaking Emily had been crying which made him put his arms around her, feeling her tremble in his arms. He led her to a chair at the table.

"What's happened?"

Whilst he made them tea she told him about the conversation with her mother and her fears from the consequences of her meeting Steve Paterson. She finished by saying, "I think my mobile phone may be a way someone with his kind of access could use to find where I am so I switched off," she told him.

"Okay, let's think about this logically," Robbie began, "Unless he goes back again to speak to her she can't give him your number," he saw Emily shaking her head.

"Unless he left a contact number, she may contact him to do just that."

Robbie tutted at her, "I can't imagine her doing such a thing, can you?"

She stared at him, the misery etched indelibly on her face. "I think she might do yes, even after I told her he was being investigated for some really bad things," a sob escaped from her. "If she can convince herself my Aunty Elsie is innocent, she is capable of thinking anything. She believes herself to be deeply wronged by Agatha and Jay taking me away from her," she stared in shock at him. "Oh God, he'll go after them won't he?" she jumped up, grabbed her phone, put it back on to look up their telephone number.

Robbie could see what she intended, "Here," he said taking it out of her hand he punched in their number to his own phone before he switched hers back off.

When the call was answered by Jay, Robbie said, "I have Emily here for you," he handed his mobile to her to explain what happened whilst he sat listening to her tell Jay the conversation she had with her mother all over again.

CHAPTER 61

John Doe's world changed after finding the entrance to the tunnel; small things began to stab at his memory like a defibrillator sending an electrical current through a dead patient's heart. Finding the bunch of keys as he explored the second tunnel flashed an array of images of clocks across his mind. There was something about the feel of them that was comforting in this now strangely empty world of nothingness – only a hospital bed with the image of a pair of sparkling green eyes playing over and over again even when he slept.

He felt safest in the small tunnel, carrying the lamp to find his way, he fetched the blankets, found the sleeping bag underneath them, to make a new bed at the end of the tunnel which was warmer than the hut. More urgent now was first the thirst followed by hunger pangs; they prompted him to explore the length of the longer tunnel where he climbed the ladder at the other end. His instinct made him search around the top for a way out into the library beyond the fire place.

It was recognition which led him through the maze of empty corridors and rooms to the source of the food he so badly needed.

*   *   *   *   *

Much to Bart's delight when Jay pulled up outside The March of Time, Agatha sat beside him in the camper. He didn't show any surprise, because Emily revealed everything about the conversation with her mother. He was shocked by what she said took place between Thelma Hobbs and Steve Paterson when he found her in Grimsby.

Bart led them through to the back room where Emily waited. Since speaking to her mother she was subdued and racked with guilt; she spent much time during the intervening days apologising to Bart for her mother's behaviour. As he already indicated to her this was hardly Emily's fault, she shouldn't feel sorry or guilty. He did feel relieved as it justified even more his part in moving Emily up to Scotland away from her. The woman was a liability. He often felt she, like a lot of people, had no business having children if they could neither set them an example nor care for them.

After the tea making was out of the way Bart enquired about any news, either about the Maola case or of the whereabouts of Steve Paterson. Jay was pleased to tell him Maola's trial was now set for mid-June being confirmed since Bart submitted an affidavit of his evidence which Robbie Cowan organised through his force and was made possible after Bart relinquished damning evidence he kept amongst his old client files when he went into the Witness Protection Programme. At the time he placed all of them in secure storage, there not being sufficient time to review them or destroy any of the files, he merely emptied his filing cabinets of everything including photographs, videos and surveillance notes, into a locked secure facility which he since maintained the annual charge for.

"There was a good deal of times, dates together with factual evidence I believe amongst my files," Bart suggested knowing if anything were to happen to him at least Maola would get the justice he deserved. Bart smiled wryly, "I'm pleased to hear it," he looked over at Jay and Agatha, "What about you two?"

Jay appeared more content than the last time he spoke about coming for his second interview, "I couldn't leave Agatha down there on her own," he admitted. "We negotiated unpaid leave for the rest of her notice….. it's not really much anyway."

"So you both can look for somewhere to live together, splendid!" Bart could see Emily was still downcast by how much damage her mother could have done.

Agatha recognised this too, ""It's okay Emily. I'd sooner be here with Jay, especially with him having his second interview tomorrow. I wanted to be here to support him. All we need to do is find a site to park 'Daisy' then we will be all set."

"Daisy?" Bart asked.

"The camper, it's her pet name!" Emily laughed for the first time in days at his puzzled face.

Bart said, "Ah, I might have a solution to Daisy's little problem," he grinned walking away towards the shop. "Come," he urged. "Emily, lock the door after us if you don't mind."

They followed him out as he indicated they should climb into the camper where he joined them, leaning between them from the rear he pointed up The Brae, "See where that white van is parked? There is a turning to the left," He sat back whilst Jay made the short journey to The Moor Hen at the bottom. Bart pointed to the side of the Inn, "Park down there."

Jay edged the camper between the gap which led to The Moor Hen's beer garden where there was a space for him to park the camper. The view was over the Memorial Games Park with a panoramic scene of fir trees on the hillside beyond it.

"How wonderful!" Agatha gasped.

"Let's go inside, I'll introduce you both to Alistair, the landlord, he says you are welcome to park here, hook up to his electricity supply, also use any of his facilities. Jay and Agatha stared in disbelief.

"There is only one downside," Bart grinned. "You will have to put up with some seriously wonderful cooking smells from the pubs kitchen!"

Bart left them with Alistair to settle arrangements. He walked back to the shop content in the knowledge they would take up Alistair's offer. He certainly knew he would feel safer having them close by whilst they were looking for somewhere permanent to live.

When he got back to the shop he tapped lightly on the door looking back up The Brae to where the white van delineated how close they would be.

CHAPTER 62

It didn't take Martin Frances very long at all to trade in his car at the car dealership, there were so many of them, he was spoilt for choice. He wasn't looking for anything special, quite the opposite. He wanted something nondescript, settling in the end for a silver second-hand Vauxhall Astra that resembled all the other silver cars on the road at the moment. He would miss his Audi. He even thought about keeping it for when his business in Scotland was complete but felt he needed to get rid in case the car enabled his movements to be traced.

Now he was back outside McKinley's Auto at Dinnet. He was reminded of his early days on stake out for the drug's squad, something he didn't miss when he left them. He'd seen the old man park his battered jeep on the next door lot where the FOR SALE sign looked older than he was. He watched him unlock the small door to the unit then open up the garage roll up door half-way as if he was expecting a delivery.

He couldn't spot the girl Nessa who he assumed was the brunette with the ponytail or Lily either who he now knew had changed her appearance. Even though he only saw her back view, he couldn't believe he didn't recognise her, she must look like the tart Shona described to him. Part of him wouldn't believe she suddenly 'turned' in favour of this Nessa girl. He knew his own wife better than anyone. She could never fancy a woman over him that was absurd. He vowed when he got hold of her he would prove it to her.

He felt a sudden revulsion that Lily, his Lily, could be intimate with a woman. The smiling face of Nessa, as he remembered her, came back to him. To think all the time the cunning bitch was laughing at him because he didn't recognise his own wife even though he held a picture of her in his hand. His temper simmered as he sat watching for her to arrive. He knew exactly what he was going to do to her when they met again.

It wouldn't be like the hotel manager that was a mistake. He regretted having lost control, taking it too far. Even when he kept insisting he didn't know anyone called Lily, he kept on with it, hardly able to talk with his mouth all smashed in. He thought, just a bit more pain would get her whereabouts out of him. The stupid bastard wouldn't tell him. He must have had a weak heart or something. He didn't think he hit him very hard.

A car pulled up at McKinley's as if expected. The old bloke got him to drive the vehicle inside the unit after which he locked everything up again driving off with the man in his jeep. Martin felt frustrated, it didn't look like this Nessa bird was coming into work today which was unfortunate because the garage was pretty isolated with no real neighbours to speak of; this would be a good place to get her to answer his questions.

Now he would have to change his plans, go to where Shona told him she was living – over the hairdresser's in Ballater. Of course, with no idea whether there was only the one hairdresser's in Ballater, he would have to do some searching which meant another stake out to find out.

*   *   *   *   *

Martin Frances parked along the street from Cheryl's hairdressers shop in Ballater having driven around for a while to identify any others. The flat above the shop was in darkness which gave him his first hint of doubt. Perhaps Nessa McKinley didn't live here. He got the whole sorry saga from Shona about how she lived with Nessa in Aberdeen until Nessa moved out leaving to go back home to her parents place at Tarland. Then she heard she was moving to her own place in Ballater.

The doubt grew the longer he sat there waiting. The drunken Shona after all was well pissed, just short of passing out completely after he bought her some more drinks. He hated drunks, especially women. This whining bitch was the very worst kind. A cruel smile crossed his face as he caught sight of a brunette walking down from the Co-op, her pony tail bouncing from side to side. She was laden with bags whilst holding a bunch of flowers across her arm. They were the expensive sort you got from a florist's rather than the ones they sold in supermarkets or a garage shop, so he knew they were meant for someone 'special'. Without oily overalls she looked much younger. He could tell she was happy from the spring in her step. *So this is Lily's choice over me?* He almost growled telling his empty car, "Not your day sweetheart and definitively not with my wife!"

He watched Nessa McKinley turn at the side of the hairdressing salon then disappear to the rear, he assumed to a separate entrance to the flat. He smiled, pleased there was no need to walk through the salon. There was less likelihood of being seen by anyone. He got out of his car to follow her.

CHAPTER 63

He woke up hearing a voice calling 'Mungo' got the flash again of those emerald eyes he remembered so well. The face came back first whilst the name took longer, like his own. There was always the underlying fear he would never remember how he got the head injury like the hospital doctor told him.

The fear stemmed not just from not knowing, it also came from the belief he may still be in danger with the absolute certainty he was not meant to have survived the 'blunt force trauma' to his head the doctor told him was caused by someone hitting him from behind with a blunt object.

Even if he saw the person who did it, he certainly didn't remember who.

What Mungo did know was he needed to be careful. The first thing was to stop using the bunch of keys he found in the tunnel to wind up the clocks he passed on his nightly trips to the kitchen to get food, because someone might notice they were still active when, in fact, they should all have stopped.

*   *   *   *   *   **

When he left Nessa's flat over the hairdresser's she lay face down across her bed, her jeans and pants mid-calf, her battered body was covered in blood, with one of her arms dislocated at the shoulder. As he walked back to the car he recently purchased he was flicking through the contact screen of Nessa McKinley's mobile phone. He found no one recorded as Lily which made his face look like thunder. What a waste of time that was. She was a tough cookie, much like the manager at the hotel. He began to doubt the drunken

Shona even after she recognised Lily's picture. Nessa didn't even have 'Shona' as a contact either. If what he was led to believe was true, they recently co-habited. What she did have was an extensive list of female names which in his now rising anger he put down to her disgusting behaviour as the dykey slut she obviously was.

He drove away even though he was tempted to sit there to wait to see if Lily turned up for her now smashed to pieces bouquet of flowers. He glanced down at Nessa's mobile on the seat beside him. He would go somewhere less conspicuous to wait to see if Lily called her. Then he remembered Shona slurring something about Nessa's 'fancy piece' drove the castle Daingneach van, maybe he should start there?

*   *   *   *   *

Downstairs below Nessa's flat Cheryl, the hair dresser was having a very busy morning, just about every workstation was occupied; two more ladies were reading magazines under the hairdryer hoods. At one point the banging coming down through the ceiling made Cheryl and two of her customers look upwards and for Cheryl herself to frown at the disturbance. She only recently rented the flat to Nessa McKinley and now began to wonder if she made a big mistake.

When the busiest of the morning passed smoothly Cheryl decided to lay down a few ground rules for her new tenant; sensing the absolute silence overhead she saw the opportunity to deliver them. She decided to pop up to have a word with her new tenant about mutual respect; when she got up there she found the door of the flat open.

Calling out to Nessa she got no response, so she pushed the door open and went inside. The silence gave her cause for concern. She froze when she found Nessa stretched face down across her bed. She was semi-clothed, covered in blood causing her to reach immediately for her mobile in her overall pocket. She called 999 for help.

By the time the police arrived Cheryl had covered Nessa partly with the bedding she was lying on. P.C Cowan was the first emergency response to arrive, he met Cheryl at the flat door.

"She's in a bad way," Cheryl was shaking. "I covered her….she's been assaulted….." She burst into tears having managed to contain herself up until this point. "I heard a lot of banging earlier, I thought Nessa was being noisy…..I came up to tell her…..tell her…."

"Nessa?!" Robbie interrupted. "Not Nessa McKinley?" He barely waited for her to nod before he rushed past her into the bedroom where he found his old friend unconscious on the bed. He felt for a pulse, found one and then radioed the control room to rush the Ambulance which was coming from miles away in Aberdeen being the only one available. He asked the Control Room for a CID response to attend because this was a serious assault being similar to another recent murder locally. When the ambulance arrived ten minutes later they rushed Nessa McKinley, with Robbie following, to Accident and Emergency.

She was admitted to Intensive Care where Robbie Cowan provided the initial police guard. The nature of her injuries, in addition to the sexual assault, were confirmed by a forensic doctor working with the hospital doctors.

D.I Leslie Morris arrived to interview Nessa only to find her still unconscious. He confirmed with Robbie Cowan apart from the noise coming through to the downstairs salon, no one could add much to the initial enquiries. The time of the assault was thought to be about 10.30 a.m. although the ladies in the salon who heard the noises couldn't say whether that was the precise time.

P.C Cowan arranged to have someone relieve him around two o'clock and since they couldn't establish the reason for the assault they were treating the incident as an attempted murder. The doctor treating her reported her condition was stable. However she needed more tests to assess for internal injuries. He couldn't predict yet when he might wake her up, for now they were sedating her.

Robbie drove over to Tarland after he was released to break the news to her parents. He didn't relish the idea knowing the reaction he would get from Jock McKinley. True to form his hostility was instant the moment McKinley answered the door, but didn't last long after he broke the news about Nessa. By the time he left them he was almost civil. Robbie promised he would do all he could to find out who did this to Nessa. He left Jock trying to comfort his wife, both believing they should have made Nessa stay with them then this wouldn't have happened.

After he left Tarland he drove over to Aboyne to break the news to Beth and Emily, he caught Beth as she was about to go out.

"Glad I caught you," he told Beth who placed the bottle of wine she was holding down on the kitchen table. They could see by the strain on his face there was something really wrong.

"I have some bad news," he began indicating they should both sit down, whilst he fidgeted uneasily.

"What's wrong?" Emily asked, her initial pleasure at seeing him unexpectedly, gave way to the concern he was there officially.

"We found Nessa this morning," he told them. "She's been very badly assaulted."

Beth gasped as the blood drained from her face, "I was going over there…..my god, Robbie, tell me she's okay!"

"She's unconscious….."

"What happened?" Emily asked clearly shocked.

Robbie toyed with how much he ought to reveal knowing how serious the assault was and the possible implications.

"She was……very badly beaten…..and she's been raped," he watched as Beth slumped back onto her chair, she seemed to crumple before his eyes. She knew immediately who had done it.

"Martin…." She squeezed through a closed mouth then began to sob uncontrollably.

Robbie waited until she recovered enough for him to ask why she thought Martin Frances would assault Nessa.

She spoke in a small steady voice as if she might have been telling them the plot of a horror film she once saw. "The first time he raped me he was forceful, not particularly violent. I was young, still a child really in many ways. I thought it was what I should let him do, you know, for giving me a home. His temper came later, then there was no doubt it was rape. He took me whenever he wanted, mostly as a means to vent his anger after a bad shift at work or if there was something he disapproved of....prostitutes or drug dealers....he somehow associated them with me. He always maintained without him I would be a slut or some other low life, after which he would beat me....." Here she stopped to get herself together to be able to carry on. "I think in the end he couldn't actually.....you know.....without he got angry. I could tell being forceful turned him on even more especially if I screamed or shouted, so I learnt to retreat into my mind, like scream inside because I thought I could lessen the punishment."

Robbie could see all this frightened Emily who was crying silently as Beth told her story.

"What about injuries? You must have had those?"

"Yes, of course. He seemed to be able to control the extent of those, so I just needed to stay hidden at home so no one could see the bruises. There was one time he dislocated my shoulder which required him to take me to A&E....to have it put back in place."

"Didn't they want to know how you got it?" Robbie again, was now convinced Martin Frances assaulted Nessa and dislocated her shoulder.

"He wouldn't leave me alone with anyone to be able to tell them anything. He always invented some story or other about how I did it. He threatened me he would kill me if I told them the truth."

Emily disappeared out of the kitchen; they could hear her in the bathroom off the hall making retching noises. When she came back she was pale.

In a small voice Beth admitted, "I know Martin did this because he would be disgusted if he thought I was having a relationship with Nessa. I know he's homophobic you see....I've heard him talking to someone on the telephone joking about beating up some 'low life'...his words, who he found to be gay," she silently recalled the actual conversation. "The rape would be his way of punishing Nessa if he thought I would want her over him....."

Robbie felt drained after hearing some of Beth's treatment by Martin Frances. He took her to the hospital as she requested telling her she would need to give CID a statement. She knew once Martin was issued with the protection order as well as be notified by her solicitor of her intention to divorce him, he would lose his temper completely. After that she would get the same treatment, or worse.

CHAPTER 64

Emily finished telling Bart what Robbie Cowan revealed the night before about Nessa McKinley, explaining that Beth suspected Martin Frances. The beating sounded too much like Phil Miller's assault to be a coincidence and he realised Beth could be in grave danger.

"Where is Beth at the moment?"

"She's at the hospital with Robbie," Emily looked grave. "They're going to bring Nessa out of her coma soon."

"Is that a good sign?" he asked. Emily nodded.

When she arrived at the shop in the morning she was carrying the cuckoo clock wrapped in brown paper cushioned by bubble wrap the same as when she came up to Scotland. Bart knew *the* clock was the one he feared and that he would find the bird with no beak when they took the wrapping off. He had mixed feelings about agreeing to try to make the bird whole again. Even after nearly two years without the clock he could still taste the fear he felt each time he came out of the unconscious state he found himself in after the noon chimes if he remained in the shop when they happened.

When he eventually began to time the bouts he found they were getting longer each time it happened. He always felt it strange believing this clock to be the cause of his blackouts. On seeing the clock again part of him told himself this is *only* a clock like any other and therefore he shouldn't be so foolish.

Together they hung the clock in a space on the wall of the shop which he kept free for any repair commissions, like the castle's Grandmother Clock Mungo MacLeod brought to him. They wound and set it to the correct time waiting for eleven o'clock to strike so they could watch the bird as expected. They stood together to wait like two children watching a Punch and Judy show expecting the crocodile to appear.

It was significantly disappointing, emphasising to Bart this was *only* a clock like all the others except for the one difference – the missing beak. They could even hear it certainly was synchronised with the rest of the clocks. They both gave an embarrassed laugh as they saw the relief on each other's faces.

Emily was the first to speak, "So have you got any idea how to give the bird a new beak?" she asked, "I have no idea."

"I have a dim memory of keeping something in my 'bits and bobs' box some time ago – at least I'm sure I didn't throw anything out," he told her. He did have an unfortunate habit of hoarding some ridiculous things 'just in case' he ever needed it. A wooden bird from a clock he no longer owned because the clock was too badly damaged seemed ridiculous at the time. He was now greatly pleased at long last the cuckoo might have a use.

"A bits and bobs box?" Emily repeated, grinning. "What's that?"

Bart laughed too, "It's what happens to you after a certain age, when you keep all manner of weird things believing one day you'll find a use for them. You are far too young to have developed such a habit."

She scanned around the shop, her eyes settling on the small seafaring chest where she knew he kept a collection of watches in need of repair.

He followed her gaze, "Err, not that one," he said. "I believe there is an old shoe box somewhere in the garage!"

"Oh, right can I go to find it?"

He nodded, "I'll get the kettle on for elevenses, we are already late for our tea."

Whilst Bart moved into the back room, Emily went in search of the box through the connecting door from the passageway into the garage. She wasn't surprised to find everything immaculate. She already knew Sirus was very organised which she always thought was more to do with the need to arrange clock parts in order to put them back together again. What she found in the garage was the same fastidiousness in the arrangement of a variety of tools, boxes with other oddments on shelves around the walls. She remembered her parent's garage back home was so cluttered with junk they couldn't get the car in most of the time. At least this made the current task easier. She found herself laughing as she searched through the boxes finding each one neatly labelled.

This made it so much easier to find the 'bits and bobs' box only it wasn't a shoebox, but a much bigger one with the Amazon smiley symbol on the side. She put the Bits and Bobs box to one side before she restored the others to their original places. She left it taped shut to ask him if this was the right one before she broke the seal.

*   *   *   *   *

The kettle began to boil. Just as Bart began setting out their cups he heard the bell on the shop door tinkle. Surprised he'd left the door unlocked he went through to the shop to serve the customer.

The first thing he noticed was the small blind over the glass panel in the door was pulled down shutting out much of the natural light to the shop. He was instantly confused because he was sure he released the blind when he opened up. He only ever pulled it down last thing at night. Anyway, it would have been open when he put the 'open' sign on the door; certainly when Emily arrived at nine o'clock. He moved out towards the door to lift it, then to search the shop for the customer. The figure stood still, his back towards him scanning the vast number of clocks hanging on the wall at the far end.

"Ah, good morning," Bart said to his back. "How can I help?" It was a while since he sold anyone an actual clock. Briefly he felt a little thrill of excitement, here was someone who might be interested. The man seemed to ignore the greeting continuing with his inspection of the clocks.

Bart's next thought passing slowly over the likelihood his customer might be deaf, gave way to a creeping shiver making his legs go numb as he found something familiar about the figure. He could hardly move one foot in front of the other as he edged further towards the door.

The man's voice came clearly across to him, "I shouldn't do that Mr Bridges, let's leave the shop closed." He turned slowly towards him, recognition settling on Bart that this was Steve Paterson, the man he knew only as his police Witness Protection handler.

He stood fully facing him. "You certainly are hard to find."

Bart edged nearer to the door as Steve moved out into the shop, his back to the counter behind which Bart knew his faithful baseball bat was hidden underneath. He didn't have a hope in hell of reaching it.

"Yes!" Bart bellowed in his loud voice, well aware Emily was somewhere inside the garage and would hopefully hear him. "I hear you've been looking for me. Let me guess," Bart suddenly wasn't at all afraid for himself, only for Emily. "You want me to give evidence against Toni Maola?"

Steve Paterson laughed, "Actually no, I don't. Or rather Toni doesn't want you to."

Bart felt the need to play for time, hoping Emily would hear and not come out.

"Now that really is a shame," Bart continued. He began to laugh which surprised Steve Paterson who frowned at his behaviour. "He's really going to be most upset with you."

"Oh, why is that?" Steve took a step closer to the shop counter leaning back against it.

"You see I've already given evidence which is one reason the trial is going ahead?" He assumed Paterson knew the trial date was set, however, his face said differently. "Oh dear, you didn't know."

Bart took a step closer to him standing away from the door only fleetingly wondering if he might manipulate him to move away from the counter so he might make a dash for the baseball bat to defend himself with.

"And also they have now come into possession of all the incriminating evidence including photographs I managed to hide away when *you*," he pointed at Steve deliberately, "took me into police protection." Steve got angry at this statement. "Remember your police oath do you?" He took another step to the side. Paterson stood up from leaning against the counter he clearly didn't like being reminded. "What on earth does Maola have on you? Or could it be pure greed, eh? I understand he does have rather a lot of inheritance to come into – unless, of course, he gets life imprisonment which is very likely."

Bart had a clear view of the passageway behind the counter having left the door open he spotted the integral garage door begin to move outwards, Emily's face peered nervously out of the gap.

There was a sudden synchronised click all around them as each of the clocks, hanging, standing or sitting on shelves simultaneously broke out into the midday chorus. Unless you were used to it, able to anticipate what was about to happen, the new experience could be somewhat of a shock, certainly disorientating. For Steve Paterson as well as the news Bart Bridges, P.I moments before imparted, together with the chaos the clocks chimes made, his senses were sent reeling. Even though he knew the door was locked (the key was sitting in his own pocket) with the bolts pulled top and bottom, he took a step towards Bart who was blocking his way out.

Emily saw the man she already feared take a step towards Bart as she rushed into the shop, bent to pick up the baseball bat all in one motion. When she stood back up Bart was lying on the floor, his body shaking, he was completely unconscious. Steve Paterson knelt next to him his arm outstretched to Bart's throat.

"You've killed him!" she yelled moving fast around the counter she hit the man a two handed swipe across his head with the baseball bat. He went down flat out at the side of Bart.

CHAPTER 65

A kindly nurse allowed Beth in to see Nessa for ten minutes only. Her face was almost unrecognisable, both of her eyelids were so swollen, had she not been ventilated or unconscious, Beth was sure they wouldn't have been able to open. The rest of her face was almost entirely black, whilst her left shoulder having been reset, her left arm was strapped across her body. The machine breathing for her made a rhythmic sound, there was a beep coming from a cardiac monitor.

Beth sat down on the low chair beside her, leaned her head against Nessa's hand resting on top of the thin sheet covering her, mindful of the tubes attached, she wept, the tears falling across Nessa's fingers. "I'm so sorry….so sorry….." she whispered as one of her fingers gave an involuntary twitch against Beth's chin.

When the nurse returned after exactly ten minutes she was asked to leave because she wasn't a relative even though the kindly nurse recognised they were close friends, "rules are rules" she muttered reluctantly.

She stood outside in the corridor not knowing what to do, lost in her anguish. The nurse found her there, told her she ought to go home, better to come back in the morning when the doctor was considering bringing Miss McKinley out of the coma.

*　　*　　*　　*　　*

The emptiness of the cottage when Beth returned there felt strangely unwelcoming, she noted Sandy's unfriendly behaviour had once again returned he was stretched out in front of the range where the fire was burning low. Absently, she threw a couple more logs amongst the dwindling embers, felt a chill in the cottage she'd not experienced before which she put down to the absence of a blaze and to her shattered spirit at seeing Nessa so broken.

Beth registered the sack of dog food now nearly completely empty, sighed knowing she forgot to fetch the new one from the stable. She opened the kitchen door to go across the yard to fetch it. Sandy didn't move or walk to the door to watch her as he usually did, *you lazy creature* she thought. Once back inside she dropped the heavy sack next to the nearly empty one and turned to lock the back door.

Sandy was standing watching her, a low growl rumbled in his throat. Beth thought perhaps he wanted to go outside, "Too late you lazy dog," she scolded.

The growl grew as Beth stared believing he was passing comment on her chastising him. He was looking not at the outside door, but the inner door to the hallway. Then he began to bark at it making Beth's skin crawl as fear began to creep up her body.

"What's wrong?" she whispered walking over to him, she placed her hand down to stroke his ears which he ignored. He continued to creep forward, ears down, tail pointing as he walked in slow motion the growl returning. He placed himself between her and the door waiting. Slowly the door knob began to turn.

Sandy froze. He was so still he resembled a statue. The growl ceased as the door moved inwards. Beth took a step backwards, her head moving around looking for some kind of weapon, until her hand found the knife block and she plucked out the biggest one, the chef's knife, from its slot holding the blade out in front of her.

The door swung out revealing Martin Frances, his eyes sparkled at the sight of her.

"There you are, Lily," he sneered. "What have you done to yourself?"

He took a step into the kitchen, heard the growl return to the dog's throat. "Now what do we have here? Call that a guard dog, do you?"

He moved sideways towards the table which was laid out with tea things. The bottle of wine which Beth placed there previously, before receiving the news about Nessa, was still there. It reminded her she was meant to spend time with her earlier before...... She looked angrily over at the man who took out his temper on her new friend, raised the knife, pointing the tip with jabbing movements at her husband.

"You monster!" she yelled. "Why did you hurt Nessa, she's done nothing to you!"

His face twisted in anger at the mention of her name, "Just look at you, she's turned you into a slut! She deserved everything she got!"

She could see the uncontrollable anger rising now knowing what to expect. He took a step closer making Sandy bark a warning.

"Shut the mutt up or I'll do it myself!" he didn't look at the dog, he was watching the heavy cleaver she held in her hand.

"You come anywhere near us and I'll......" she jabbed the knife in the air towards him again warning him of her intention.

He moved a step closer, didn't see the dog pounce towards him. Sandy leapt at him, catching him full in the chest with his front paws, sufficiently to knock him off balance against the wall with a heavy blow, winding him for one moment before both of his hands pushed the dog sideways smashing the foxhound against the floor where he yelped and lay hurt.

Beth moved nearer to the range seeing the new logs begin to burn brightly and where she could see the heavy kettle still sat on the self in front was showing wispy steam rising out of the spout, if she had to she would pick it up and throw it at him.

Martin watched her reading her intention, his voice changed into the smooth charming man she knew he hid behind, "Now why don't we sit down, let's talk, have a cup of tea like you were about to do?"

She knew better than to be fooled by his slick pretences even if other people were taken in by them; she knew they were a prelude to his sadistic games. She kept the knife where it was, chanced a glance towards Sandy, trying to judge how injured he was. He lay still, his eyes open now not making a sound.

"Shall I make the tea or will you?" he asked with a subtle mocking to the tone. He reached forward, picked up the bottle of wine, "Or do you want to share this?"

"Put that down!" she ordered not wanting to be reminded how she was meant to share the wine with Nessa, a thank you for her helping with the legal stuff. It reminded her he should have been served the papers by now, "Did you get notice of the injunction preventing you from making contact with me?" she asked, "Which incidentally you have broken, now they'll arrest you." She had completely forgotten they would be arresting him for his attack on Nessa.

Martin began to laugh, "Really? You think they'll believe *you* over me? Look at you....you whore....!"

"So why are you here?!" she screamed at him. "If I'm such garbage, you'll be pleased with the divorce papers won't you? Good riddance to bad rubbish - then you can get on with the rest of your life, eh?"

Martin Frances had sat down on one of the kitchen chairs at the table, his face twisted again with malevolence. He thumped the table hard, "No! No! No! You don't leave me! You belong to me....you are coming home!" he yelled. "Do you really think I'd let you leave me.....for a woman?!" Beth sensed Sandy's subtle movement as he rolled onto his belly. He raised his ears listening. "And when I get you home I'm going to teach you many many lessons; believe me you won't ever want to try this again." He glanced around the

456

kitchen inspecting it. "Whose house is this anyway?" he asked as if clearly puzzled by the set up.

"It's mine," Beth said testing the truth on herself. "Yes, mine, so I have no intention of coming back with you," she pulled her body more upright, stood her ground, saw the knife in her hand as if seeing it for the first time. She placed it down on the work top. "You, on the other hand, will be going to prison for the awful things you've done......not only Nessa, eh Martin?" She could see a flicker of doubt cross his face. "That poor man at the hotel was you, right?"

He didn't answer. She could tell he realised what she meant, "And such a waste of a life. He didn't even know me, Martin." He glanced sharply at her searching her face for the truth. Then his face changed to anger knowing no matter how hard he hit the man he couldn't tell him anything about where she was living because he didn't know.

"You can't hurt me here, Martin," Beth suddenly knew the truth. "This cottage doesn't like you – can't you feel it, I can – well it's not going to let you hurt me." She smiled sweetly.

"What are you talking about? You're raving mad!" he leaned on the table for leverage to stand up. Beth saw Sandy out of the corner of her eye rise slowly onto his legs, the growl in his throat returning loudly as he pounced. He sprang up from the floor only this time Martin Frances was rising from a sitting position. This time the dog went straight for his neck sinking his teeth into soft flesh, tasting the blood as it gushed into his mouth like he was used to doing with a fox. He dragged him down onto the floor.

Beth caught a glimpse of flashing blue lights through the closed kitchen blinds over the window before she sprang across to the dog shouting, "Leave Sandy!"

Sandy let go. Martin's hands grabbed his neck as blood spurted out. Beth reached him, went down on her knees to clutch the wound to stem the blood. When the kitchen door burst open they found her leaning over Martin Frances as if she were trying to strangle him; she was covered in blood from the open wound.

*   *   *   *   *

Emily heard about what happened to Beth later from Robbie Cowan. She could see he was greatly shaken when he arrived in response to the panic alarm Sandy pushed Martin Frances against when he leapt for him the first time and discovered Beth leaning over his bleeding body. At first he thought she must have attacked him with a knife because of the amount of blood everywhere, but there was no sign of one other than a clean one on a work top near the kettle. She looked to be trying to strangle him. Her hands were around his neck. He was convulsing whilst trying to prise her fingers away.

Beth immediately yelled to him as he burst through the door, "Call an ambulance, the dog attacked him to save me!"

The truth came out later after Beth recovered from the shock of him finding her. He was there to harm her as well as to take her back she had no doubt. Ironically, the ambulance crew attending him told Robbie she saved his life by her quick reaction to staunch his bleeding neck because Sandy's tooth caught his jugular and he would have bled out otherwise.

Much later when Beth was interviewed by D.I Morris, she was able to tell him Martin admitted to the assault on Nessa McKinley and though he did not admit it, she knew by his face he was responsible for killing Philip Miller which he hadn't denied when she accused him. The forensic evidence from the manager's bungalow matched at least one finger print to Martin Frances which put him at the scene; the finger print was an imprint in Philip Miller's blood. He was cautioned at the hospital, placed under guard until he could be taken into custody.

She was a little sad at the thought Nessa may have given into his ferocious attack on her by telling him where she was living. Beth asked Robbie if he knew how Martin found her.

"Certainly not from Nessa if you've even thought it. I would stake my life on it, I know her well, she wouldn't," Robbie spoke with great conviction sounding like the friend he was and nothing like a police officer. "Ness is as stubborn as hell, this isn't the first time she's been assaulted by someone's irate partner or husband……"

Beth gasped at his words, the vision of her broken body lying in the hospital flashed before her. She began to cry.

"She's a tough cookie, but I have to tell you this is the worst I've seen her," he confessed. "She thinks the odd black eye or split lip is worth her efforts to protect abused women from domestic violence."

Beth's heart ached at the thought of her injured. She asked him if he would take her back to the hospital, "I don't care if I have to sit in the waiting room all night because I'm not a relative, I need to be near her." And so he did.

CHAPTER 66

Bart sat up in the hospital bed surrounded by his friends who were piecing together the events of the day before, his memory only up till he lost consciousness as the noon day chimes began. Emily clearly thought he had been killed by Paterson because of him leaning over him looking like he was releasing his throat which was why she grabbed the baseball bat to hit him across the back of the head.

Paterson later admitted he thought Bart Bridges had suffered a heart attack because he charged across the shop towards him as the clock chimes began. He saw him go down whilst making for the door to get away from the dreadful noise they made.

After Emily's intervention, they lay side by side, as Jay came charging in from the back having received a text from Emily telling him Steve Paterson was in the shop. She heard Bart talking about Maola wanting him dead. Jay found Emily standing holding the bat, which he took away from her.

"You could have killed him," Bart said from the hospital bed. "Is he okay?"

Agatha revealed she took charge of arresting Paterson who came round shortly after she arrived. Even though she wasn't yet working for Police Scotland she summoned them to take over the arrest.

"I couldn't read him his rights if he stayed out cold for long," she said grinning.

"Thank goodness!" Bart's relief was due to not wishing Emily to be responsible for Paterson's death. "I thank you all for coming to my rescue."

"Mostly Emily," Jay conceded. "It was all over by the time we arrived. That's some formidable assistant you have there I would say." Emily blushed of course.

"Is there any news about Nessa?" Bart remembered Emily's description of how badly she was injured.

The door to Bart's side room opened. Beth came in pushing Nessa in a wheel chair.

"My goodness!" Bart exclaimed as he saw her blackened swollen face with one eye closed entirely.

Robbie Cowan followed behind them holding his police hat under his arm. He moved over to stand next to Emily.

*   *   *   *   *

Robbie Cowan was able to fill everyone in on Steve Paterson's involvement with Tony Maola having liaised with the police who escorted him back to England. He was now prepared to give his full evidence in exchange for protection for his wife and children. Up until his arrest Maola was able to use him to find key witnesses by threatening his family. He even had one of his children kidnapped to prove what he was capable of doing if he didn't comply. Paterson didn't dare do anything else. He made it clear he played no part in what happened to any of the witnesses after he found them for Maola. However, Paterson was able to identify Maola's associates who were responsible for eliminating some of them and intimidating others.

He also filled in the gap about how he managed to find Bart. Specifically by using Emily's mother who was more than ready to tell him how Jayson and Agatha took her away - she didn't know where to – but she was able to give him sufficient information about them for him to find them. He pretended to take her complaint which is how he found out Agatha McLeary was a police officer and Jayson Vingoe a CSI. It took practised patience to watch them to wait until they led him to Bart Bridges. He told the investigating team he hadn't meant to harm him. He was mortified when he thought his presence in the shop made him have a fatal heart attack.

In exchange for a great deal of information Steve Paterson and his family were given a new start through the Witness Protection Programme which brought a subtle smile to Bart Bridges face.

CHAPTER 67

Robbie finished updating everyone, then looking down at Emily standing beside him, he smiled conspiratorially. She smiled back nodding a silent agreement, "We also have some other news," he announced. Those gathered stared back expectantly as most of them knew Emily and Robbie were an 'item' or so they believed. Now they anticipated something of a personal nature to be delivered. Only Bart wasn't smiling because he believed Emily was far too young and it was altogether too soon for anything of a permanent nature.

"We've 'found' Mungo MacLeod!" Emily announced. "Well thanks to Beth," she smiled across at her friend who seemed greatly surprised and pleased at the same time.

"I'm assuming by the grins he's alive as we suspected?" Bart enquired of Emily.

"You knew he was alive?" Beth asked.

"I suspected he was because we found the hidden tunnels under the castle where we saw someone had been sleeping." Bart sought Emily's agreement and she nodded.

"We also found the bunch of keys for the castle clocks which we knew Mungo must have left in one of the tunnels and which Thomas Galbraith was unable to hand over to Sirus. Mungo must have used them to keep some of the clocks wound up *after* he disappeared."

Nessa tried to speak through her swollen lips, "He's really alive? I thought that awful man the Laird's secretary might have….." She lost her voice in her effort to speak so Beth squeezed her shoulder gently to comfort her.

Robbie's update revealed to Bart, Emily was keeping him informed about some of their findings at the castle. After the van Mungo' was driving over to pick up the clock was hit by the stag, he stopped to inspect the damage, finding the stag barely alive and very badly hurt. He dragged it across the snow into the woods away from the road in case anyone should pass by seeing him do what he knew he must do. In the absence of his shot gun he used a fallen tree branch to put the stag out of its misery.

That was as much as Mungo could remember for a very long time. It was when he was prompted to remember Mary Macaulay by the nurse's green eyes he got the confidence to go to find her which was when he abandoned his bed in the castle tunnel. With her help to prompt him his memory recovered over subsequent days.

He was unable to remember who hit him or even if he saw them. The police eventually got a confession from Thomas Galbraith after Mungo recalled having an argument with him regarding the castle artefact collections he was employed to record for valuation purposes. Unexpectedly, Galbraith revealed Laird Munro intended to sell them all, stripping the castle of its assets. Mungo became angry telling Galbraith he couldn't do that because legally the Laird didn't own them, they belonged to his father who inherited them just as he would when his father died. He had seen the document to prove it. Seumus Grant gave ownership of Castle Daingneach to the Munro's he thought in settlement over a personal dispute, however, the contents were not included as this historic document verifies.

Thomas Galbraith was shocked when he heard this because in return for undertaking the valuation he was expecting to receive 10% from their sale. He really believed Duncan Munro wouldn't have promised him this if he wasn't able to meet it. Mungo assured him he was the rightful descendent of Seumus Grant specified in the deed his father showed him and which was recorded as the Grant 'treasure' people talked about. A number of the artefacts he knew to be extremely valuable, with some being priceless.

At this point Emily took over explaining her research into Mungo MacLeod's family tree had been very revealing. Seumus Grant, like Old Jim suggested, had been more than a collector of armoury, he had used them in many clan rivalry battles and took whatever he wanted through brute force. Unfortunately, this involved a personal appetite for any woman that took his fancy. The Munro settlement had not been connected to a clan battle as was thought but the result of one of Seumus's indiscretions with a young castle servant from the Munro clan whom he took by force and impregnated; having no children of his own he gave the Munro clan the castle on his death and the artefacts in a legal document to her offspring if she concealed the fact and married to cover up his part in it. She became a MacLeod and her subsequent line remained as ghillies to the Laird in order to keep the family line at the castle and the artefacts known as Seumus Grant's treasure to remain there also, never to be sold off separately.

*   *   *   *   *

"What about Duncan Munro, is he aware of this document Mungo's father has?" Bart asked.

"That isn't clear yet.....the Laird hasn't been available for comment," Robbie said. "Or even if he knows anything about Thomas Gailbraith's assault on Mungo, part of which is also to do with Mungo's relationship with Mary Macaulay. Another motive we believe for the assault."

"Doesn't it prove intent, Robbie?" Bart asked. Robbie didn't answer saying he couldn't comment. Bart continued, "I do think it is unlikely Duncan Munro would know about the assault, he did genuinely seem concerned at Mungo being missing."

*   *   *   *   *

Robbie explained after Sirus told them Thomas Galbraith was a strange man they kept a close eye on him. He admitted during the interview he believed the castle to be haunted by Seumus Grant because he'd seen him rising out of the fire in the library on one

465

occasion; then one night he saw him 'floating along the corridor'
down near the kitchens.

Of course, Robbie admitted it was Emily who suggested perhaps
he saw Mungo (looking wild and the image of Seumus Grant) coming
out of the tunnel under the fire basket looking for food which seemed
more realistic after Emily told him about Sirus finding the tunnel. It
certainly confirmed why there were some of the clocks still working
long after he went missing and why Thomas Galbraith always seemed
to be nervous.

Robbie went in search of Mungo after Beth told them she thought
there was someone now living with Mary Macaulay whom she also
found to be much more cheerful since the last time she visited her.

After Mungo's assault, he recovered enough to walk away from
the stag later to be found lying in the road by a passing motorist who
called for an ambulance and was taken to hospital. When he was fully
conscious he saw his name written up as John Doe which he believed
for some time. The nursing staff overlooked the requirement to report
these types of cases to the police, when someone recognised the error
phoning the information through to the police, Mungo had
disappeared. He was recorded as a 'self-discharge' so when the police
arrived they didn't get to interview him.

After leaving the hospital he was drawn back to his old haunts by
the barking of the deer in the woods. This brought flashbacks of killing
one with a tree branch which led him to believe he was a poacher, not
a ghillie putting one out of its misery after the accident.

*   *   *   *   *

Beth sat listening intently a curious expression on her face.
"Does the family lineage down from Seumus Grant mean that
Mungo MacLeod not only inherits Seumus Grant's treasure, the
artefacts, but is the rightful heir to the Castle as well? It sounds to
me like he also has that right being partly descended from the
Munro clan?"

Everyone stared at her and a subtle smile came to Bart's lips, "You could very well be right there," he said triumphantly. "I think it will take much legal work to sort that one out I suspect and one thing's for sure......no one can dispute he comes from the Seumus Grant genes, they are like two peas in a pod!"

A touch of sadness came across Emily's face as she looked over to Sirus, "We thought old Jim MacLeod didn't realise his son, Mungo was missing," Bart nodded his agreement. "Of course, Mungo wasn't aware his father had died. Up until he went missing he took care of the old man, keeping his house tidy for him, making sure he had meals or money for the pub."

"I see - Jim didn't seem to show any distress at his absence though, did he?" Bart asked.

"We think because Mungo arranged with the health centre for him to receive nursing support," Emily explained. "Maybe he hadn't missed Mungo because of all their comings and goings at home."

"He did look a bit sad when we approached him in the pub. Even given he owned all the treasures at the castle, I'm more than sure he couldn't afford to buy himself a meal," Bart added. "He was greatly pleased when we offered him some dinner." Bart knew it was the reason he'd left the twenty pound note under the candlestick when they left him sitting in his chair. Sadly he was still there when they found him next day having died in his sleep. "Mungo must have been really upset Jim died and he wasn't with him." Emily said.

"Yes, he was. No one should have to die alone like that he said."

They all agreed with Bart whose jovial mood on their arrival had now disappeared entirely. He felt a little self-conscious with all of them staring at him.

"I have some news also," he tried to smile which came over a little forced. "I don't wish to alarm anyone. I have been given a lot of tests since I arrived in hospital. You will be pleased to hear I did not have a heart attack as Steve Paterson thought."

No one welcomed the news sensing Sirus wasn't cheered by the knowledge as they would think he ought to be. They stood in silence waiting for the next part to be delivered.

"They have, however, found the cause of my bouts of unconsciousness which I'll admit I have had.....oh, for some time," he took in the room full of his friends standing silently waiting. He suddenly felt very lucky he wouldn't die alone should that be the worst case scenario. "They found a meningioma, a brain tumour," everyone tried not to show their shock. "The good news is these things are usually benign although because I have been in hiding for some time I haven't had a general practitioner to refer myself to, consequently the tumour has grown beyond the size any other form of treatments can be given, so they need to operate to remove it......which they are doing soon." He searched their faces, his gaze stopping on Emily's grave face, "I will need my most excellent associate to take over the reins of the business for a while, until I am fully back on form."

Emily left Robbie's side, moved over to Bart, threw her arms around him hugging him close. Bart embarrassingly patted her shoulder, "Now that's enough sadness for today!" he bellowed loudly. "I have spent most of my life alone and look....." his hand moved taking in everyone around the room. "I am here surrounded by all my friends," his eyes went straight over to Nessa, "And some look much worse than I do!"

Everyone laughed relieved to make a sound and one which clearly hurt Nessa who could barely smile.

"I am truly blessed!" Bart said.

THE END

EPILOGUE:

A small crowd of local people, who had gathered, were standing together at the bottom of the hill named The Brae. They were talking in hushed whispers, speculating on why there was a sheet covering the clock shop's sign, wondering if yet again the premises had changed hands given it had only been a couple of years since it ceased to be an art gallery being bought by that funny little man, the clockmaker.

Several cars arrived, parking up around the shop leaving space directly in front of the shop doorway. The locals spotted people they knew like Max and Steph from the Griddle Iron around the corner at the 'turning circle'. Alistair, the landlord from The Moor Hen was walking down from his pub together with a couple of people some heard were Jayson and Agatha Vingoe. They stopped, stood together as if waiting for something significant to happen.

A girl with short light blonde hair stood beside her friend with a long auburn ponytail, her right arm held across her body by a white sling. Her face still showed the faint signs of severe bruising she received from the man who's soon to be ex-wife was tightly holding her other hand. They walked up The Brae until they stood outside the clock shop.

The crowd began to swell as a few more curious locals joined them having heard 'something significant was happening at The March of Time'; perhaps it was no longer to be called that. A few nudges drew attention to the local police Defender stopping just short of the hill and parking up. P.C Robbie Cowan got out being joined by his passenger, a young girl, those who knew them believed to be his girlfriend Emily who worked for the man at the clock shop.

She seemed intrigued by the gathering of so many people, looking up at Robbie Cowan for an explanation, but was met with a shrug of non-comprehension. They walked together, the crowd allowing them through to join the two women standing holding hands.

"What's happening?" Lily Johns (once known as Beth Grant) asked Emily.

"I've no idea," she replied glancing up at the sheet stretched across the shop's sign. "I was told to be here at eleven o'clock."

"Us too," Nessa McKinley said, her ponytail flicked as her head also turned to the sign.

The door to the shop opened as the cacophony of sound from the clocks inside began the eleven o'clock chimes, a fanfare for the small stout figure of Sirus Jeffries emerging and standing in the doorway, his face a serious mask above the bright red paisley bow tie that matched the waistcoat pulled tight across his well-proportioned stomach. He stood, waited whilst the clocks went through their cycle. He held up a finger to indicate the sounds were tightly synchronised looking directly at Emily for confirmation; she smiled, nodded her approval.

The clocks finished, the last cuckoo sounded all went quiet. He stepped forward onto the pavement.

"Ladies and gentlemen," his voice boomed above the assembled chatter until all whispers of those collected there died down. "Thank you for being here," he marvelled at how many people were gathered knowing he personally invited only a handful of them. "Although I have no actual family left, I am pleased to say I have some exceptional friends," he glanced and nodded from Jay and Agatha, to Emily and Robbie then to Lily (Beth) and Nessa. "I count myself blessed.....I welcome everyone here today."

His arm stretched out towards the gathered crowd, "You are all welcome to join us today at The Moor Hen for a buffet lunch...."

A young voice shouted, "What's the celebration?" everyone laughed at the eager youngster who couldn't wait any longer to know.

"Indeed, that is exactly what this is, a celebration of gratitude to be here today," he held back any tearful response that wanted to intrude, "Thanks to some really good friends we are here today," his heart ached at the absence of Philip Miller, whom he also called friend, but knew he couldn't dwell on his loss. "Before we do, you will be wondering about the subterfuge," he pointed above his head at the sheet over the shop which everyone could now see was attached to a long rope dangling to one side with a tassel at the end. "I have a new sign," he announced, holding his hand out towards Emily, "I would ask you to officially reveal it, if you would?"

Emily looked up at Robbie who appeared as mystified as she was, then she stepped forward to join Bart. He smiled at her encouragingly, pointed to the tassel whispering, "Just pull hard."

She took a step, held the end of the rope and tugged.

The sheet fell to the side revealing The March of Time original name, with the same caricature of a white rabbit in bow tie with matching waist coat resembling Bart. The new addition of a caricature of Alice in Wonderland complete with blue dress and ribbons in her hair with a face resembling Emily herself was now painted on the other side of the shop name. New also was 'Proprietor's Bartholomew Bridges and Amelia Hobbs substituted for Sirus Jeffries which had been removed.

Emily stood backwards into the road to take in the new sign, her hands clasped in front of her, a smile on her face.

Bart Bridges continued, "This young lady," he pointed at Emily, "I would be proud to call daughter is my business partner in this shop and whatever else we may decide to undertake!"

He winked at Emily who he knew would be thinking, 'Bartholomew and Hobbs, Private Investigators', who knew what the future held?

We'd like to know if you enjoyed the book. Please consider leaving a review on the platform from which you purchased the book

Lightning Source UK Ltd.
Milton Keynes UK
UKHW010629080422
401285UK00001B/9